The White Rose of Scotland

The White Rose of Scotland

a Scottish Island Novel

Audrey McClellan

Beaver's Pond Press, Inc.
Edina, Minnesota

ISBN 1-59298-053-8

Library of Congress Catalog Number: 2003116349

Cover art by Carla McClellan.
Eilean Dubh map by Jane Gordon.
Book design by Mori Studio.

"Jamie MacDonald's Compliments to His Sheep," "Jamie's Lullaby/Jamie's Lilt/Rosie's Reel," "Cemetery Hill," "The Emigrant's Lament," and "Return to Eilean Dubh" are original compositions by and copyright to Sherry Wohlers Ladig. Used by permission. Lyrics to "The Emigrant's Lament" and "Return to Eilean Dubh" are by Audrey McClellan.

The Scottish country dance, "Snow on the Mountain," was devised by and is copyright to Lara Friedman-Shedlov. Used by permission.

Printed in the United States of America

First Printing: February 2004

08 07 06 05 04   6 5 4 3 2 1

Beaver's Pond Press, Inc.   7104 Ohms Lane, Suite 216
Edina, MN 55439
(952) 829-8818
www.beaverspondpress.com

to order, visit www.BookHouseFulfillment.com or call 1-800-901-3480. Reseller discounts available.

To M1, M2 and A2, A3, and John and Carla, with love.

The Andrew Simon Fraser Memorial Scholarship has been awarded by the
Saint Andrew's Society of Minnesota to Audrey McClellan for
Westering Home, the first Scottish Island Novel,
for furthering the Society's objectives in promoting
and nurturing Scottish history and culture.

The author is grateful to the Society
for its support and encouragement.

Contents

The little white rose of Scotland, the white rose
That smells sweet and sharp,
And breaks the heart.

Hugh MacDiarmid

PART I

Jean and Darroch

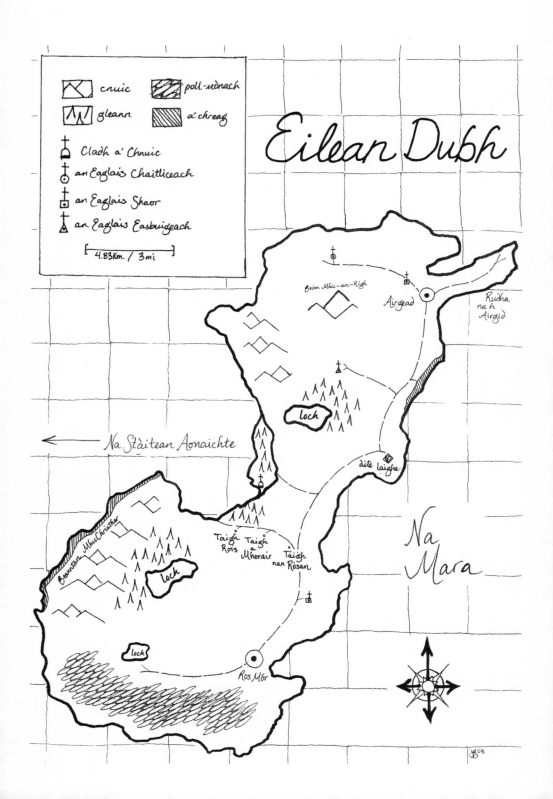

One

*Eilean Dubh (pronounced ale-en dew), a small island located in the
Hebridean Sea off the western coast of mainland Scotland; it is the
largest island in the Middle Hebrides group. N. B.: geographers
do not recognize a "Middle Hebrides," arguing that all of the
islands so-called, with the exception of Eilean Dubh,
are simply rocks in the sea.*

Robertson's Relics and Anomalies of Scotland, 1923

*I*t was raining on Eilean Dubh. It had been raining for two days, beginning on Friday afternoon with a light mist that soon changed to a heavy drizzle. In the middle of the night the *Eilean Dubhannaich* had been awakened by claps of thunder that rattled windowpanes, and lightning flashes that ricocheted off the dark western mountains and seared through bedroom curtains. Then the deluge poured down.

By morning the rain settled to a steady driving force that spilled small burns over their banks and flooded streets in Ros Mór and Airgead, forcing the cancellation of the usual Saturday market in both towns. The vendors packed up their crafts, the produce from their croft gardens and their homemade jellies and meat pies, and moved to the pubs, the cafes or the hotels for nourishment and *craic*. Whatever the weather, they would not be denied their Saturday morning chance to get caught up on the latest gossip. And maybe start a new story or two circulating.

On Sunday morning, as if in deference to the Sabbath, the rain faded to a soft patter. Warm mist rising from the soaked ground met cool air above to create waves of fog that drifted over the narrow Island roads and slowed driving to a crawl. Stragglers drifted into the Island's four churches all through the services.

At precisely twelve o'clock as the bell peals from Our Lady of the Island Catholic Church rang over the hills and the last notes from Protestant throats echoed off kirk walls, the rain began again, steady and determined.

There was no lingering in churchyards today.

In *Taigh a' Mhorair,* the Laird's house, Jean Abbott MacChriathar and Darroch Mac an Rìgh were in bed. Hot showers had helped chase away the lingering chill of Minister Donald's gray stone Free Presbyterian kirk and cups of tea and plates of scrambled eggs, gammon and toast had completed their rehabilitation.

They were cozily ensconced side by side, propped up with pillows and surrounded by piles of papers and books. Sunday afternoon was their special time for making love but like vegetables before dessert, a cuddle was preceded by work.

Darroch's beautiful blue, slightly far-sighted, eyes were aided by black-rimmed reading glasses that had slipped halfway down his long elegant nose. He was reading a Co-Op committee report, having already finished two television scripts featuring possible acting roles for him, one letter requesting a personal appearance at a shopping mall opening and a batch of newspaper articles from his clipping service.

Jean had completed her tasks. Reports and letters lay on the floor by the bed and a romance novel lay beside her where it had fallen from her hand. She'd slid down in bed, her hair spread over the pillow, her bright green eyes staring dreamily up at the skylight, watching the rain fall, waiting for Darroch to finish his work.

They were very relaxing, these Sunday afternoons, long and dreamy, a fire of peats and coal crackling in the room below, the bedroom warmed by the stolid presence of night storage heaters, their brick and oil contents radiating heat collected during the night when electric rates were low. Today a chicken roasted in the oven, nestled among potatoes and carrots, and the fragrance wafted through the cottage.

Wonderful as their nights were, there was something special about making love in the daytime, under the skylight, bright sunlight shining on his black hair, catching the whisky-gold highlights in hers, warming their bodies as they kissed, caressed, teased, laughed. When it rained, like today, the drops clattered on the glass above, making the bedroom intimate and cozy, the bed their private sanctuary.

Even though she knew they'd end up making love, Jean had not been able to bring herself to slip into bed naked on these afternoons, as Darroch did. He'd persuaded her to go to bed at night without clothing by the simple expedient of immediately removing whatever she was wearing. But Sundays, in broad daylight, were different. She'd said, "What if somebody comes to the door? Or we have to answer the telephone?"

He'd laughed at her. "Have you forgotten where you are? This is a Scottish Presbyterian island, Jean. No one goes anywhere on Sunday afternoons. And I've turned the phone off."

"Màiri and Jamie . . . " she'd begun. The MacDonalds, their best friends and neighbors down the lane in their cottage, *Taigh Rois*, were prone to pop in for a chat and a cuppa at any time.

" . . . spend Sunday afternoons in bed, just like we do. I got the idea from Jamie, remember?"

But she still couldn't do it. "There's all those army jets flying overhead on their practice runs, looking down through the skylight," she'd muttered.

He'd laughed and diverted his energies into finding her something pretty to wear for their afternoons. Today she had on one of his prize finds from an Edinburgh antique shop, a man's silk smoking jacket from the 1940s, heavy with embroidery and soft and slippery against her skin.

Languid and happy, she stretched and sighed. She slipped out of the jacket and put it carefully on the elderly oriental rug on the floor. Then she turned on her side and began to move one hand over Darroch's long, lean body, tugging at chest hair, drifting over ribs and flat belly, and lower.

Darroch realized suddenly that the report he was reading made no sense. He tossed it on the floor and moved down in bed to pull her into his arms.

I love Island Sunday afternoons, Jean thought contentedly.

Two

And hear my vows o' truth and love,
And say thou lo'es me best of a'.
Robert Burns

*D*espite Darroch's most persuasive efforts they were still not married. His gentle, malleable Jean, usually so amenable to reason, had set herself stubbornly against marriage, coming at last to the point where she refused even to discuss it. "We are perfect just as we are," she said and that was the end of it.

Darroch had given up, at least for the time being. They were handfast, had been for almost five months. That ancient ceremony of commitment was good enough for everyone on the Island except Minister Donald of the Free Presbyterian Kirk, who took a dim view of handfasting, especially when it involved Darroch Mac an Rìgh, the Laird, and his beloved American lady. "It is setting a bad example for the rest of the Island, the two of you living in sin. I do not understand why you cannot make her see reason," he said in exasperation to Darroch. "Do you want me to talk to her?"

Alarmed, Darroch snapped, "No! Under no circumstances! I absolutely forbid it, Minister." If anything would set Jean against marrying him it would be interference in their lives from the Minister. She would be so alarmed and embarrassed that she might bolt, if not to her homeland, certainly back to her own little thatched cottage up the hill. And we are not living in sin, he thought crossly. The handfasting ceremony in which they had sworn to be together for a year and a day, promised before two witnesses, Jamie and Màiri MacDonald, was perfectly legitimate in Eilean Dubh custom.

But there was no arguing that with Minister Donald. "The Laird should set a good example."

"I have set a good example. All my life I've set a good example; my parents brought me up that way. Now it's time for people here to stand on their own feet. If they misbehave it's nothing to do with me." Darroch strode to the Minister's study door, then turned back.

"And I am not the Laird. My great-grandfather gave up the title a hundred years ago." He stalked out.

The Minister looked after him fondly. A fine lad, he thought. The Laird from head to toe.

Darroch's comments did not stop the Minister from preaching a sermon on the merits of Holy Matrimony next Sunday, his eyes fixed firmly on the sole occupant of the Mac an Rìgh pew, who squirmed uncomfortably. At the end of the sermon Darroch stood up, red-faced, glared at the Minister and stalked out, not waiting for the final psalm to be sung. The congregation stared, nudged and whispered.

The Minister smiled in satisfaction. While he could not compel the independent-minded Laird to behave as the Kirk deemed proper, he could certainly keep the pressure on.

The rest of the population of the Island confidently looked forward to celebrating the Laird's wedding but it was not in their nature to rush things. "All in good time" could have been the Islanders' motto. The pace of life on a tiny Hebridean island was slow and deliberate and nothing speeded it up. It was one of the things Jean liked best about her new home.

She could not explain her aversion to marriage. She had found the man with whom she wanted to spend the rest of her life, she loved him and trusted him completely, but she would not agree, yet, to marry him. Her American marriage had ended in divorce, his marriage had ended in divorce, even though both were sanctioned by government license and blessed by their churches. She now believed that the only lasting union came from what was understood and promised by the two people involved. What they were to each other was their business and theirs alone.

They lived in his cottage and used hers as an office where they kept their computers and their papers. Darroch prepared for his television acting roles there before going to London for filming. Jean kept her collection of Eilean Dubh fairy tales there. She was re-writing and polishing Darroch's translations from the Gaelic and hoped to put the stories into printed form one day.

Once a month, when her period came, she moved back into her small house and slept alone.

It was hard to explain to Darroch and harder for her to understand herself, but she had a need to be independent before she married again. Except for a few months in an apartment when she was in college, she'd never lived by herself until she came to the Island, fleeing the wreck of her first marriage in the pretense of looking for an Eilean Dubh ancestor.

She'd learned a lot about herself, living alone, and she wasn't through with the learning process.

It was good for her to spend a few days a month alone, to draw into herself, especially when she was having her period, when she felt most the need for privacy. And it helped her in the continuing transition from her life in Milwaukee to her life on a small Scottish island. She loved her new friends and neighbors but sometimes they seemed so different. So Scottish. Sometimes she missed America and Americans.

Sometimes she needed to step back from her present life and review the past, to think about her relationship with her first husband Russ, to deepen her understanding of what had gone wrong with that marriage, so that she did not make mistakes with Darroch. She intended that relationship to last the rest of her life. She had intended the first one to last that long, too, and it had gone horribly wrong. Of course, Russ and Darroch were completely different people, but they were both men, after all.

Darroch did not quite understand. If it was modesty about her period that concerned her it was entirely unnecessary as far as he was concerned. In his three-year marriage to his first wife Adrienne he'd gotten quite accustomed to dealing with that time of the month. Adrienne had become depressed and tearful, had needed lots of cuddling and reassurance. And his long-ago lover, Morgan, with whom he'd lived for two years, had craved sex. "It helps with the cramps," she'd said. They'd spread towels on the bed and made love, laughing, and she'd been hotly, messily, exquisitely female. He'd felt himself privileged to be initiated into the ultimate mystery of womanhood.

He wanted to be with Jean, with or without sex, found it hard to sleep at night without her warm body snuggled against his. He'd get up, finally, tired of restlessly tossing and turning, stalk to the bedroom window and stare up the hill at her cottage. Often there was a light on and he had the satisfaction of knowing that she too found it difficult to sleep alone.

He'd think about walking up the hill and knocking gently. He'd never presume to open her door and walk in, even though *Eilean Dubhannaich* doors were never locked. He didn't think he'd open the door. Well, he might open it and call gently to her. If she came to him, put her arms around him and turned her face up for a kiss, he'd carry her to the bedroom, lift her into bed and crawl in with her.

When she was finally wrapped in his arms he could get a good night's sleep.

He knew he'd do no such thing. Instead he'd walk up in the morning, knock and wait to be admitted, sit down at her kitchen table and share cups of coffee. She'd not become so acclimated to Scotland that she preferred tea to coffee in the mornings.

And he'd wait out the six long nights until she came back, walking into their cottage with her little carry bag of clothes. "Hello, lovie. I'm baaack!" she'd call.

He'd turn from the stove, smiling. "*Feasgar math, mo chridhe.* Dinner's almost ready. Come to the table."

"Smells wonderful. What is it?"

"Beef stew. I didn't know when you'd be home so I fixed something that will get better the longer it sits."

"*Miorbhuileach*. I made bread."

Afterward they'd do dishes together, Jean leaning her head occasionally to brush against his shoulder. Sometimes his arm would steal around her waist and she'd sigh in pleasure, then yelp because his hand was leaving a cold dishwater-wet print on her hip.

Then she'd say, "I'll go upstairs and take a shower and get ready for bed."

"Grand. I'll shut things up down here," he'd reply casually. He'd move to the fireplace and smoor the fire, whispering the traditional prayer in the Gaelic, the Island's own language.

And a few minutes later they'd be in bed together, and life could resume its accustomed pattern.

The monthly separations were hard, but he didn't protest. Whatever was going on in Jean's head, he was willing to let her have space until she was ready for marriage, the ultimate commitment. He would do that for her because he loved her.

Apart from that small ripple, the months they'd been together had been remarkably good. They were very compatible, both well-organized, hard-working, good-natured individuals with shared interests, the largest one being the care and preservation of their little Island, its language and its remarkable folk music. They enjoyed every minute they spent with each other, in and out of bed.

So Darroch could ignore the Minister's frowns and his friends' expectant looks and be happy with his Jean. At least they were handfast and he knew her commitment to him was unshakable. One of these days they'd get married, he knew, and he wasn't going to rush her into it.

This afternoon's lovemaking had been especially delicious and her yielding to him had been all he could have ever wished. They'd fallen asleep in each other's arms.

Jean woke first. She had not intended to nap and she immediately remembered the roasting chicken. I hope it's not burned, she thought guiltily, and scrambled up, throwing her feet over the side of the bed.

She was immediately overcome by a wave of nausea so intense that she could only think of getting to the bathroom in time. She made it just as her breakfast came up.

Darroch heard her retching. He followed the sound and found her crouched by the toilet, her face white. He wet a washcloth and knelt by her to wipe her face.

She felt too ill to be embarrassed. When he lifted her up and carried her to bed she wanted only to lie flat until her stomach settled down.

He sat by her. "It's that flu that's going around, I expect," he said reassuringly.

It did not seem like flu to Jean. She did not feel feverish or achy and once she was flat on her back the nausea was disappearing. Something else occurred to her.

"Would you get me a handful of crackers, lovie?" she asked.

"Do you think you should eat anything?"

"Yes, please. And pull the chicken out of the oven." The idea of the chicken, golden-brown, sizzling in its own fat, made her feel ill again. "Crackers first, lovie."

He frowned but got up and went downstairs to the kitchen. When he came back with the crackers and looked down at her, worried, she said, "Don't forget the chicken." After he'd gone she ate the crackers one by one, lying flat on her back. Crumbs spilled down her front and tickled her neck.

After a bit she sat up slowly. The nausea did not return. She looked down at herself. Surely her breasts seemed fuller. They had been sensitive lately, they had ached but she'd thought it was because her period was due. It was, she realized suddenly, almost a week late. She was seldom late, as regular as clockwork. She'd been too busy to think about it till now.

And suddenly she knew. She was pregnant.

Three

And they twa met, and they twa plat,
And fain they wad be near;
And a' the world might ken right weel,
They were twa lovers dear.

Old ballad

*P*regnant.

She lay very still, thinking about it, staring up through the skylight into the cloud-filled sky.

She had wanted it so much and now that it might have happened she was quite overwhelmed. Her jittery mind began to scroll through the negatives, beginning with the obvious: morning sickness. The urgent need to pee, the backaches, heartburn, mood swings, fatigue . . . and then a swollen belly, distorting the svelte figure she worked diligently to keep trim.

Did she really want a baby? Even more important, did Darroch? She hadn't given him a choice; she'd simply announced her intention of getting pregnant, had refused to use anything to prevent it. She knew he yearned for a family and the *Eilean Dubhannaich* yearned for an heir from their Laird, and she intended to do her best to gratify both constituencies.

But she and Darroch hadn't talked about it. Did he really understand what it would mean, how it would change their lives?

Middle of the night feedings, dirty diapers, colic. Ear infections, tantrums, report cards, first dates.

An end to the tender intimacy they prized so much, with a third person always to be considered, from now on.

She began to panic. Suppose he hated the whole idea?

And what about the hazards of having a baby when she was forty. No, forty-one. Would the baby be all right? Would she?

She'd be sixty by the time the baby was grown up. Old enough to be a grandmother, not a mother.

And what about sex? Lord, she loved sex with Darroch. They'd made love in every room in the house, in the shower, in front of the fire, standing up in the kitchen with her bottom perched on the sink, her legs wrapped around his waist, both of them laughing helplessly. They'd discovered in each other a deep hunger for loving sex. It was more than fulfillment of physical desire, it was the sacrament of their relationship. Sex was their private world that no one could invade.

Except a baby.

Would Darroch still want to make love? Would he be afraid of hurting the baby? Would he still want her when she grew large and ungainly?

Russ had been freaked out by the idea of making love to a pregnant woman and she'd been so full of hormones she'd wanted sex desperately and it had been awful; it had caused a rift in their relationship that had never completely healed. Suppose Darroch felt the same way?

If he rejected her she'd curl up and die.

Darroch came into the bedroom, carrying a tray. "Want to try a cup of tea?"

Cautiously she raised herself up. The nausea did not return. "Yes, thanks."

He handed her a cup and sat on the edge of the bed, looking at her anxiously. "Perhaps you should see Ros MacPherson. Although there won't be much he can do, if it's flu."

"I know." But Ros, the doctor, could tell me if I'm pregnant, she thought. She knew that chemists sold do-it-yourself pregnancy tests, but if she bought one it would be all over the Island before she got home, thanks to Eilean Dubh's well-developed gossip network. She shuddered at the thought. "I'll see him, though, just to make sure."

"I'll ring the surgery." He came back in a few moments. "They've a cancellation. Ros can see you at two."

Darroch wanted to come into the examining room with her but she convinced him to go and do the marketing. "Then we can go right home afterwards."

Ros listened quietly while she related her symptoms. Then he examined her. Afterwards he said, "I can't be sure until the test comes back. But I think it very likely that you are indeed with child."

He took his glasses off and wiped his eyes. "I attended Darroch's mother during her pregnancy. May I be the first to congratulate you, *mo leadaidh*.

The Island will be delighted." Better than that, he thought, they'd be ecstatic that their beloved Laird would have an heir to the Mac an Rìgh name.

"Thanks, Ros. I've wanted it. But it's sort of scary, at my age."

"I understand. We'll do our best to see that you get the finest care. Unless . . . " He hesitated so long that she grew puzzled. "You may prefer to go to Edinburgh, or London. I would understand that."

Leave Eilean Dubh, be surrounded by strangers? Leave the loving companionship of her friends? Not a chance. "No, I want to be with people I love and trust. And I have confidence in you, Ros."

She decided to wait until she got the test results to tell Darroch but it filled her head so completely it was all she could do not to blurt it out. But she kept her secret until Ros called. "The test was positive. You are six weeks pregnant," he said. There was silence on both ends of the phone until she said, "Thanks, Ros," and hung up.

She sat, lost in thought. Considering the frequency and enthusiasm with which they made love, she was surprised it hadn't happened sooner. She'd almost begun to believe that it wouldn't happen at all, that she was too old at forty-one to get pregnant.

When had she conceived, she wondered, and got up to look at the calendar. She checked the dates. There was a tiny "x" on a Wednesday six weeks ago, a mark she always made to note a remarkable event. Weeks later she would scan the calendar, looking for the "xes", teasing her memory for what had been special about that date.

She didn't have to strain her brain to remember that "x"; it had been one of the most extraordinary lovemaking experiences of her life.

She had been sitting at the kitchen table writing out a grocery list, completely absorbed in thoughts about what to have for dinner the next evening. She'd been only dimly aware of Darroch, on the sofa, tossing aside the script he'd been reading, getting up and stretching his six-foot-three-inch frame. He walked over to her chair and knelt beside her, wrapping his arms around her waist. "What are you doing?" he whispered in her ear.

His warm breath tickled her down to her toes. "Oh, something very important," she teased.

"How important?" He nibbled her earlobe until she giggled. "Pretty important."

"More important than this?" His hands slipped under her sweater, under her blouse and moved upward. Long fingers tugged at her bra. "Why do you wear these things?" he grumbled.

"You're supposed to," she said. "Because the breasts need support."

"Like this?" He lifted her breasts with his hands.

"Just like that," she gasped.

"You've got me for support, you don't need this." He unfastened the bra and pulled it open, then filled one hand with her breast and turned her with the other arm, so his mouth could find hers. Time slowed and the kiss went on and on, until he coaxed, "Come down here with me," and tugged her down into his arms, then put her gently on the hardwood floor.

In a haze of pleasure she felt him pulling her dress up. "You surely don't need to wear these around the house," he said, sliding her panties off.

"No," she agreed dreamily. "I suppose not. You've got them off most of the time, anyway."

He fumbled with his trousers and moved on top of her. He eased himself into her with deliberate slowness, knowing he was increasing her enjoyment. And she was enjoying it: her body was arched up to him in a perfect bow of pleasure and inside she was liquid and hot. Her orgasm was instantaneous, he felt her rippling and convulsing around him as he began to move with increasing urgency to his own release.

She felt naked and raw inside, stripped of all artifice. She had given herself to him completely and the emotion was so intense that she wanted it to last forever.

He raised his head. "The floor is hard, *mo chridhe*," he whispered. "Did I hurt you?"

"Oh, no, never," she sighed, then cried out in alarm when she felt him beginning to withdraw. She couldn't bear it if he didn't stay inside her. "Don't leave me." She pressed her hips up against him urgently. "Please . . . "

He came back, going deeper and deeper. She wanted him deeper still and wrapped her legs around him, raising them higher and higher until her ankles were clasped behind his head. She peaked again, spiking so intensely that she shuddered violently in his arms and tears sprang to her eyes.

She felt his increasing need and moved against him till he flooded her with his climax, and her womb opened to take in his life.

Afterwards they'd lain quietly together until Darroch was at last able to lift himself from her and say tenderly, "Making love on the kitchen floor. Will there be no end to this madness?"

"I certainly hope not."

He helped her to a sitting position and they sat tangled together, kissing and laughing until it was time to start supper. Before she took the salmon out of the fridge she marked an "x" on the day's date. Wednesday, July 4, she'd noted. Wonderful Wednesday, with fireworks.

Yep, that had been the one, all right. She hadn't been the same since, there'd been an acute new sense of anticipation, the restless feeling that she was trembling on the brink of something exciting. And now she knew what it was.

A baby. Perhaps a miniature version of her darling Darroch, with his startlingly blue eyes and jet-black hair and long elegant nose. And smart, like Rod and Sally, her grown-up children from her first marriage. Sweet and cuddly, nursing contentedly at her breast. Her mind conjured up a baby's first smile, first laugh and she went all mushy inside. Mothering hormones flooded her.

She'd have to brush up on her repertoire of lullabies. Maybe there were some Eilean Dubh lullabies she'd never heard. She'd ask some of the elderly ladies. They'd be delighted to help her, clucking and muttering fondly while they searched their memories for beloved old songs.

Ah, the *Eilean Dubhannaich* would love it. A new generation of Mac an Rìghs to fuss over, worry and gossip about, an heir to the Mac an Rìgh dynasty. She giggled, thinking of Darroch's reaction to that word. He'd spent his adult life trying to rid the Island of the idea of the lairdship and now she was perpetuating it.

Oh dear, Darroch. What would he think?

She had refused wine for dinner the last few nights, pleading a touch of the flu, but tonight she was going to have a whisky, a small one, her last taste of alcohol for seven and a half months. She poured them both a dram and brought it on a silver tray to the leather sofa in front of the fireplace.

"I have something to tell you," she said.

He took his glass and looked at her inquiringly.

"I'm . . . we're . . . I'm going to have a . . . we're pregnant!" She blurted it out. "I hope you don't mind."

"Mind?" In his astonishment he seized on the last thing she said. "Why would I mind?"

"It'll change our lives . . . "

He put his glass down and pulled her into his arms. Neither said a word for the next few moments. Then he relaxed his hold. "I'm sorry, did I squash you? I'll have to be more careful now. No more bear hugs." He smiled down at her.

She began to cry, nerves and pregnancy sending the tears spilling from her eyes. She wiped them away angrily. "I don't want you to be careful, I'm not glass, I won't break. Please don't say you won't hug me any more, I couldn't stand that."

Darroch's heart swelled with tenderness. He lifted her legs, pulled her on his lap and rocked her like a child. "Hush, my lovely darling, my bonnie wee lass. I'll hug you all you want, I promise. Every day. And kiss you till you cry for mercy." He tilted her head up to his. "I couldn't live without kissing you, Jean. You know that. Now, *mo chridhe,* tell me why you're crying."

"I don't know. Hormones, I guess. I feel all weepy. I was so afraid you wouldn't want a baby."

He said, surprised, "Why would you think that? Haven't we been trying our best to get you pregnant? Not that I regret a moment of the trying, mind you."

"You don't know how much it will change things. Our life will be turned upside down."

He chuckled. "So we'll get a look at things from a different direction, aye? Might be fun."

She said darkly, "Wait till those two A.M. feedings. See if you still think it's fun."

He took her shoulders firmly and turned her to face him. "Jean, why are you worrying about all this? Other people have babies and they survive. You've had two. We can handle it. We'll handle it together. Even the two A.M. feedings."

She looked into his eyes and he looked back, his gaze steady and unwavering. Of course he was right. She flung her arms around his neck and kissed him. "You're so sensible, lovie."

"And you are *miorbhuileach.*" He brought her hand to his lips. "I haven't the words to tell you how happy you've made me. You and our baby. I can't imagine a better life. Except . . . can I still make love to you? Because right now I want you very much." She was the mother of his child and he wanted her in bed with him, wanted to be inside her, as close as two human beings could get to each other.

Jean wriggled off his lap and stood up. "That's your answer to everything, isn't it." When he looked at her, eyebrows raised, she grinned and held out her hand to him. "It's a good one and mine too. Come on, let's go to bed."

When Jean was in bed he sat down by her. He put his hand on her belly. "You're so flat. It's hard to imagine that there's a baby in there."

"Right now it's about the size of a peanut. Wait a couple of months. I'll swell up like a balloon."

He said softly, "Like a seedpod. Or a rose, getting ready to bloom." He stroked her belly, then bent to kiss her there. "*Feasgar math, mo nighean,*" he said, his mouth close to her skin. Good evening, my daughter. Jean understood only bits and pieces of the rest; it was all in the Gaelic. Though she'd been studying the language diligently, her comprehension was sometimes slow to kick in.

"What are you saying?"

"I am introducing myself. I told her that I was her father, that I loved her, that her mother and I love each other very much. That we will take good care of her. That we look forward to meeting her, when she's ready to greet the world."

Touched to tears, Jean swallowed the lump in her throat and said, "You're sure it's a girl?"

"No. Tomorrow night I will talk to our baby as if he's a boy. That way I will—what is it you Americans say?—cover all the bases." He smiled at her, then lay down and gathered her in his arms. "The size of a peanut, hmm. I think I will get a book, Jean, so I can see what she is like as she grows inside you."

He thought about how he'd envied other men walking with their pregnant wives, or pushing prams, or holding the small hand of a child. He'd envied his friend Jamie as he sat in his rocking chair, a little redheaded girl standing on one side, a yellow-haired boy on the other, arguing as to whose turn it was to sit on Daddy's lap, Jamie settling the argument by lifting them both up, one in each arm. He'd sat, grinning broadly, his lap full of giggling children.

Darroch had thought he'd never have that happiness. A wife and a child of his own. A thousand questions flooded his mind. When would the baby come? Would it be a boy or a girl? *A Dhia*, was the cottage big enough? He'd heard that babies required enormous amounts of paraphernalia. Should he start planning to build an addition? He sighed with the pleasure of a new project on which to expend his boundless energy.

"It is a miracle," he murmured and felt so deeply content that he did not even have to make love to her to find satisfaction. Right now he was happy just to lie in bed holding her, looking up through the skylight as twilight deepened into night. A year, he thought, a year since we met. Look how far we've come.

Drowsiness crept over Jean, warring with her desire for sex. I'll just doze for a moment or two, she thought, remembering another symptom of pregnancy: the ability to fall asleep anywhere, anytime.

Darroch sat up suddenly. He leaned over her, captured her hands, held them firmly and stared into her eyes. "We're going to get married, Jean. As soon as possible. No more waiting."

She smiled at him drowsily. Time to move on, to something new. She was ready. She'd had time to prepare. "Okay." Her eyes drifted shut.

Darroch looked at her, asleep in his arms. So this is how it begins, he thought. A new life.

Mozart theme—"Voi che sapete"—Marriage of Figaro, Act II

(in public domain)

Jamie MacDonald's Compliments to His Sheep, and His Apologies to Mozart

Var. 1 on Jamie MacDonald . . .

Var. 2 on Jamie MacDonald . . .

Var. 3 on Jamie MacDonald . . . (works as a counter melody to the original Mozart)

Four

Welcome babe wi' music,
Welcome babe wi' charms,
Welcome babe wi' herb an' flo'er,
Make safe the mither's arms.

Eilean Dubh pregnancy blessing

Jean woke early the next day and thought she was still asleep when she heard the distant music of a violin. What on earth, she thought, and lifted her head to listen. Just in time she remembered to reach under her pillow for crackers, and nibbled them slowly.

Darroch was still asleep. She slipped out of bed quietly, dressed and went down to the kitchen for a cup of tea and cinnamon toast.

She heard the music again. It had not been a dream. She took her cup and went out the kitchen door.

It was coming from the field across the road where their friend Jamie MacDonald pastured his prized flock of Jacob's sheep. The fiddler had to be Jamie, she thought, there was no one on the Island who played so brilliantly. When she walked to the garden wall she could just get a glimpse of a tall figure, bright golden hair glowing in the sun, standing in the pasture surrounded by sheep: Bonnie Prince Jamie from the Isle of Skye, the handsomest man on the Island and the best Scottish fiddler in the world.

Jean smiled and put on her coat. She poured the rest of the tea into a thermos and picked up two mugs.

The music began again as she climbed the stone fence and made her way through the field, skirting piles of sheep droppings. Jamie was leaning against an enormous rock and he was playing something she recognized.

When he finished she said, "Mozart? I didn't know you knew Mozart."

He looked up, not surprised to see her. "I don't know it very well, but the sheep can't tell the difference. A very uncritical audience, sheep."

"Do they really like music?"

"You don't see them running away, do you?" He smiled at her.

It was true, the four-horned, black-spotted Jacob's Sheep were not all over the pasture as usual; they were grouped near Jamie and had not scattered at her approach. "I've heard you some mornings. I thought it was my imagination, or the fairies making music. Do you do this often?"

"Only when I take a notion that the sheep need a tune or two. This is the one they like best." He played a lovely gentle melody of his own devising.

Jean thought she heard a soft satisfied "baaa" coming from the flock.

Jamie put his bow down. "Why are you carrying two mugs?"

"Tea." She poured and handed the mug to him.

They sipped in silence. Then Jamie tucked his fiddle and bow back in the case. He straightened and looked her over. "Well," he said, smiling.

She felt herself turning pink. "You know, don't you."

"*Thà gu dearbh, mo fhlùr.* I am very happy for you." He stretched out his arms and she walked into them. "Does Darroch know yet?"

She nodded. "I told him last night."

"And . . . ?"

"He's very happy too."

"And you?"

"I must admit I had my doubts but Darroch put them to rest."

"Never fear, Jean, all will be well." He kissed her cheek, then let her go. "Time to get back. They'll both be up by now, wondering where we are."

He walked her back to the cottage. Darroch was standing in the kitchen staring into the empty, still warm, teapot with a puzzled look. He raised his eyebrows at the sight of them. "What's this, an early morning rendezvous?"

"For sheep music," said Jamie. He extended his hand. "Congratulations, *mo charaid.*"

"Jean, you told him," began Darroch and she laughed. "Since when has it ever been necessary to tell Jamie anything?" Every Islander knew that Jamie had the Sight, the ability to see into the future, though no one, especially not Jamie, would talk about it.

Darroch shrugged his shoulders in resignation. "It's a good job there's no military secrets on the Island, with you around." He shook his friend's hand.

"Will you stay for breakfast, Jamie?" said Jean.

"No, I'm away home. It's my turn to cook today and herself will be ravenous. Appetite of a tiger, that woman." At the door he paused and turned. "I won't say anything to Màiri, and if you'll take my advice you'll keep this quiet for a bit."

"I know. If you tell people too soon it will seem as though you've been pregnant forever."

"That, and the fact that everyone will have something to share with you."

"Such as?" said Darroch.

"Advice on what to eat, what to drink, why you should exercise, why you shouldn't exercise. Good omens, bad omens. Cures for morning sickness, charms for an easy labor, charms for this and cures for that. Gifts of sprigs of rowan, shells shaped like wombs, bunches of juniper. There'll be no end to it."

"Never tell me they'd still believe in that old nonsense," Darroch said, astonished.

"With the prospect of the Laird's baby in their minds? There'll be no telling what they'll get up to."

Darroch looked dismayed but Jean chuckled. "That's really sweet," she said and both men swung around to stare at her in surprise.

"Jean, you shouldn't have to put up with this superstitious foolishness. I'll get Minister Donald to preach against it," Darroch said firmly.

"That'll just drive it underground. You'll be finding anonymous bunches of rowan and perfectly shaped eggs on your doorstep every morning."

Darroch groaned. "Jean, you must think you've landed on an Island full of dafties."

"No, I don't. I think it's nice. And very interesting. I'll be happy to listen to what they have to say."

"It's a complete waste of time . . . ," Darroch began.

Jean said, "I don't know that and you don't either. There's lots of attention paid to old folk remedies today. Some of them even turn out to be useful."

"Shells shaped like wombs? Perfect eggs?"

"Not to mention the jelly made of hares' brains. It's supposed to be good for pregnant women, Jean," Jamie said, grinning.

She shuddered but looked at them defiantly. "I'll listen to all of it. Maybe I'll collect the stories. Maybe I'll write a book about it. Folk remedies of Eilean Dubh."

When Darroch looked unconvinced she added, "Let me make sure I understand all this. You're saying that everyone will be interested, will want to give advice and presents. And this is supposed to be a bad thing."

"Gossip, chatter, nosy interference," growled Darroch.

"Listen. Do you know what the reaction of my friends would be if I were back in Milwaukee and pregnant at forty years old, with two grown kids? Half of them would congratulate me but they'd still snicker behind their hands at the idea of someone my age starting all over with diapers and babysitters. The other half would offer their condolences and would find one way or another to ask why I don't get rid of it."

"Rid of it?" said Darroch, horrified. "Because you're forty people would laugh and want you to get rid of a baby? Even if you're married?"

"Don't get me wrong," said Jean. "I wouldn't presume to tell another woman what to do. But I'm healthy, I have money, I could look after a kid, I could enjoy having it. Sure, it would change my life, but who cares? But people would laugh at me; they'd think I should be embarrassed to get caught being careless. And you two think I should be upset because the *Eilean Dubhannaich* will be interested in our baby?"

She looked at them. "If they want a share in this child it's theirs. I think it's *miorbhuileach* that they're interested and I intend to listen to every word of their advice. I may not take it, but I'll sure listen."

Darroch shrugged. "I still think it's a damned imposition and a bloody cheek, but if you don't mind, Jean . . . "

Jean grinned. "Wait and see how impossibly spoiled I get. I've always wanted to be the center of attention. The queen of the May. Just watch me!"

Jamie took her hand and kissed it. "I salute you, *a Shìne*, queen of the May, queen of Eilean Dubh."

"Do you know how odd that seems to an American, to be called that?"

"Do you know how odd that seems to a confirmed republican, to say it?" Jamie grinned.

"That bloody Laird business. Go away, Jamie," Darroch growled. "Go fix Màiri's breakfast."

"At your command, *a Mhic an Rìgh*. My lady." He bowed to Darroch, then to Jean.

"Always taking the mickey," Darroch mumbled as Jamie left. "Fancies himself a wit, does Jamie."

"Well, I think it's . . . "

Darroch groaned. "I know. Sweet. Sentimental rubbish." He pulled her into his arms. "This is our baby, Jean. Not the Island's, ours."

She smiled to herself, but answered docilely, "Yes, darling."

Five

The King's most humble servant I,
Can scarcely spare a minute;
But I'll be wi' ye by an' bye;
Or else the Deil's be in it.

Robert Burns

*W*edding preparations began and moved along swiftly. Having finally secured Jean's consent, Darroch was taking no chances that she'd change her mind. And Jean had refused to celebrate her wedding anniversary with her first husband Russ so that her kids wouldn't realize she was pregnant when she'd married, and she didn't want to go through that with another child. She wanted to get married as soon as possible.

True, it was no disgrace today being pregnant before marriage, thanks to the movie stars and rock musicians who'd made it popular, but who knows what morals would rule in fifteen years when the child would be old enough to be embarrassed. Besides, it would be easier to fit wedding clothes if she wasn't bulging with bairn.

The first hurdle was an administrative one. They gathered up their birth certificates, divorce decrees and Jean's passport and took them with their marriage notice form to the Registrar's office in Airgead in the north of the Island.

An awed clerk passed them immediately on to the inner office. Such an important and much anticipated event as the Laird's marriage would be dealt with by the Registrar himself. Besides, the clerk wanted to be free to hit the telephone and be the first to spread the word: the Laird and Mrs. Jean are getting married, at last.

Jimmy Buchan was a small man in a brown suit, with brown hair and a bristly brown mustache. He was an incomer to the Island, from Glasgow.

When he spoke, his Glaswegian accent was so pronounced that Jean thought at first he was speaking a foreign language.

"Guid dae to yez," he said. "Laird Mac an Rìgh, an' ye'll be the Amuricun lassie? Gaun, sit yez daown."

Darroch explained their errand. They had come seeking the certificate that only the Registrar could issue and which was needed before Jean, a foreign national, could marry in Scotland: the paper certifying that there was no impediment to their proposed marriage.

"Aye, aye, I knae fine what ye're wintin'. Kinna sae yer papers, then?" Darroch passed them over and the Registrar scrutinized them carefully for a long time.

At last he looked up. "Aw 'n ordaer. Whan's th' waeddin'?"

"We haven't set a date because we didn't know how long it would take to get the certificate."

"Gie's a coupla weeks. Tha high heid yins in Edinbro 'll hafta hae a nebby. Ah'll put the wind up, rummle 'em a bit, and we'll get ye fixed aout the week or twa. Gaun on w' yer plannin'; it'll aw cum right."

Darroch stood up and held out his hand. "Thanks, Jimmy."

"Nae tother." The Registrar shook Darroch's hand and turned to Jean. "Glad tae meet ye, Missus. Wif aw this Gaelic mince it's a plasur to hav another wan here whit speaks Anglish, as waell 's me."

Jean smiled politely, realizing she'd not understood more than a third of what he'd said.

The second hurdle was about where to hold the wedding and who would perform the ceremony. They didn't have much choice about that. Minister Donald had presided over most of the major events of Darroch's life except his first wedding and look how that had turned out.

Left to herself Jean would have liked a Unitarian service, as in the church she'd attended in Milwaukee, or maybe a Quaker ceremony. But she realized how deeply hurt Minister Donald would be if he was left out and she knew that he had to be the one to officiate. Luckily he wasn't a fire-and-brimstone sort of Free Presbyterian, and much less dour than most of the Wee Free clergy. And perhaps they could persuade him to alter the service a tiny bit. She wasn't going to promise to obey, for example, nor would Darroch expect it. They would be equals in this marriage.

But the Minister's old stone kirk was small. Everyone on the Island would want to attend the Laird's wedding. Where would they put them all? Nearly 800 people, and a kirk that seated 200 at most. Who could be left out?

Jean said, "Could we have it outdoors? And the reception in the Citizens Hall?" The Minister, consulted with trepidation, looked at them thoughtfully out of his icy gray eyes. "The Lord is present everywhere. He doesn't need a kirk to signify His presence. I'll marry you in the kirkyard."

The reception, at least, posed no problems, once Jean and Sheilah Morrison, the gourmet cook who ran the Rose Hotel in Ros Mór with her husband Gordon, put their heads together.

Sheilah began to tick off the items on her fingers: game pies, roast beef, Jean's special lasagna, ham. Then the desserts: trifle, cranachan with raspberries layered among whisky-soaked oatmeal crumbs, shortbread, apple pies, Sheilah's killer chocolate cake. Pots of heavy cream, ready to augment anyone's dessert choice with a few more calories.

"We'll make as much as we can ahead and store it in my freezers. Everyone will help cook."

Jean fretted that they'd never be able to prepare enough. Darroch said the entire Island would come, the reception would last all afternoon and mellow into a *cèilidh* lasting well into the long autumn night. Tons of food and drink would be needed.

Sheilah said, "Don't worry, these are just the basics. Everyone will bring something to share and a bottle or two."

Jean was horrified. "It's our wedding. Darroch and I will provide everything."

Sheilah laughed and said, "No, be reasonable, Jean. No one expects you to provide for that many people. Besides, you won't allow them to give wedding presents, so they need some way to contribute, to show their affection." Then she clinched her argument by saying, "There's no way I could cook that much. Do you want to kill me?"

Darroch, reluctant to let the women have all the fun, made up gallons of what he called his American "bar-be-que" sauce. The recipe had been given to him by a Charleston lady, a fan of his hit BBC television series *The Magician* that had become a cult classic wherever it was shown. The "receipt" had been handed down in her family since plantation days, she'd said.

He marinated and cooked batches of meatballs and tiny pork ribs. The meat's flavor was spicy, hot and sweet all at once. "Just like you, Jean," he whispered in her ear.

Jamie was drafted into service to make the Atholl Brose, a concoction of whisky, honey and the "juice" from oatmeal soaked in water for several hours. "I'm doing this under protest," he grumbled. "What a way to treat whisky."

But Jean's friend Barabal Mac-a-Phi insisted and her mother concurred that it was traditional at a laird's wedding.

"All the more reason to drop it," growled Darroch, irritated as usual by the bloody laird business. He agreed with Jamie about the whisky and said (but not where Barabal could hear) that it was highly unlikely that her mother would be that familiar with his family's wedding customs. "Made it up, most likely. Her mother's family's MacShennachs; they wouldn't even have been invited to a Mac an Rìgh wedding for the last century because of the feud."

But Barabal prevailed and the Atholl Brose was made and decanted back into the empty whisky bottles. All the cooks were offered a dram to taste.

Barabal drank hers with relish, smacking her lips at the end. "Very nice, laddie," she said to Jamie, to his annoyance. He hated being called "laddie." "I'll have another wee sip just to make sure." She held out her glass and drained the refill happily. "My mother will be pleased."

"That makes it all worthwhile," said Jamie sarcastically.

Events had moved so swiftly that Jean had not had time to think about what she was going to wear to be married. She brought it up to Màiri, who stared in disbelief.

"Has Darroch not talked to you?" Jean shook her head, and Màiri said, "Men! You'll want to have a kilted skirt made in the Mac an Rìgh tartan and we'd best get on it straightaway."

When Jean looked bewildered Mairi explained. "For anyone who can afford it, a long skirt, ankle-length, made like a kilt, is traditional, in the groom's tartan."

"Who will make it?"

"Elspeth MacShennach, Barabal's mother. She's a seamstress; didn't you know? Let's hope she's got enough yardage of Mac an Rìgh tartan. It takes forever to have a mill weave it and they need an order of several bolts before they'll even warp their looms, or whatever it is they do."

They were in Elspeth's house early the next day and Jean was measured for her skirt. Luckily, there was enough tartan left. Then Darroch took her to Inverness to Duncan Chisholm's shop to select her white lace-frilled blouse and to order her velvet jacket, in green to match her eyes and complement the colors of the Mac an Rìgh tartan. Jean sucked in her tummy when she was being measured and wished she could do the same with her breasts which had begun to swell with her pregnancy.

Mr. Chisholm himself waited on them and promised to have the jacket ready in two weeks. "For a wedding we pull out all the stops," he said.

That night, in bed with Darroch at his favorite B and B where he always stayed when he came to Inverness, Jean couldn't sleep. So much to arrange; what had she forgotten? I wish I had a little more time to plan, she fretted. But it was her own fault; she'd adamantly refused to think about getting married until the baby had come along.

She put her hand on her belly, testing its contours. Don't grow too fast, she told the baby. I've still got to get into that kilted skirt in a month.

Six

How often didst thou pledge and vow,
Thou wad for aye be mine!
And my fond heart, itsel sae true,
It ne'er mistrusted thine.

Robert Burns

The wedding guests began to arrive on Eilean Dubh, by Caledonian-MacBrayne ferry and by Murdoch the Chopper's helicopter. Jean and Darroch found themselves scurrying often to meet one or the other. Today it was a group coming from London on the helicopter.

"Who's in this batch?" Jean asked as Darroch's elderly Bentley sped towards the helicopter firm's landing pad.

"Actors. My friend Max Summers. He was Edgar Linton when I did *Wuthering Heights* on *Classic Theatre*, remember? He organized this group but he didn't tell me who is coming. He thought there would be about eight, but of course if someone's gotten an acting job they'll have dropped out. Anyway, they've rented Barabal's house. It's the only one on the Island big enough for a group that size."

"Where's Barabal and company gone?"

"She's farmed out the kids to relatives—I didn't know she had that many relatives—and she and Tòmas are staying with his mother. She's not over fond of her mother-in-law, but she said the money for the rental was too good to pass up."

They arrived just as the chopper was landing. Hand in hand they watched as the door opened and the first of the wedding guests got out. "That's Max," Darroch said, nudging Jean.

"My dear old chap, how are you?" called Max, bounding over. "And this ravishing creature must be the bride-to-be." He raked her up and down with a lascivious look. "Umm, just my type, all long hair and curves. Your servant, ma'am."

Jean almost lost her composure, but managed to say, "I'm pleased to meet you. I remember you from *Wuthering Heights*. Such a good performance."

"Beautiful and possessed of exquisite taste. I must kiss you." He put his arms around her with a flourish and saluted both cheeks with resounding smacks. Jean blushed.

"Steady on, Maxie, watch that famous charm," said Darroch.

"Oh, dear, yes. Gary's with me and he's so dreadfully jealous!" he said, throwing a mock glance of terror over his shoulder toward the chopper. "He thinks I'm a wicked flirt, but it's only that I have such a friendly nature. Aren't men just so difficult?" he sighed, looking at Jean for sympathy.

Flustered, Jean looked away and saw the woman just alighting from the chopper. Her eyes widened. "Darroch, who is that?"

The woman was a white-skinned vision in a vivid turquoise sari, scarves and shawls flowing, her curvaceous figure topped by improbable strawberry-blonde hair. She's gorgeous, Jean thought. But a bit over the top. Well, more than a bit, actually.

Darroch groaned. "*A Dhia beannaich mi.* Who invited her?"

"I did, old dear, " Max said, grinning. "She was desperate to come. How could I say no? You know I'm a soft touch for lovely ladies, and especially for Adrienne."

Adrienne, Jean thought. Darroch's ex-wife, at my wedding.

The woman stopped dramatically, looked about her and then ran towards them, all fluttering fabrics and wind-blown hair. Ignoring Jean and Max, she flung herself at Darroch.

"Darling Darroch!" She was kissing his cheeks with passionate little pecks. Jean stared.

Darroch growled into the blonde mass of hair, "Steady on, 'Rienne. You're overacting . . . as usual." He plucked the red-nailed hands from his shoulders and held her at arm's length.

Beyond the spectacle of Darroch's ex-wife Jean saw a man descending from the chopper. He was brown-skinned and simply dressed in a white tunic and trousers. His rounded face was crowned by impeccably cut straight black hair that stayed neatly in place in the wind that was blowing both Darroch's and Max's hair in their eyes.

Max said, "We've brought the Prince too."

"But of course. We can't bear to be separated," said Adrienne petulantly.

Jean remembered from an article in *Hello!* magazine, which she'd read on the sly, hiding it from Darroch who disapproved of gossip in general and royal gossip in particular, that Adrienne last year had married a prince from a tiny country on the Indian subcontinent. He was an enigmatic figure, both astonishingly wealthy and astonishing powerful in the area's politics.

He watched coolly as his wife flung herself at her ex-husband. Jean felt sorry for him. She moved forward. She folded her hands prayer-style under her chin and bowed slightly. "*Fàilte gu Eilean Dubh*, Your Highness." She had no idea of how to address an Indian prince but she hoped that was right.

He smiled. His face was too round to be handsome but it was illuminated by the most beautiful brown eyes Jean had ever seen, deep liquid pools holding secrets and warm passionate currents of pure sexual tension. She was mesmerized; she could not look away. She saw a sudden flash of amusement in the depths of those eyes and a smile curved his mouth.

"*Tapadh leibh gu dearbh, mo leadaidh*," he said in a flawless Gaelic accent. Steepling his own hands, he returned her bow.

"My goodness," she said. "You have the Gaelic."

His smile was warm and so entirely for her that she felt like the only woman in the world. "I spent my summers in the Highlands as a child, and if I had not had the Gaelic I would have had no playmates."

"We are honored to have you here, Your Highness. A most pleasant surprise."

A slight frown wrinkled that smooth brow. "Max did not send word? Naughty Max. He likes to set the cat among the pigeons. No doubt it amused him to surprise Darroch with his ex-wife. You are the bride-to-be, I assume? Lovely, and so American." He extended his hand.

"My name is Jean MacChriathar, Sir," she said. She put her hand in his and shivered when he kissed it, a soft sexy caress.

He tucked her hand in his arm and they moved forward to the others. "Introduce me to your so-wonderful fiancé, of whom I have heard much."

"Sir, may I present Darroch Mac an Rìgh?" She had no idea where her royal manners were coming from. Perhaps she'd seen them in a movie?

Darroch inclined his head. "You are most welcome to Eilean Dubh, Your Highness." Jean watched with amusement as Darroch's jaw dropped when the Prince responded in fluent Gaelic. "Sir, I'm overwhelmed that you know our language."

The Prince smiled serenely.

Adrienne cleared her throat, annoyed at being upstaged by her husband. Darroch turned toward her and said gruffly, "Jean, this is Adrienne. We used to be married. 'Rienne, my fiancée, Jean MacChriathar." He put his arm around Jean.

Jean said, "Hi," and held out her hand. She had no idea what Adrienne's title might be but damned if she was going to call her princess. Or curtsy, either.

Adrienne put her hand out as though she expected it to be kissed. Jean seized it and shook it vigorously.

Adrienne withdrew her hand and gave Jean an indignant look. "So pleased to meet you," she said regally. Jean had never heard anyone sound less pleased.

Behind them the others had spilled out of the helicopter. Murdoch the Chopper was reuniting them with their luggage and Max was herding them toward Murdoch the Taxi's mini-bus.

Darroch said, "Are you staying at the Rose Hotel, Sir? We'd be pleased to take you there."

"So kind," murmured the Prince. A slight wave of his hand brought two brown-skinned people, a man and a woman, to his side with suitcases.

The Prince extended his arm to Jean. "Lead on, my dear," he said and the procession of maid, valet and suitcases followed them to Darroch's elderly Bentley. Adrienne seized Darroch's arm and urged him after them.

They set off for the Rose, the Prince in the front seat next to Darroch, Adrienne reclining languidly in the back seat by Jean, maid and valet on the jump seats.

Jean found herself sitting rigidly upright, back straight, in contrast to Adrienne. "Is this your first visit to Eilean Dubh?" she asked, knowing perfectly well that Adrienne's refusal to visit the Island had been a factor in the divorce.

"Yes. I find rural areas amusing, but I don't care to spend time in them. Except, of course, for my friends' country estates."

Snob, thought Jean.

"My dear," said a gently reproving voice from the front. "You must see that Eilean Dubh is beautiful, a tiny jewel. Such richness of color in the vegetation, so many shades of green. You must be blessed with much rainfall, *a Mhic an Rìgh*."

Darroch murmured pleasantly, answering questions, pointing out the sights. Jean wondered what he thought about being addressed formally as the Laird, and knew where it came from. No doubt Adrienne was quite familiar with her ex's views on the subject.

Several days later they were back at the helicopter pad, this time to welcome Jean's daughter Sally from Milwaukee and her son Rod and his wife from California. Jean could barely contain her excitement as the chopper settled down for a landing. Sally had come to Eilean Dubh for a visit last January, met Darroch and approved of him, but Jean hadn't seen Rod since the summer of the previous year when he'd married Lucy Thompson in her home town of Ames, Iowa. Then he and Lucy had gone back to Berkeley, where she'd resumed her upper-management level job in a large bookstore chain, and Rod had immersed himself once again in his computer science studies. He'd been so involved in writing his master's thesis that he and Lucy hadn't come to Milwaukee or Ames for Christmas.

Jean and Rod had corresponded, first by letter, then by e-mail after she was settled on the Island, but she'd not had the frank, full discussion of her crashed marriage with him that she'd had with Sally. His communications with her had been reserved and formal, and she had very little idea of what he thought about her relationship with Darroch and their forthcoming wedding.

Sally was first out and ran straight to her mother's arms. Next came Rod, helping a woman carefully down the stairs.

"Hi, Mom. Lucy and I have a surprise for you. We're expecting." Rod could never keep a secret; there'd been hell to pay if he got a whiff of anything special planned for Christmas and birthdays.

And I've got a surprise for you too, Jean thought, but said nothing. Instead she warmly embraced her daughter-in-law. "How wonderful. When are you due?"

"Seven months, minus a few days."

"And you didn't tell me?"

"We wanted to tell you in person at the . . . wedding," said Rod, remembering he wasn't sure whether or not he approved of his mother's remarriage.

It occurred to Jean that perhaps she'd be a grandmother before she was a mother. Again. This line of thought made her woozy so she introduced Rod and Lucy to Darroch, cautiously watching Rod's face for signs of trouble.

Rod stared at Darroch sternly. "I've heard a lot about you from Sally. We'll have to have a talk."

Darroch felt as though he were being appraised by a Victorian father. "Ummm . . . I'll look forward to that." *I think,* he added silently to himself. He turned to Lucy. At least with a pregnant woman he was on familiar ground, thanks to Jean. "How are you feeling, *m'eudail*? I imagine you're looking forward to a nice lie-down in a proper bed. We have the car right here."

Sally cleared her throat. "There's someone else with us. A surprise." She turned around to the chopper.

A handsome blond man was descending the chopper's stairs. Jean gasped and clutched Darroch's arm.

"Oh, my," she said faintly. "Whose idea was this?"

Sally said, "Mine. Plus Daddy really wanted to come."

Darroch thought, *Daddy?*

Russ Abbott found his eyes drawn immediately to Jean. Still as pretty as ever, he thought sentimentally, and looked at the man standing with a proprietary arm draped around her shoulders. He'd formed a picture of Jean's lover in his mind. An actor, she'd said. Russ had thought disdainfully, he'll be about five eight, sharp dresser, stuck on himself, a real wimp.

Nothing had prepared him for the reality of the tall man who was kissing Sally affectionately, shaking hands with Rod, bending tenderly over Lucy. He could have used a few more pounds packed onto his lean frame but his slimness served to call attention to the width of his shoulders and to his height.

He's taller than I am, thought Russ with a pang. Must be six foot three or so. Damn.

True, Darroch was not handsome but there was something about his face that drew and kept the wandering eye: a lively, intelligent expression and the humor lurking in what even Russ had to admit were spectacularly blue eyes, even from a distance.

Russ strode forward, put his hands on Jean's shoulders and kissed her mouth.

"Hi, Russ," she said nervously. "Darroch, this is Russ. My—umm—ex-husband."

The two men stared at each other. Then the funny side of it struck Darroch and he began to grin. "Sauce for the goose, Jean," he said and she smiled back, relieved.

"Let's see," said Jean. "An ex-husband, an ex-wife, a new husband, two children, a daughter-in-law and a grandchild-to-be. I guess the gang's all here."

Darroch grinned. And baby makes ten, he thought to himself. He stuck his hand out to Russ. "*Fàilte gu Eilean Dubh*," he said. "To everyone."

Seven

She is a winsome wee thing,
She is a handsome wee thing,
She is a bonie wee thing,
This sweet wee wife o' mine.

Robert Burns

Sitting in the hotel lobby, waiting for Sheilah to untangle herself from her guests so that they could discuss plans for the wedding food, Jean thumbed idly through a magazine. When the Prince entered she stood up instinctively.

She had no idea why he invoked this response in her, she felt sure she'd never accord it to a member of the British royal family, except, of course, the Queen.

"*Feasgar math*, Your Highness," she said.

"Good afternoon, my dear Jean. May I call you Jean? It seems quite natural to do so. The informality here is quite delightful. So un-British."

"Of course, Sir. Would you like tea? Shall I get Sheilah?"

"Please sit down, my dear. And no, thank you, the lovely Sheilah has seen to our tea. A splendid cook, Sheilah. I would quite like to lure her away to assure myself of constant access to her pastries."

Jean laughed. "I'm sure she'd be flattered, but . . . "

"But the oh-so-worthy Gordon has her heart, hence her pastries. I understand. A pity, it does seem a waste of her talents." He sighed. "But then, love conquers all, does it not?"

"It would appear so, Sir."

He turned his liquid brown-eyed gaze full on Jean and she shivered with pleasure. "You will tell me if I presume, but you and your Darroch . . . I think you are very much in love. Am I right?"

"Quite right. I adore him."

"And your adoration has persuaded you to make your life on this—forgive me—extremely tiny and unimportant, but undeniably beautiful Island, as love has trapped Sheilah here."

Jean laughed. "Neither Sheilah nor I feel trapped, I assure you. We're both happy with our lives."

"Hmm." His eyes on her were thoughtful. "I assume you are familiar with the details of the marriage between your fiancé and my wife?"

Warily, Jean said, "Well, some of them. The details of the divorce, anyway."

"Adrienne did not see fit to sacrifice her life in London to join her husband here. Her love was not strong enough. I fear she is a woman of fickle and inconstant passions."

Reluctant as she was to say anything good about the woman who had made Darroch so unhappy, Jean could not help but protest. "That's not really fair, Your Highness. Adrienne's an actress; her career depends upon her being in London. Both Sheilah and I have our work here. It's not a fair comparison."

"Indeed, you make a good point." He hesitated. "I assume you are aware of my wife's other little failing."

"It's hardly my business," Jean protested, embarrassed, remembering that Adrienne's infidelity had caused Darroch to divorce her. Jean had divorced Russ for the same reason.

"Permit me to be the judge of that. May I continue?" He waited until Jean nodded. "My country has several beliefs that are different from others in our Indian subcontinent. We believe, for example, that sexual pleasure in a marriage is as important for a woman as for a man. Perhaps even more so, for pleasure in lovemaking is believed to produce strong healthy sons."

Conscious of the brown eyes on her, Jean knew she was blushing.

"So our young men, as well as our young women, are trained in the art of making love." He leaned back in his chair. "Thus it seems not unreasonable to me to expect my wife to be faithful, since she cannot complain of being unsatisfied."

Jean felt a ridiculous impulse to hide her face behind a magazine. She was sure her color must amuse him.

He persisted gently, "As a woman, do you not agree with my reasoning so far?"

"Sir, I'm sorry, I don't think it's that simple."

He waited politely for her to continue.

"My ex-husband assured me that it was not sexual satisfaction that motivated infidelity. It's the thrill of the chase, the excitement of the capture, or so he said. It's hard to sustain that sort of thrill in a marriage, if that's what you're looking for."

"Wisely put. However in my dear wife's case such thrills must be curtailed. Unrestrained sex today can bring a death sentence. Perhaps it always has; sexual diseases are not new. My wish is to protect her from the consequences of her own impulses. You understand that she is not capable of that by herself?"

"It's not for me to judge her." The conversation was making Jean increasingly uncomfortable.

"In addition," he went on, "she has become an embarrassment to her family. Her father is very close to Her Majesty's Household and you will no doubt understand why that circle is wary of scandal that comes anywhere near the Queen's people. A daughter who is a tart is not . . . fashionable. So my father-in-law and I have joined forces to reform our dear Adrienne."

He drew a deep breath and the expression in the brown eyes hardened. "Infidelity will mean that I will immediately sever our relationship and her family will not take her in. She will be alone, destitute, without resources. She will have to earn her living as an actress, an unlikely circumstance. Do you think I am cruel, my dear?"

"Sir," Jean said, "I can't imagine why you are telling me this."

The Prince sighed. "There are people in this world who have a great capacity for love. I think your Darroch is one of them. He is a serious man and he still feels something for his former wife. Not sexual love, not romantic love, perhaps not even liking. But he feels something. My guess is that it is responsibility. In his mind and heart he will worry about her. He will wonder what he could have done to keep her from her self-destructive course.

"It is my wish that you will acquaint him with what I have told you. I cannot do it. It is not the sort of thing men say to each other. Tell him that the foolish little Adrienne has found a protector, one who will do his best to ensure she comes to no harm."

He smiled at Jean. "You are American, independent and strong, you will not like the idea that a woman needs protection. Believe me, there are women and men too who cannot manage their lives alone.

"My demands upon Adrienne are simple. I wish a beautiful, charming, companion and lover. I wish a woman who can manage my households, arrange my parties and entertain my associates. Someone who will spend my money. And she is very good at that.

"I do not want or need a child from her. My dear late first wife provided for the succession well. I have two fine sons and two beautiful daughters. More children would only complicate matters. I wish passion in my bed without the complication of pregnancy." He smiled at Jean, knowing she was embarrassed.

"So, my dear bride, there is a wedding present, one for your husband. Adrienne is no longer, as you might say, a monkey upon his back. She is well looked after. I love her, you see. In my own way I am as deeply in love with her as you are with your fiancé. Sometimes a misfortune for me, but there it is," he said ruefully.

"Your Darroch is a passionate man . . . I do not speak in this circumstance of sexual matters, you understand. You will wonder how I know this and I will tell you: I had him investigated when I contemplated wedding Adrienne. She was to become my princess, a role requiring certain standards. It was my duty to know as much as I could about her and her life before our marriage.

"And so I know that your Darroch lives intensely. He has much he thinks he should achieve; he is a man who shoulders the responsibility for many lives. I hope to have relieved him of one worry. Now it is up to you. You must help him focus on what is important so that he does not burn himself out with yearning to accomplish the impossible."

Jean whispered, "Yes, I understand, Your Highness. You are very wise."

He smiled at her. "I am, after all, a spiritual leader of my people, and it is my duty to be wise. I cannot solve all problems but I must try to help."

The brown eyes gazed on Jean and she felt herself growing weak at the knees. Really, the man's effect on her was alarming. "I am grateful, Sir, for all you have said and I will see that my fiancé understands your message."

"My wife knows that she has lost her power over Darroch and she does not take the loss well. She likes to retain her hold on her men. Do not worry; I will see she creates no mischief. And if she tries . . . I think you and I could create some mischief with each other. I am very fond of American women."

The Prince's smile was intimate. Jean did not know which way to look. He said softly, "Now, my dear, do you think you could bring yourself to dispense with 'Your Highness' and the sirs? My name is Amar."

Jean bowed her head. "Yes, thank you, Amar."

"Good. Now may I obtain a wee dram for you? Fortunately my religion is one that allows alcohol in moderation and so I am allowed to partake of the delightful whiskies that are the flower of Scotland."

"Of course. Shall we go to the residents' bar? I warn you, there'll be music beginning before long. Thursday night is traditional music night."

"Excellent." He rubbed his hands together in anticipation. "I have not sung '*Fear a' Bhata*' in twenty years. I hope I can remember the words if there is a sing-along. Will there be Scottish country dancing this week? I quite long for the rigors of the 'Eightsome Reel'. I last danced it at Balmoral at the Ghillies' Ball," he said as they headed through the door into the bar.

Eight

Happy be the husband an' wife,
happy be the bairns in the hoose.

Eilean Dubh proverb

*J*ean knew that she would have to tell her kids about her pregnancy but she wasn't looking forward to it. She had told Russ and he'd looked at her with a mixture of horror and outrage. He glowered so fiercely that she was taken aback.

"I thought you'd be happy for me," she said.

"You thought I'd be happy that my wife is expecting another man's baby?" Russ said incredulously.

"Read my lips, Russ, I am not your wife. I have not been your wife for a year."

You'll always be my wife, he thought furiously, but said, "You're not even married to him. It's disgraceful."

She stared at him. "You got me pregnant before we were married."

"That was different."

"How?"

He gave her the look she'd dreaded when they were married, the look that preceded a two-day sulk and the silent treatment. "It just is."

She was surprised that after a momentary quaver in the pit of her stomach, Russ' anger no longer had the power to alarm her. Hey, you're a grown-up now, she said to herself in wonder. Got a real nice guy and a baby coming and a whole new life. Anything that Russ says or does is water off a duck's back, as mother used to say.

She narrowed her eyes and gave him a look right back. "Get used to it."

After Russ' temper tantrum she dreaded telling the children about her pregnancy; heaven alone knew how they would react. After dinner several nights after their arrival they all gathered around the Mac an Rìgh fireplace: Jean, Darroch, Sally, Rod and Lucy.

Jean began, "I want to talk to you all about Darroch's and my relationship. We are handfast. That's an old Eilean Dubh custom, and it means we swore before two witnesses to be together for a year and a day. It's as binding as marriage, on the Island."

The Americans looked puzzled. "Why didn't you get married right away, Mom?" asked Sally.

Darroch said, "Your mother wanted her independence, and I respected that."

Rod said accusingly, "You've been living together."

"Yes. As I said, handfasting is like marriage." Jean looked up at Darroch, who was leaning against the fireplace. He smiled at her.

She said, "We have decided now to get married. I'm ready to take that step. And it's the right thing to do, because I'm pregnant."

The word fell into a pool of silence and lay there. Then Sally threw her arms around her mother's neck. "Oh, Mom! That's so cool. Congratulations!" She jumped up and embraced Darroch. "I'll bet you're pleased as can be, you rascal. You're going to be a daddy!"

"I am thrilled senseless, Sally," he said. "And terrified, and awed."

Lucy said softly, "How nice, Jean. When are you due?"

"In about six months."

"Oh, we're due around the same time. I wonder which of us will be first?" She smiled timidly at Jean. "And our baby will be your grandchild and your baby's nephew; is that right?"

Rod had said nothing, so far. Now he turned to Jean and said, "Mother, how could you?"

"It was quite easy, really," said Darroch, and could have bitten his tongue off when they all turned to him: Sally grinning, Lucy blushing, Rod angry and Jean—his darling Jean—looking horribly embarrassed. Fool, he thought. You've got twenty years and a ton of experience on this young prat. Why are you letting him get to you?

Say something, fix it. "Your mother and I love each other very much and it's natural that we would want a family of our own."

"But at her age . . . " Rod began.

The balance had shifted. Jean said indignantly, "What do you mean? I'm only forty-one! Lots of women are just starting families in their forties, after they've established their careers."

Rod said, "You already have a family, Mother."

"I want a baby with Darroch," she said flatly. "And that's just what's going to happen."

"But at your age . . . it's so undignified," Rod said primly.

Annoyed, Jean glared at him, then caught Lucy's eye. "It's not all that dignified at any age," she said.

Unexpectedly, shy Lucy began to giggle. "Morning sickness. A shape like an elephant. And imagine being dignified when you're in labor!" She was laughing outright now and Jean was joining her.

Jean said, through her giggles, "That's why women have the babies. Men can't stand being undignified."

And they were off again, this time with Sally joining them. The three women were whooping with laughter. "Having to pee all the time!" shouted Lucy. "Wanting pickles and ice cream at three in the morning," cried Jean.

Lucy wiped the tears of laughter from her eyes and stared at her mother-in-law. "Do you really?"

"No, thank God. But I'm ravenous, I just crave food, any kind of food. I'm going to weigh three hundred pounds by the time the baby weighs eight."

"But you're so lucky you can eat at all. I have this friend whose morning sickness is so bad that . . . " She leaned closer to Jean and lowered her voice to a confidential whisper.

"Move, Rod," ordered Sally and when he got up, offended, she plopped herself down on Jean's other side and craned her neck forward to listen.

Rod and Darroch stood staring at each other. Then Darroch sighed and said, "Come outside, Rod. This is no place for us."

"Feminine bonding," muttered Rod as he followed Darroch out the kitchen door. "Silly females."

"They're not." There was no way he would permit Jean to be slighted, especially by her stiff-necked son. "They're not silly, they're happy. Giddy with happiness. I feel the same way about this baby."

"I hope Lucy has a boy. I'll have reinforcements at home, at least." He looked at Darroch. "I suppose you want a boy, to carry on your ancestral name. That's important to you English people, isn't it?"

Darroch, a proud Scot, gritted his teeth at the English reference but made no attempt to correct Rod. Instead he said softly, "I would like a little girl, just like your mother. Green eyes and all."

"Well, I think it's pretty weird to have a mother who's pregnant at the same time as my wife. It's just that . . . well, you know. Sex. I don't like thinking about it in regard to my mother."

"Perhaps your mother feels the same way about you."

"What?" Rod turned to him, astonished. "What do you mean? It's perfectly natural, for Lucy and me. It's a perfectly natural thing, sex."

Darroch grinned.

Rod paused. Then he said, irritated, "I thought you were an actor, not a philosopher."

I really don't like him, thought Darroch. For that matter, he didn't like either of Jean's menfolk. Russ was too arrogant, too aggressive, too opinionated. And this kid was a prude.

Rod said accusingly, "How long have you been living with my mother?"

"We've been handfast for six months. And before you ask, we didn't become lovers until her divorce was final. Neither of us approves of adultery and it would have offended the moral code of the Island."

He stared at Rod, watching in the light from the open doorway as the young man turned red with embarrassment.

"Do you have any more questions?" Darroch asked, letting his anger and disdain show in his trained actor's voice.

"No," said Rod.

"Then let's go back in. It's cold out here."

Darroch went through the door without looking back to see if Rod was following him. His eyes met Jean's and he smiled to reassure her.

Rod cleared his throat and said, "I'm sorry, Mom." He went to Jean and put his arms around her. "Congratulations. About the baby. If it's what you want, then I'm happy for you."

He stood up and extended his hand to Darroch. "Congratulations. I hope you'll be very happy. All three of you."

Darroch shook his hand. Perhaps this young man has some redeeming qualities after all, he thought.

Despite his acceptance of his mother's pregnancy, Rod felt he needed more information about what he regarded, quite naturally, as the unfortunate breakup of his Milwaukee family. True, he'd left home at eighteen to go to the University of California in Berkeley, and thus had been emancipated for four years, but he was old-fashioned enough to believe that his parents should have remained in their time capsule of happy wedlock, puttering around in Milwaukee, where he could go back at any time and be received into the warm family bosom as if he'd never left home.

Rod could be as canny as any Scot, or his father, when it came to finding out something that he wanted to know. He and Lucy were staying with Sally in the thatched cottage, the pair of them in the bedroom and Sal in the living room, on a cot borrowed from the Rose Hotel. He encouraged his sister to take Lucy out for an afternoon of what he called "girl talk."

Sally ignored the sexism of that remark, and said she'd take Lucy to lunch at the Rose and introduce her to Sheilah Morrison, the gourmet cook for whom she worked part-time, who was teaching her culinary secrets. Lucy loved to talk about cooking.

Having gotten rid of the younger women, Rod politely but firmly summoned his mother up to the cottage for a little chat.

Jean came, filled with apprehension. She'd been aware of the cool, appraising glances Rod had given Darroch, despite his outward acceptance of his stepfather-to-be, and she fully expected to be subjected to an interrogation.

She was quite right.

She made a pot of tea and sat down at the kitchen table with Rod. She cast a wistful look down the hill at the cottage she shared with her beloved, sighed, and said to her son, "All right. Out with it. I know you've got questions."

Rod decided against dissembling. "Why weren't you frank with me about why you left Dad?"

Taken by surprise, Jean said, "I wrote you that I had left him."

"But you didn't say why."

She could be frank too. "It wasn't any of your business." In reality, she could not bear to upset Rod's relationship with his father by telling him about Russ's infidelity. The boy had a high opinion of Russ and she'd hoped to get through the whole messy situation without damaging that opinion. Besides, it hurt too much to tell the kids that their father preferred other women to his wife of twenty years.

"You told Sally."

"Only after she came to Eilean Dubh and surprised it out of me. Besides, she had her suspicions about the whole infidelity thing."

"I was suspicious too."

"You were?" Her children's perspicacity amazed Jean. "How did you . . . "

"You're very naïve, Mother, and very trusting. I saw them, the last Christmas I was home, Dad and that Mary Lu woman, at your holiday party. He was pretty cool and didn't give her any encouragement, but I noticed how she kept sending him those coy looks and eyeballing you so smugly. She even got him alone in the sun porch for a few minutes. They came out in a hurry after I walked by. Dad was straightening his tie, looking embarrassed, and she was grinning like she was putting something over on all of us, damn her."

"Why didn't you tell me?" Jean's eyes, quite unexpectedly, filled with tears.

Rod shrugged. "What was there to tell? That Dad's office manager had a crush on him? I figured you already knew that, and it didn't bother you." Then he noticed the tears. "For God's sake, Mom, don't cry. It was a long time ago, and it's all over now."

"Yes." Jean regained her self-control and dashed the tears away. "I didn't want you to know about that. I wanted you and Sally to think that Russ and I had just grown apart, and that we'd decided to go our own separate ways and were going to get an amicable divorce."

"All very neat and tidy but it didn't add up for either Sally or me." He said bluntly, "What was Darroch's part in all of this?"

"He didn't have anything to do with the divorce. He was my friend, and then after I'd been here a while and got my head straightened out about your father, we realized that we loved each other." She took a deep breath. "But if it hadn't been for Darroch, I might have gone back to Russ. He can be very persuasive, and I would have been very lonely."

"That's what Sally said." Unexpectedly, he smiled. "She said Dad was like a wounded tiger after you left, skulking around, muttering about how he'd been abandoned, making it sound like it had all been your fault, plotting how he was going to get you to come home.

"She called me, you know, after her visit to you, and said you'd left him because he'd been unfaithful. I thought you'd forgive him, eventually, and take him back."

"I couldn't." Jean shook her head. "I could never trust him again, and I couldn't bear to live with that."

"That's what Lucy said." At Jean's look of surprise, he added, "She said that it would be hell, living with a man who'd betrayed his wedding vows. That a woman would never be secure in her marriage after that happened, that she'd always be terrified when her husband was an hour or two late coming home, or when he went out of town on business trips. There'd always be that nagging suspicion that he had another woman, even if he'd promised to be faithful. She said you were perfectly right to leave him and to stay gone."

He grinned ruefully. "She gave me such a ferocious look that I was shaking in my shoes, and said if I ever did that she'd be gone so fast I wouldn't even hear the screen door slam. She meant it, too."

"Well." Jean shook her head, imagining her gentle little daughter-in-law issuing such an ultimatum to her imposing, self-assured husband, who liked to think he was the boss in his marriage. Lucy was obviously not as much of a mouse as she seemed, and Jean was glad of it.

"Is there any more tea?" said Rod, peering into his cup. It did not occur to him to pick up the teapot and look for himself. When Jean poured fresh cups, he announced solemnly, "Dad is a very difficult man."

"Amen to that," murmured Jean.

"That's why I got straight As in high school, why I was president of two clubs, and why I was the star pitcher on the school baseball team. Dad never put on any overt pressure, but I knew he expected high achievement from me. That's why I went away to college in California, instead of Milwaukee or Madison. I knew that if I stayed here I would be sucked into Dad's business, and I didn't want to be the boss's son."

Jean offered the plate of cookies without speaking, unwilling to interrupt this surprising flow of confidences from her usually reticent son.

Rod took a cookie, then put it down. "I'm not cut out for academic life, and I could learn a lot, working with Dad, and it would be really challenging. He knows everything about computer software and he gets some fascinating problems to solve. He's a terrific businessman, too. Knows all the angles. But I don't think I would be happy under his thumb, and he's not about to give up control."

He sighed. "Maybe someday. Right now I'm going to wrap up my master's degree, and then I guess I'll have to look for a job. Where, I don't know, because Lucy doesn't like California, or big cities, and that's where employment is in my field." He picked up the cookie, took a large bite, and sighed again, wiping crumbs from his mouth. "Thing is, she really likes this Island."

As do we all, thought Jean.

"She's shy, and a place like this would suit her down to the ground, where she could get to know everybody, just like in Iowa. She'd like to live in a small town, but that's not where the jobs are. I suppose I'll join Dad's firm eventually, but I've got to make it on my own first, no matter how much pressure he puts on. I have to meet him as an equal, not just as his kid."

Rod was quite right, Jean knew. The only way to deal with Russ was with chin up, on a level playing field. If she'd realized that earlier her marriage might not have taken such a disastrous turn.

Nine

I hae a wife o' my ain,
I'll partake wi' naebody;
I'll tak cuckold frae nane,
I'll gie cuckold to nobody.

Robert Burns

In the midst of the wedding preparations Adrienne felt herself lost and ignored. Eilean Dubh was already as disappointing as she thought it would be, all those years ago. Darroch paid absolutely no attention to her. Any attempt on her part to flirt with him brought the response she hated, coolly lifted eyebrows and a fleeting look of scorn which dissolved into boredom. No, there was nothing left there. It was disturbing, when she remembered how much in love with her he had been.

At the Friday night *cèilidh* she began looking for another flirt. Perhaps jealousy would elicit a more flattering response from Darroch.

Her first choice was Ian the Post, the mail carrier. He was young, good looking and charmingly gawky, with thick sandy blond hair, a sturdy muscular body and blue eyes that reminded her, sentimentally, of Darroch. She began planning her campaign.

Before she could set up an accidental encounter with him, however, his wife, known on the Island as Ian's Catrìona, appeared on the scene. Ian's eyes went to hers immediately and he crossed the room quickly to give her a quick, shy, but to Adrienne's experienced eye, passionate kiss. Then they smiled at each other intimately and linked hands.

Ian's Catrìona was exactly the kind of competition Adrienne preferred to avoid: young (about fifteen years younger than herself), beautiful, a natural blonde, who moved with assurance and quiet elegance and whose eyes showed both intelligence and good humor.

She wrote Ian the Post off, reluctantly.

Her choices were limited, she thought, among Island men. There were several who were attractive in a rough, unpolished Scottish way, who would look good in their kilts, whirling around in some wild rustic dance. These men all seemed to be married or otherwise spoken for and not worth the effort of detaching from a spouse or girlfriend.

Her game had an element of danger, after all. She dared not promise too much for fear of triggering some unpleasant action from the Prince, or worse, her father.

It had been her father the Earl who had issued the edict about her behavior with men. The Prince had gracefully turned the task over to him. "For you see, dear Papa,"—Adrienne's father had been flattered by the Prince's respectful assumption of a filial relationship—"I must not alienate Adrienne by seeming unkind. She will accept it if you lay down the law. You are her father. She must obey you."

Buoyed by the Prince's artful suggestion that English girls would obey their fathers as unquestioningly as Indian girls would, the Earl assumed his most patriarchal and stern aspect when he called Adrienne into his study and announced that her days of sleeping around would be over, once she married the Prince.

He had adored this only daughter since birth, had guarded himself against becoming her slave and treated her with a heavy hand, kept her at a distance. As a result, instead of showering on him the daughterly affection he craved, she treated him with a fearful respect and came home less and less as she grew older.

She had taken his order to heart and she was very discreet now. But she would have her flirts, she was entitled to the admiration she evoked in men, she would not do without it.

Her inspection of the Island men brought her quickly to another candidate: Jamie MacDonald. The handsomest man on the Island, with his spectacular body, sunshine-colored hair and Skye blue eyes. (Blue! did all Highland men have those gorgeous blue eyes? Perhaps she should spend more time in Scotland.) She liked his quick smile, his confident way of carrying himself and the obvious respect with which he was treated. Adrienne never liked her courtiers to be downtrodden, they must be men of worth. It was more satisfying, that way, to reduce them to adoring puppets.

Bonnie Prince Jamie, she had heard that he was nicknamed. The idea suited her fancy. Bonnie Prince Jamie and Princess Adrienne.

So she watched for her opportunity to engage him in what she was sure would be a mutually interesting chat. Seeing him sitting alone, lost in thought—he was mentally rehearsing a new fiddle and mandolin duet he and Jean were working on—she strode confidently across the room and sat down by him.

"Hi," she said. "You're Jamie, aren't you."

Jamie froze. He possessed a very great sense of loyalty and he had an excellent memory. In his mind he could still see Darroch, in that summer of his betrayal, eyes dark with pain, shoulders drooping and lines forming around his mouth, as he faced the fact that the wife he loved had played him false. Jamie remembered with great clarity his own sense of helplessness, knowing that there was no way to comfort his friend.

And here she was, the cause of all that misery and heartbreak. He looked at her with loathing and drew away.

"My name's Adrienne," she said and held out her hand.

Jamie's innate Island politeness would not allow him to ignore that gesture so he cautiously took her hand and shook it. He shuddered. Her hand was ice-cold.

Sure of her own charms, Adrienne put his reaction down to shyness. "Aren't you the fiddler? I hope I'll get to hear you play. Everyone says you're just wonderful."

No one on Eilean Dubh, with the exception of American Jean who had quickly learned better, would describe Jamie's playing as wonderful. "All right" or "not bad at all" would be an Islander's choice of words. Too much enthusiasm marked one as a gusher.

Jamie's mind worked vigorously, trying to think of a way to get to the opposite side of the room from Adrienne without being openly rude. Rudeness would be very satisfying to him; he had longed for years for a chance to tell her off, but it was, after all, a wedding, and she was a guest on the Island.

Her very presence was disturbing to him. He could sense what Jean would have called in her jokey, old-fashioned slang, "bad vibes" emanating from Adrienne, currents of shallow, self-seeking, hurtful emotions. She depressed him, made his head ache.

"*Tha mi duilich*," he said. "*Chan'eil Beurla agam.* No English." It was quite literally an expression of his feelings: no English, whether language, people or government. And he got up and moved away, leaving Adrienne staring after him.

She was too stunned to think of trying again with him; she had been so sure everyone on the Island spoke English. Incapable of carrying on a bilingual romance, she decided to look elsewhere and crossed him off her list with regret. It would have been very satisfying to show Darroch she had enchanted his best friend.

Màiri had the pleasure of witnessing this brief encounter. She said, later, to Jamie, "And how did you manage to escape the clutches of the blonde *bana-dhiabhol*? She seemed to have her eye on you."

Jamie shuddered, remembering that cold hand. "*A Dhia beannaich mi*, the woman is like death. What could Darroch have seen in her?"

Màiri said, "How did you get rid of her?"

"I told her I didn't speak English."

"What?" Màiri was horrified. "You told her that? She'll think you're an uneducated peasant. You know how that class of *Sasannachan* always thinks of us."

"*Mo ghràdh*, next to her I am an uneducated peasant, and very glad of it." And he refused to discuss the subject any further.

In the end Adrienne found someone receptive to her charms. It was Russ.

Russ was not having a good time. He had wanted to come to Jean's wedding, wanted to see her new man, but the sight of her happiness made him feel lost and alone. He forgot that his infidelity had been the cause of their marriage breaking up and he felt himself very much the injured party. His darling daughter Sally was obviously extremely fond of the interloper and even his cautious, cool son Rod seemed to be getting along with him. And his shy daughter-in-law Lucy was enchanted by Darroch, who treated her with loving consideration, gentle teasing and great respect for her pregnant state.

Jean's pregnancy was the final straw. Nothing could have stoked his jealousy to a higher flame. He thought frequently how satisfying it would be to bury his fist in his rival's lean belly.

He found himself sitting next to Adrienne at the *cèilidh*. Anyone watching them from across the room would have noted exactly the same expression on both faces: petulant, jealous and scornful.

They were watching their ex-spouses dancing together in the Scottish country dance called "The Flowers of Edinburgh." Jean and Darroch were flying down the length of their set in the figure called "down the center and up" and they were both laughing so hard they had scarcely enough breath to dance. The other dancers were laughing too, clapping their hands and shouting out comments.

Russ and Adrienne stared at them glumly.

Russ said, waving his hand in front of his face, "God, it's smoky. This must not be the non-smoking side," not realizing that at an Eilean Dubh *cèilidh* there was no non-smoking side of the hall. Many people smoked and everyone breathed the same air.

Adrienne did not reply.

Not one used to being ignored by a beautiful woman, Russ turned to her. "Hi. I'm Russ Abbott." He extended his hand.

She looked at him appraisingly. Good-looking, well dressed, confident. Definitely a candidate. She recognized the name suddenly: he was Jean's ex-husband. Perfect. She gave him her most delightful smile and Russ' face warmed in acknowledgement. "I'm Adrienne. Well, Princess Adrienne, really; my husband's Prince Amar. That's him." She waved her hand in the direction of the Prince, who was surrounded by a bevy of admiring Eilean Dubh ladies whom he was keeping in a frenzy of giggles. The sight made her furious, and she responded with more coquetry aimed at Russ.

"But just call me Adrienne. You're American, aren't you? You won't care a thing about titles." She smiled again, the full thousand-watt treatment.

This is more like it, thought Russ and his answering smile was intimate. "I don't know. I've never met a princess before. What should I do? Am I supposed to kneel? Should I kiss your hand?" He reached for her hand, managing to brush her thigh at the same time, and brought it to his lips as he looked into her eyes.

"That's a good start," said Adrienne.

"I'd ask you to dance," said Russ, "but I don't know how to do this stuff. I'm strictly a waltz and tango man."

"I don't know them either." That was not entirely true. She'd taken a crash course in Scottish country dancing in London back when she was a debutante, planning to go to the grandest event of the Scottish social season, the Skye Ball in Portree. But she'd gotten her first modeling job then and abandoned the debutante whirl, never looking back.

"The smoke is really bothering me," said Adrienne, delicately fanning herself.

"Would you like to step out for some air?" Russ got up, looking hopeful.

"I think I would." She stood and put her hand on his sleeve in a confiding gesture.

He took it and tucked it in his arm. "Here we go," he said.

I certainly hope so, thought Adrienne and cast a little triumphant smile back into the room.

No one noticed.

Ten

O, whistle and I'll come to you, my lad;
Tho' father and mither and a' should gae mad . . .
Robert Burns

The waterfront was almost deserted. Everyone was inside enjoying the *cèilidh*.

"Would you like to stroll? Or do you prefer sitting on the bench?" Russ asked.

"Oh, let's walk." She looked down at her dress and made a self-deprecating gesture. "This dress isn't made for bench-sitting. I shouldn't have worn it tonight, but I didn't know what was appropriate . . . " She let her voice trail off wistfully.

"It's a beautiful dress. I've been looking at it—and you—all evening." He leaned a little closer to her. "I've been wondering who you are." That was not the truth. He had not noticed her until he ended up sitting next to her; he'd been too preoccupied with Jean and her damned Scottish lover.

"Let's talk about you. Since you're American I assume you're part of the bride's family?" She wasn't going to reveal she already knew who he was.

"I am the bride's family. Uh, that is . . . umm . . . Jean is my former wife."

"Oh, I see. You must have parted on good terms to be invited to her wedding."

"Our kids wanted me to come," he said gruffly.

"And that would be that pretty Sally. And that young man Rod must be your son; he looks just like you. He's so handsome." An indirect compliment, and she thought it would work.

It did. Russ preened a little, then said, "Yeah, they're attractive kids, the pair of them. They're good kids, too; they didn't want me to feel bad about Jean getting married again. They want us both to be happy."

"How sweet."

"Yes. I admit, it's been a little awkward, meeting . . . um . . . Darroch." The name still stuck in his throat. "Under these circumstances."

"I imagine it is," she cooed sympathetically.

"How about you? I suppose you're one of his actor friends from London."

"Well, more than a friend. We used to be married."

"You did? Say, you're just the person I want to talk to. Let's sit down." Forgetting her dress, he drew her over to a bench and pulled her down beside him. "Tell me about him. What kind of a guy is he?" Russ demanded.

"Oh, he's very nice . . . "

"Well, there must be something wrong with him, if you divorced him."

This was becoming embarrassing for Adrienne. "He divorced me."

"Yeah? Why?" Russ stared at her.

"You Americans are so direct," she pouted prettily.

"Sorry. I just want to make sure he's an okay guy. You know, that he'll treat her right."

"I see. You're still in love with her."

"No! But she's a friend. We were married twenty years and I still feel I should look out for her."

Adrienne sighed. "Well, to be frank, he divorced me because I was unfaithful."

"You too? Well, we have that in common. That's why Jean divorced me."

"They're not very forgiving, those two, are they. It was just one teeny mistake I made, just once."

He ran a hand through his hair. "I can't say that. I was foolish enough to have a string of affairs."

Her eyes wide, Adrienne said, "Oh, dear. How did she find out?"

"I told her."

"I told Darroch."

They looked at each other. Then Russ laughed. "Well, honesty isn't always the best policy, is it?"

Adrienne was silent.

"Well, go ahead, talk about him. I suppose he's as wonderful as my daughter keeps telling me. No tact, that girl."

She would not trash Darroch even if he had dumped her. "Yes, he is. He's a very good man. Too good for me, I guess. Your Jean must be an exemplary woman for him to have taken up with her." She let her voice show a little sarcasm.

She's not my Jean anymore, he thought. "She's a wonderful mother, a great wife. I was foolish to have played around on her but I just couldn't stop myself."

Adrienne leaned closer. "I know. People like you and me . . . it's hard to confine ourselves to just one person. It must be a character flaw."

He picked up the nuances in what she said. So she was looking for some action, was she. That wasn't quite what he had in mind right now. "You married again, though," he reminded her.

She sighed wistfully. "I'm one of those women who needs security, someone to care for me. And the Prince is very sweet."

"Sweet. And dull?"

Remembering the exciting life she led as a jet-set princess and the exotically sensuous life she led in his bed, Adrienne could not bring herself to label the Prince as dull. "Not at all. He's very complicated. Just when I think I understand him, something will happen and I'll realize that I don't know him at all."

"Keeps you guessing, eh. Sounds like just the ticket."

"But he's so sophisticated, so cool. Sometimes I feel the need for a little quiet time, simple things. A cuddle on the sofa, a walk holding hands. You know what I mean." Nothing could have been further from the truth but she thought it might appeal to this lonely American. She looked up at him wistfully and let her hand stray lightly to his.

He looked at her. What a liar, he thought. Why is she putting the moves on me? "Come off it, toots. What's your game, really? Like a little variety in your bed?"

The Prince offered her plenty of variety and she blushed bright red thinking about it. "No! I just thought . . . you seemed lonely. I thought we could offer each other some comfort."

"What did you have in mind?" he said bluntly.

She was spared the embarrassment of answering when Sayed, the Prince's valet, materialized suddenly beside her. Damn the man, he was always sneaking up on her, and his eyes were always suspicious.

"I beg pardon, Your Highness, for the interruption. But His Highness asked me to find you. He wishes to waltz with you."

She stood up gracefully. "Do forgive me, Russ. My husband awaits."
And she floated off, followed by Sayed.

Whew, thought Russ. What a little tart, as people here said. And she
spelled trouble with a capital T. No wonder Darroch got rid of her. But she
certainly was pretty and he had enjoyed flirting with her. He looked forward
to their next meeting and wondered, uneasily, if that Indian servant of the
Prince's carried a knife.

Eleven

I will not let thee go,
I hold thee by too many bands . . .
Robert Bridges

*D*arroch was adamant about accepting no wedding presents from the *Eilean Dubhannaich*. During his marriage to Adrienne he'd been a houseguest in her aristocratic friends' stately homes. There he'd had the dubious pleasure of contemplating any number of expensive gifts from years past, honoring some event in an aristocrat's life, purchased with pennies collected from estate tenants who lived in unimaginable poverty.

He remembered one item in particular at Dunrobin Castle in Scotland: a lavish silver epergne the size of a coffee table, richly engraved and decorated, presented to a long-ago heir when he reached his majority at the age of twenty-one.

He'd stood and contemplated it for a long time, remembering the desperately primitive conditions in which those tenant-contributors had lived. Remembering how the Duke and Duchess of Sutherland had cleared some five thousand of those tenants, forcibly removing them from their homes and transplanting them to the barren coast, in the name of charity, and so His Grace could use their lands for sheep-raising. The unspeakable cruelty practiced by the Duke's agents still echoed in the memories of Highlanders and threatened the existence of the majestic statue of that duke, perched on a hillside gazing benignly over his erstwhile estates.

Darroch was having none of it, no wedding presents for the Laird, any more than he would tolerate the rest of that bloody laird business. His family had been lairds of Eilean Dubh for two hundred years until his great-grandfather had become a socialist, renounced the title and given his lands to the Islanders. *An Tighearna Dearg,* the Red Laird, had retained only the small croft where Jean and Darroch now lived, in the cottage he'd rebuilt with his own hands.

Darroch refused the title but accepted the attached responsibility of looking after the Island and the Islanders. The income from his acting career had started and continued to fund the Trust that supported many projects to improve Eilean Dubh's quality of life. His classic BBC series *The Magician* was still shown around the world and now, in his status as a beloved actor, face and voice familiar to nearly every viewer, he was much in demand for television roles and commercial endorsements.

At the dinner for the honored guests on Wednesday night, Jean was seated next to the Prince. He said to her softly, "Did you convey my present to your bridegroom?"

She whispered back, "Yes, Amar. He didn't say much but I know he was pleased."

"Good." He smiled, letting his gaze stray over his wife, looking beautiful and chattering away, seated between Darroch and Russ. "Here is something else for you, in commemoration of your wedding." He handed Jean an envelope.

She tore the envelope open to discover a check for a substantial amount made out to the Island Trust. "Sir . . . I mean Amar . . . what on earth . . . ?"

He shrugged and looked at her ruefully. "I had a chat last night in the residents' bar with Màiri MacDonald. What a glorious creature, I could scarcely listen to her talk for feasting my eyes on that magnificent red hair. She was telling me about her Gaelic Playschool. It is my wish that this gift go first to any needs her school might have. Anything left over I leave to your Trust's discretion."

When Jean tried to stammer her thanks he said, "My Indian subcontinent has over 300 languages, each one precious to its speakers. I admire any attempts to keep a native language alive; it is the heart of its people. As I support such efforts at home, I must also support them here. It is a token of my respect for the Gaels of Scotland."

"Amar," she said. "You're *miorbhuileach.* If you weren't married and I weren't about to be I could really go for you. In a big way." She meant it, too, those eyes of his promised so much to any woman lucky enough to gain his attention.

She thought he was blushing but she couldn't tell for sure, his skin was so brown. "My dear, I assure you the feeling is mutual." He squeezed her hand.

Across the table Adrienne eyed them uneasily. What was that American tart up to with Amar? She redoubled her efforts to enchant Russ. He was responding, she thought. His eyes held both interest and amusement. Or was he laughing at her?

It didn't matter. She liked a challenge. She would show them all, Darroch and his precious Jean, and Amar, for ignoring her and treating her like a petulant child.

Right, Russ, she thought, here we go. Thinking of her favorite movie, she said to herself, fasten your seat belts. It's going to be a bumpy night.

Twelve

After the dinner there was Scottish country dancing, lively, vigorous jigs and reels and stately strathspeys. Darroch found himself sitting next to Russ, who was watching the dancers morosely.

Russ said suddenly, "God, that Màiri's got a luscious body."

Darroch went rigid with shock.

"I'll bet she's a hot armful in bed," Russ said.

Darroch, keeping a tight hold on his temper, said, "You're lucky Jamie's not around to hear you say that. You'd be flat on your back with your head halfway through the wall in a minute."

"Jealous, is he? He doesn't like me anyway. What's he got against me?"

"You made Jean unhappy. He's very fond of Jean."

"Yeah, I've seen the way he looks at her. Doesn't it bother you?"

"No. We're friends. We know each other's limits."

Russ said, deliberately goading, "Jean's got a wonderful body too. Great hips. A man likes something to hang on to when he's . . . "

Darroch ground his teeth, trying to remember the duty owed to a guest, even one as obnoxious as Russ. "We don't talk about our women that way."

Ignoring the comment, Russ said, "I miss having Jean under me in bed . . . "

Darroch rose, furious. "You need to learn some manners. Get up, damn you."

Jean, wary of the interpersonal dynamics between Russ and Darroch, had been keeping a cautious eye on them. She materialized by Darroch's side.

"What's wrong?" she said.

Darroch scarcely saw her in his fury. "Not your affair. We're going outside for a little talk."

"Hey, it's okay," Russ said. "I was just yanking your chain. Having you on, like you Brits say."

Darroch snarled, "Then apologize, damn you."

Russ spread his arms wide in a conciliatory gesture. "I apologize. I meant no disrespect."

Jean said, "It's all right, darling. He likes to tease." She sat down, pulling gently on Darroch's arm until he sank back into his chair.

Russ said, "Yeah. Just trying to see if there's a human being inside that starchy interior. Damn, you English are stuck-up."

"*A Dhia*, I've had enough." Darroch shot to his feet. "Get up and come outside."

Genuinely bewildered, Russ said, "Take it easy. What did I say?"

Jean hissed, "He's not English. You're in Scotland, you fool. You don't call a Scot an Englishman."

"Not if you want to live to say anything else," said Darroch, glaring down at him.

"I didn't know. I really didn't. How could I?" He stood up and offered his hand. "Look, somebody's going to have to explain why what I said was wrong, but I'm sorry."

Darroch looked at the extended hand as if it were a snake, then shook it reluctantly. Russ smiled, pleased to have found a weakness in the man he regarded as an opponent. "At least I know all you English . . . sorry, Scotch . . . have more than ice water and tea in your veins."

Jean, still uneasy at the set of Darroch's jaw, tugged at his sleeve. "Let's dance, lovie. Excuse us, Russ."

Darroch growled as they walked away, "That man's got a poisonous tongue."

Jean squeezed his hand. "Yes, lovie, I know. I was married to him for twenty years, remember?"

He finally smiled. "You're a saint, Jean."

"Yes, lovie. Be sure you remember that."

He said suddenly in her ear, "I'm looking forward to making love to you tonight. I hope you won't be too tired."

"When have I ever been too tired?" She smiled at him, and as they joined the set he gave her a quick kiss before he took his place opposite her.

A collective sigh of pleasure went up from the watching *Eilean Dubhannaich*. They loved romance, almost as much as they loved music and dancing.

Adrienne appeared suddenly before Russ, lured by his dissatisfied expression. "I don't usually ask men to dance but I'll make an exception in your case."

"Baby, you know I can't do those dances." He stretched a hand up to her. "Come sit down and keep me company." All this talk about luscious women had turned him on and he looked her up and down with appreciation. "You sure are pretty tonight."

"If you don't want to dance let's take a walk instead."

"Best offer I've had all evening."

They moved casually to the door. Adrienne glanced around for Amar. He was sitting in the middle of what she had come to think of, resentfully, as his harem: Barabal, Sheilah, Ian's Catrìona, and several others. She tossed her head and followed Russ.

Amar's gaze followed them out the door but he did not leave his chair.

Outside, Adrienne slipped her hand into Russ's.

"All this lovey-doveyness," she said plaintively.

"Yeah. I'm getting tired of it too."

Somehow they found themselves on a bench overlooking the harbor. Adrienne shivered in the cool night air and moved closer to Russ. Her head drifted down to his shoulder.

What's this? he thought. She sure is trying hard. And moving fast. She was beginning to irritate him. He preferred being the one to start the action; he didn't like a woman who came on to him so obviously.

"You and the Prince—are you happy?" he asked.

"He is very good to me . . . "

"And that's not enough, eh. So you thought you'd screw around with me," he said brutally. She wasn't really interested in him; she was just trying to punish her husband. He resented being used.

Adrienne sat up and looked at him. "Why, no. It's just that we have a lot in common. And I find you attractive. And sympathetic."

"Is that right," he said, his voice hard. "Just how sympathetic do you want me to be? Is this too much for you?" He pulled her into his arms and kissed her roughly.

Just for a moment he felt her responding. Then she pulled away and glared at him. "What the hell do you think you're doing?"

"Just being sympathetic, honey," he said sarcastically.

"Damn you and damn all men," she snarled. "You don't care what I want but you all want something from me, don't you. Darroch wanted me to live here and be earth mother to his blasted Island. Amar wants me as a decoration at his parties and a toy for his bed. And you think I'm a slut."

"I don't know if you're a slut but you're giving a pretty good imitation of it. Back in high school we'd have called you a tease. Try to get a man hot for you, then get all outraged when it works." He had no idea why he was being so cruel but she seemed to symbolize suddenly all that had gone wrong in his life. Flirting, teasing, cheating. Losing. "Do you ever put out?"

"Not for you I don't," she snapped.

"That's okay. I don't fancy you, like you Brits say," he said cruelly.

She stared at him, then burst into tears.

"That won't work . . . " he began. He realized abruptly that she wasn't faking. Her sobs were passionate and from the heart. He felt awful.

"Adrienne, I'm sorry," he said awkwardly. "Come here, baby." He pulled her into his arms and patted her on her back. "Don't cry. I'm a rat, to treat you like this."

She was weeping so desperately that he was alarmed. He said, "It's just this damned wedding. Seeing Jean so happy with that guy. It just gets to me but I shouldn't take it out on you."

He heard her gasp something and he bent closer, trying to understand what she was saying. "Why couldn't he have given me another chance? It was only once. I loved him. Why did he walk out?"

"We picked the wrong people to cheat on, baby, that's all. Jean did the same thing to me. But you'll be okay; you've got your Prince. He's a nice guy, isn't he?"

"He's so cold, he treats me like a possession, he never listens, he never shows me any affection, all he wants is sex. If I could just have a little kindness . . . Darroch was always kind to me. I need it. I need Amar to tell me he loves me." It all tumbled out and she sobbed as though something inside her had broken.

The Prince appeared in front of them like a genie from a bottle. An angry genie, finding Adrienne in another man's arms. "What the hell are you doing with my wife?"

His tone was so harsh, so unlike the calm and self-controlled Prince, that they both stared at him in astonishment. Then Adrienne gave a little scream and burst into sobs again, sobs of fear this time.

Russ glared. "What you should be doing. Comforting her. Can't you see she's upset?"

Suddenly uncertain, Amar said, "Adrienne, what's wrong?" He turned on Russ. "What have you done to her, you bastard? I'll kill you if you've tried . . . "

"Does it look like I've tried to hurt her, fool?" growled Russ.

"Did she make a play for you? You've been warned, Adrienne, about what would happen . . . " The Prince's voice was cold with fury.

Adrienne trembled and shrank against Russ. He snarled, "She didn't do a damn thing wrong, Prince whatever-your-name is. We were talking about our ex-spouses and it just got to her."

Adrienne whispered, "Thank you, Russ," and he tightened his arms around her protectively. "Don't worry, baby, I won't let him hurt you."

The Prince looked from Russ to Adrienne and back, his expression hard.

Darroch had just put Jean into Jamie and Màiri's car with a promise to follow them soon. She'd been on the brink of falling asleep while they waltzed but he felt he couldn't leave without saying good night to all the wedding guests. Now he found three of them by the harbor, confronting each other angrily. Uh-oh, trouble, he thought. Why am I not surprised? Adrienne was in the middle of it, sobbing her heart out, and he knew immediately that she was not faking.

He brushed past the Prince, went straight to Adrienne and knelt before her. "It's Darroch, *m'eudail*. Be easy, love," he said gently. She looked at him from eyes puffy with weeping and a wave of sympathy swept over him. The barriers he had constructed against Adrienne in his mind crumbled. He gathered her hands in his and looked up at Russ. "What's happened?"

Russ said, "It's this wedding thing, it's bugging us both. We never should have come."

Darroch said, "She's very fragile. She puts up a good front to hide it but she can't handle her emotions. Once she gets started, she goes to pieces." He crooned to Adrienne in the Gaelic.

Adrienne lifted her head from Russ's shoulder and gave Darroch a teary smile. "That's that funny language of yours, isn't it, darling? You always could comfort me with it."

He smiled back. "I remember. You still haven't grown that hard shell, have you. We used to talk about it, how we needed to toughen you up."

Their eyes met in perfect communion. "I loved you, Darroch," she whispered. "You should have given me another chance."

"I couldn't, *m'eudail*. I had to be able to trust you. It nearly destroyed me when I couldn't. And it wasn't working. I couldn't have you and the Island too. I have responsibilities here."

Adrienne said, "Your rival was only another man. My rival was a whole Island."

He nodded. "We should have talked about it, but I think we would have come to the same conclusion. It couldn't work. We had different priorities. I'm sorry, 'Rienne. I treated you badly."

"We treated each other badly," she said. "I'm sorry, too, Darroch." They smiled at each other sadly.

Russ said, "Yeah, you should have worked this out sooner, like Jean and I did."

Amar said helplessly, "I don't understand what's going on."

The other two men stared at him accusingly.

Russ said, "You're a cold fish, man. A woman needs a guy who can be tender with her. It wouldn't hurt you to drop the dignity thing once in a while, be sweet. You can see she needs it."

Darroch said, "She's not strong emotionally, Amar. You must be kind to her."

Amar said, "I can't help being cold, that's the way I was raised. A prince must always be in control of his feelings." Then he straightened his shoulders and looked at his wife. "But I will try. Adrienne, let me help. Whatever is wrong, we will fix it."

She sat up, away from Russ. "I love you, Amar." She drew a deep breath. "And I'm not a slut. I've never been unfaithful to you and I never will be. It was just a game, a way of getting another man's attention when I couldn't get yours. And I'm tired of it." She sniffled and made the ultimate admission. "Maybe I'm getting too old for it."

Amar strode forward and pulled her up into his arms.

As an actor Darroch could always recognize an exit cue. "Come on, Russ." The other man stood up and the two of them walked back to the Hotel.

"God, I could use a drink," said Russ.

"Follow me, I'll see what I can find." Darroch led the way to the residents' bar.

The bar was dark. Darroch went in, sure of his way, and clicked on the light behind the bar, leaving the rest of the room in darkness. "Whisky?"

"Great."

Darroch poured him a dram of Bruichladdich and one for himself. "Water?"

"No." Russ took a large swallow. "I needed that. I can't deal with women's hysterics."

"Nor I. Jean never has hysterics."

"No, she never did. Not even when I told her I had slept with someone else."

Darroch looked at him. "I'm sorry, this is none of my business, but how could you do that to Jean?"

"Damned if I know. Dumbest move I ever made in my life." He gulped his whisky. "And the funny thing is, I knew she'd go bananas but I couldn't stop myself from telling her. She'd never have known otherwise. I'd been getting away with it for several years. She never suspected anything."

"You're a bastard, Russ," Darroch said.

That was the second time he'd been called that tonight and he was getting tired of it. "Yeah, okay." He finished his drink and pushed his glass forward for another. "Funny thing is that it cured me when she walked out. If she'd forgiven me I'd never have cheated on her again."

"She couldn't stand being betrayed. No more could I."

"Yeah. Poor Adrienne."

"Poor Adrienne, poor Russ. Some would say they got what they deserved." Darroch poured himself another dram, a small one because he had to drive home.

"Well, if it makes you feel better, you self-righteous jerk, I've suffered for my mistake and so has she."

They glared at each other, fists clenched, each man flashing on the pleasure of stretching his opponent flat on the ground. Self-righteous, Darroch thought. Well, maybe I have been. He said, "Sorry. I know you suffered. So did Jean, so did I. Nobody won. Can we bury the hatchet, as you Yanks say, and be friends? You were kind to Adrienne tonight and I appreciate it. I'm still fond of her." He extended his hand.

Russ looked at it for a long moment, then sighed. "Okay. It's all water under the bridge, anyway." He shook Darroch's hand. They were quiet for a bit.

Russ said, "What the hell is he prince of, anyway?"

Darroch shrugged. "Some place in India." They were quiet again.

Finally Russ said, "So you're going to be a daddy. How's Jean doing?"

"She's fine, except for the morning sickness."

"Yeah, she has a hard time with that. Crackers help if she eats them before she gets up. Watch out for chicken; it made her sick to deal with it. The fat and skin and stuff."

"Thanks for the tip. Maybe I'll have to learn how to fix her famous fried chicken."

Russ smiled. "Yeah, she's a great cook. Do you cook?"

"Aye."

"I had to learn how after she left me. It was damned hard but I finally got the basics down. I'm no expert but I don't starve." There was pride in his voice.

Darroch said suddenly, "Why don't you come for supper with us tomorrow night? The kids are coming and our friends Jamie and Màiri. Have to warn you, though, we usually end up playing music afterwards."

Russ looked at him with interest. "Thanks, I'd like that. She's still doing the folk music thing?"

"Yes, she's wonderful. Sings like an angel."

"Yeah, I know. Okay. Around six?" Darroch nodded and Russ got up from the stool. Then he turned and stared directly at the other man. "Treat her right. If I find out you haven't . . . "

Darroch looked him in the eye. "I love her, Russ. She's safe with me. She'll always be safe with me."

Russ sighed deeply. "I trust you, Darroch." He turned and walked out. On his way upstairs he thought about Ruth, the woman next door with whom he was cautiously developing a relationship. Maybe it's time for me to think about marriage again, he said to himself. I'm tired of being alone.

Home in the cottage, Darroch undressed and slipped in beside Jean, careful not to wake her. But she roused and said sleepily, "What time is it? Where have you been?"

"I've been chatting with Russ, but it's a long story. I'll tell you tomorrow."

"Russ?" Even in her drowsiness she was astonished.

"By the way, he's coming for supper tomorrow night."

"He is? That's—um—six, I think."

"Maybe I'll invite the Prince and Adrienne too." He thought about that for a moment. "No, I don't think I will. I've had enough fireworks for one wedding."

He tightened his arms around Jean. "Go to sleep, *m'aingeal*." But she was already asleep.

Thirteen

My heart is like a singing bird
Whose nest is in a watered shoot;
My heart is like an apple-tree
Whose boughs are bent with thickset fruit.
My heart is like a rainbow shell
That paddles in a halcyon sea;
My heart is gladder than all these
Because my love is come to me.

Christina Rossetti

*J*ean woke to the sound of rain on October 22, the morning of her wedding. She looked at the clock: six A.M. She listened to the raindrops pelting down on the roof, groaned, pulled the pillow over her head and went back to sleep.

When she woke two hours later, light was peeking around the edges of the shades. She gobbled her crackers, jumped out of bed and ran to the window. The day was full of bright sunlight.

Outside, the Island looked as though it had been washed. It sparkled with raindrops everywhere: glistening on the cottage's golden thatch, shimmering in the grass, trembling on the open faces of wildflowers.

She took a deep breath of the clean, warm, moist air. Perfect, she thought, and scampered back inside to fix breakfast for herself and Sally and get ready for the big day.

Obeying the tradition that the bride and groom should not see each other until they meet before the Minister, Jean had moved back into her tiny thatched cottage with Sally the night before the wedding.

In the kitchen, she found that Sally was already up. "I'm fixing breakfast, Mom. Go do what you need to do to get ready. Wash your hair." She knew Jean's propensity for hair washing before an important event.

"But I washed it last night. Isn't it all right?" Jean hurried off to the mirror to inspect herself.

Darroch's black Bentley stopped in front of the cottage at ten-thirty to decant Màiri and her daughter Eilidh, the female half of the MacDonald twins, then continued on its way to the kirk, Jamie at the wheel, Darroch beside him.

"Are you nervous?" Jamie asked.

"Why should I be nervous?" Darroch replied.

"Well, I was terrified at our wedding. I thought Màiri might change her mind. If she'd thought twice about it she might not have wanted to tie herself to a gormless fiddle player. It was a relief to see her at the kirk."

"I'm not worried," Darroch said smugly. "She has to marry me. She's pregnant."

"Ah. Clever Dick. I didn't think of that."

"And it's no accident. She wants my baby. She insisted on it." He sighed with satisfaction.

Jamie and Màiri had both been amazed that Jean was willing to go through all the hassle of raising another child, since she already had two grown children. "A grand woman," Jamie said. "The Island's delighted."

"What, you mean they already know?"

"Know, or guess. They've been watching Jean's waistline for as long as you two have been together."

Darroch muttered a curse and said, "Don't tell Jean that. She thinks it's still a secret. She actually thinks that it's possible to keep a secret here."

Jamie chuckled. "Optimist."

In the thatched cottage Jean sat in front of the dressing table mirror while Eilidh did her hair. It was to be worn down, at Darroch's insistence, and Jean had eschewed flowers and ornaments woven into it as too juvenile. So the seamstress, Elspeth MacShennach, had fashioned a small hat out of green velvet, Robin Hood style with a feather, and a tiny veil. It perched jauntily on Jean's head, the green deepening the color of her eyes. Beneath it her whisky-colored hair rippled down her shoulders.

She'd slipped into her underwear, a pretty lacy bra and panties, and struggled with stockings and garter belt purchased from a Victoria's Secret catalog. The increasing roundness of her belly had made tights a tricky proposition: they tended to slip down and she didn't intend to spend the day surreptitiously tugging them up. Hence the garter belt.

But she had trouble twisting around to the angle required to fasten the back garters, so Sally did it for her. "What an odd thing to wear," marveled Sally.

Jean had trouble with the kilted skirt, too, because she couldn't see over her expanded bosom to fasten the buckles that held the skirt on. Both Sally and Màiri had to help her, one holding the skirt on and the other buckling. "Suck it in, Ma," said Sally.

"I am sucking it in," Jean said with dignity. "Tell your sibling to suck it in."

They finished buttoning the lace blouse up Jean's back, each woman taking a ceremonial turn with the buttons. Then Sally held the green velvet jacket for her to slip into, and all three watched warily as she pulled the jacket forward over her breasts.

One button, two, three . . . the fourth button was over the fullest part of her bosom. Jean wiggled, tugged, grimaced and finally slipped the button home. "I look like a stuffed sausage," she announced. "Another good reason not to be pregnant when you're getting married. Your wedding clothes don't fit. You'd think I would have learned that the first time."

Eilidh and Sally flew at the jacket, pulled it down in back, up in front and adjusted it so it fit comfortably at last. Jean turned this way and that in front of the mirror. "Is the Marilyn Monroe look fashionable this year for brides?" she muttered.

Màiri said firmly, "You look perfectly splendid. Quite beautiful, in fact." Jean and Eilidh looked at her in surprise. She had never been known to gush.

"You look terrific, Mom," said Sally, and Eilidh nodded in agreement.

Jean was secretly pleased with her appearance. The flowing hair, the little cocked hat, the green velvet princess-cut jacket, the long pleated kilt skirt that swirled when she turned, all combined to give her the dashing look of a Renaissance noblewoman. If she could just keep her stomach held in, she thought, it should do nicely.

Bridesmaid Màiri was wearing a white blouse and a long kilted skirt in her MacDonald tartan. Sally, the maid of honor, didn't have a tartan skirt so she'd had Elspeth MacShennach make her a long pleated one in sapphire taffeta, and it swished around her ankles in a satisfying manner. It was just the color of Darroch's eyes, she thought romantically. She had a little crush on him.

They were ready by the time the Bentley returned, this time with Murdoch the Taxi at the wheel.

Jamie, the best man, stayed at the kirk as moral support for Darroch. They had been invited into the Minister's office for a wee dram to bolster the bridegroom's nerves.

"*Slàinte mhath*," said the Minister, raising a glass of a pungent, elderly Glenlivet. The summit of his career, he thought happily, presiding over the Laird's wedding. At last.

"*Misneachd, a Dharroch*," said Jamie, joining the toast. Courage.

"I am not nervous," insisted Darroch, though his palms were damp with sweat. Jamie noticed, amused, that his friend's hand trembled when he raised his glass.

The crowd had been gathering around the kirk for several hours. Most Islanders had walked to the kirk, parking down in Ros Mór, leaving the spaces in the lot and along the road for the aged, the infirm and the *Sasannachan*, whom all the *Eilean Dubhannaich* knew couldn't walk any distance at all and would insist on driving or being chauffeured. A number of Island men had offered their vehicles and their services as drivers and the visitors found themselves loaded into a variety of elderly Austins, old trucks and one miniscule, even more ancient Morris Minor. It was hard to tell who were the more bemused, Islanders or visitors.

Chairs were set up in front of the kirk but many people brought travel rugs and spread them on the ground. There they sat, talking and laughing, while they waited for the ceremony to begin.

When the Bentley appeared with the bride's party a murmur of excitement swept the crowd. The children jumped up and followed the car to the back of the kirk and had to be shooed back to their parents by the ushers, Barabal Mac-a-Phi's husband Somhairle and his three oldest sons.

At last all was ready. The Minister, waiting in the front of the kirk with Darroch and his groomsmen, Jamie and the doctor, Ros MacPherson, looked at his watch. "It's gone noon," he announced, just as Sally stuck her head around the door of one of the Sabbath school classrooms, where the bride's party waited.

"We're ready," she said.

Groom and groomsmen adjusted their jackets, straightened their sporrans, ran nervous hands down the pleats of their kilts. Then young Angus and Cailean Mac-a-Phi opened the kirk's doors and the men, led by the Minister, walked solemnly down to take up their positions in the center of the kirkyard.

A thrill of anticipation ran through the crowd. Eilidh put bow to violin and began to play the wedding march. The crowd scrambled to its feet.

Jean, on the arm of her son Rod, appeared in the doorway. She lifted her pleated skirt carefully in her free hand. This was tricky and she'd practiced it, because lifting it made the pleats flare out around her ankles, ready to trip her. With Rod's support she made it down the steep kirk stairs and stepped out into full sunlight. The crowd clapped in delighted admiration.

Darroch felt his knees trembling and clutched his best man's arm for support. "*A Dhia, a Sheumais*, have you ever seen a woman more beautiful," he sighed, barely hearing Jamie's murmur of assent.

Jean glanced downward as she left the last step and realized that a long red carpet stretched out in front of her, leading the way. Wherever did that come from, she thought.

Preceded by Sally and Màiri she made her way slowly down the carpet until she came to stand by Darroch. They exchanged a look of perfect love and satisfaction. He bent and whispered in her ear, "Delicious hat, *mo chridhe*."

The Minister opened his book and began the words of the marriage service. He read them in the Gaelic and then repeated them in English for the benefit of the foreign guests. It made the service twice as long but no one cared. They were enjoying every minute.

Darroch's voice, repeating the vows, was loud and clear, as befitted an actor, and Jean tried to speak up as he did, so that everyone in the crowd could hear them pledge their lives to each other.

When the Minister at last solemnly declared that they were man and wife Jean felt like throwing her hat joyfully up in the air. Instead she turned to Darroch, flung her arms around his neck and kissed him with a resounding smack.

The crowd applauded, whistled and shouted.

As Jean and Darroch started back to the kirk to sign the register they were engulfed in a mass of *Eilean Dubhannaich*, all eager to express their good wishes. Finally they were so surrounded they couldn't move forward.

Jamie had stepped back to Eilidh, who handed him his fiddle so that he could play the recessional with her. But he stopped after a few notes, and began to play the Island's own song, "The Emigrant's Lament." The *Eilean Dubhannaich* drew themselves up straight and began to sing solemnly. The crowd parted and let the newlyweds walk up to the kirk door. At the top of the steps they turned and waved.

The crowd cheered.

After signing the register and having pictures taken they drove the Bentley to the cottage to change clothes. Jean knew she could not bear to remain in her wedding outfit for the reception; it was so warm and so tight around bosom and tummy.

Upstairs they began to undress. Darroch took off his jacket and white shirt. Jean took off the heavy kilted skirt. He unbuttoned, lovingly, the lace-trimmed blouse that the women had buttoned, lovingly, that morning, and slipped it off her shoulders.

Jean ran her hands down to her hips. "I'm all wet with sweat around my waist; that skirt is so hot. How do you men stand having nine yards of wool wrapped around your hips?"

"Air conditioning from down below." He turned her around to face him and pushed the slip straps off her shoulders, over her breasts and down to her hips. It slithered to the floor at her feet.

He stared at her. "What's that you're wearing?"

"It's a garter belt, to hold up my stockings. I didn't want to keep tugging up tights during the ceremony."

He licked his lips. "Do you have any idea how sexy that is?" he said.

"Well, no. Is it?"

"Men hate tights, you know. They're hard to strip off and you're always afraid you'll ladder them, and your lady will be cross with you, afterwards."

"Ladder?"

"Run them, you'd say. But this is *miorbhuileach*." He bent and ran his hand up her legs. "Lovely long sexy legs in stockings. And naked above them, this bit right here." He ran his hands across the tops of her thighs. "And then all this silk and lace above. Quite enchanting."

He said, "Ah, *mo Shìne, m'aingeal*, I had intended to wait until tonight, till our wedding night. But if you wouldn't mind, I'd like very much to ravish you."

"Let's think of it as practice. Ravish away."

They undressed each other. Jean said, "Do you want the garter belt and the stockings off too?"

"No, I want to feel your silk covered legs wrapped around me."

He was right. It was very sexy, very erotic.

Afterwards she took a quick little nap in his arms until it was time to go back to the Citizens Hall for the reception. She put on a soft green full-skirted dress with a rounded neckline, and pinned her Mac an Rìgh sash to her shoulder.

"Can we have the hat on?" said Darroch, and she laughed and pinned the little Robin Hood hat to her hair.

The first person they encountered when they went back into the Citizens Hall was Jamie. Of course he knew where they had gone and what they had been doing, and he grinned at them.

He said in the Gaelic to Darroch, "So you couldn't wait."

"No," said Darroch. "Could you?"

"No. Delicious Jean. I'm surprised you came back at all."

"Jean's hungry," he grinned. "And not just for me."

"What are you talking about?" Jean asked. "I know it's something about me, I heard my name." A mischievous impulse seized her tongue and she said to Darroch, "Are you telling him about the garter belt?"

Jamie's eyes opened wide. "*A Dhia beannaich mi,* I thought they were extinct." His eyes flicked downward over her legs. "And those would be stockings. Not those damned tights." He shook his head in wonder. "It's been a long time since I've seen a woman in stockings and a garter belt. I suppose I couldn't have a peek . . . " He looked at Jean coaxingly.

She smiled. Her hands went to her skirt and began to lift it.

Scandalized, Darroch said, "Stop that at once, Jean. Jamie, what the hell do you do to women, hypnotize them?"

Jamie and Jean grinned at each other.

Darroch said firmly, "Would you get me a cup of tea, please, *mo chridhe*?"

"Yes, darling," she said and walked demurely to the kitchen.

Darroch turned to Jamie, his expression stern.

Jamie glanced uneasily at his friend. "It's just a bit of fun, Darroch. I don't mean anything by it," he began.

"Aye, I know that," Darroch said, and grinned. "You're still on your feet, aren't you? But women like a touch of jealousy. Even Jean."

"You're pretty smart about women, for a newlywed," said Jamie.

"Aye," said Darroch. "It's my favorite line of study. I've spent years at it."

"Careful," said Jamie. "It's when you think you know it all that you get the surprises."

"I love surprises," Darroch replied.

Together they watched Jean walking across the floor to the kitchen, head high, hips swaying, skirt flowing around her. Darroch frowned. "I never should have let her wear that dress," he muttered. "It's too sexy."

"It's not the dress, she could wear a flour sack and still look positively edible. It's what the Yanks call attitude."

Darroch looked at him in surprise. "However do you know that, Jamie?"

"*People* magazine," Jamie said smugly. "I read it last week in the dentist's office."

In the kitchen Jean encountered a barrage of teasing. "And where have you been so long?" demanded Sheilah.

"Changing clothes," Jean said.

"She had help. That's why it took so long," said Barabal.

The women laughed. "I wouldn't mind that kind of help," said one. "It's not so long since I was a bride that I don't remember how helpful a man can be, when you're changing clothes."

"Getting out of them goes pretty fast. It's putting them back on again that takes all the time." Another woman added something in the Gaelic that sent the rest into whoops of laughter.

Sheilah and Jean looked at each other and Sheilah demanded, "Come on, none of that. What did you say, in English?"

Barabal leaned over and whispered in her ear and Sheilah's eyebrows rose, then she collapsed in laughter. "You cheeky hussies," she gasped between giggles.

"Tell me," begged Jean. Màiri glanced at Sally, who was listening with wide eyes. She whispered in Jean's ear.

"Oh, my goodness!" said Jean, bright red.

"What are you talking about?" demanded Sally.

"Not for virginal ears," said Barabal and Jean nodded agreement.

"Damn," said Sally.

Fourteen

I have spread my dreams under your feet;
Tread softly because you tread on my dreams.

W. B. Yeats

The question of where they would spend their wedding night had puzzled them for a while. Setting off right away on a journey would be too exhausting for pregnant Jean, so they decided to defer that for a week until she was rested from the wedding. Sheilah had offered her finest room at the Rose but they had finally decided that their cottage, with its fireplace and skylight, was best, coziest and most private.

The reception had been grand, turning into a mad evening of Scottish country dancing and wild music, but they'd finally managed to slip away and it was *miorbhuileach* to be safe and secure at home and alone together. When they were changing their clothes in the bedroom, Darroch presented Jean with an elaborately wrapped package. When she opened it and parted the tissue paper she cried, "Oh, I do love pretty lingerie," and lifted from the package a red nightgown. She pulled it slowly from the package, spread it out on the bed and looked at Darroch with her eyebrows raised.

The nightgown was so sheer it was transparent. It had a low neckline with tiny straps and there were ribbons down the open sides to hold them together.

"There's more," he said, and she noticed with amusement that he was blushing.

The next layer was a silk robe to be worn over the nightgown, opaque instead of sheer, in a red and pink floral pattern. Beneath it lay the tiniest panty imaginable.

Jean's eyes were wide. "I thought you didn't want me to wear anything to bed," she said.

"It's not for bed. Put it on now, Jean. Wear it while we eat supper. I'll put the supper on the table while you dress," he said.

"More like undressing," she murmured.

Supper was cold lobster salad, fresh rolls, lemon tarts, all from Sheilah. Jean ate heartily despite all she'd eaten at the reception.

Darroch was hardly able to touch a morsel, so bemused was he by Jean in her new outfit. Considering how luscious she looked he thought it had been worth the embarrassment of buying it.

He'd seen it in a window of an exclusive Knightsbridge lingerie shop on one of his rambles around London and had instantly imagined it on Jean. The thought had given him enough courage to enter the terrifyingly female world of the shop.

The lady manageress and her assistant, behind the counter, and three lady customers all stared at him. A six-foot-three, broad-shouldered man with gorgeous blue eyes was not the type usually seen in the shop, which catered to properly suited, predictable City types. This man was certainly not in the City, he was wearing a turtleneck and jeans and he did not look at all predictable.

For a moment Darroch was tempted to run back out. *Misneachd*, lad, courage, he told himself and marched forward.

"May I assist you, sir?" asked the manageress.

He had to clear his throat before he could talk. "The . . . um . . . nightgown . . . in the window. I'd like to buy it. For my fiancée," he added quickly and thought, fool, they certainly wouldn't think it's for your grandmother.

Scottish, the women all thought. What a sexy way of speaking Scots had. And this one had a beautiful deep voice.

The assistant, at her boss's nod, scampered into the stock room and returned with a box. "It's a set, sir. There's a robe." She drew that out and spread it over the counter. "And the nightie." She pulled it out with a reverent flourish and held it up by the slender straps.

He had not realized how sheer it was. He could see every detail of every object behind the gown, including the assistant's wide-eyed stare.

"And . . . ," the manageress cooed, "there's the panty."

It was tiny and it had ribbon ties on each side. Darroch swallowed hard.

There was absolute silence in the shop. The manageress and her assistant looked at him with expectant expressions. The three lady customers had given up any pretense of doing their own shopping and were staring at him openly.

Darroch cleared his throat again. "I'll take the set," he said firmly. All the women in the shop sighed with pleasure. He put his credit card down on the counter.

"I'll wrap it for you, sir," said the shy young assistant and began bustling around with paper and ribbons. All Darroch wanted to do was to get out as soon as possible. He endured the manageress' polite chitchat, conscious now that everyone in the shop was listening avidly. "And will the wedding be soon, sir?" she asked.

"Not soon enough," murmured Darroch without thinking and a gasp, then a sigh, echoed from five female throats. Scarlet, he grabbed the package, muttered his thanks and bolted.

The lady manageress looked after him, eyes narrowed in thought. "I'm almost sure he's somebody," she announced. The assistant and the customers agreed heartily. Oh, he's somebody, all right, they thought.

He couldn't think of that shopping expedition without embarrassment but it had been worth it, he thought, watching as the robe slipped seductively from Jean's shoulder and revealed a tempting glimpse of the contents of the sheer gown. He wished she'd hurry with her supper.

At last she pushed her plate away with a satisfied sigh. "I shouldn't be so hungry, but I am," she said. "It's that baby." She noticed the direction of his gaze and blushed. She'd never worn a garment so revealing and it made her feel different. Wanton. And hungry again, but not for food.

He got up and swiftly cleared the table, then turned to her. "Let's go and sit by the fire," he said.

On the sofa he pulled her into his lap and caressed her, feeling like a Turkish sultan with his favorite wife. His hand covered her belly and she sighed with pleasure. "I was holding my breath all day inside that kilted skirt," she said.

He chuckled. "I've been admiring your round little tummy. It was all I could do to keep from patting it during the ceremony."

"What, do you mean I'm showing? What will people think?"

"They think you're *miorbhuileach,* just as I do." She smiled dreamily and leaned back against him, offering up her lips while her hair and the silk robe spilled down his arm.

He took eagerly with mouth and hands what she offered. My woman, he thought. My wife. Although he would have denied it vehemently, at that moment he was every inch the Laird, commanding and possessive. And every inch of him wanted every inch of her.

"I want you to be comfortable while I make love to you. Shall we go up to bed now?" he whispered.

"I thought you'd never ask," she replied. She wriggled off his lap, stood up and extended her hand to him. "Come on."

Upstairs he slipped the robe from her shoulders and laid it across a chair. Then he picked her up in his arms and carried her to the bed. Being carried, she thought happily, was so delightful, so comforting, so erotic. It was like being a child and a woman all at the same time.

He sat on the edge of the bed, looking at her. "I know you're tired, *m'aingeal*. Let me love you. You don't have to do a thing. You can even fall asleep if you like."

"Fall asleep? Not on your life. This is my wedding night." She stretched her arms out to the sides, arched her back. "I intend to enjoy every minute of it. I'm going to pretend it's the first time we ever made love."

They smiled at each other, remembering that wonderful first time, on the fur rug in front of a blazing peat fire in her little thatched cottage.

Darroch started with her feet, taking one in each hand, massaging them. They were swollen and she groaned as he worked them deeply and played with each toe. "So much standing," she sighed. "Should have worn tennis shoes."

He moved to her legs, working his way up her thighs with kisses. He kissed her lingeringly through the tiny panty. Then he untied the strings on each side and pulled it away. Jean was shuddering with desire and he did not make her wait: he took her with his mouth. She screamed as ecstasy ripped through her.

The nightgown was held on by three ribbons on each side and he untied them one by one as he worked his way up her body, lingering on her belly where their child lived, moving with exquisite slowness to her breasts. He kissed each one, then scooped them into his hands and thrust his face into the valley between them, a valley where he could happily lose himself for days.

By the time his mouth moved to a nipple she was trembling with anticipation, her hands buried in his black hair, stroking and caressing his scalp. He suckled her hungrily and felt her arching into another intense, shuddering climax.

When his lips reached her throat she wept and begged for more. "Please . . . "

He pulled the nightgown off over her head. "Please what? Tell me what you want, my darling *Shìne*."

"I want you inside me."

"What else do you want?" He caressed her throat.

"I want you hard and deep, touching my womb, tickling our baby."

He smiled and captured her hands in his and held them on both sides of her head.

He was so strong, so vividly male and his blue eyes were filled with love and passion. It was like being in the middle of a storm, with thunder and lightning crashing all around them, and herself safe and warm beneath him.

He'd been teaching her to talk love talk and she adored it, though she thought she wasn't very good at it yet. It was like a game, each trying to take the other to a higher peak of enthusiasm. She whispered something sexy in his ear.

He shivered with desire.

She whispered something else, even sexier.

Maddened, he drove into her, taking her with one fierce thrust. She shrieked and he yelled and buried himself in her. Both gave themselves up to waves of pleasure.

Ahhh, they both thought afterwards, lying together in a heap. It's even better when you're married. Jean fell suddenly, deeply asleep where she lay, worn out by the day. He grinned and arranged her in a neat little comma shape and wrapped himself around her.

Darroch was awakened the next morning by rustling noises outside and snatches of a song vaguely familiar to him. He got out of bed and peered down out of the window, then drew back hastily, aware that he was naked and that there was a large crowd of his fellow *Eilean Dubhannaich* outside the cottage, gathered around the door. Bloody hell, he thought, what are they doing here?

He dressed hastily and went downstairs, ready to do battle. They'd been left alone last night and he supposed it was too much to hope for that they'd be left alone from now on. There was a quick rap on the door and before he could answer it Jamie slipped in.

Darroch stared at him accusingly. "I suppose you're here to tell me what's going on."

"Aye," said Jamie. "They're floo'rin' th' hoose." He said it with a broad Scots accent. "It's a grand old Island custom. Surrounding the newlyweds' house with flowers is supposed to bring good luck."

"The only good luck I need is to get lucky enough to be ignored," said Darroch bitterly. "*A Dhia*, can I never have a normal life? Other people get married here and this doesn't happen to them."

"You're the Laird," said Jamie. "These old customs are important when you're involved."

Jean appeared, yawning, at the head of the spiral stairs. "Darroch?"

Darroch said furiously, "Fuck the old customs and fuck the bloody laird business. They're disturbing my honeymoon and they've waked up my pregnant wife."

Jean did not know there was anyone in the house but Darroch until she was halfway down the stairs. She was wearing her new robe and when her eyes met Jamie's appreciative stare she wrapped it tightly around her, not realizing that she was just accentuating her curves and the sensuality of the garment. "Who's disturbing who? Or whom, as the case may be?" she said.

Darroch spun around, running his eye over the robe. "It's nothing for you to worry about," he growled. He'd never intended for anyone else to see her in that outfit, especially not randy Jamie.

Surprised by the gruffness of his voice she gave him a puzzled look, then said, "Good morning, Jamie."

Jamie moved forward and gathered her into his arms for a tender kiss. "*Madainn mhath, m'eudail*," he murmured. You look very beautiful this morning. Married life must agree with you."

She blushed, as he knew she would.

Darroch said, "Take your hands off my wife, please, Jamie, and tell me what we're going to do about this damned foolishness."

"Not to worry. Màiri's outside talking to them."

Curious, Jean slipped away from Jamie and went to the window. "My goodness! Look at all those people! And the flowers. What's going on?"

"They're floo'rin' th' hoose," said Jamie.

"Floo'rin' . . . oh, I get it. Whatever for?"

"It's an old Eilean Dubh custom," growled Darroch. "Surrounding the newlyweds' house with flowers is supposed to bring good luck or some damn fool thing."

"I don't know the meaning of all of the flowers but the broom is for good luck, the heather for long life, and the gorse is for fertility. Not that you'll be needing that one." Jamie smiled aggravatingly.

Darroch looked at his wife, expecting her usual delighted reaction to yet another quaint old Eilean Dubh custom. Instead, she was horrified.

"Where did they get those flowers? They've never gone and picked them from the wild flower preserves, have they? They mustn't do that. Oh, Anna Wallace will be furious. She'll go mad."

"There's a good idea," said Darroch. "We'll set Whiplash Wallace on them." He moved to the telephone. "Anna will sort them. When it comes to protecting those wildflowers, she's got a tongue like an adder."

"No need for Anna," said Màiri, coming in the door. "They've assured me they've just taken a couple of each flower, except for the heather and the broom, and God knows we've plenty of those." She looked at Jean. "What a pretty robe."

"Darroch bought it for me," said Jean. "You should see the nightgown that goes with it."

"I'd love to," said Jamie, and laughed when Darroch glared at him. "How did they get round the trucks?" he asked. He and Tòmas Anderson, their neighbor down the lane, had parked their trucks crosswise across the head of the lane, to guard against any intrusion in the newlyweds' privacy last night.

Màiri laughed. "Quite clever, really. They boosted Somhairle Mac-a-Phi *as òige* over the truck and he opened the door on the other side. You didn't lock that one, Jamie. Then they all slithered through."

"My poor truck. My upholstery," sighed Jamie. "Well, at least they didn't push her downhill into the sea."

Darroch ran a hand through his hair. "I give up, I absolutely give up. Superstition, tradition, laird-worship, and now flower power. *A Dhia*, can they never let us be?"

Jean said soothingly, "Never mind, lovie. Look, they're leaving now. It was kindly meant. Their intentions were good, really."

Màiri said, "Well, there's a bit of a hitch. They want to see the bride and groom before they leave."

Darroch cursed under his breath. "Tell them to go away, Jamie. If I go out there I'll just shout at them like a madman."

Jean's hands flew to her hair. "Oh, dear. I must look awful."

Jamie slid an arm around her shoulders. "You look like a bride should look," he whispered in her ear.

"How's that, Jamie?"

"Hot and sexy."

She giggled. "Is that right?" Bonnie Prince Jamie could always turn her on.

"Aye. But you might just show a bit more skin." He eyed her robe.

"Like this?" She lifted one shoulder and the robe slid slightly down the other one.

"Very nice," he murmured. "Here I am in a fine cozy cottage with the two bonniest women on the Island—maybe on the planet—and a mob outside to cheer me on. Go away, Darroch. Come back in a few hours."

"Only a few hours, Jamie?" Jean murmured. "I had you figured for an all-day man, myself."

Jamie grinned and opened his mouth to reply but Màiri cut him off. "That's enough of that. Don't encourage him, Jean, he's bad enough without help. Go outside and talk to them, you two, so we can go home. I've a thousand and one things to do today."

"All of which involve a strong back and a weak mind—that's me—and none of which will end us up in bed before midnight tonight," Jamie mourned and rolled his eyes at Jean, who smiled sympathetically.

"Go and get dressed, Jean," Darroch ordered, "and we'll get this over with. Jamie, remind me to knock your head against a wall one of these days to settle your libido down." He looked at his wife, who hadn't moved. "Now, please, Jean."

"Marry a man and he goes all bossy and domineering," Jean grumbled, but she headed obediently toward the stairs.

"It's that bloody laird business," said Jamie, to Darroch's annoyance.

Upstairs, Jean brushed her hair, dabbed on lipstick, and dressed in a green sweater and skirt. When she came back down both men looked at her admiringly. Darroch said, "Shut up, Jamie. It's my turn." He went to her, took her shoulders in his hands and quoted:

She walks in beauty like the night
Of cloudless climes and starry skies,
And all that's best of dark and bright
Meet in her aspect and her eyes.

Màiri said, "Why do you never recite poetry to me anymore, Jamie?"

"Women," he grumbled. "Having the best sex in the world isn't enough for them. They want poetry too." He pulled his wife into his arms and kissed her soundly. "Here's a choice for you," he whispered in her ear. "We can go home and fuck each other silly, or I'll read poetry to you for an hour. Which is it to be?"

She said, "And what if I choose the poetry, Jamie?"

"I'll just have to think of a way to change your mind." He ran a hand down her back to her bottom and pressed her against him.

Màiri wriggled sensuously.

"I see you've made your choice," he said, grinning.

Darroch said, "Is sex all you think about, Jamie?"

"Aye. Sex and music. What else matters?"

"How about love?" Jean asked, secure in Darroch's arms.

"Oh, that's in the both of them. You can't have sex without love, or music without love. I can't, anyway."

"Quite the philosopher, our Jamie." Darroch kissed his wife, then said, "Come along, *mo chridhe*. Let's give them what they want."

"I'll announce you." Towing Màiri by the hand, Jamie went outside. "Ladies and gentlemen, the bride and groom." He flourished his hand back toward the door and Darroch and Jean came out.

To Jean's complete astonishment every man there bent in a slight bow and every woman dipped a little curtsy. She heard Darroch's quiet, resigned sigh.

But he raised his beautiful actor's voice and said pleasantly, "*Madainn mhath, a charaidean.* You are most kindly welcome to our house."

Young Somhairle MacPhi stepped forward with flowers in his hand. "*A Mhic an Rìgh,*" he saluted the Laird. "Lady Mac an Rìgh," he said, bowing to Jean and presenting her with the bouquet.

Astounded to be greeted with a title, Jean stammered, "*Tapadh leat, a Shomhairle.*" Impulsively she leaned forward and kissed his cheek. He turned red. She looked at the faces around her. There was the MacDonalds' daughter Eilidh, Barabal and her family, Ian the Post and his Catrìona, Cailean the Crab and his lady, Seonag and Murray the Meat, Beathag the Bread, Sheilah and Gordon and so many others who'd become her friends in the last year. Behind her she felt the warm loving presence of Jamie and Màiri.

And beside her, Darroch's tall figure. Sweet, strong, sexy and completely hers. "Oh, *mo charaidean,*" she blurted. "I love you all so much, and our Island!"

Fool, she thought, gusher. Now you've done it; you've embarrassed everyone.

But she was the only one embarrassed. Smiles broke out on every face and there was a ripple of applause. Our lady, they thought proudly. So American.

"Away with you now," Jamie said, making a shooing motion with his hands. "Off you go. Let's give the newlyweds their privacy so they can get better acquainted."

Laughing, the crowd began to disperse. "Uh-oh." Jamie snapped his fingers. He felt in his pocket for his keys. "Best move the truck so they don't all crawl over my upholstery again." He hurried off up the hill.

"You'll stay for a cup of tea?" Darroch said politely to Màiri.

"No, indeed," she said. "We've all imposed on you enough today."

"It's no imposition," Jean began.

"Aye, it is. You need your privacy; it's your honeymoon. I'll just collect Jamie and take him home." She grinned wickedly. "I'll have a few chores out of him before he gets what he wants."

She kissed Darroch and then Jean. "Come down and see us when you've a mind to. Maybe in a week or so."

Alone at last, Darroch thought as they went back inside. He eyed Jean, then sighed. No, he thought, with the way things were going the Minister would likely pop up on their doorstep as soon as he'd gotten her undressed.

"Would you like some breakfast?" said Jean cheerfully. She had a pretty good idea of what was going on his head.

But he surprised her by saying, "Aye. Got to keep up our strength. Tiring work, honeymoons."

Jamie drove his truck down to *Taigh Rois*, arriving as his wife was walking up their path. She turned and threw him a backward glance and went in, her hips swinging seductively. Whistling, he put his keys in his pocket and followed her.

He caught up to her just inside the door, put his arm around her waist and swept her off to their bedroom. She sputtered but her indignation was merely a formality; she was as eager as he. But it wouldn't do to let him know that, not at first, anyway.

He pulled her down on the bed and kissed her while her clothes magically disappeared under his busy hands. Then he moved on top of her and when he heard her soft murmur of assent he plunged. She arched up to him as he shouted and exploded in her.

Jamie had these tumultuous outbreaks of passion often, even after twenty-some years of marriage, and she loved them. She'd nothing to do but lie back and take him and he always made sure she had her pleasure too. She'd asked him, once, what prompted them, and he'd looked at her, surprised. "Lust, mainly. And what's a wife for but to satisfy your lust?" She'd used her shocked look on that remark and it had led to another hour of lovemaking.

Now she stroked his hair as he lay on top of her. "What set you off this time?"

He nuzzled his face in her throat. "Jean."

"What? She writhed beneath him, pushing at him with her hands, furious with jealousy. "You get hot for another woman and take it out on me?"

"Hush yer whist, ye silly bitch," he said affectionately and rolled over, pulling her on top of him. He gave her a sharp smack on her bottom. "You know I'd never be hot for another woman when I've got all the red-headed fury I can handle right here in my bed. It wasn't her body, it was the expression on her face this morning. She reminded me of you after that first time I had you up on the hill above Sabhal Mór Ostaig. Like a woman who's been well fucked and liked it. Remember?"

"Aye." She unbuttoned his shirt. "You were wonderful, Jamie, and I did like it."

"You gripped me so tightly that I thought we might have to stay up there forever, me buried inside you. *A Mhàiri, m'aingeal, mo ghràdh*. How much I love you, *m'eudail*." He kissed her warmly and ran his hands down her back to grip her bottom. "I love weddings, I love honeymoons, even other people's. They make me crazy for you."

Màiri was losing interest in anyone else's sex life but her own. "Get undressed, Jamie. Let's go to bed properly."

And they did and didn't fall asleep for a couple of hours.

Fifteen

Then be not coy, but use your time,
And, while ye may, go marry . . .

Robert Herrick

The wedding party dissolved quickly after the wedding. The last to leave were the Americans, and Jean and Darroch accompanied them to the Glasgow Airport where they departed amidst tears and hugs.

Then the newlyweds went to London, planning to stay just a few days in Darroch's flat while they decided where to go for their honeymoon. The wedding had occupied them so totally that they'd not had time to make plans. Now they could think about it and decide: Paris, Florence, Venice? Darroch's travel agent would make arrangements for them once they'd made up their minds.

But the flat on the Thames had a fireplace and a balcony overlooking the river, and it was so cozy and so welcoming that they both relaxed into it and ideas of leaving disappeared. Jean was still tired from all the excitement of the wedding and Darroch thought a few days of rest were what she needed. And London offered so much, once she felt up to it: plays, opera, ballet, social life.

Neither his agent Liz nor his accountant Blodwen the Welsh Wizard had been able to come to the wedding. So Blodwen held an intimate dinner party for them and Liz a cocktail party for the theatrical set.

Jean was an object of much curiosity to the women who attended the cocktail party. They drifted over, one by one, to inspect this American who'd captured one of their most eligible bachelors, and Jean found herself surrounded by the beautiful, talented and clever ladies of London theatre and television.

Jean recognized many of them. That woman had been in one of her favorite Britcoms, that one was the star of the play she'd seen last night, that one's picture had been in the tabloid she'd read this morning. She sipped her soft drink, trying not to feel overwhelmed, and looked around furtively for Darroch.

He'd been buttonholed by one of the most garrulous men in his profession who always had useful information to share about upcoming productions and roles. Every time he tried to escape another nugget was produced that held him.

"Darling, do tell," said a striking little brunette to Jean. "What is it like being married to the divine Darroch?"

"It's wonderful."

"I'm sure. Tell us, is he as fabulous a lover as I've heard?"

"I don't know what you've heard . . . ," Jean began, astonished at the question.

"I can answer that. You don't have to ask his wife." A lovely blonde preened.

"Madge, did you really? Do tell, sweetie."

"He was incredible. Heartbreakingly sweet, and so passionate. Of course, it was years ago, when we were both so touchingly young." She sighed tragically. "It was just a brief fling, it couldn't last, of course."

"Why not?" asked Therese, the petite brunette.

"We had different plans for our careers," she said primly.

"Madge, love, do you go around telling the wives of every man you've slept with about it?" said Therese.

"It would take months and she'd be quite hoarse afterwards," murmured a redhead. Then, as Madge looked at her indignantly she said, "Well, I'm sorry, sweet, but everyone knows you're the most dreadful tart. You've never kept it a secret."

Madge tossed her head. "I believe in being quite frank about my *affaires de coeur*."

"Well, I fancied Darroch something rotten," said Therese. "So tall and lean, and such a gentleman. And those eyes! How lovely to wake up next to him and watch him open those eyes and gaze longingly at you."

They all looked at Jean expectantly and she blurted, "Well, yes. It is lovely." And she turned red.

"Darlings! Look at her blush. What a sweetie." Then taking pity, Therese steered the subject into different waters. "But he insists on living in Scotland, on his little island. Adrienne couldn't bear it, you know, so desperately rural. How are you holding up?"

"I quite like it," said Jean.

"But you're an American . . . "

"It's a beautiful place and the people are great. Everyone's been so kind to me."

The others twittered and returned to a subject far more interesting to them.

"Simply everyone adores Darroch, you know, my dear," said Therese. "And in this profession, that's very unusual; we're all so competitive. But even other actors like him. He's so good no one can really begrudge him all those brilliant parts he gets, and he's never been pompous or conceited. Quite unlike an actor, really," said Therese. The others chorused their agreement.

"How nice of you to say so," said Jean. "Everyone on the Island loves him too."

"Is it true . . . " Annie, the redhead, leaned closer. " . . . That he's really a laird and he's renounced the title?"

"His grandfather did years ago and Darroch agrees with it."

"How terribly Tony Benn-ish," said Madge loftily.

"Is it true he gives all his money to the poor and needy?" whispered Kate, a young actress who'd been standing on the fringe of the group.

"Well, not all of it, of course, he needs something to live on. And there aren't any poor and needy on our Island; everyone has enough to get by on. His earnings help fund the Trust which pays for projects that benefit the Island, like our Gaelic Playschool." Jean was hoping to switch the focus of the conversation but they were too quick for her.

"No diamonds or fur coats for you, then, darling," said Madge. "How sad!"

"Not at all," began Jean. "I don't want . . . "

"Every woman wants . . . "

"I don't," said Jean firmly.

"You are terrible, you girls, to tease her so." Annie looked at them all sternly. "There are other things in the world besides jewels and furs."

"Such as?" said Madge, eyebrows raised.

"The volunteer work you do with the Schools Theatre Project, Therese, and the fundraisers you headed for the Mermaid Breast Cancer Campaign,

Madge, darling. You mustn't give our friend here the idea you're all empty-headed tarts."

"No, we'll leave that to Adrienne," said Madge and everyone laughed, including Jean.

"Getting back to sex," began Therese. "Someone told me that Darroch has the most astonishing . . ."

Darroch arrived to rescue Jean. "Good evening, ladies." They looked at him, speculation in their faces. "Umm . . . should my ears be burning?"

"So like an actor, to assume he's being talked about. And quite right, of course." Madge slipped her arm through his companionably.

"Hello, Madge." He patted her arm, removed it from his and deftly slipped the freed arm around Jean. "Are they treating you nicely, *mo chridhe*?" he said to her.

"It's been a most enlightening conversation," she said.

"I was afraid of that," he said and grinned at them. "How much explaining do I have to do in the taxi on the way home?"

"A diamond bracelet's worth, love," said Madge, and all the women giggled at his baffled expression.

London nightlife was fun, and London day life, with its museums, shopping and walks, was even more fun. But it was just as much fun to stay in the flat on a rainy afternoon with a fire in the fireplace and music on the CD player, and Chinese takeaway to look forward to for dinner.

Jean had worked her way through Darroch's bookcases and had moved to his videotape collection where she discovered to her great joy an entire set of episodes of *The Magician* recorded for him from BBC masters. To her delighted amazement she found two she'd never seen before, even though she'd watched the series avidly on public television years ago in Milwaukee.

Darroch, sitting at the dining room table balancing his checkbook, said, "Aye, those were never broadcast. 'Whispering Death' was only about two-thirds done when production was halted by a technicians' strike. We never finished it. And 'Laughter in an Empty Street' is the pilot for the program; it's only about forty minutes long. We always intended to do it properly for the series but we kept finding stronger scripts to do instead."

"May I watch them?" At his nod, she popped the pilot tape into the VCR and watched, enthralled, as a much younger Darroch, the character of the Magician not fully formed, appeared on the screen.

Lured by her appreciative chuckles and sighs, Darroch set his checkbook aside and sat down with her. He was soon adding sidelights. "Oops, there's an overhead mike in that shot." "My hat was too small; I didn't dare put it on. It would have bobbled around on top. What a bighead, everyone would think." And he winced when he saw himself pull the rabbit out of his pocket and hold it up by its ears.

"We caught hell from the RSPCA for that after the first show; it's not at all the proper way to handle a rabbit. Scruff of the neck, they said, and support its hind feet. Quite nasty, those hind feet. That rabbit had a kick like a mule and claws like razors."

When the show ended Jean turned to him, her eyes soft with hero worship. "How I loved that program! And I had the most terrible crush on you. I used to dream that I'd run into you one day."

"And the rabbit too?" He opened her blouse, his long fingers brushing over her skin.

"No rabbit, just you."

"And what would we do, after we'd met?" He lifted her so that he could ease her blouse off her shoulders.

"Just what you're doing right now."

"An easy daydream to fulfill." He slipped her skirt off. "Except it's only me and not the legendary Magician."

"From what I heard the other night, you're pretty legendary too."

"So I've a lot to live up to, have I?"

"I'm not worried. You've given a good account of yourself so far."

"No complaints, then?" He kissed her tenderly.

"Well, just one. You've got too many clothes on."

"I can remedy that." And he did, and took her in his arms.

Jean said, "Darling, what's it like, having had lots of lovers?"

He sighed. "So they gave you an earful, did they. I was afraid of that. Well, it was nice, frankly, me being a young man and trying to come to grips with the fact that I couldn't have what I truly wanted. Which was Màiri, of course, as well as an acting career.

"You mustn't think it was just the sex, although that was quite lovely. It was companionship, and sweetness, and someone to talk to. Ours is a transitory profession. You get attached to someone and then she's got to move on, because of her career." He paused, thinking of Morgan, whom he'd loved years ago, and who had gone to Australia for a job as a director. "So it was . . .

make love, and be friends, and not take each other too seriously. Because you might wake up in the morning and she'd be gone."

"It sounds sort of sad."

"All a learning experience, for an actor. Emotional turmoil is a good tool. But I've had enough of it." Looking down at her, he said, "You get more beautiful every day. Such lovely full breasts with swollen nipples. For the baby, I assume."

"Yes. I'd appreciate it, lovie, if you'd toughen them up."

"What?"

"A baby's jaws have the grip of an alligator and if the nipples aren't tough they crack. It's very painful; it happened to me with Rod. I would have quit nursing if I hadn't been so stubborn. I just gritted my teeth and nursed through it and eventually they healed. With Sally, the doctor advised rubbing a wash-cloth over my nipples to toughen them. But if you'd help out . . . it would be more fun."

"I am happy to oblige." He kissed her breasts tenderly.

"Like an alligator, lovie."

"Like this?" He suckled her until she moaned, "Just like that."

"Anything for the baby." He circled his hand over her belly. "You're rounder, *m'aingeal*. Swelling like a ripening fruit. How long will it be until I can feel her kicking?"

"Another couple of months."

"Wonderful child, I can't wait to feel your little feet against my hand."

"In the middle of the night, kicking like a football player. Rumpety-rumpety-rumpety."

"We'll get her a tryout with Partick Thistle. The first woman footballer."

"Umm." Jean looked up at him and his heart swelled with love. She was different, now that she was pregnant. A dreamy sensuousness like nothing he'd ever experienced with a woman before, and she moved against him so erotically his head reeled and his whole body ached with his need to be inside her.

Hormones, Jean said. Incredible, he called it, and lived for the moments when she surrendered to him completely, arched her back and took him deep. She was both abandoned and innocent, as though she were being made love to for the first time, and so trusting that she held nothing back in her response. She gave him everything in her and he took it like a thirsty man takes water, nourished by sex with a woman who loved him, and only him, with all her heart and body and soul.

He murmured, "Are you comfortable? Do you want to go upstairs to bed?"

"No, right here on the couch, just like at home."

Afterwards Darroch rolled onto his side to take his weight from her, and pulled her close. They'd debated together whether or not they needed a honeymoon, since they'd been lovers for months. Now he realized that it was just what they needed: a chance to be alone, unworried by everyday life, daily duties. Plenty of time for talking and cuddling. Making love whenever they wanted, as often as they wanted, with no interruptions.

Except that the phone had begun to ring.

"Leave it, the ansaphone's on," he whispered in her ear when she moved beneath him.

But the voice on the machine was instantly recognizable. "Màiri," said Jean. "Shall we get it?"

"I can't move right now. Give me a minute or two and I'll call her back. But I think I'll do this first . . . do you like it?"

"Oh, yes," she sighed.

The answering machine was forgotten.

Sixteen

Na trì rudan as briagha air an t-saoghal:
Long fo h-uidheam, boireannach leatromach,
Agus gealach làn.
The three most beautiful things in the world: a full-rigged ship,
A woman with child, and a full moon.

South Uist proverb

Back home from London, they settled happily into married life and Darroch to the task of learning to live with a pregnant woman. His inexperience led him to be overprotective and that, coupled with Jean's raging hormones, led to the first clashes of their time together.

Exasperated with being treated like a piece of fragile glass, when she felt as healthy and strong as one of Jamie's Jacob's sheep, and almost as aggressive, she growled one evening, "I don't want to go to bed yet. I'm not tired."

"You need your rest. "

"I had a nap this afternoon." Jean pushed the broccoli on her plate around with her fork.

"All right, one more hour and then it's bedtime. Finish your supper. Eat your vegetables."

"I hate broccoli," she muttered sulkily.

"It's full of iron. You know you need extra iron for strong blood; the books all say so. I was just reading about it last night."

She forked a mouthful of the despised vegetable into her mouth. I'm going to burn those pregnancy books, she thought crossly. Sneak them all out and throw them in the rubbish pile, bury them in the compost heap. "Ugh," she said, chewing and grimacing. "It makes me want to throw up."

Darroch pushed his chair back hastily. "Perhaps you'd better lie down after all."

"No, I'm all right," she said, faintly ashamed of herself, and choked down another bite of broccoli.

Worried, he stared at her. "If you don't like that I'll look for another green veg. Maybe sprouts, or spinach. I think the Co-Op has canned spinach. I could fix creamed spinach tomorrow night."

Jean detested creamed spinach even more than broccoli, and the thought of it made her feel really sick. She gulped and put her hand over her mouth.

He jumped to his feet. "Jean . . . "

By a tremendous effort of will she controlled the attack of nausea. "I'm all right. Don't fuss so much."

He looked at her, hurt. "I only want to do what's best for you, *mo chridhe*."

She was deeply ashamed of her behavior. "I know you do," she said and burst into tears. Tears were so close to the surface these days and she hated it, hated losing control over nothing and upsetting Darroch.

He was by her side, pulling her up into his arms. "Leave that nasty stuff, Jean. You don't have to eat it. Come sit by the fire." He steered her to the sofa and settled her on his lap. "I'm sorry, *mo chridhe*, I'm a brute. Darling Jean, don't cry."

"No, you're not, it's me, I'm a bitch. I hate it, I'm so sorry, I just can't control my awful tongue."

He grinned. "I love your tongue, Jean. It's not awful at all, it's delicious. Come on, give me a taste," He coaxed her mouth open, tangled his tongue with hers in a long delightful kiss. She giggled and relaxed against him. She was not reluctant to go to bed, when he suggested it a few minutes later.

But it was a delicate balancing act, keeping them both happy. He did not want to engage in verbal combat with her. He knew she was miserable because she was so snappish. He consulted his books and learned that mood swings and irritability were common in the early months of pregnancy. That knowledge gave him courage.

He also consulted Màiri and Jamie, veterans of the birth of twins, Ian and Eilidh. Màiri had simply shrugged her shoulders. "If men only knew what it's like," she said dramatically and would say no more.

Jamie, on the other hand, was deeply sympathetic. "Ah, *mo charaid*, there's nothing more terrifying than a pregnant woman. You never know which way she's going to jump."

"Be serious, Jamie."

"I am serious. If you only knew what that woman of mine put me through when she was carrying the twins . . . " He lifted his shoulders in an expressive shrug. "I didn't know what to do. She'd go from giggling to scolding, from cuddling to sudden floods of tears."

This sounded so much like Darroch's experience that he was heartened. Perhaps he wasn't losing his mind after all. Perhaps it was all perfectly normal.

"The worst of it was . . . " Jamie paused dramatically. "Sex."

Now Darroch was tense with a sudden worry. Was there something that he was not expecting, that had not been covered in his books? "What about sex, Jamie?"

"She thought I didn't want her." Lost in memory, he was back at *Taigh Rois*, in the third month of Màiri's pregnancy. They had just finished dinner and she was doing the washing-up. He was suddenly aware that she was crying, hands in the dishwater, tears dripping, head bowed. He moved quickly to put his arms around her. "What's wrong, *mo Mhàiri*?" he whispered.

"You don't want me. You think I'm fat and ugly."

Jamie looked at Darroch. "What gets into women's heads, anyway? She'd always been the most beautiful creature in the world to me but now that she was pregnant she was splendid. A Rubens painting. Her skin like milk slipping through my fingers. Her hair a darker, richer red, like a Titian, and wild with curls. And her breasts . . . " Jamie licked his lips. "Like the globes of perfect blown glass vases."

Darroch whispered, "She always did have beautiful breasts," then stopped guiltily.

But Jamie was too lost in memory to be jealous of Darroch and Màiri's time as lovers so many years ago. "Everything about her body was fuller, rounder, softer. She was just beginning to show and her belly curved outward . . . "

He looked at Darroch and raised his hands in an un-Jamie like gesture. "*A Dhia*, it makes me hard just thinking about it. I was crazy with lust for her and she thought I didn't want her because she was fat and ugly. Now how is a man to respond to that?"

Darroch said, "What did you do, Jamie?"

"I carted her off to bed and made love to her. Well, Ros had said it was all right and I was daft with wanting her. It was the most terrifying and glorious experience of my life. Do you have any idea what it's like to make love to your woman who's had two miscarriages and is pregnant with twins?"

Darroch shuddered. At least he didn't have to worry about that; the ultrasound Jean had had in Edinburgh had revealed that she was carrying one baby, perfect and normal.

"We had to stop making love when she was about six months along. Ros said it was too dangerous. Three months before, two months afterwards. I was climbing the walls with frustration." Jamie sighed deeply.

Darroch said, "What do you mean, two months afterwards?"

"Well, you can't just leap on a woman after she's had a baby," Jamie said patiently. "The . . . uh . . . is . . . umm . . . sore. And she's torn, when the baby's head comes through her . . . ummm. She needs time to heal." He looked at Darroch in amusement. "Haven't you read that, in all your books?"

Darroch ran an agitated hand through his hair. "I've skipped that part, about the actual birth." He had, in fact, read about it in one book that was graphically illustrated with photographs. He'd been so traumatized that he'd hidden the book in the bottom of the stack, figuring he could go back to it later—much later—when it was relevant.

Besides, he reasoned, Jean had had two babies and Ros was a very experienced doctor. They'd know what to do, between the pair of them. He pictured his role in the event as the hand-holder, the brow-wiper, saw himself murmuring tender words of encouragement in Jean's ear. A very satisfying role and he would play it well, supporting his darling Jean, just like in the videos about husband-coached childbirth that he'd bought, there being no childbirth classes on the Island.

Jamie said, "My advice is to relax and enjoy it as much as you can. Be patient and gentle; don't argue with her no matter how exasperated you get. Look after her health. And make love to her as often as you both want. Enjoy your time as a couple because it will all change, once you have a baby."

"Thanks, Jamie." He felt better, although one thing still worried him. "How long did you say after the birth, before . . . "

Jamie looked at him sympathetically. "It was different with Màiri because she had twins. With a normal birth I suppose it's around five or six weeks. And of course the same before."

"Oh." There was a world of feeling in the word.

"My advice for you is to get a hobby. Something to keep your mind busy and your hands occupied." Jamie grinned. "How about learning to whittle?"

Jamie's Lullaby

play 3–2–2 as written

(like a waltz)

Jamie's Lilt

(hornpipe or play-song feel)

Rosie's Reel

Seventeen

Broom is a-bloom, gorse is a-glow,
Baby sleeps soft in arms white as snow.
Heather and foxglove blow on the heath,
Father leans close, mother sings sweet:
"Island babies all shall know
Love is around them always."
Traditional Eilean Dubh lullaby

*E*veryone on Eilean Dubh knew about the baby now. They'd told Màiri, Catrìona and Ian the Post, Sheilah and Barabal, and all of those individuals had kept their secret, but the Island knew somehow that the Laird's wife was going to present them with a Mac an Rìgh heir and there was quiet, satisfied rejoicing.

No one mentioned it, of course. It was not their place to say anything about it until the official announcement was made. They waited, and simmered with expectation.

In Murray the Meat's butcher shop one morning, Jean had nearly reached the bottom of her grocery list. All that was left was Murray's special free-range chicken breasts that she intended to fry for supper tonight.

Jean took one look into the butcher's case and was instantly nauseated by the sight of the chicken: yellow-skinned, moist, delicately ornamented by globs of thick golden fat. She turned pale, then green, and uttered a single strangled moan.

Mrs. Murray the Meat, mother of six, recognized the symptoms and sprang into action. She was around the case in a second, putting a comforting arm around Jean while she urged her into the back of the shop. "Loo's right there, love," she advised, pushing open the door to a small bathroom.

Jean stumbled in and gave up the contents of her stomach to the toilet. When she came out a few minutes later, white-faced and sweating, Mrs. Murray steered her firmly into the kitchen behind the shop. "Don't look," she advised as they sailed by the room where meats were cut and packaged. A faint odor of blood hung over it. Jean shuddered.

Her hostess looked at her with a sharp eye and said briskly, "Cup of tea will settle your stomach. Sugar, no milk, and here's some crackers, get them down you. You've missed lunch, haven't you. Mustn't do that," she scolded gently. "Got to keep food inside you all the time. It keeps the nausea down."

"I was running behind. I thought I could wait for lunch. I won't make that mistake again," Jean said, and meant it.

Mrs. Murray set a cup in front of Jean. Then she sat down with her own cup and waited quietly.

Finally Jean said, "I guess you've figured it out."

"Figured what out?" said Mrs. Murray, all innocence.

"That I'm pregnant."

"Are you just!" the other woman exclaimed. "Isn't that *miorbhuileach*!" With the secret out she felt free to probe a bit. "When are you due? And how's your health, apart from the sickness?"

"Oh, I'm fine, most of the time. And I'm about three months along," she added, facing bravely the fact that now everyone would know, officially, that she'd been pregnant before she was married.

"Lovely, only six months to wait," said Mrs. Murray. "Mind you," she said comfortably, "we've all been hoping for it, ever since the pair of you were handfast."

With that one remark she banished Jean's fears of scandal. So it was true, as Darroch and Màiri had assured her. She wasn't going to be regarded with raised eyebrows and disapproving glances because she'd been pregnant before the wedding; the Islanders regarded the handfasting ceremony as the legitimate start of their relationship. The embarrassing ghosts of her first marriage's prenuptial pregnancy faded into memory. She felt a relief so profound that she could have burst into tears, but managed to control all but the immediate tears that filled her eyes.

Mrs. Murray saw the tears but attributed them to a mother-to-be's wayward emotions. "More tea?" she said, turning away to give Jean a moment to regain her composure.

"No, *tapadh leat, a Sheonag*, I'd better get out and find Darroch. He'll think I've been whisked away by the fairies."

Mrs. Murray chuckled, imagining anyone confusing her plump little form with one of Eilean Dubh's legendary sylphs. "So he might," she agreed.

As Jean rose to leave she added casually, "So when will you make the official announcement, then? Never fear that I'll keep your secret until you do."

Jean turned back to her. "Do you think we need an official announcement?"

"Well, it would be more fun, wouldn't it. Pick an occasion, let everyone know at the same time, get all the congratulations over and done with. Then you can settle down to the business of having your baby." She added thoughtfully, "Perhaps at a *cèilidh*?"

"That's a good idea. Everyone's there."

"Except Minister Donald, of course. But you'll already have told him, I'm sure."

"Uhhh . . . not yet," Jean said guiltily.

Mrs. Murray stopped dead, clasped her hands over her stomach and said seriously, "Oh, no, *m'eudail*. That will never do. The Minister must be told, right after your family and dearest friends, and definitely before you tell the world."

"I suppose so," Jean said. "Unless—perhaps he's already guessed?"

The other woman exploded in giggles. "Oh, no, *m'eudail*, not the Minister. He doesn't think of such things, his thoughts are so exalted, and his poor sweet wife, rest her soul, couldn't have children. I imagine he thinks babes grow on the lowest branches of gorse bushes."

Taken aback, Jean looked at her, then nodded her head. That certainly presented an interesting new view of the Minister, she thought.

Later, when she related the whole experience to Darroch as they sat together at their kitchen table, she concluded, "And Seonag Murray thinks we should tell Minister Donald right away."

Darroch put his hand over hers. "I've told him. He cried."

"What?"

"Aye. We both pretended it wasn't happening, but I saw the tears glistening on his eyelashes. Sentimental old *diabhol* he is," he said to hide his own emotion. He'd been deeply touched by the Minister's reaction, and uncomfortably aware that once again he was the Laird, the focus of the Island's hopes and dreams.

"Perhaps you and I should have told him together, but I wanted to spare you that ceremony. A near royal occasion, you ken, telling the Minister that there will be a Mac an Rìgh heir." He shook his head ruefully.

Jean shuddered. "Yes, thank you. But it would have been fascinating, seeing the Minister in tears."

"Ach, no, *mo chridhe*. That was private, just between the Minister and me." He grinned. "Kind of a guy thing, you know."

So they made the long-awaited official announcement at the following Friday's *cèilidh,* standing with arms around each other on the dance floor in front of the stage. Darroch said simply, "*Mo chàiradean*, I want you all to know that Jean and I are expecting a baby in six months."

Pandemonium broke out in the crowd, carefully controlled because they were, after all, Scottish and no one wanted to be thought a gusher. But they smiled and called out congratulations, then burst into delighted applause.

Jamie was up on the stage, fiddle and bow in hand. He let the celebration go until he thought Jean and Darroch were becoming uncomfortable with all the stramash. Then he cleared his throat and announced into the microphone, "I've a new tune. For our friends here, and their baby."

The hall quieted immediately. A new baby and a new tune from Jamie MacDonald. *Miorbhuileach.*

The tune was soft when it began, like a lullaby heard from an adjoining room, gentle and soothing. It changed slowly into a lilt that children would sing in their play, and ended in a soaring melodic song that spoke of happiness and hope, a song that despite its essential Scottishness, managed to convey in subtle rhythm and phrasing an American feeling that was a tribute to the baby's mother.

Jamie finished, took his bow from the fiddle, and surveyed his audience. A roomful of people was staring at him, mouths open, speechless with awe. A satisfied smile played around the edge of his mouth and he thought, you've got the touch, Jamie, my lad.

At his feet, below the stage, stood Darroch, clapping his hands in admiration of his friend's talent, and Jean. She was gazing up at Jamie with hero worship in her eyes. It pleased him mightily that his respected fellow musician, dear friend and favorite flirt would look at him like that.

He winked at her.

Jean turned red and giggled. Recovering, she mouthed at him, *you are miorbhuileach.* Then she mimed swooning into Darroch's arms.

Jamie grinned as the Eilean Dubh murmur of approbation rose lustily around him.

A Dhia, he thought. What a satisfying evening.

Eighteen

Softly, in the shadows, a woman is singing to me . . .

D. H. Lawrence

*J*ean entered the second trimester of her pregnancy and to her relief and her husband's her emotions settled down. The morning sickness was gone, except for occasional flare-ups, and her need for sudden dashes to the bathroom had declined. She felt healthy and full of energy.

One day in the kitchen she turned on the radio to BBC Radio One.

She heard her own voice.

She froze, clutching her teacup so tightly that it rattled in the saucer.

Her voice, and Darroch's. Jamie's fiddle and Màiri on the piano. A Citizens Hall full of Eilean Dubh voices, joining in on the chorus of "The Emigrant's Lament."

When the song finished she felt behind her for a chair and sat down blindly. Darroch, coming in from outdoors, saw her sitting white and still.

"Whatever is wrong? You look like you've seen a ghost. Are you in pain?" He threw himself down beside her and seized her hands.

She blinked and looked at him. "You're not going to believe this," she said, "but we're on the radio."

When he stared, she added, "BBC One. All of us, singing in the Citizens Hall. 'The Emigrant's Lament.'"

The phone rang and he snatched it up. "*Tri coig tri coig. A Chatrìona?*" He listened, said something in the Gaelic and hung up. "You're not going to believe this, Jean," he said. "We're on the radio."

"Thank God for Catrìona," she said. "I thought I was hallucinating. How in the world . . . ?"

The phone rang again. "*A Bharabal* . . . aye, Jean heard it too, and Catrìona."

When the phone rang a third time, he answered it and after he hung up he unplugged it. "It seems the whole Island listens to Radio One," he said. "So much for our Gaelic programming on Four."

"It doesn't start till twelve," Jean said, "because that guy on One is so popular, there's no use to put anything on opposite him. Darroch, how could this have happened?"

He thought for a moment. "Gary—I forget his last name—Maxie's boyfriend. He's in the music business, he's a talent rep or producer or something. He quite liked our music, remember? He asked if it was okay to record our set at the *cèilidh* on our wedding day and I said yes. He did say something about playing it for a friend and he asked me if 'The Lament' was under copyright. I remember that because the very idea made me laugh, it's two hundred years old if it's a day. But they must have cleaned it up, remastered it or something, if they used it on the radio because there was all that noise in the background at the *cèilidh*. And the Citizens Hall is not the Albert Hall, though its acoustics are quite good."

"No," Jean said slowly. "That was the odd thing; it wasn't changed at all. It was as though I were standing in the Hall. There was even that baby crying."

"Oh, yes. Marsali MacShennach's latest. However did she get her to stop, I wonder. Her screams were deafening."

"Stuck a nipple in her mouth . . . ummm . . . began to nurse her."

Darroch was flipping through his Rolodex. "I'll call Max; see what he knows." After a moment he said, "His ansaphone. Probably still asleep, it's only noon. You know actors." He left a message and before he could turn the phone off again another call came in. "Oh, hullo, Liz."

"Darroch," said an aggrieved voice on the other end. "I really would appreciate it if you would tell me when you start a new gig. I've had three calls already this morning and they all want to know about this recording you've made. What is a poor ignorant agent to tell them?"

"You know more about it than I do. I haven't even heard the song on the radio. My wife nearly fainted when she heard it. Aye, okay, *ceart math*," he said into the phone. "I'll call you when I sort this, Liz. Cheers, bye."

Jean had turned the radio back on. "Why is this guy so popular? He quacks like a duck. Oh, Darroch. Listen." She turned the radio up and a chorus of *Eilean Dubhannaich* voices filled the room.

"And that's the hot hot *hot* new sound from—Scotland! Bye-bye, guys and dolls, dig you tomorrow!" said a voice over the music. It swelled and faded and a new voice said earnestly, "This is BBC Radio One. The time is twelve noon. And now for the news."

Jean turned off the radio. They looked at each other. She said, "How about . . . "

"Tea," finished Darroch. He'd forgotten to turn the phone off and it rang again just as he was lifting his cup.

"Hullo, old darling. Whyever are you calling me at the first flicker of ghastly dawn?" said Max.

Darroch said, "Max, you have ten seconds to tell me why my wife, my friends and I are suddenly the hot hot *hot* new sound of Scotland."

"You are?" his voice rose to a squeak and he dropped the phone. "Gary, Gary, get up, you slug-a-bed! Old what's-her-name has come through! They're a success!"

A new voice came on the phone. "Hullo, Darroch," it said cautiously. "Are you on the radio?"

"We are, Gary. Would you care to explain?"

There was the sound on the other end of someone drawing in a deep breath. "Well, I listened to the tape I made at the *cèilidh* and it seemed to me it had commercial possibilities. There's a market for Scottish music; remember how 'The Mull of Kintyre' took off years ago. And Jean has a terrific voice; it grabs the ear. So I gave the tape to this friend of mine who's the Sunday evening deejay. She must have gotten a good response when she played it if The Duck used it on Monday morning; he's really tuned in to anything that might fly. Give me a few minutes, Darroch. I'll find out what's happening and call you back, okay?"

The phone off, Darroch turned to Jean and relayed the conversation.

"My goodness," she said. "This is just about the weirdest thing that ever happened to me."

"Weirder than marrying a Scot?"

"No, that holds the all-time record," she said. "Darroch, Màiri won't have heard us on Radio One. She never listens to English language broadcasts and she's been at the Playschool all morning so no one could tell her. What is she going to think when she hears about this?"

He groaned. "The worst, I'm sure. We'd better break it to her gently."

They both stood silently, imagining Màiri's response to their very personal Island song being aired for all to hear.

"Let's meet her at the Playschool and take her to lunch. We'll get a glass of wine into her first."

Darroch turned on the phone when they were ready to leave the cottage. It rang immediately.

It was Gary. "I've got it all arranged, Darroch. An appointment on Wednesday at a dear little studio in Brixton; we use it all the time. We need you and Jean and the fiddler and the piano player. I asked my associate about re-doing the audience participation with a London choir but he said the homegrown choruses, even the baby crying, helped create the appeal of the tune. So we'll re-master it and clean up the sound and lay you four over it.

"Our appointment is for two-thirty. That should give you plenty of time to get down here."

"Wait a minute," began Darroch.

"Can't wait, my darling, must strike while the demand is hot. That's the music biz. It's not that slow old television stuff you're used to. We've got to get a single in the stores before the lovely public forgets all about you and moves on to some new excitement. Oh, and bring a second number to record."

"I have to check to see if the others are available."

"Of course, love. Just have them in the studio Wednesday at two-thirty. I'll e-mail you the directions for getting there. Cheerio." And he was gone.

Darroch said to Jean, "We're to be in London Wednesday ready to re-record 'The Lament.' With Màiri and Jamie. To sell in music shops."

Jean said, "She'll never do it, darling."

"Umm. Maybe two glasses of wine before we tell her, do you think?"

Màiri balked at being dragged out to lunch. "I have too much to do."

But they were relentless and soon all three were seated in the Rose's dining room. Sheilah came in with menus and said, "Was that us I heard on Radio One? I couldn't believe it."

"Sheilah, can we have a bottle of white wine? Right away?" Darroch cut her off.

"Yes, of course." She left, looking puzzled.

Màiri looked at them suspiciously. "What is going on?"

Darroch said, "I never could keep a secret from you, *m'eudail*." The wine arrived and he poured her a glass. "Take a bit of this, now, and we'll tell all."

He waited until she'd had some wine and then he told her the whole story, very carefully. Both he and Jean could see the anger growing in her; she'd gone quite red in the face. Even her hair seemed to be bristling.

"That is absolutely outrageous. He took something that was ours and gave it to the BBC? To Radio One," she said with loathing.

"Aye." Darroch sat back in his chair, resigned to the fireworks that would follow.

"And you approve of this?"

He said, slowly, "I do not see that it is such a bad thing, to share our culture with the rest of the world. As long as it is done with respect."

"With respect? On Radio One?" She turned to Jean. "And you agree?"

Before Jean could answer, Darroch said "You haven't heard all of it." We are wanted in London. On Wednesday. All of us, you and Jamie included. To make a proper recording, so that it can be sold in stores."

She was scarlet with indignation. "For the English to buy, and laugh at?"

Darroch said, "Why do you think they'd laugh?"

"Because they always laugh at anything Scottish. Especially in the Gaelic."

Darroch said, "*A Mhàiri*, be reasonable."

She folded her arms across her chest and glared. Sheilah, approaching to take their menu selections, hesitated. She had no desire to get caught in the middle of one of Màiri's firestorms.

Jean said plaintively, "Can we order first? I need something to eat. I feel a wee bit peely-wally."

Darroch looked at her anxiously.

Sheilah moved in on cue.

Màiri returned to the attack. "I will not be a party to this. I will not prostitute my culture. Jean, surely you don't approve."

Jean said, "Oh, I don't know. It might be rather fun."

Darroch sent her a glance of thanks. "Aye, think of it that way. It will be a chance to have a bit of fun. You've never seen London, *a Mhàiri*."

She shuddered. "Nor ever wanted to see it."

Sheilah waited uneasily, notepad and pencil in hand.

Jean said, "I've often thought that Jamie should be heard by a wider audience than just the few of us here on the Island. He has so much talent. The world should hear him."

That was a new idea. Màiri looked at her, suddenly uncertain.

"And everyone will hear how *miorbhuileach* the music is on Eilean Dubh. Surely that's worth some effort," Jean added.

Darroch said, "We won't do it without total creative control. We will present the music the way we feel is appropriate. If that's not acceptable, we won't do it."

Màiri opened her mouth to object again and Jean said softly, "If the recording sells, we can give the money to the Trust. Or to the Playschool. Remember how high the estimate is to replace the Playschool roof, even with our own people volunteering their labor? And that's not fair anyway. We should pay them for their time; they've got tons of their own work to do.

"We got a good start on fundraising with the jumble sale. This might earn us enough to finish the job. Darroch, isn't that right?"

He said, "We can certainly dedicate the profits to fixing the roof. Or anything else the Playschool needs. And if it sells well, we could make a wee bit, I imagine."

The three looked at each other.

Sheilah said plaintively, "Would you like to order now?"

They waited for their meal in an uneasy silence, punctuated by Màiri's mumbling.

When lunch arrived Jean said, "Food, thank heavens. I'm starved."

Màiri said, "Darroch, surely it can't be good for Jean, in her condition, to drag her all the way to London."

"As long as I have a suitcase full of sandwiches I'll be okay. Remember, Darroch and I went to London for our honeymoon and nothing bad happened."

Màiri growled and ate her lunch without speaking again.

Jean put her fork down. She said, "I have an idea. Let's see what Jamie thinks. If he opposes it, then I'll side with Màiri."

"Fair enough," said Darroch. "We'll let Jamie cast the deciding vote."

Jamie was there when they returned Màiri to *Taigh Rois*. He listened to what they had to say. Then he grinned. "It was really a success, on Radio One?"

Darroch nodded. "Gary said they'd had a ton of calls, all wanting to know where to buy the recording."

"Was it The Duck who played it?"

Màiri looked at him suspiciously. She'd had no idea he listened to Radio One.

"Aye."

His grin grew broader. "Well, well, think of that. We're right up there with the rappers and the hiphoppers. What shall we call ourselves? I rather fancy Jamie and the Islanders, what do you think?"

"So you want top billing, do you?" said Darroch, chuckling.

Màiri said, "Jamie, you don't mean to do this . . . "

"Oh, aye, *mo ghràdh*. And I plan to enjoy every minute of it. Will we go down in enough time to visit the Victoria and Albert Museum, Darroch? I've always wanted to see their collection of antique musical instruments. And will we record in a proper studio? Like the Beatles and Eric Clapton?"

"Of course."

Jean said, "I think it's incredibly exciting. Let's go home, Darroch, I need to start packing. What does a recording star wear in London, do you know?"

The three of them grinned at each other. Màiri looked stubborn. Darroch said, "Don't sulk, *m'eudail*. Just think about the Playschool roof."

Nineteen

Though Eilean Dubh is but a tiny and insignificant Island,
its music is celestial.

Robertson's Relics and Anomalies of Scotland, 1923.

The four of them tumbled out of a cab in front of a large Victorian house in the south London suburb of Brixton. The street was very quiet, with two or three pedestrians walking by. In Brockwell Park, across the way, skateboarders zoomed along on their way to the Stockwell Road.

"Are you sure this is right, Darroch?" said Jamie. He had been expecting an ultra-modern building, all concrete and glass.

"This is the address," Darroch answered, striding up the steps and ringing the bell.

A smiling sari-clad Indian woman answered the door. Gary came forward to greet them. "So you found us," he said. "Welcome, everyone."

Inside, beyond the hall, an oval room was dominated by a huge white fireplace at one end. On the marble mantle sat a collection of vintage microphones, and on one side of the fireplace was a grouping of potted plants. A vivid oriental rug covered the floor.

The windows were fitted with drawn white shades illuminated by the sun behind them, so that the room seemed to glow. Banks of electronic equipment, stacked ten units high, and a large desk with two computers were at the far end of the room. Over the desk were abstract paintings and old photographs in antiqued brass frames.

The Indian woman brought in a silver tea tray and set it on a side table. Gary said, "Imira, darling, take their coats. Tea, everyone? I'll be mother. Sit down and make yourselves at home."

When they all had their cups Jean said, "This doesn't look the way I imagined a recording studio would look."

"Scotty and Dom like to keep it homey; it relaxes everyone. And this room has wonderful acoustics, very warm and live. We thought it would be just right for you. We've recorded other folk music here."

"Here? You mean we're going to record in this room?" said Jamie.

"Yes, this is Studio One. And if everyone has finished their tea we'll get started."

As Gary took them through the preliminaries, Darroch whispered to Jean, "Are you nervous?"

"You bet. How about you?"

"Terrified. Remember, I'm an actor, not a musician. When it comes to music I rely on Màiri or you to tell me what to do."

They worked through the afternoon. The choice of the second recording had caused intense debate. Jean thought it should be an instrumental showing off Jamie's fiddle playing, while Darroch and Jamie favored a traditional ballad sung by Jean. Màiri remained aloof. They had not made their decision by the time they were ready to record it.

"What's the source of the appeal of the original recording?" said Gary, when they described their dilemma.

"Damned if I know," said Jamie. "It's just the same music we play at home every other Friday night."

"Exactly," said Gary. "That's what catches attention. It draws people in, makes them feel they are right there with you. I think an instrumental is too risky standing alone. The music needs a voice."

The front door opened and closed and a young woman appeared in the threshold, smiling at them. She had the bright red hair, blue eyes and alabaster skin of a Highland Scot. "And here is Fiona, our arranger, right on cue," Gary said.

She smiled. "*Feasgar math. Ciamar a tha sibh an diugh?*" Good afternoon. How are you all today?

Four sets of jaws dropped in amazement. Màiri, who'd been grimly silent all afternoon, spoke first. "*A bheil Gàidhlig agad?*" You have the Gaelic?

"*Tha. Tha mi bana-Uibhisteach.*" Yes. I am from Uist.

Gary said, "Fiona's one of the best arrangers in London and we're very lucky she's available." He winked at Darroch. He had noticed Màiri's stubborn silence and truculent expression. "And I thought that since she's from one of the Scottish islands herself, you'd feel at home with her. Introductions all around, then we'll get to work."

Màiri was now positively voluble, for her, and she, Darroch and Jamie began an earnest discussion in their own language with the arranger.

Finally Darroch took pity on the other two and said, "English now, *mo chàiradean*. Fiona, we can't decide what our second tune should be."

"Let me hear what you're considering," she said. They ran through their nominations. She said, "I agree, there definitely should be a vocal, with both Darroch and Jean, but let me see what we can work in to take advantage of the fiddle and piano."

She put together an arrangement of *"Mo Ghille Dubh Ciar Dubh"* that showcased both instruments and voices and they soon had a recording that satisfied all of them.

"Brilliant," said Gary. "Now, off with the four of you, get some food, and let us mix what we've got. Come back in an hour or three. We've got the studio till ten tonight so with luck we can wrap this up today."

"Food," sighed Jean. "That sounds *miorbhuileach*. What's to eat around here?"

"There's Thai and Satay just around the corner, and a very nice Japanese noodle bar a block further. Imira, coats please," and he hustled them out.

After dinner they came back and listened to the finished product.

"Is that really us? It sounds like we're back in the Citizens Hall," said Jean.

"Just what we hoped. We've kept the Islanders' choruses on the original tune. Wish we had them for the second; it gives a nice note of authenticity. I was thinking, Darroch, we should come back up to Eilean Dubh and record at a *cèilidh* if we do a CD."

"What?" said Màiri blankly.

"If the first recording sells well we'll need to record an entire CD."

"You mean we have to do more of this?" she said and her expression grew menacing.

Gary grinned, but said only, "Coats, Imira, darling. Our visitors are all finished for today. Darroch, I'll be in touch about the press gathering for the recording's release. Don't leave town; we'll be ready to go by Friday."

Màiri's eyes grew huge. "Friday?"

Jamie threw her coat around her shoulders. "Hush yer whist, wummin."

"Imira's called you a cab; it'll be at the door in a twinkle. Bye-bye, darlings, enjoy your stay in the big city," said Gary and ushered them out the door.

They were quiet in the taxi going back to the flat, Jean and Jamie thoughtful, Màiri simmering and Darroch watching her cautiously.

Finally he said, "Màiri, there's no reason to subject you to the press preview; it's all meaningless chatter. You and Jamie can start back home. Jean and I will handle it."

"What!" said Jamie. "Miss all the fun when Jamie and the Islanders are unveiled? Never! We're in."

Darroch said, "About that name, Jamie . . . "

He grinned. "It's open to negotiation." And as Màiri opened her mouth to protest, he added, "But not the grand unveiling. We'll not miss that. And that's final, *a Mhàiri.*"

She glared but said no more.

Darroch whispered in Jean's ear, "Do women love a masterful man?"

"This one does." Then she said, "I have a thought about a name."

They looked at her expectantly.

"Well, we sing traditional music. Why not call ourselves *Tradisean?* The Gaelic for tradition. And it's pronounced almost the same as in English and it looks like it's pronounced. People shouldn't have any trouble saying it, even if they can't spell it."

"I like it fine," said Jamie, and Darroch nodded.

Màiri shrugged. "I don't care what we're called. I just want to go home."

The recording was soon released to considerable airplay and successful sales. There was a demand for more by *Tradisean.* When Gary and his staff arrived on Eilean Dubh to record the rest of the CD at a *cèilidh* Darroch began to think he had bitten off more than the group could chew.

The *Eilean Dubhannaich*, of course, were thrilled. Their music, them-selves singing, to be heard all over Britain. Jean suggested that a couple of recordings be made at the Thursday night residents' pub get-togethers at the Rose Hotel. Nearly everyone except Jean and Darroch and the recording staff were well lubricated for the occasion and excitement ran high. Even Màiri accepted a dram, glaring at Jamie when he insisted she take it "for your nerves, *mo ghràdh.*"

"I don't have nerves," she snapped and gulped the whisky.

The recordings turned into jam sessions. Gary, grinning broadly, played them back for those assembled. "We don't sound half bad," said Somhairle MacPhi *as sine*, and everyone nodded solemn agreement. That was not gushing; it was the simple truth, they all knew.

The Emigrant's Lament

words: Audrey McClellan
music: Sherry Ladig

chorus: A — way, a — way o'er the steel grey sea, a — way from the be lo — ved Is — land.

1. Up before dawn, seeking the fish, watching the schools fill my net. My

chorus:

life it is wai — ting there on the shore, my — Island holds all that I love, A —

way, a — way, o'er the sun — rise sea, going home to the be — lo — ved Is — land.

2. Then came a dawn, fish came no more, love ended in hunger and death.

chorus:

Seeking a new life in the New World, an exile am I from my home — land. A —

way, a — way, o'er the cruel empty sea, a — way from the be — loved Is — land.

3. Now my day ends, I seek but this, a re — turning to my be — gin — nings. Oh

chorus:

Listening One, lead my life and my death to the peace of my own lovely Is — land. A —

way, a — way, o'er the sun — set sea, going home to the be — lo — ved Is — land. A —

way, a — way, o'er the sun — set sea, going home to the be — lo — ved Is — land.

(Instrumental)   (last chord)

Twenty

Away, away, over the steel-gray sea,
Away from the beloved Island.
"The Emigrant's Lament." Eilean Dubh folk song

*G*ary and Liz, Darroch's agent, began importuning them to do a series of appearances to support the recording. "Concerts are terrific for CD sales; people want to see the music makers. Just London, and Cardiff, and Edinburgh. And maybe York and Shrewsbury. Manchester, of course; there's a great folk club there."

Jean fussed and worried over her outfit for the concerts. She definitely couldn't get into her wedding skirt, not if she were going to sing without gasping for breath. Liz took her to a little dress shop and after much thought they picked out a long flowing dress of turquoise silk. It slithered over her curves, just hinting at the pregnant belly beneath. She would pin the Mac an Rìgh sash to her left shoulder.

Màiri would wear her MacDonald skirt and sash, and the men their kilts.

Everyone but Jamie was taut with nerves for the first concert, in London. They were second on the program, just before the headliners, a well-known folk act. When she peeked through the stage curtains and saw the crowd Jean was alarmed. "I've never sung for so many people before," she muttered.

"*Misneachd*, everyone," Jamie, never nervous, said cheerfully. Màiri muttered and growled her apprehension. Even Darroch was a bit unnerved by the large audience.

To their surprise and relief, the debut went beautifully. They gained confidence as they sang and played, and the audience's applause spurred them on to new heights. When they left the stage after their third encore Jean knew she'd never sung so well, and the half-admiring, half-jealous glances of the headliners confirmed *Tradisean's* success.

Sales of their CD in the lobby were brisk and reviews of both concert and recording were excellent.

The reason for their success was not hard to understand. They were a stunning combination on stage, visually as well as musically.

Màiri had resigned herself to doing the concerts but she was determined to keep everything secret about herself, reasoning stubbornly that all she was forced to share was her music. She came on stage on Jamie's arm but refused to go to the front for a bow. Instead she plunked herself on the piano bench, back to the audience.

If she thought that made her invisible, she was wrong. The stage lighting ricocheted off the wild red-gold curls tumbling to her waist, making her figure shimmer and glow as she played. Her particular fans took to seeking out the side seats where they just might, by craning their necks, get a look at her face. Their best moments came whenever she got caught up in a riotous piano-fiddle duel, forgot the audience and threw mischievous glances over her shoulder at her husband.

Jamie would fade forward on stage like a tight end waiting for a bullet from the quarterback and angle himself so that Màiri had to turn towards the audience to see him. And when they finished their duet he would swoop down on her, seize her hands and force her to turn and bow, acknowledging the applause.

For Màiri's fans, those were the best moments of the concerts.

Jamie's admirers were never deprived of his presence. Blond hair gleaming, blue eyes flashing, he took to the stage like a cat to cream, always in control of his person, his instrument and his listeners. He liked lots of audience eye contact, especially with females, and it didn't matter to him whether it was a pretty young girl, a sedate matron or an elderly lady. In the midst of the most dazzling solo he would lift his head and scan beyond the footlights, looking for someone with whom to exchange a secret little smile. The recipients of those smiles always straightened up and blushed, thrilled to have had an intimate moment of contact with the man the British folk world was now calling Bonnie Prince Jamie.

Darroch was the anchor of *Tradisean's* stage persona. His face was known to almost everyone in Britain with a television set. They'd seen him in dramas,

Britcoms, commercials and magazine ads, and many had grown up watching him as the Magician; they'd shivered in safety behind their couches as he fought evildoers. Tall, self-assured, smiling and friendly, he was also a bit of a surprise: no one had imagined that he could sing as well as act.

If Màiri was the enigma, Jamie was the star and Darroch was everyone's beloved big brother, it was harder to pigeonhole Jean, the Yank. She was not flashy or dominating. She was quietly dignified when she entered with Darroch and took a bow, then stepped back to let Jamie play the opening number, just like at home. She was shy and oddly virginal, despite the bulge of pregnancy beginning to show amidst the shimmering folds of the turquoise silk dress. And her beauty was the type that grew slowly in the minds of the watchers.

When she sang the audience quieted to a reverent hush as her voice fell perfect and crystalline into the silence.

Angelic, one critic called her. "Ridiculous," said Jean. "Newspaper hyperbole, they're terrible gushers," said Darroch, although he privately thought the comment was right on target.

They always concluded their concerts with "Eilean Dubh," Ùisdean and Mòrag's song, the beautiful haunted tune that had stayed on the Island and at the same time traveled to America with Jean's emigrant ancestor. It was the tune that had confirmed once and for all Jean's link to the Island.

It employed all four of them, with a sweeping overture by piano and fiddle, segueing into Darroch singing the Gaelic words that began,

A maiden fair as the Island sky, beneath the oak tree softly sleeping . . .

It concluded with Jean playing the mandolin and Jamie fiddling as she sang her Appalachian version in English, the words and rhythm different and uncannily the same. Bringing the song to its ending, Jean warbled,

We will remember our true love, down by the banks of the Ohio.

The audience would go nuts.

The first time it happened the foursome was taken aback. They knew the tune and their rendition were good but they hadn't expected such a tumultuous reaction. To settle their listeners down and end the concert, they chose for an encore the song from their first recording, Eilean Dubh's and their signature tune, the poignant "Emigrant's Lament." And everyone, audience and performers alike, went home pleasantly sad but happy.

Jean, Darroch and Jamie made a practice of coming out on stage after the concerts to talk to their fans and answer questions.

Jamie sat on a chair at stage right, fiddle and bow in hand, always ready to demonstrate should anyone want a few pointers on playing traditional music. The fact that some of the people surrounding him might be interested in something other than music did not occur to him.

So it was a surprise when a very pretty brunette invited him out. "Cup of coffee? There's a cafe just across the street," she said.

Surprised, he said, "Thanks, love, but the others are waiting for me."

"Later then? I'm in the hotel just down the street." And she slipped a piece of paper into his hand.

Suspicion took root in his mind. No one had made a pass at him in years, despite his beauty, and he had forgotten that he used to be a sex object. All the *Eilean Dubhannaich* women knew he was married, and more-over married to the fearsome Màiri. No one dared trespass on her turf.

Jamie waited until he was back in their dressing room to unfold the paper. The women were behind a screen, changing clothes, and Darroch, in jeans and turtleneck, sat tilted back in a chair, long legs propped up on the make-up counter.

"What do you make of this?" Jamie said to him. "A girl gave it to me."

Darroch looked at the paper, frowned, then grinned. "Looks like a hotel room number. Your first groupie, *mo chariad.*"

"What?" Jamie didn't know whether to be pleased or alarmed. "You mean she thinks I'd meet her in a hotel room?"

"Aye. Get used to it." Darroch was enjoying the look on Jamie's face and the faint blush that was beginning to show around his ears.

"Well, I'll be damned."

"Only if you take her up on it."

Jamie said stiffly, "My wife's right up on stage with me. Everyone knows I'm a married man."

"Knows, and doesn't care."

Jamie shook his head. Despite his successful career as Jack-the-Lad on Skye before his marriage, once he'd met Màiri all thoughts of other women had left his mind. He didn't think of himself as straight-laced, but he was shocked to his very fingertips.

Darroch took pity. "You'll have to learn to deal with it." In his career as the very popular Magician he'd had many such offers, in fan mail and in person.

"What should I do?"

"Stay cool. Cultivate a look of polite disinterest. Look over them, through them, never directly at them. Never make eye contact. If all else fails, walk away. Quickly."

"Walk away from what?" said Màiri, coming from behind the screen.

"Uhh . . . ," Jamie stopped, unable to think of anything to say.

"Jamie's just had his first encounter with a groupie," said Darroch.

"Oh, that." She sounded so unconcerned that both men stared at her. "Persistent, aren't they." She sat down at the mirror and began to brush her long red hair.

Jamie said, "You mean someone's tried it on with you? But you never stay out front to talk."

"Some of them manage to slip backstage." She lifted her hair and let it fall through her fingers.

Jamie scowled, furious. "You mean someone's had the damned . . . the infernal, colossal cheek to try and pull my wife?"

"Several someones." She put the brush down and smiled at her reflection, the secret female smile that always drove Jamie crazy.

"You should have called me . . . "

"I took care of it," she said smugly.

Darroch and Jamie exchanged glances, imagining exactly how she had taken care of it. Her whiplash tongue was well known to both of them; they'd both felt its sting.

Jean came from behind the screen, peered at herself in the mirror, then went to stand by Darroch. "What are you talking about?" she asked.

"It seems we've all made the acquaintance of groupies," said Darroch.

"What? Well, I haven't. What am I, chopped liver?" Jean said indignantly.

"You're pregnant, *mo chridhe*. No one would suggest such things to you." Darroch patted her belly fondly.

Màiri turned around to look at them, her eyes narrowed and cat-like with satisfaction. "Oh, didn't I mention it, Jean? The last one that tried to chat me up said I should bring you along, that he had a friend who quite fancied you."

Jean's jaw dropped.

Darroch said angrily, "But she's pregnant. She's showing, for God's sake."

"Aye. And more beautiful than ever," said Jamie.

"That settles it," said Darroch firmly. "I'm not letting you out of my sight, Jean. No one's going to make improper suggestions to my wife."

"Or mine," growled Jamie.

They glared at their wives and the two women looked at each other. Nothing like a bit of competition to keep a husband on his toes, Màiri signaled with her eyes, and Jean, understanding perfectly, grinned at her.

For two months they led the life of wandering minstrels, playing concerts around Great Britain. Then Jamie began to worry about his Jacob's sheep and Màiri fretted about the Playschool, even though it had been left in the competent hands of Barabal Mac-a-Phi.

In a hotel room—it was in York, Jean thought, though she'd gotten a little dazed from the rapid pace of their travels—matters came to a head. They were together in Jean and Darroch's room, gobbling Chinese takeaway, another quick meal squeezed in before a pre-concert sound check.

One of them mentioned the Island and abruptly Jean began crying, tears dropping from her eyes into her shrimp stir-fry.

Darroch realized it first. "Oh, damn. Whatever's wrong, Jean?" He put his plate down and wrapped his arms around her.

"I'm sorry," she wept, furious at the reappearance of a hormone-fueled loss of emotional control. "I miss Eilean Dubh. I want to go home," she wailed.

"So do I," said Jamie.

"At last you've come to your senses," said Màiri.

Darroch looked at the other three. Liz and Gary had been importuning him to add dates to their performance schedule. CD sales were brisk and they wanted to keep the momentum going. He had in his briefcase a new list of proposed concerts. It had made his head ache, just thinking about it. He'd begun to dream about Eilean Dubh, as he always did when he was away for very long, and misty visions of pines, ocean and mountains had stayed with him through the mornings. And he'd sensed the growing melancholy in the group as each one thought about the beloved Island.

"I've had it, too," he declared. "We're going home. No more gigs after the last one on the schedule."

"Oh, can we really?" breathed Jean. "Even a short visit would be *miorbhuileach*."

"For good," he said firmly. "We've done enough. We have things to do at home. The Playschool. And babies. And sheep," he added, grinning at Jamie, whose devotion to his prized flock was known to them all. He'd brought with him books and pamphlets about sheep raising and spent his spare time reading, mumbling, and making notes.

"We've done more than enough," said Màiri. "We have our own lives to lead."

"It's been fun, though," sighed Jamie. For the first time in his life he had been able to play his fiddle just as he wanted, before an audience of non-Islanders, listeners who had to be won over at every concert, and his improvisations had gotten more daring and dazzling at each performance. He'd never known such freedom and it intoxicated him. Even the attentions of groupies had ceased to worry him, once he'd learned how to deal with them.

And he loved every aspect of the performances, loved watching the admiring faces of fans, loved their rapturous applause, loved the radio interviews and the magazine and newspaper reporters hanging on his words. The tabloid newspapers' pathetic attempts to dream up scandal in their lives had amused instead of angering him. An article headlined, "Bonnie Prince Wows Chicks, Redhead Wife Says Hands Off My Man," had made him laugh out loud, and had made a *miorbhuileach* weapon for teasing Màiri. She'd stuck her nose in the air and snubbed him as thoroughly as she snubbed the reporters.

But even Jamie was getting tired of the hotel rooms and the restaurant meals, and being stuffed into the car they'd rented to get to their gigs. Aye, it was time to go home, but he had plenty to think about and remember the rest of his life, of the time when he'd been a star.

The indefatigable Liz coaxed them into one last concert at Inverness, and they agreed, with the proviso that all the proceeds were to go to the Playschool. Word spread that *Tradisean* was going to retire at a benefit concert for their Island, and soon folk acts all over Britain with whom the four had made friends were volunteering to donate their services. The farewell concert, titled, "Raising the Roof," quickly sold out. A second concert, called *"Suas leis a' Ghàidlig!"*—"Up with the Gaelic!"—was hastily scheduled for the following night, and that sold out as well.

Fans from all over Britain flocked to Inverness for the folk event of the year. The concerts were brilliant, but the music-making didn't stop there: the weekend turned into a giant *cèilidh*, with impromptu *seiseanan* springing up in pubs all over the small city. Merchants, B and B proprietors, hotelkeepers and bar owners rejoiced in the groundswell of business.

Tradisean rejoiced, as well. Not only were they going home to Eilean Dubh, they were going back as a success. And they had made enough money on the weekend to put a new roof on the Playschool, with enough left over to buy playground equipment and give all the teachers a bonus in their pay-checks.

Even Màiri rejoiced, in her gruff way. "I told you three this was a good idea," she said. "I'm thinking we might do a wee bit of this concertizing next year. We could use an addition on the Playschool."

The other three looked at her, dumbfounded. Then Darroch muttered something to Jamie in the Gaelic about the unpredictability of women, and Jamie shook his head in wonder.

Jean just smiled. Rubbing her rounded belly, she said, "I sure hope baby likes music. And traveling."

Twenty-one

I heard Tradisean *play in York and it changed my life.*
I've bought a guitar and I'm going to learn how to speak the Gaelic.
Fan letter to Jean Mac an Rìgh

*T*he four returned home, wanting nothing more than to rest up and resume their normal activities, and discovered sacks of fan mail waiting. Some of it had been sent on from their official address, Liz's firm, but some of it came directly to the Island, since their fans knew they lived on Eilean Dubh.

Most letters were sensible, containing polite expressions of respect for their music and gratitude for the pleasure *Tradisean* had given. But a number were decidedly peculiar, and addressed in the same way, to "The Magician," or "The Yankee Queen," or "The Red-Headed Wonder Woman."

The ones to Jamie were the most bizarre. Most were sent to "Bonnie Prince Jamie," which excited no more than a few mild chuckles. Some, however, to Jamie's deep embarrassment, were addressed more fancifully: "Beautiful Jamie," "The Angel of the Fiddle," or the worst, the most humiliating of all: "The Yellow-Haired Fiddle God."

Jamie moaned when he saw that one. "I'll never live this down," he said. "Even old sobersides Ian the Post snickered out loud when he delivered this letter. I'm finished on the Island. No one will ever take me seriously again."

"We never did take you very seriously," said Darroch.

"It's a good job they don't send me postcards. Everyone on the Island would howl if they knew what was inside this letter. It's unbelievable, what some of these lasses write. Is there no modesty left in the women these days? Read this one. And it's illustrated. Look at the little drawing." He gave Darroch the letter.

Darroch had had his own share of outrageous letters as the Magician but he raised his eyebrows as high as they would go when he read that one. He said, "The writer seems to be quite familiar with Indian temple carvings."

"Aye," said Jamie bitterly. "I always did attract the art lovers."

Darroch pursed his lips and read the first two paragraphs again, then shook his head. "Mind you, I'm no expert, but I don't believe that's anatomically possible."

"Possible, maybe, but damned uncomfortable," muttered Jamie.

Jean, stretching up on tiptoe to read the letter over Darroch's shoulder, gasped. "We're not trying that at home," she warned her husband.

Jamie snatched the letter back. "You shouldn't read it, Jean. It's not fit for a woman's eyes."

"A woman wrote it," she pointed out.

"Not your kind of woman," said Darroch severely and Jamie nodded.

"I'd a notion to answer the letters—except that one—but Màiri's forbidden it. She says the postage would ruin us. What will I do with all this mail?" mourned Jamie.

"Damned if I know," said Darroch. He'd always had the BBC secretaries to deal with fan mail, sending a routine autographed picture in response, giving him only the special ones to reply to personally. "We can't dump this all on Liz."

"Cheeky devil," said Màiri crossly, surfacing from one of her own letters in which the writer had taken her to task for being so withdrawn on stage. She tore the letter to shreds. "Use them to light the fireplace this winter."

"We can't do that," said Jean. "These nice people have taken the time to write."

"We don't have the time to reply to them all or the money for postage."

In the end they solved the problem with Liz's help. Her office issued a statement written by Jean and Darroch in which *Tradisean* apologized for not being able to answer each letter personally, stressing the work and responsibilities they had on Eilean Dubh. It was widely published in newspapers and entertainment magazines, though the tabloid papers continued to refer to them as "The Mysterious Recluses of the Secret Island."

All the *Eilean Dubhnnaich* got a chuckle out of the "secret island" reference, and Cailean the Crab ventured the opinion that it might increase tourism. "Everybody loves mysterious places," he said confidently, and encouraged Mrs. Cailean to spruce up the two tiny bedrooms of the B and B she operated in their home.

The letters trickled to a manageable flow, where they could actually read and reply to some of them. They were vastly relieved.

Màiri was soon happily deep in plans for raising a roof. And the Playschool itself was once more firmly under her thumb.

After a while the *Eilean Dubhannaich* got tired of subtly teasing Jamie about his rock god status.

Jean and Darroch turned their energies to preparing the house for a baby.

Life was, more or less, back to normal.

Twenty-two

He was a great actor . . . he could just do it.
Never overdone. Just perfection.
There was no complication. The performance was unguarded.
Katharine Hepburn on Spencer Tracy

*F*ive weeks later, early in Jean's sixth month, Darroch had an acting job that required his presence in London for six weeks. He hadn't wanted to go, but there were bills to be paid and the Trust's income to bolster. He'd contracted for the part months ago, before Jean's pregnancy, and the contract had to be fulfilled.

"Of course you're going with me," he said firmly to Jean. "I'll not leave you alone so far gone with child."

Jean didn't mind. She liked his spacious, modern London flat—it was a refreshing change from their cottage—and she found the city fascinating. She'd miss Eilean Dubh, of course, just as he would. But with each day that went by interest in her pregnancy increased, just as Jamie'd predicted, and she was beginning to be overwhelmed by the attention the Islanders showed to her and the contents of her womb. At a visit to the Seniors' Residence only last week half a dozen elderly ladies had cornered her, all talking at once in their cozy Island voices, the Gaelic and English so intertwined that Jean was thoroughly confused.

She figured out at last that what they were arguing about were the signs and portents that foretold the sex of her baby. One woman insisted that a magnet dangling over a pregnant belly was the best sign. If it spun clockwise the child was a boy, counterclockwise, a girl. Another based her prediction on the movements of the baby in her womb. "Boys are like jumping jacks inside you, never still," she said and demanded to know if the bairn woke Jean up at night dancing reels and jigs.

Jean did not have the heart to tell them that the ultrasound exams she had in Edinburgh revealed the baby's sex much more accurately, and that she and Darroch had insisted that the doctor not tell them whether it was a boy or a girl, just that it appeared to be healthy despite the mother's advanced age.

Darroch decided that they would take the Bentley aboard the Cal-Mac ferry so that they could drive down to London in style and comfort, then park the auto in his flat's garage until time to drive home. So they had a pleasant, meandering journey down through Scotland and England, taking side roads, avoiding the treacherous and crowded M1 where trucks and autos competed fiercely at eighty-mile-per-hour speeds. They'd stayed at charming country B and Bs, taking long walks every night for Jean's and baby's health, and making love tenderly under deliciously warm duvets.

They took over a week to get to London and at the end Jean was exhausted and exhilarated. Once in the flat she collapsed in a comfortable armchair facing the balcony and the enchanting view of the Thames in front of her.

Darroch struggled up the stairs to the bedroom with their luggage but Jean wasn't up to unpacking yet. "Leave it, lovie. Let's have a cup of tea and relax." For dinner he went down the road and got Chinese takeaway and they gorged on eggrolls, shrimp toast and seafood. There was no ethnic food on Eilean Dubh though Darroch had been negotiating steadily with a Chinese restauranteur in Inverness to open a café on the Island, so far without success. Jean looked forward to making up her deficiencies of soy sauce and curry during their London stay.

Monday morning Darroch was off to rehearsals at the BBC's Wood Green studios. Jean puttered around the flat, finishing the unpacking, running the Hoover over his beloved oriental rugs and making a grocery list.

She'd never been with Darroch while he was filming and had never realized what hard work acting was. He came home at night drained and depleted, ready for a sit-down with a whisky. He tried valiantly not to show it but she realized quickly that he really didn't want to eat out each night no matter how appealing the restaurant. She added chicken, fish and chops to her shopping list and baked bread so the flat would have the same delicious odor as their cottage at home.

She walked along the Thames in the daytime. When she got up the courage to tackle the rest of London, she devoted herself to learning the Tube map and made excursions to the museums she'd heard so much about: the Victoria and Albert, the Museum of London, the Museum of the Moving Image, the Imperial War Museum. She went to Harrod's and Fortnum and Mason's for groceries. She explored Chinatown for exotic cooking ingredients and Bloomsbury for bookstores. She walked through Chelsea and down the Kensington High Street, bought sandwiches and ate them in London's parks.

She didn't quite have the nerve to venture into the smart, exclusive shops in Knightsbridge, although she was trying hard to work herself up to it. Nothing would fit her now, of course, but she could always browse.

One Sunday morning they got up early and went to the Portobello Road street market and wandered among the array of junk and treasures there.

In one stall she found a true treasure, a children's game based on *The Magician*. It was like new and had all its playing pieces, including a figure of Darroch dressed as the Magician, complete with top hat and cloak depicted in brilliant red enamel. She was less enamoured with the playing piece of ex-wife Adrienne in her role as his assistant, clad in tight blouse and brief skirt. Jean raised her eyebrows and put the piece back in the box.

She insisted they play the game when they got home and they spent a hilarious two hours locked in competition which he eventually won, but narrowly. She gave him a good battle though, for she knew the Magician scripts cold. She'd begun watching them again from his videotape collection every afternoon when she took her little lie-downs in front of the television set.

She enjoyed watching him work on his character for his new part. One day he was out on the flat's balcony, striding its length back and forth, each passage across changing a bit as he refined his movements. People's walks are different in different time periods, he'd told Jean. Mostly it's because of the clothes, but other things play a part: social class, nationality, whether or not you carry a sword and have to be ready to use it.

He carried a sword in this part, a different sort of role for him, a Regency romantic comedy-thriller in which he, as the hero, had to rescue a beautiful Englishwoman masquerading as a French spy. Jean looked at the costume sketches and sighed with pleasure, imagining her darling Darroch in a velvet coat, embroidered vest and tight doeskin britches, playing a dashing rake.

"You should have curly hair," she teased him. "All Regency heroes have curly hair."

"How do you know?"

"I read a lot."

He said, grimacing, "I did overhear the costume people talking. The designer said she was going to put curlers in my hair while I'm having my make-up done. Not that it'll do any good. My hair's as straight as string."

"Perhaps they'll try a curling iron. Or perhaps a perm."

Horrified, he blurted, "Never! Can you imagine the flap on the Island if I came home with a perm?"

She giggled, then laughed outright. "You'd look like a very large Shirley Temple. We'd have to change our *cèilidh* act. You'd have to learn to tap dance."

"Oh, I know how already. Let me think a moment." He thought, made an exploratory gesture with his foot, then executed four time steps, a spin and sank to one knee facing her, arms spread.

"Where did you learn that?" she said, impressed.

He shrugged. "Some role or other. It's quite easy, really. Come on, I'll teach you." He reached for her hand.

She stepped back nimbly. "Oh, no, you don't. Not till after dinner, anyway. The pork chops will burn up."

He knew she was curious about the process of television production so when rehearsals were finished, everyone's characters well established and all the blocking set, he invited her to come with him to the studio.

After he'd gotten Jean settled on the far edge of the set he looked at his schedule for the day's work and realized they were filming a love scene. He hoped Jean wouldn't mind watching him make love to another woman.

For Jean it was a rude introduction to the world of theatre to see Darroch turn on someone else the loving, passionate look she was used to having directed only at herself. At first there was the shock of disbelief. She'd been thoroughly engrossed in the scene and it wasn't until she saw that look that she was jolted into awareness. That's my husband, she thought, forgetting the character he was playing.

He and the actress playing opposite him were in a bed of hay in a set meant to be an abandoned barn. Jean went cold all over as he kissed his co-star, then hot as he fumbled desperately with the woman's clothing. Waves of jealousy flowed over her. She thought she might burst into tears.

Then the baby kicked sharply and began a little dance inside her. Gasping with surprise Jean found herself jolted back into the real world. Uh-oh, reality check, she thought. It's only acting.

Darroch possessed the actor's gift of involving himself totally in his role and it wasn't until the passionate scene was completed that he remembered that Jean was watching, wide-eyed.

The director said, "Very nice. Take a quick break and we'll film it. Darroch, a word in your ear."

"Coming, Wills. All right, Janet?" he said to the actress playing opposite him.

"Lovely, darling," she replied, still breathless. She buttoned her blouse, smiled seductively at Darroch, then went to the edge of the set and threw herself into a chair beside Jean.

Jean looked at her. She was beautiful, with long black hair, deep brown eyes and a slender, full-bosomed body. Jean felt a pang of envy, and renewed jealousy.

"God, that Darroch's a gorgeous man," the actress sighed.

"Yes, he is," said Jean.

"Kisses wonderfully. Too bad he's married," said Janet.

"His wife's pregnant, too," said Jean.

"Is she? I hadn't heard that." She looked at Jean for the first time. "My name's Janet Somerville. We've not met."

"I'm Jean."

"American?" When Jean nodded she said, "Are you a friend of someone here?"

"Friend of Darroch's. Well, his wife, actually."

"Lucky old you." Janet looked at Jean carefully, then said, "Is all this new to you? I mean, have you ever watched him play a scene like this before?"

"Ummm . . . no."

"Odd, isn't it. Seeing your man make love to another woman. I remember watching my second husband rehearsing a film we were both in. Absolutely torrid love scenes. I was furious with jealousy."

"So it bothered you?"

"Actually we were divorced right after the film was finished." Looking at Jean's face she added hastily, "Not because of the love scenes, not the ones in the film anyway. I found out he was doing a little extra-curricular rehearsing with his co-star. That's why the scenes had that touch of authenticity." She sighed deeply. "Actors, you know."

"Well, no, I don't. Darroch's the only actor I know."

"Dreadful skirt-chasers, except for the ones who are gay. No self-control at all."

Darroch had more self-control than anyone Jean had ever met but before she could say so the director called, "Ready now, please. This one's for real."

Janet hauled herself out of the chair with an extravagant sigh. "Nose to the grindstone." Then, glancing at Jean, she said, "Don't worry, darling. It's all make-believe, remember. If it gets too bad, just close your eyes."

"I'd rather see just what's going on," Jean muttered and forced herself to watch every second as they repeated the love scene twice more before the director was satisfied.

Darroch took off his make-up and changed clothes before he came out to face Jean, a little worried about his reception. But all she said was, "Tired, lovie?"

"Aye."

"All that kissing," she murmured. "It must be exhausting."

"My lips are sore," he said, and grinned at her. "They'll need some of your special loving care tonight."

"Don't you think you've had enough for one day?"

"Oh, no. Just whetted my appetite," he said, relieved that she was taking it so well. Leaving, they encountered Janet. "Bye-bye, Darroch, darling," Janet called gaily as she headed for the elevator arm-in-arm with the director. "Bye, Jean."

Darroch looked at Jean in surprise. "You've met?"

"Yes, we had a little chat. She seems very nice."

"Aye, and very sweet. She's engaged to William, the director. He's desperately in love with her and madly jealous. He hinted that I didn't need to show quite so much enthusiasm in the romantic scenes." He grinned down at Jean. "I'm glad you're not the jealous type, *mo chridhe*."

Jean smiled demurely back. She let her hand stray down to her belly for a surreptitious caress. Thanks, kid, she thought. I owe you one.

Twenty-three

Men know nothing about birth.
Nothing at all.
Kemp Battle

*J*ean woke up on April 4 and knew something was different. To begin with, she had an appalling backache that had started in the last hours of sleep, giving her awful dreams. And second, she had a tremendous desire to clean the cottage.

Watching her trying to sweep the floor, pausing frequently to put one hand on her aching back, Darroch grew worried. "Leave that, Jean. If the place wants cleaning I'll clean it. Come and sit down and I'll fix your breakfast."

"Don't want any breakfast," she mumbled but she put the broom in the closet. "I'm going to wash clothes." After the clothes were in the dryer she announced that she was going to wash her hair.

"Wash your hair? It looks perfectly fine to me."

"It's filthy. I haven't washed it in days, three at least." She headed up the iron spiral staircase to the bathroom with determination, Darroch following with arms outstretched in case she stumbled.

He helped her shower, terrified she'd lose her balance. He steadied her while she shampooed her hair and rinsed it. He plugged in the dryer, since it was difficult for her to bend over, and held it while she brushed her hair dry. After that she got out the suitcase she'd packed for the hospital and took everything out of it, then put it all back in.

Darroch put his foot down. "Stop that, Jean. You haven't eaten a thing. Come downstairs and sit in the comfy chair and I'll bring you a cup of tea and some toast. You need some food."

"Have to go to the bathroom first," she said.

He heard her cry out when he was putting tea into the teapot. He ran upstairs.

"My water's broken," she said.

"What? We've got to get you to hospital right away!" Frantic, he tried to remember what the pregnancy books had said about the onset of labor. "Where the hell are my car keys? Jean, go out and sit in the car. I'll get your case. No, wait, I'll help you down the stairs."

But she was heading for the bedroom. "No, can't have baby in the Bentley. Ruin the upholstery. Got to lie down." She knew only too clearly what would happen next. She'd never seen the inside of a hospital labor room; both her other babies had come with lightning speed. Her uterus was contracting strongly and rapidly now. She crawled into bed. "Get me pillows, prop me up. Oh, God, that hurts," she cried as a contraction ripped through her. "Get me a whisky. A large one."

He looked at her in astonishment. "What?"

"Whisky, damn it." She gritted her teeth as the contraction peaked. "Haven't you ever—been in a movie with a battlefield scene—ow—where they'd run out of drugs and had to use—ow, ow—whisky as an anesthetic—when they were cutting off—ow, ow, ow!—somebody's leg."

"The baby . . . alcohol . . . "

She shouted, "It's not going to hurt the baby, she's finished! Bring me whisky, you big galoot!"

She had never raised her voice to him and had certainly never before called him a galoot, whatever that was. He ran downstairs and poured a large whisky, his hands trembling, the liquor splashing on the table. When he brought it to her she gulped it down. "Put pillows behind my back. I want to be in a sitting position."

Another contraction slammed into her and she shrieked. "Call Ros, tell him the baby's coming. And bring me another whisky."

He was nearly incoherent on the telephone but managed to blurt out the news to the astonished receptionist. "Tell Ros to hurry, please!" he shouted.

"Where's the damned whisky?" she called. The liquor was taking effect and she felt a bit more relaxed in between contractions, which were coming steadily and painfully with scarcely a minute separating them. "And bring towels. I don't want to ruin the mattress."

She drank half the whisky in the second glass, then smiled dreamily at him while he tucked towels around and under her. "Don't worry, darling, everything will be fine. Soon we'll have our . . . " The next contraction was so intense her words died in her throat.

Darroch stared, appalled, as her body arched in agony. Then he wrapped his arms around her. He held her while the contraction ripped through her. It was so strong he could feel it against his body. So much for his envisioned back rubs and breathing coaching. He trembled with fear, a prayer to the One Who Listens bouncing through his brain: Let her be all right, please, let her be all right. And the baby. "What can I do, *mo chridhe*? Tell me what I can do . . . "

"You've done enough, don't you think?" She laughed out loud at his expression. "This is all your fault . . . oh, darling, don't look like that, I'm just kidding . . . " She screamed again, a long agonized wail. "Here's another fine mess you've gotten me into! Oh, lovie, give me your hand!"

She squeezed his hand so hard he felt the bones rubbing together, then abruptly let it go and used both hands to brace herself on the bed. She felt a tremendous downward pressure and then momentary release. The baby's head had crowned.

"Pull my skirt up. Oh, why didn't I get undressed! What's happening?"

He lifted her skirt and stared in terrified wonder as the baby, propelled by another strong contraction, emerged between her thighs. "The baby's coming. Oh, Jean."

Another contraction gripped her, so intense that she did not have the breath to scream and she felt a popping sensation, like a cork exploding from a bottle. She sank back into the pillows, completely spent.

The baby lay on the towels, blood all around. The umbilical cord stretched from its navel back inside Jean. Darroch stared. "*A Dhia beannaich mi,*" he said.

He didn't dare touch the baby. Instead, he leaned over and solemnly inspected her. "Oh, *mo chridhe*. It's a girl and she's perfect."

"Is it really a girl?" Jean realized suddenly that the baby had not made a sound. "Is she breathing?" she gasped in terror. "Wipe her mouth, clear her throat, make her breathe."

Galvanized into action, he wiped the baby's face, covered her nose and mouth and blew hard into her. Abruptly she opened her mouth and wailed.

"Ohhhh," cooed Jean. "Give her to me, lovie. Wrap a towel around her and give her to me. Careful of the cord; it's still attached inside of me. And support her head."

He slid both hands under the baby, put her on a towel and wrapped her up. Then, with the cord dangling down like a snake, he put the child in Jean's arms.

"Oh, my," sighed Jean.

"*A Dhia,*" sighed Darroch.

Wonder was succeeded by an immense curiosity. They bent together over the baby.

"She's got your eyes, darling," said Jean.

"Do you think so? But that's definitely your mouth, *m'aingeal*, so full."

"Big, you mean," said Jean and they both laughed.

"She's so tiny," he said. "Just a wee scrap."

"She felt like an elephant inside me," said Jean.

"Look at those little fingers. Oh, Jean, she's got fingernails."

"Toenails, too. Look." She uncovered a baby foot and held it up for his inspection.

"She's pink as a rose. I thought newborns were red."

"Oh, she's quite lovely. Her head isn't even misshapen. I suppose that's because she came so fast."

"I thought it was supposed to take hours, *m'aingeal*. It couldn't have taken more than fifteen minutes after your water broke. How did you manage so quickly?"

"Practice, I suppose."

The baby uttered a mewling cry and turned her head from side to side. Jean scooted herself up against the pillows and put the baby to her breast. For the next few minutes mother and child were utterly distracted as Jean taught her daughter how to nurse. When the baby's mouth clamped, at last, around her nipple, Jean gasped, then began to cry.

"Alligator, *mo chridhe*?" said Darroch tenderly.

"Angel," wept Jean. Darroch swallowed hard and he too was engulfed by tears. He bent and buried his head in her hair. She rubbed his shaking shoulders and crooned, "We had our baby, darling. All by ourselves."

"You did it," he said, lifting his head. "All I did was follow orders and say, '*A Dhia*.'"

"The whisky was a tremendous help."

"I love you, Jean," he said. "Are you sure you're all right? There's blood . . . "

"It's not pouring out, is it?"

Alarmed, he examined her. "No."

"I'm okay, then. Blood's normal, lots of little things get torn. I'm fine. I'll be back in the fields plowing tomorrow morning."

He stared at her, puzzled, and she laughed. "Rod came quickly too. I was only in the hospital for about an hour before he started and it only took about forty-five minutes to deliver him. The doctor almost didn't make it. He was furious with me, seemed to think I should have waited for his gracious presence before I started labor. Sally came even quicker. Must be that sturdy Eilean Dubh peasant stock from great-great-something grandpop Ùisdean."

The door to the cottage banged open and two people rushed up the staircase, shouting, and stopped abruptly. Ros MacPherson said, "Dear God."

Nurse midwife Elasaid Morrison said automatically, "Dinna take the Lord's name in vain, Mr. MacPherson."

Ros said, "Certainly I didn't. That was a prayer of thanks. Everything all right, Jean?"

"I think so, Ros. Baby seems fine and she's learned to nurse already." The baby's sucking had stirred something up inside Jean and she frowned. "More contractions, ow! Am I having twins?"

"The placenta's coming. Away, Darroch, let me tend your wife. I've cut the cord; Nurse, take baby and have a look at her."

Sent off, Darroch lurched downstairs and poured himself a large whisky. He drank it standing up, leaning on the fireplace. He thought if he sat down he might not be able to get up again, his legs were so trembly.

Nurse Elasaid, bending over Jean, caught a whiff of her breath. "Heavens above, Mrs. Jean, you've no been drinking?" she said in shock. She was a very strict Presbyterian and a devout teetotaler.

"Battlefield anesthetic," said Jean. Ros got it and chuckled. Nurse Elasaid looked puzzled. "Have you ever had a baby, Nurse Elasaid?"

"Certainly not. I'm a maiden lady," said Elasaid primly.

Jean smiled at her. "Well, it hurts. We're fresh out of morphine so we used whisky as an anesthetic."

Nurse Elasaid pursed her lips, clicked her tongue and said no more.

Jean screamed as another contraction sliced smartly through her. Ros said, "There, that's the placenta out and you look fine, Jean, just a wee tear. I think it's along the line where you had stitches before, would that be right? Nurse, tidy up Mrs. Jean and let's have her away to the hospital."

Within a few minutes mother and child were ready to travel. Darroch helped his wife down the stairs, then swept her up in his arms and carried her to the ambulance, Nurse Elasaid following with the baby.

He went back inside for Jean's suitcase. The phone rang just as he turned to leave and the voice of his stepson said, "Hi, Darroch. Is Mom there?"

"Well, she's a wee bit busy right now," began Darroch, but before he could tell Rod the glad tidings, Rod spoke, his voice trembling with excitement.

"She'll want to hear this even if it interrupts something. Lucy's had our baby and Mom is a grandmother. A big healthy boy, seven and a half pounds, named Andrew Russell for his two grandfathers. Lucy's just fine. She had a long labor, though . . . "

Darroch, conscious of Jean and baby waiting, finally had to interrupt Rod's recital of the details. "Rod, you've a baby sister. Just born here in the cottage and we're just taking her and your mother to hospital now. No, no, all's well, don't worry. I'll ring you later, " he said firmly to the voice sputtering with surprise on the other end of the phone.

Climbing into the ambulance, Darroch motioned to the driver to wait, and he bent over to kiss his wife. "Congratulations, Grandma," he said, grinning.

Jean said drowsily, "Huh?"

"A fine wee boy, named Andrew Russell. Rod called just as I was leaving the cottage. What do you think of that, *mo chridhe*? Lucy's well, but it took her twelve hours of labor to accomplish what you managed in fifteen minutes."

The whisky was just catching up to Jean. She smiled and murmured, "Ah, she'll get the hang of it once she's had a wee bit more practice. But well done, Lucy, just the same." And she kept her eyes closed for the ride to the hospital, meditating on the wonder of two babies born just minutes apart, and so closely related, all because of her. And she was a grandmother, and the mother of a new-born baby. *Miorbhuileach*. That was the only word for it. The One Who Listens must have gotten an earful.

Later, staggering out of the hospital room in which Jean had been ensconced, Darroch was surprised to find Jamie in the waiting room. Jamie wrapped his arms around his friend. "Well done, lad. How's our lady and the bairn?"

"They're fine, Jamie, but I'm about to pass out."

"Had it at home, did she? Clever Jean. I'm sorry I couldn't get there in time to help. I was away down in the lower pastures and the truck stalled the first time I tried to start her."

"How did you know, Jamie? And what are you doing here?"

"Where else would I be?" said Jamie, neatly sidestepping the first question. He did not intend to talk about the fierce presentiment that had overwhelmed him and had brought him running from his pasture to his old truck, that had fuddled him so thoroughly that he'd stepped on the gas pedal too hard and flooded the carburetor.

"It's a girl, is it?" Jamie said for form's sake, though he knew already.

"Aye, and she's beautiful, Jamie. You've never seen such a perfect little creature, like a pink rose. Why do people always say newborns are ugly?"

"Aye, Eilidh was lovely enough to be on a magazine cover. Ian . . . well, that's another story. Red as a sunset and yelling from the moment he entered the world, or so Ros said. I wasn't allowed in the delivery room; such things weren't done then. Lucky you, to be in on all the action."

Darroch said, "Lucky isn't exactly the word I'd use. Terrified, baffled, utterly useless. She did it all herself. I just stood around and wrung my hands and prayed. *A Dhia*, Jamie, aren't women miracles."

"They are that." He looked up as Màiri burst into the room. "Here's my own little miracle now."

Màiri gasped, "What's happened, what's happened? Is Jean all right? How's the baby? The nurses are saying that she had it at home. Darroch, why didn't you get her to hospital?"

"She wouldn't go." He shrugged his shoulders helplessly. "It all happened so fast. One minute she was fine and the next minute she was yelling at me."

"I'd have yelled at you, too, if you made me have a baby at home."

"Don't scold, *a Mhàiri*, can't you see the poor devil's nearly dead from the experience. Men aren't like you women, we're delicate creatures. We can't take all these stresses and strains."

Màiri flung herself suddenly into Darroch's arms, nearly knocking him over backwards. "I'm sorry. I was just so worried. Is Jean all right? And the baby?"

He put his arms around her and they rocked back and forth together. "Aye, all's well."

They held each other for a moment, each acutely conscious of the poignancy of the event. It might have been the two of them, twenty years ago, rejoicing over the birth of their own baby. Jamie knew it too and did not interfere with their moment. After a bit he said, "I should like very much to see Jean and the wee rosebud."

Recovering, Darroch said, "Aye, come ahead. Jean's told me she plans to sleep for fifteen hours straight. She says she's going to nurse the baby with her eyes closed. But perhaps she's not dozed off yet."

Jean opened her eyes to see Jamie. "Am I dead? Here's an angel come to visit me. Hello, darling Jamie."

He grinned and bent to kiss her. "You've nearly done for our Darroch, you know. He's all nerves," he whispered in her ear.

"He's a father now; treat him with respect. Hello, my darling Màiri. Take Darroch home, please, and give him a nice big whisky. He's earned it." Darroch gave her a farewell kiss as her eyes began to close.

As they tiptoed out of the room Jean opened her eyes and shouted, "We've got two babies to celebrate. When you come back bring a bottle of champagne! And don't let Nurse Elasaid see it!"

Twenty-four

If you then will read the story,
First, prepare you to be sorry
That you never knew till now
Either whom to love or how;
But be glad as soon with me
When you know that this is she . . .

Ben Jonson

*T*he MacDonalds took Darroch home in their old red Austin, folding him and his long legs into the back seat. When they reached the Mac an Rìgh cottage Jamie got out. "Go along, *m'eudail*. I'll be there directly; I'm just going to settle Darroch."

Inside *Taigh a' Mhorair*, Darroch paced restlessly.

"You need to get some sleep," said Jamie.

"I'll not sleep, I may never sleep again. My mind's a muddle. It keeps going round and round."

"Sit down. Where's your whisky?"

Jamie brought the bottle and glasses to the table and when Darroch would have sprung up to pace again he was firm. "Sit down, for God's sake. You're making me seasick."

Darroch flung himself in the chair. "I'm all about in my head. I made a right cock-up of things, Jamie."

"What're you talking about, man?"

"I should have gotten her to hospital. I should have insisted."

"How do you figure that?"

"She had the baby here. She could have died, the baby could have died . . . "

"Ridiculous. She insisted on staying here, right?"

"She didn't want to have the baby in the Bentley."

"Damned good sense, if you ask me. Jean knew what she was doing.

Staying here in safety and comfort, with her man to watch over her, letting the doctor come to her."

"She could have hemorrhaged . . . "

"And she could have hemorrhaged in the Bentley. What would that have done to you? Torrents of blood and you looking at her instead of the road. You'd likely have put the three of you and the car over the cliff into the ocean."

He poured a large whisky for Darroch. "Drink that. All at once."

Darroch drained it and shuddered and Jamie poured another. "It worked out fine, if you ask me. Having her baby at home, just like in the old days, and you with her. A rare experience." He gulped his own whisky. "They shoved me out, remember? Wouldn't even let me hold Màiri's hand. I could hear her scream, now and again. *A Dhia*, women suffer a lot for our pleasure, don't they?"

"Aye." He finished his second drink. "Do you think they hold it against us?"

"I've never understood what's in the head of a woman, least of all in Màiri's head. She smiles sometimes, that mysterious smile of hers. But she'll never tell me what she's smiling about."

Darroch looked up in surprise. "Jean does that too."

"Aye. A woman's mystery enough to make you believe in God, isn't she."

"Enough to make me sure that if there is a God, it's a female one."

They were quiet for a few moments, drinking. Then Darroch said, "We're not going to get drunk like we did that other time, are we?"

Jamie shuddered. "That next morning was the worst head I ever had, I wanted to die. We killed the bottle."

"To the last drop. And I don't even remember the next morning."

"Lucky you." Jamie poured another round.

They drank again. Darroch's eyes began to close and Jamie stood up. "Off to bed with you, man. You need all the sleep you can get. You won't get much the next few months."

He took his friend's shoulders in a firm grasp. "Can you make it up the stairs?"

"Maybe I'll just rest a few minutes on the sofa . . . "

"Upstairs." He urged Darroch to the spiral staircase and prodded him up it. "Do you want your clothes off?"

Darroch laughed with his last remaining bit of strength. "No, thanks, nurse. I'll just lie down for a bit first." He threw himself on the bed. "*Tapadh leat, mo charaid.*"

"A favor returned. *Feasgar math*. Sleep well, Papa."

Lying in bed Darroch felt sleep slipping away from him. He lay there and let his mind drift back to a similar time when he and Jamie had been together, celebrating the birth of the MacDonald twins, Ian and Eilidh.

It had been a nightmarish experience. Màiri had been in labor for hours and Darroch and Jamie had paced the waiting room in agony. Afterwards they'd gone back to *Taigh Rois* to recover.

They'd opened a fresh bottle of whisky that Jamie had been saving to wet the babies' heads and had proceeded to get very drunk.

Halfway through the bottle Jamie had lifted his head and stared at Darroch, bleary-eyed. "Tell me about that first time with her."

"What?"

"The first time you made love to Màiri."

"Jamie, in the name of God, how can you ask me that?"

"Because I need to know. It should have been me. She's mine, she's always been mine. Tell me what I missed."

Darroch sat silently, conscious of Jamie's eyes intent on him. Then he sighed. "It'll kill me, to tell you. I go over and over it in my head, sometimes."

"Tell me and get it out of your head and into mine."

Dreamily, Darroch said, "It was her seventeenth birthday. We'd made a pact when we were sixteen that we'd become lovers on her next birthday. We knew they wouldn't let us marry before we were eighteen but we had to have more than just kisses, we had to join our bodies and join our souls. We had to have each other.

"As the days ticked away to her birthday it was all we thought about. Getting away together to make love. Going to a hotel in Oban, finding someplace private. In the end we went up Cemetery Hill."

Jamie shivered. "*A Dhia*, I hate that place."

"Do you?" said Darroch absently. "I don't know why. It's so quiet and peaceful." He drank deeply of his whisky. "It was midnight, the first hour of her birthday. I sneaked out of our house, waited outside for her to sneak out to me. We didn't dare wake everyone by taking a car so we walked all the way to the Hill and up to our bench, where we always went to cuddle.

"I had an old tartan rug for us to lie upon. Think of that, Jamie. The most sacred experience of our lives and we had to have it on an old travel rug in an old deserted cemetery. Why is life so cruel to lovers?"

Jamie shook his head.

Darroch said, "The ocean went wild that night; we could hear the waves pounding the cliff like battering rams. And the wind was cold. I was so afraid I wouldn't be able to keep her warm. But she made me undress her anyway." He closed his eyes. "She was naked under her outer clothes."

Jamie gulped his whisky, poured another and gulped that too. "Go on," he said, through gritted teeth.

"There she lay with the moon painting light and shadows on her body, the most beautiful sight you've ever seen." He laughed softly and Jamie looked at him in surprise. "And me, poor fool. I hadn't a clue about what to do.

"There was no sex education in our school then; we were supposed to learn it all at home. A fine idea, unless your parents can't teach you. It was not the sort of thing my father could talk about; he was very repressed and dignified. You couldn't even imagine him with his clothes off. You remember him, Jamie. A fine man, he was like God to me and I loved him dearly but I couldn't ask him about sex. He gave me a book. *What Every Young Man Should Know about Sex and Marriage.*"

Jamie laughed out loud. "Aye, my father gave me that one too. Some help it was. I got all the wrong ideas from it."

Darroch looked at him, curious. "So how did you learn?"

Jamie smiled gently, remembering. "From a fine lusty Englishwoman staying at the hotel where I worked. Say what you like about the *Sasannachan,* I've had a soft spot for Englishwomen ever since."

Darroch said, "My father told me to read the book and then ask him if I had any questions. Imagine asking God how to make love to a woman. I'd sooner have asked the Minister."

"Get on with it, man. What did you do?"

"Ah, Jamie, you're relentless, aren't you. Well, I lay down beside her and took her in my arms and then wondered why she was laughing at me. 'Don't you want to undress, too?' she said and she began to unbutton my shirt. I hadn't thought to leave off my underwear as she had, I was wearing a flannel undershirt. Thank God I hadn't worn my long flannel drawers as well; she would have laughed herself sick. She helped me take my clothes off and I lay back down and she moved into my arms again.

"We kissed for a long while and then I began to touch her. Have you ever thought, Jamie, how the curve of a woman's breast is just shaped to fit into a man's hand? And those rounded hips and that plump little bottom. She was a goddess.

"Here I was, a gormless, overgrown gowk of a boy, and I was going to make love to a goddess. My courage failed me, my imagination failed me. Luckily, my body took over thinking for me.

"I moved on top of her. I was so much taller I had to bend like a pretzel so as not to smother her against my shoulder." He said quietly, "And then she took me inside her, and I was her first lover, and she was mine."

Jamie was crying, the tears running down his face and dropping into the glass of whisky he was steadily demolishing. He would have done anything to keep from hearing what Darroch was saying, but the voice was insisting that he listen. You wanted to know, Jamie, was the message between them.

"She closed around me and although she was very tight I had no trouble slipping deep into her. In my lust I forgot about her maidenhead so when I came up against that barrier I didn't think, I just thrust through it. She cried out and the sound went through me like a knife. But then she wrapped her legs around me and pulled me deeper."

Darroch was crying too. "Ah, don't make me tell the rest of it, Jamie. Use your imagination."

Jamie was using his imagination and it was killing him. He poured the whisky into his mouth so fast that he choked. Then he folded his arms on the table and dropped his head into them. His shoulders shook as he wept.

Darroch said, "The next day we went to my grandmother and got Màiri's grandmother to come up too and we handfasted ourselves to each other, in front of our two witnesses. Then I went to her father and told him what we'd done."

Jamie lifted his head. "*A Dhia,* you told him?" He was remembering his terrifying father-in-law.

"Aye. Màiri wanted to talk to him too but he took her by the shoulders and put her outside, then sent her mother out and locked the door behind them. Then he turned to me."

Darroch's face was white. "He shouted at me for half an hour, then he talked to me quietly. I'd sooner have had the shouting. He quoted the Bible and when he couldn't remember the chapters he wanted he got their family Bible. You know, Jamie, that huge old leather-bound one. It must weigh twenty pounds. I was terrified he was going to belt me with it. He read to me about sin and debauching virtuous maidens until I thought I'd sink through the floor with shame.

"And all I could think of was that I had the same thing to look forward to from my father. And probably the Minister as well. Debauching virtuous maidens. Me, the Laird's son, the Minister's prize pupil, always the shining example for the other boys. Sunk beneath reproach, as the saying goes.

"I kept trying to figure out what the hell we'd done that was so wrong. I loved her and she loved me and we were old enough to be lovers. And we'd gotten handfast right away, and we wanted to get married. It wasn't that I carried her off and raped her, or even seduced her. I hadn't a clue about how to seduce a woman.

"The last thing he said to me was that if I got her pregnant before we were properly married he'd cut off my balls and feed them to the fishes."

He grinned suddenly and ruefully. "It was all her idea, anyway. Left to myself I'd not have had the courage. I'd probably have kept it at kisses and feeling her up under her skirt and moping around till we got married."

Jamie lifted his head and grinned too. "Once she gets an idea in her head there's no deterring her."

"She wanted us to be lovers and that's all there was to it. I hadn't a chance." He poured another whisky and drank it down. "And that's how it happened and I believe I am very drunk."

"I believe I am drunker," said Jamie with dignity. "Why is the damned room spinning? I believe I will just go lie down a while."

He staggered to the sofa and collapsed.

Darroch stood looking down at him. He said softly, "I loved her then and I love her now, Jamie. We're both men enough to understand that."

Jamie's eyes were closed and Darroch never knew whether or not he had heard those last words. He took the sofa blanket and wrapped it over his friend. Then he lurched into the bedroom and collapsed onto Màiri and Jamie's bed. His last conscious thought was that the pillow held the fragrance of Màiri's hair.

He didn't understand why Jamie had wanted to hear all that but he knew why he'd told him: for a last desperate wallow in the joy of Màiri's love and the days when she was all his. Before he gave her up forever, now that she was a mother.

Now as he lay in his own bed, the one he shared with his own darling wife, he smiled. A favor returned, Jamie had said. Damned right, he thought, and slept.

Twenty-five

My babe so beautiful! it thrills my heart
With tender gladness, thus to look at thee . . .
Samuel Taylor Coleridge

A steady steam of *Eilean Dubhannaich* trooped through the hospital to peer through the nursery windows at the baby whose cot was labeled "Baby Girl Mac an Rìgh." Jean's visitors were limited so that she could get some sleep. Unable to voice their congratulations in person the visitors all brought flowers and her room soon resembled a garden. The nurses distributed the flowers throughout the hospital.

When the fruit-and-veg seller ran out of flowers other gifts appeared: bouquets of heather, plucked from the hillsides, hand-embroidered baby garments, hand-whittled rattles and teething rings. For the first time Jean realized the full impact of her baby on the Island.

Overwhelmed, she begged Darroch to make them stop. "I don't need anything else. I'll have to change baby's clothes twelve times a day to use all this stuff."

So he got Minister Donald and all the other Island clergy to announce from the pulpit that anyone wishing to pay their respects to the Laird, his lady and their offspring could contribute to a fund to benefit the Playschool.

After they got home from the hospital it seemed that the stream of visitors would continue at the cottage. There were knocks at the door all day. "Just popped in to say hello," the visitor would say. "And may I have just a wee peep at the bairn?"

It became apparent to Darroch that nobody was going to get any sleep in the cottage.

"*A Dhia beannaich mi*," he complained. "Do they not remember what it's like, having a baby in the house?" Nothing, not even the knowledge that it would happen, had prepared him for being awakened every two hours during the night by the child's crying. Both he and Jean were ragged from having their naps interrupted by visitors and their faces ached from smiling. Baby was cranky from the unfamiliar voices and faces that appeared before her constantly.

It was Joe Munro, the young veterinarian, Ian MacDonald's friend, who came up with a solution. "They just want to see her. Would you permit me to take pictures and post them? If they can get a good look at her, perhaps they'll leave you alone."

Joe was a talented photographer. He brought up his camera and took a series of pictures, developed them in his darkroom and distributed them around Airgead and Ros Mór. Competition was intense to display the pictures until he hit upon the idea of giving each merchant different photos. The *Eilean Dubhannaich* moved happily from place to place, enjoying pictures of baby and proud parents as they did their shopping. When they'd seen all the pictures in Ros Mór, that village's residents went up to Airgead and vice versa. "Wonderful for trade," the merchants chortled happily to each other.

Joe changed the photos frequently so that the *Eilean Dubhannaich* would have something new to look at. Unannounced visits to the cottage declined but just to be on the safe side Darroch posted a sign on *Taigh a' Mhorair's* front door that read, "Baby sleeping. Please do not disturb."

In reality, or so it seemed to him, baby did not do much sleeping. She fused day and night until it seemed to Jean and Darroch that their whole life was a panorama of baby feeds, baby screams and baby laundry.

By the end of the third week Jean's milk supply was well established and baby began to sleep for as long as four hours at a stretch. It seemed like heaven to them and they both collapsed on their bed whenever baby slept, Darroch getting up now and then to check on her.

They still hadn't named her. If she'd been a boy she would have been Alistair Darroch, just as her father was Darroch Alistair. It was a Mac an Rìgh tradition that those names, alternated each generation, would go to the eldest son.

But they hadn't been able to decide on a girl's name and had finally given up worrying about it. A name would suggest itself when baby was born. Her middle name would be Mòrag, of course, for it was Jean's middle name, anglicized to Marian, and a Mac an Rìgh family name, all the way back to their shared ancestors Ùisdean and his Mòrag. But her first name eluded them until one night when they watched Jamie holding the child.

"You're a wee rosebud," he crooned to her. "The little white rose of Scotland."

"Rose," said Darroch.

"Rosamond," said Jean. "The rose of the world."

"Rosamond Mòrag Mac an Rìgh," lilted Darroch.

"Wee Rosie," crooned Jamie. And the baby was named.

With a name Rosie began to take on more of a personality and changed from a crying, wetting, defecating, contrary bundle to a small person with her own preferences. She was more contented being held on the left side of a person's body. "She hears the heartbeat," said Jean. She liked lying naked in a patch of sunlight. She liked hearing Jamie's fiddle but screamed at Ian's button-box accordion.

"Wait till she hears her first bagpipes," said Darroch.

She developed an intense fascination with the Minister, who was one of the few whose visits were welcomed. He had no qualms about holding a tiny baby, having done hundreds of baptisms, and Rosie would lie back in his arms, peering up at him, listening intently as he stared down at her, his gray eyes warm under their fierce eyebrows, and spoke to her in sonorous Gaelic.

"What is he talking about?" wondered Jean.

Darroch said, "He's telling her Bible stories. He's up to Genesis, chapter 19. I had rather hoped he'd skip all that business about Sodom and Gomorrah but I think she's getting the unexpurgated version."

Joe's pictures showing the Minister holding the baby were a sensation in the villages and Murray the Meat, the lucky displayer of that set, estimated that business was up by twenty per cent that week.

The weeks passed and life in the cottage settled down to a manageable regimen. At the age of five weeks Rosie slept through the night three days out of seven, terrifying her father the first night it happened. Darroch had wakened, realized it was morning and that Rosie had not cried all night. Fear overwhelmed him and he staggered to her cot, dreading what he might see.

She lay on her back, eyes open, staring accusingly at him. You're trying to starve me to death, her gaze said. You forgot to wake me for my middle of the night feeding. She opened her mouth and wailed.

Darroch snatched her up and held her to his breast, next to his pounding heart, half crying, half laughing in relief. "Hush now, hush now, *mo fhlùr, mo ròs beag,* let your mother have a few more moments of rest." He laid her down on her changing table and whisked on a fresh diaper, talking to her the whole time. She quieted and stared up at him. I haven't forgiven you yet, her look said.

He bent down and put his face squarely in the middle of her belly. Taken by surprise Rosie squeaked, then gurgled happily.

Darroch straightened up and looked down at her with wonder. She had laughed, he thought, for the first time.

He picked her up and carried her to her mother, who was just opening her eyes and struggling to a half-seated position. Jean settled the baby at her breast.

Darroch said, "She laughed, Jean."

Jean's eyes widened. "At five weeks old?" Then she grinned. "It must have been one of your better jokes."

PART II

Eilidh and Joe

Twenty-six

Eilidh, Eilidh, Silk o' the Kine;
Happy is he whose hand shall twine
Thy warm wild beauty of shadow and shine.
Like the glossy waves of a golden sea,
Eilidh, thy deep hair covers thee:
Oh, Eilidh, Eilidh, a deep, deep sea,
A golden sea,
A deep, deep sea.

Alfred Noyes

*E*ilidh MacDonald was beautiful from the day she was born and so fragile in appearance it seemed a stray breeze might waft her away. Màiri, normally the least superstitious of women, put rowan boughs over *Taigh Rois's* doors and windows to keep the fairies out. Eilidh was just the kind of baby they'd hunger to steal away and replace with a changeling.

Her twin brother Ian was large and sturdy, very active, with a vigorous howl when he wanted food or attention. Màiri soon learned to put them together in one cot whenever she needed to soothe Ian. Side by side with his sister, he grew contented and the two of them cooed and babbled at each other, developing their own secret language in which they conversed until they were old enough to go to school.

Jamie, leaning over the cot and worshipping the babies, could not believe his luck: two of them at once, one red-haired, the other yellow, just as the Sight had showed him, a boy and a girl and his Màiri alive and healthy after their birth.

He took Eilidh's tiny hands in his. He studied them intently, then looked at his own blunt, workman's fingers. Then he looked at Màiri's small square hands as they moved competently to change Ian's nappy.

"Her hands are like Darroch's," he said suddenly.

Màiri fastened the nappy, then hoisted Ian to her shoulder and walked over to stand by Jamie and Eilidh. Silently she examined the baby's long slender fingers with their tiny pointed tips.

"So they are. Well, she'll be a good violinist, that's for sure. Or a pianist, with that reach." She patted Ian on the back absent-mindedly.

"*A Mhàiri*, how do you explain the fact that my newborn daughter has hands like Darroch's?"

"I've no idea." She smiled at him. "*Le droit du seigneur*, perhaps?"

She grew into the most beautiful girl the Island had ever seen. She was close to six feet tall, and slender, as delicately-made as a willow tree. She had the smallest wrists, the slenderest fingers, the longest legs and the daintiest ankles of any Island woman. Even in her gawky adolescence she was as beautiful and supple as a young deer.

Like her brother, she resembled Jamie, with his high forehead and cheek-bones, straight nose and Viking strength, but she had Màiri's full-lipped mouth and the effect was amazingly sensuous. But she had a shy untouched look, innocence shining from her large blue eyes, a striking contrast with her sexy mouth.

Her hair was truly amazing. It was as if every other hair on her head was Màiri's brilliant red and the rest were Jamie's gold. It was like a flickering flame.

If the young men of the Island had not been awed into immobility by her astonishing beauty she would have had to beat them off with a stick. And the awareness of what Jamie and Ian would do to anyone who tried to take liberties with their Eilidh kept even the brashest young man in line.

Jamie adored her, Ian worshipped her and Màiri loved her devotedly. She was called by her family, and Darroch, whom everyone considered her uncle, "darling Eilidh," sweet-tempered, cheerful and gentle. A peacemaker, like Jamie.

It was obvious from a very young age that she was a gifted violinist. Darroch gave her a tiny violin when she was five years old. She loved it, carried it everywhere with her, slept with it at night. Jamie taught her how to play.

When she and Jamie played their instruments together at *cèilidhean* men wept and women swooned.

When she finished high school her parents sent her to an important music academy in Edinburgh, their hearts torn at the separation, but knowing that her destiny lay away from Eilean Dubh. Ian was in Edinburgh too, at university, preparing for a medical career. They had dinner together frequently, sharing their homesickness.

When she graduated from the Academy she was offered a position with the Edinburgh Chamber Orchestra. She welcomed the opportunity but it filled her with terror, until she met Simon.

Simon was everything an aspiring young virtuoso should be: self-centered, petulant and leanly, dramatically handsome. Slightly built, of medium height for a man, he was not quite as tall as Eilidh. He had intense gray eyes and a wild shock of dark hair that fell fetchingly over his eyes when he played.

He liked fireworks and dramatic rhythm changes and slashing bow work when he played and his interpretation of some of the orchestra's classical repertoire was dashing, to say the least. At times he so annoyed the long-suffering conductor that he would halt the entire orchestra while he delivered to Simon a stinging lecture on the lack of discipline in his playing, a lecture replete with sarcasm and dripping with venom, and finishing with "bloody show-off."

Simon would merely bite his lip, smooth back his unruly hair with a long slender hand, hold up his head and look tragically misunderstood.

It was useless to scold him, the conductor knew. His antics were going to take him—the sooner the better, in the conductor's opinion—to a larger, less-disciplined orchestra which preferred showmanship to discipline and where he would inevitably become the pampered darling of the local artistic set.

Hopelessly spoiled by a doting mother and three adoring sisters, all in awe of his talent and convinced he was a genius, he was utterly charming. And though he was gay he was devastatingly attractive, and attracted to, women.

He encountered Eilidh on her second morning with the orchestra when she was at the height of awkward shyness and vulnerable confusion. He had lately taken to wearing a black cape over his black turtleneck and black trousers and when he swept into rehearsal that morning there was a muffled, half-sarcastic, half-admiring ripple of applause from the orchestra's younger members, though one of the young men was heard to murmur, "Ah, Dracula returns."

Taking his seat in the violin section, he saw Eilidh struggling to put her music in order after dropping it. Nervous tears lingered in her beautiful blue eyes. Her full lower lip trembled. Simon was enchanted.

He stared at her intently—it was one of his favorite techniques with women—as she fumbled with the music. Finally she became aware of the piercing gaze on which he prided himself.

She looked up. They stared at each other. She blushed bright red and dropped her music again. She dropped to the floor between the crowded chairs and began to pick up sheets of music, muttering. Simon bent down to help her by picking up a sheet or two. His head close to hers, he said, "What are you talking about?"

"I'm swearing. In the Gaelic," she said, her eyes downcast.

"How wonderful. Will you teach me?"

She looked up and their eyes met. Both were instantly charmed. "Give me that," he ordered and plucked the music from her hands. With a few deft touches he put it all in order, stacked it on her music stand and steadied it while she climbed back into her chair.

They ate their lunches together on the Concert Hall's front steps. Her sandwich was prawns Marie-Rose; his was sprouts and veggies. He fed her bits of it and lectured her on vegetarianism.

It was the beginning.

Simon bossed her about, teased her mercilessly, scolded her, played tricks on her, exactly as Ian had done. When she began to think that their relationship would always be a big brother/little sister one, he changed tack. He began to pay her lavish compliments, stare longingly at her and seize every opportunity to whisper intimately in her ear, usually things that made her turn pink, to his enjoyment. Eilidh was hooked, a slender brown trout wriggling on his line.

He let her sew on his buttons and cook him wonderful meals, forgetting his vegetarianism when she served an exquisite fish. He advised her on her wardrobe, making her throw out things he hated (which she later surreptitiously retrieved from the trash, being too much the thrifty *Eilean Dubhannach* to throw out perfectly good clothes just because they weren't stylish).

He went with her when she bought her white blouse and black skirt for her performance costume. He impatiently rejected lace, frills and ruffles and made her buy a white silk blouse that was very plain and cut low and square across her bosom. He made her buy it one size too small so that it drew tightly over her breasts when she played. He whispered in her ear, "It makes your nipples stand out. All the men in the first six rows will be squirming with lust," and was amused when she blushed.

Back in his flat he made her put on the white blouse and model it for him. Then he told her to take off the blouse. She did. "Take off the bra, too," he ordered. When she obeyed, pale and trembling, he ordered, "Come here."

She stood between his legs for several moments while he stared at her. Then he pulled her down across his lap and began to kiss her. When his mouth moved to her breast she screamed and moaned like a wild thing.

It became a regular feature of their relationship. Several times a week he would undress her to the waist and pet her while she writhed and yearned for more, although she was too innocent to know for what she hungered. He taught her to open her mouth when they kissed and to tangle her tongue with his in a delicious mating.

Curiously enough, he had little desire to make love to her. He much preferred men but he enjoyed her mouth and her sweet little breasts. Her slender muscular body reminded him of statues he'd seen in museums of beautiful young Greek boys.

And there was the tiresome matter of her virginity. It did not seem quite fair to relieve her of it when he had no intention of taking their relationship any further than a delectable bedding.

He did not think she would become a success as a concert violinist. She lacked what he called, tritely—he was a musician, not a wordsmith—the killer instinct: the need to achieve stardom whatever the cost. She would be defeated by the endless cutthroat competition of the professional music world and would eventually go back to her little Island, find a man and get married. And virginity was no doubt very important to such men. Her chances of a good marriage would be diminished if she were "soiled," or so he thought.

He was not a complete bastard, he told himself righteously. Besides, women were so much trouble to make love to, needed so much foreplay, so much sweet talk. Men were so delightfully direct.

Eilidh walked the first four months of the orchestra season aroused and in love while Simon grew increasingly impatient with the conductor's harangues and his own small-time status. He was desperate for change and for a man with whom he could establish a real relationship, not these fumblings with a silly woman.

He got both. The man who came to Edinburgh to poach promising young musicians for an important English orchestra was dynamic and sexy and he and Simon hit it off right away. Within a week Simon knew he was going to the concertmaster's chair in Manchester and to live in his new friend's apartment. "You can stay with me until you get settled," the man had said but both knew what they had in mind.

He could hardly wait.

He caressed Eilidh furiously that last evening. He thought madly of plunging himself into her but restrained himself. It would be a test of his fidelity, at least for now, to his new love.

As she lay quivering, disheveled and glassy-eyed in his arms he told her he was leaving. He added casually that he had fallen in love with the man who had recruited him for Manchester.

She was too stunned to cry. It had never crossed her mind that he was gay.

Simon did not mean to be cruel. He truly believed that passion and heartbreak were good for an artist. And never having experienced heartbreak himself he took a rapacious, vicarious interest in her devastation and stored it up for his own artistic development.

Wounded to the depths of her loving soul, she crept back to Eilean Dubh for the holidays. Aware now of sex, quivering with frustrated passion, she cut a swathe through the Island's young men. They flocked around her and did everything but gather in packs in her parents' front garden to howl for her. She ignored them all.

When she went back to Edinburgh in January, mourning for Simon, she was resolved never to fall in love again.

In March Eilidh and Ian were both home for two weeks holiday. A friend of Ian's was already there: Joe Munro, a young man who would graduate from veterinary school in June. Ian's plan was to lure Joe to the Island as an assistant to the Island's beleagured and overworked vet Alastair Cunningham. He'd arranged for Joe to spend six weeks as an intern in the practice and found him a tiny cottage just down the lane from *Taigh Rois*. Its owner had recently died and the cottage was vacant.

Joe was a serious-minded young man and an excellent student, devoted to his work. He had offers to join veterinary practices in Edinburgh, but he did not think he wanted to devote himself to the care of cats, dogs, and birds, as much as he liked them. He thought he might like the challenge of a mixed practice, with everything from companion animals to farm animals, in a place where he could be of real use to a community that needed him.

He came from a small town in southern Scotland. He enjoyed the quiet of the countryside, liked hiking and fishing and long periods of solitude. He'd been the man of his house since his father died when Joe was fourteen. He had sustained his mother through the sad early years of her widowhood, had helped her raise his two younger sisters. Now his mother was settled into a pleasant job in their hometown, with both sisters, one married, living nearby. He felt, at last, that he could begin to make a life for himself.

And he liked Eilean Dubh; he felt he could fit in there. He especially liked the Island's music and he loved the *cèilidhean*, where he could sit quietly and listen and no one bothered him or pressed him to make conversation.

One night he saw Eilidh for the first time.

Eilidh was sitting on the sidelines, as usual. The young Eilean Dubh men, though panting with lust for her, were too shy to ask her to dance in the times when she sat alone, distant, wrapped in sadness. She looked so forlorn that Joe's tender heart went out to her. Drawn by something he couldn't resist, he approached her, wondering if he actually had the nerve to speak.

"Hullo," he said. His tongue felt too big for his mouth and his hands were wet with nervous perspiration. She was so beautiful and he was so ordinary. How did he dare to approach this goddess?

She looked up in surprise. She was used to being left alone at the dances.

"Hullo," she replied.

"Would you like to dance?" Then, as she looked at him with limpid blue eyes he felt he had to add, "I'm not very good at these Scottish country dances. We learned them in school but the footwork is beyond me. I can keep up, though, if you'd like to try."

"No, thank you." She looked down.

"Put you off, have I," he said sadly and when she lifted her head, ready to apologize and stammer out an excuse for her refusal he added, "You're probably right. Tell you what, I am good at waltzes. Maybe you'll give me a waltz later tonight. May I sit down?"

His request disconcerted her. "If you really want to."

"What I really want is a breath of fresh air. Will you join me?"

He seemed harmless enough and she was happy for an excuse to leave the *cèilidh*. She was tired of being stared at longingly by the young Eilean Dubh men. "All right."

Outside the hall he headed for the bench opposite the water. "Ah, that's better," said Joe as he sat down. "Dancing's fun but sometimes I like to get out of the noise and the smoke and the crowd."

Eilidh sat beside him, at a total loss to know what to say. After a bit she realized it wasn't necessary to say anything at all. She relaxed into his silence.

Joe said, "Beautiful night. What are you thinking about?"

His abrupt remark threw her off balance and she was startled into a frank answer. "I wasn't thinking about anything." Airhead, she thought. He'll think you're a complete airhead. "Ummm . . . I was thinking that it's a beautiful night, too."

"Too beautiful to think about anything at all." He turned and smiled at her, a gentle, calm smile. Taken by surprise, she smiled back.

Ah, that's better, thought Joe.

Eilidh looked at him, really looked at him for the first time. She saw brown hair, warm brown eyes framed by glasses, a wide, sweet mouth. She was fascinated by the way the lights of the hall reflected off his glasses. It was as though the lights were shining from his eyes. She had to say something. She could not keep staring at him. "You're new here," she blurted.

"Aye, I am. My name is Joe Munro. I'm a friend of Ian MacDonald's."

"I'm Eilidh MacDonald. Ian's my brother. My twin."

"Oh, aye. He told me he had a sister." She's beautiful, Ian had said, and Joe had shivered. He didn't like beautiful women, except from a distance; they made him nervous. He wondered now how he'd had the nerve to speak to her. Because she looked so sad, he realized. He added, "Ian invited me to the Island for a visit."

She finally thought of something to say. *Eilean Dubhannaich* could always talk about their Island. "Do you like it here?"

"Aye. It's really pretty." He turned to look back at the water. "I'm a veterinary medicine student. Ian's the devious sort. I think he's hoping I'll fall in love with the place and come to work with the local vet. Seems he needs a partner because the work is too much for one person."

"Oh." After a moment she blurted, "Are you going to? Stay, I mean."

"Don't know." He stretched his long legs out and leaned away from the bench. "I might. I haven't decided."

She waited for him to start flirting with her, as most men would. Would you like me to stay? he'd say. Or, I might stay if you asked me. Something like that, trite and predictable.

Instead, he said, "There'd be a lot of challenge in the work, real variety and a chance to get plenty of experience. And animals are important to the people here. I like that; they're important to me, too. But I don't know. It's different from any place I've ever lived. Cut off. Isolated."

For some reason she suddenly wanted him to stay. "But it's a brilliant place to live. The people are friendly, once you get to know them. And the climate's the best of any place in Scotland." At his raised eyebrows she said, "It's true. It's a microclimate, warmer and sunnier than anywhere else. Something to do with the mountains."

"Is that so," he said. He looked at her, serious and intent, and she realized that he had actually been listening to her. Most men looked instead of listening. She hurried on, feeling it her duty to list the negatives. "There's not a lot to do outside of work, though. Only one cinema and *cèilidhean* every other Friday. It's not very exciting."

"Oh, well. Guess I'd have to make my own excitement. I like hiking and bird-watching. And I spend a lot of time reading. And messing about with cameras. Photography's my hobby."

"This is the place for you, then." Her smile lit up her face. Joe, watching her, felt a tiny tug in the neighborhood of his heart and realized why the other men were both wary of and attracted to Eilidh. Smiles like that made her a dangerous woman, he thought.

Carried away by her enthusiasm, Eilidh thought she was close to making a sale. "Is there anything else you're wondering about?" she asked.

I'm wondering why your eyes are so sad, he thought. Wondering why a girl like you isn't spoken for. Wondering if I'm going to fall in love with you. Aloud, he said, "No, I think you've covered it all. Shall we go inside for that waltz? I am good, I wasn't exaggerating. My sisters forced me into service as a partner in our dining room when they were learning to dance." He stood up and offered her his hand. "Come on, take a chance on me."

I might, thought Eilidh. I might take a chance on you. And she took his hand and stood up. As they entered the hall she blurted, "Would you like to go hiking tomorrow?" As he looked at her in astonishment she stammered, "It's a bit chilly; you'd need a warm jacket. But I could show you some really pretty places. Especially if you like wildflowers. There's some very early ones just blooming now. You have to know where they are to find them."

Joe smiled into her eyes. "I love wildflowers but I can never remember their names," he said. "I'll bring my flower book along."

"Oh, I know them all," she said.

"Then I'll just bring my camera," Joe said happily.

After their hike the next day both were exhausted and chilled. He invited her down to his tiny cottage for a cup of tea. When they opened the door a shaggy black and white Border collie got up and walked to them with slow dignity. Joe knelt and took the dog's large head in his hands and rubbed his ears.

Eilidh loved dogs. "What's his name?"

"I don't know. No one knows. He came with the cottage. When the old man who lived here died, the neighbors bundled the dog up and took him off to a croft several miles away, thinking it would be a good home for him. He was back in a couple of days, tired and hungry and determined to stay.

"I told Ian I'd take care of him as long as I was here. He's quite old and arthritic. He really can't work sheep any more, though he'd like to, and he deserves his retirement. But nobody knows his name. So I just call him Old Dog."

Eilidh went to her knees and extended her hand for the dog to sniff. "*Cù aosda,*" she crooned and Old Dog, recognizing his native language, wagged his tail in grave pleasure.

"He likes you," said Joe, delighted. "What's that you said to him? Is that Gaelic?"

"Aye. *Cù aosda.* It means Old Dog."

Old Dog wagged his tail harder and Joe, watching Eilidh's long fingers move over the grizzled head, thought if she ever touched him like that he'd wag his tail, too.

A very young black cat jumped down from a kitchen chair and approached them on delicate paws. She chirruped a greeting to Joe and butted her little head against his leg. He sat quietly while she climbed into his lap and stretched her slender body to an amazing length so that she could put her paws on his shoulder while he whispered a greeting in her dainty ears. Then she turned and looked at Eilidh, having made clear her ownership of her human.

Her eyes were a vivid shining violet-blue. Eilidh was entranced.

"Her name's Pansy," Joe said. "For her eyes, of course."

Pansy stepped down and approached the stranger, inclining her head gracefully to sniff the outstretched hand. She permitted a gentle caress on her head.

"I found her mother over in the pasture, in labor, the first day I was here. I couldn't leave her; the hawks would have finished off both her and the kittens. Turned out she belonged to Mrs. Beathag the Bread and she'd just wandered off. Cats do that sometimes when they're near birth. I kept the family here for her till they were weaned and she let me have a kitten."

Eilidh laughed. "You have a regular menagerie. Where are the birds?"

Joe blushed. "In Edinburgh. A friend's taking care of them. I had to give the snake away, though, she was growing fast and my cage was too small for her." He added, unnecessarily, "I like animals."

"So do I."

Joe looked at her. She was sitting cross-legged on the floor. Old Dog's chin was resting on her shoulder and one of her arms was wrapped around his neck, her hand ruffling his ears, his nose ruffling her amazing hair. Pansy had decided she liked the stranger and was butting her head against Eilidh's other hand, asking for a caress.

His hands hungered for his camera, his eyes plotted camera angles.

Eilidh smiled and crooned to both animals in the Gaelic.

Joe knew beyond any shadow of doubt he would never be the same again.

They spent the next ten days of Eilidh's holiday together. She went with him when he filled in on an emergency call for Dr. Cunningham. It was a difficult labor, the calf turned in a breech position, the young inexperienced cow loud in her distress.

"You understand I'm not fully qualified, yet, till June," Joe advised the crofter who said, "Just get on with it, man. If you can help her I don't care if you've learned everything you know by post."

Eilidh watched, awed, while Joe put his arm inside the cow, wincing as the bones and muscles tightened around him, reaching, stretching, pulling until he'd turned the calf into the proper position for birth. Finally the calf slipped out, the cow mooing in relief.

Eilidh looked at the wet, blood and mucus-smeared animal at her feet, and at Joe, crouching down, cleaning the calf's face, making sure it was breathing.

He looked up at the crofter in satisfaction. "A fine young bull. A beautiful animal."

"Aye. Well done, young man." It was high praise, coming from an *Eilean Dubhannach*. They never gushed.

After he'd washed up, Eilidh held his coat for him to slip on. "Look at him, Eilidh. Did you ever see anything more beautiful?" said Joe, looking at the young bull now standing on trembling legs.

"No, *m'eudail*," she said and kissed his cheek. He blushed.

Parting at the end of their magical ten days was very hard for both. They'd hiked and talked and cooked together. She'd played her violin for him and he'd taken countless pictures of her. He'd sat by the fire and read a book while she'd practiced a new piece the orchestra would perform that spring. They'd given each other the gift of quiet reflection, quiet time together.

Eilidh felt herself beginning to heal. Simon's intense gray eyes were replaced in her mind with Joe's brown ones, warm behind his glasses. She was refreshed and eager to get back to her music. And she looked forward with equal eagerness to returning to Eilean Dubh in June, knowing that Joe would be there.

He'd made his decision. He would stay on Eilean Dubh, stay forever as long as there was a chance Eilidh would come back to him.

Jean and Darroch, on a walk one morning with Rosie strapped in a sling on her father's broad chest, were caught in a sudden rain shower. Joe, peering out his door at the rain, saw them and invited them in for shelter and a cup of tea.

Sitting by the fire, Jean noticed a pile of photos on the table. Stunned by the beauty of the top one, a close-up of bright yellow creeping cinquefoil, she picked it up for a closer examination, saying, "Oh, this is lovely. Did you take this, Joe?" Looking at the next one, she said, "Look, Darroch, it's the sea, at the end of our lane."

Absorbed, they looked at the photographs one by one, marveling at their beauty and craftsmanship. There were photos of a field of harebells swaying gently in the wind, one of a tiny Eilean Dubh robin, another of a flock of swifts circling high in the bright blue sky. All the pictures showed Joe's growing love for Eilean Dubh, revealed the hours he'd spent walking the hills.

Too late Joe remembered that photos of Eilidh, lots of them, were in the stack.

Jean picked up the first one of Eilidh. "Oh, Joe, you've captured that wistful look in her eyes perfectly."

Joe blushed, remembering when he'd taken that shot. He'd been lying on his belly in the grass, camera aimed at a marsh orchid, waiting for the right gust of wind to position the flower just as he wanted. Eilidh had flopped down beside him, watching intently. When he'd snapped the shutter she'd chuckled at his little sound of satisfaction, then flung herself down on her back in the grass, arms outstretched in his triumph.

He'd sat back on his heels and taken pictures of her, each one more exquisite than the last. She'd made faces at him, pursed her lips, squiggled up her nose. She'd done her Marilyn Monroe imitation, flicking her tongue over her mouth to make it wet and gleaming, and pouted sexily.

Overcome by an impulse he couldn't resist he'd leaned over her, balancing himself carefully on his elbows so their bodies didn't touch, and kissed her. Then he'd pulled back, grabbed the camera and taken her picture again.

When he'd gotten the pictures back from the chemist in Airgead he'd had no trouble in identifying that photo. "Girl who's just been kissed," he'd called it to himself, relishing how he'd captured her look of sweet surprise, and remembering the taste of her full, soft, sun-warmed mouth.

He was going to enlarge that one and frame it and he'd hang it in a private corner where only he could see it. Maybe with a vase of flowers, and a little candle underneath. A shrine. Fool, he called himself, but he couldn't help it.

Jean looked at that picture and realized suddenly that Joe was deeply in love with its subject. Poor Joe, she thought, but then she came to the photo of Eilidh staring full into the lens, eyes glowing at the man behind the camera. She recognized that expression as the one she'd seen in her own eyes, in the mirror, when she thought of Darroch.

Maybe it's lucky Joe, she thought.

Cemetery Hill

slow reel
e minor

rpt.

(last note,
last time)

Twenty-seven

Tears, idle tears, I know not what they mean,
Tears from the depth of some divine despair
Rise in the heart, and gather to the eyes . . .

Alfred Lord Tennyson

*J*oe went back to Edinburgh at the end of his internship and Eilidh attended his graduation in June. He came to Eilean Dubh and she arrived soon after. She helped him move permanently into the tiny cottage, with Old Dog, Pansy and two budgerigars named Puff and Smoke. She washed his cupboard shelves while he arranged clothes in the closet and books in the worn old bookcases. He carried equipment to the old shed behind the cottage that was going to be his darkroom.

They made the bed together and he put his shaving gear in the bathroom while she cooked a huge platter of fish for their supper.

She announced that she was going to take him for a very special hike the next day, up to the top of Cemetery Hill, which she said was called *Cladh a' Chnuic* in the Gaelic. "You can see almost all the way to America from there, and all of Eilean Dubh in the opposite direction. It'll let you see what you've gotten yourself into."

He picked her up the next morning at her parents' cottage and they hiked the road to the lane that led up Cemetery Hill.

Near the top of the hill his footsteps began to lag. Where was she taking him? He was conscious of a distant roaring in his ears that grew louder as they neared the top. He couldn't see anyone around but he could hear the sound of multiple voices.

He shook his head in disbelief. He could hear people talking, but there was no one in sight.

Her slender fingers entwined in his urged him onward. The roaring grew louder. People were talking, shouting, moaning. Heaviness overwhelmed him, his feet weighed a ton. He stumbled. "Wait a minute, I have to catch my breath," he gasped

She stopped, then urged him on.

The noise was becoming intolerable. "Eilidh . . . what's going on?"

She turned and looked at him. "What's wrong, Joe?"

A baby was crying now, a long despairing wail. He began to tremble. "I have to sit down. Is there a place to sit down?"

She put an arm around his shoulder and urged him forward to the bench at the hilltop. He was dimly conscious of a view that encompassed the sea and the sky stretching out forever. He sank down onto the bench and buried his head in his hands and willed the voices to be silent.

Eilidh said, "You hear them, don't you."

"Oh, God, who are they? What do they want?"

"They're the dead. And I don't know what they want. They probably all want different things, just like people who are alive all want different things."

"All those children . . . "

"Aye, they're the worst." She took his hand.

He looked into her Skye blue eyes. "You hear them too?"

"Aye. I've always heard them. I'm used to them now; it's just sort of a quiet murmur."

She stroked his hand reassuringly. "They don't mean any harm. This hill . . . it's been a burial ground for centuries. I think it's one of those places where the veil between life and death is very thin. Sometimes the veil is torn and their voices come through, for those who have the ears to hear them. Sometimes they laugh. Can you hear that, too?"

He listened. "Aye." He was not trembling as much now.

"It bothered me a lot when I was a child, until Daddy explained. He hears them too; that's why he hates to come up here. Only for funerals, then he leaves as quickly as possible."

He looked at her, dazed. "Eilidh . . . do you know . . . there's a sort of pink haze around your head."

Delighted, she said, "Tell me about it."

"It's incredible. It shimmers and there's touches of gold around the edges."

"So you see auras, too, darling Joe." She took his face between her hands and kissed him delicately and he trembled again, for a different reason.

He stammered, "Is that what it is? An aura? I've never known what to call it." He'd tried, as a child, to tell someone about it and had never forgotten the blank look he received in exchange. After that he'd not mentioned it again, had tried to ignore it. "I've always seen them around people but it's so much stronger here on the Island. Everyone has one. But especially you. I've never seen such a color as there is around you."

She kissed him and stroked his cheek. "You're psychic, aren't you, my lovie."

"Oh, no," he said, horrified. His Presbyterian upbringing revolted at the idea. "You mean things like seeing the future . . . "

"No, that's the Sight. Daddy has it and I have too. What you have is different. You're just very sensitive. Don't you want to kiss me back?"

"Oh, aye."

"Don't you want to put your arms around me, sweet Joe?"

"I'm afraid to touch you. You'll disappear, vanish into the wind."

"No, I won't. I promise."

Somehow she was on his lap and her arms were around his neck. He put his arms around her and held her gently. She was slight but by no means insubstantial; she warmed him all over. He pulled her closer and kissed her and she opened her mouth to his tongue. She tasted like—what was it? Honey, or Demarara sugar? Something sweet. He explored inside her, gasping with pleasure, hearing her little sighs of happiness.

Suddenly he drew back and looked at her with astonishment. "They're singing, now."

"What are they singing?" Her hands ruffled through his hair.

"I don't know, but it's beautiful."

"I'll play it for you tonight, on my violin. After we've made love."

He shivered. "Are we going to make love, darling Eilidh?"

"If you want to."

"I've never wanted anything so much in my life."

"Let's go to your cottage, then."

"No, wait." He took a deep breath and looked into her eyes. "We won't make love unless you promise to marry me. It's the way I was brought up, it's the right thing to do."

She smiled at him. "So you want to marry me, do you?"

He wanted—what did he want? He wanted it all, wanted her in bed with him, wanted her for the rest of his life. Wanted this astonishing creature to be his forever, wanted her body, her heart, her soul. He put a hand behind her head and kissed her deeply, possessively. "Please, Eilidh. Marry me. I love you."

She whispered, "I can cook. I can't sew very well but I can keep your buttons attached to your shirts. I'm not naturally tidy. During the week you may have to wade through piles of my things. I let it all go till the weekend. But every Saturday morning I whisk around the house and straighten everything up, do the laundry, put everything away, to have a clean house for Sunday and the next week." She looked at him teasingly. "I hope you won't mind that by Wednesday everything is back to a shambles."

"I'm a good picker-upper. I'll follow you around and put away everything you drop."

She laughed, delighted. "I'll have to spend Saturday mornings looking for it all, won't I."

He put his hands on her shoulders and looked at her sternly. "Answer me, Eilidh. Is it aye, or no?"

"It's been aye since the first night I met you. I've just been waiting for you to realize it." She chuckled at his look of astonishment, wiggled off his lap and stood up. "I'm starving and I'm dying to cook you supper. Let's go shopping." She glanced at her watch. "Come on, get a move on, before Cailean the Crab closes up. I'd love some fried fish, wouldn't you?"

She could have suggested rats' liver and seaweed pie and it would have sounded delicious. He got unsteadily to his feet and followed her down *Cladh a' Chnuic*. Behind him, the voices stopped singing and there was a sudden burst of applause. He glanced over his shoulder and grinned. "Thanks. See you later," he said softly.

Twenty-eight

As wan, as chill, as wild as now;
Day, mark'd as with some hideous crime . . .
Alfred Lord Tennyson

*A*fter supper she pushed her plate away and looked at him seriously. "There's something you have to know about me, Joe," she said. She stood up. "Let's sit in front of the fireplace and talk."

Puzzled, he followed her to the sofa. When he tried to take her into his arms she pulled away. "Listen first," she said. She took a deep breath and began to talk.

"My orchestra doesn't have enough money; orchestras never do. We have to rely on fundraising to make up the deficit." She turned her head to look into the fire. "There's a man . . . he's an excellent fundraiser, a businessman who knows everybody with money and knows how to talk them out of it.

"The orchestra director called me into his office one day about two months ago. He said he would appreciate it if I would take on an extra job. He said that I was an asset to them because I was pretty and that lots of people liked me, not just because I played well but because I was different. From a tiny little Scottish island, with an adorable accent, and young. I was exotic, he said, and that always played well with the moneyed crowd. He asked me if I would help with fundraising, do a few personal appearances at cocktail parties, chat people up and help relieve them of some of their cash.

"When I said I'd like to help but that I didn't know anything about how to raise money he said that didn't matter; all I had to do was smile a lot and be charming and play a couple of tunes on my violin. He said they had an experienced man who'd go with me and take care of the fundraising part."

Her eyes glazed over. "Then he called the man in and introduced us."

He was tall and stocky, and more than twice her age. He advanced and held out his hand. "Hi, I'm Chase Campbell. I understand we'll be working together." When she put out her hand he covered it with both of his and smiled.

She shivered. His hands were cold and so were his eyes; there was something in their depths she couldn't like. "Hello."

"I'm a great fan of yours. I could listen to you play the violin all day. We'll make a good team."

She smiled back, timidly. "I'll do my best."

She sat in silence while the two men talked. Then Chase turned to her. "Next Thursday night, then, Eilidh. I'll pick you up. Give me your address."

She was excused early from Thursday's rehearsal so that she could get ready for the cocktail party. She fussed over her wardrobe; she didn't really have much in the way of dress-up clothes except the white blouse and long black skirt she wore for performances. Dubious, she put that on.

The evening was a great success, just as the orchestra manager had predicted. She smiled till her face ached and played a Bach partita and then, as an afterthought, an Eilean Dubh folk song. Her listeners were enchanted, and money changed hands.

"You've done a brilliant job, Eilidh," said Chase when he dropped her off at her flat. "The cash flowed in. The folk song was a great touch. Drop the Bach and play a couple of those next week."

"Next week? I thought this was a one time event."

"Oh, no. Talk to Archie. He's got a whole schedule lined up for us." He patted her cheek in a fatherly fashion and saw her to her building door. He said, "This isn't a good neighborhood for you, Eilidh."

"It's all right. Besides, it's all I can afford."

He said thoughtfully, "I've a friend who's an estate agent. I'll ask her what's she's got available."

Eilidh didn't mind the neighborhood but she hated the flat. The bathroom was grubby no matter how much she cleaned it, only two burners on the stove worked and she didn't trust the lock on the door. When Chase

Campbell called her the next week and gave her an address from his friend, she was delighted to find a snug, cozy flat in a well-kept-up building in a good neighborhood just off Minto Street. And she could afford the rent. Ian helped her move, raising his eyebrows when he went inside. "How much do you pay for this? It's *miorbhuileach*."

The fundraisers became a weekly event. Chase Campbell would pick her up and they'd attend a posh party where she'd smile and play and he'd collect the checks. "This is brilliant, Eilidh," said Archie, the orchestra manager. "You're the best draw we've ever had. Keep up the good work."

Sometimes they had dinner together, when she was late getting out of rehearsal. He insisted she eat before going to a party. "Otherwise you'll get silly from drink and make terrible mistakes when you play." He took her to elegant restaurants and watched her, smiling, while she ate wonderful food, awed at her surroundings and uneasily flattered by his scrutiny.

He was so self-assured, he overwhelmed her with his sophistication and his casual taking for granted that she would do what he said. He pronounced her name "Ellie", not "Aylie", which made her feel gauche and rustic, like something out of an American television hillbilly comedy.

When he dropped her off several weeks into their fundraising, Chase said, "A big one next Wednesday, Eilidh. Have you got something posh to wear? Other than the orchestra gear, that is. Something really swank."

She shook her head. "This is all I have. I haven't had time or money to shop for anything else."

He tilted his head and looked at her appraisingly. "Perhaps I can help. My daughter used to be your size before she put on weight and she's got some expensive frocks just hanging in her closet. Let me see what I can liberate."

"I couldn't . . . "

"Of course you can. I spent plenty on her wardrobe and the greedy cow can't wear any of them now. I'd like to see them being used." When she hesitated he said, "It's just a loan. Do it to please me, Eilidh. And for the orchestra."

She was taken aback when the parcel arrived on Monday and she pulled out of it a beautifully cut cerulean blue silk dress. When she tried it on and looked at herself in the mirror she was astonished. The dress shimmered on her slender body and was cut so cunningly it seemed as though she had curves. The neckline was low across her small bosom, hinting mysteriously at the treasures within. She didn't have a bra that would work with the narrow straps so with much trepidation she did without. When she looked down at her breasts she saw that her nipples made tiny indentations in the silk.

She turned back and forth in front of her mirror, the dress swirling about her hips.

She didn't recognize herself. She was innocent and seductive at the same time. The dress seemed to reveal more of her than she was willing to share. Uneasily, she wondered what her parents would think.

When Chase Campbell took her sweater from her shoulders at the party he grimaced. "I should have thought of a wrap. This sweater is awful. Maybe something in fur. Would you like a little fur jacket, Eilidh? To go with the dress?"

She shuddered. "Oh, no, I don't approve of wearing fur."

"Velvet, then. Or cashmere. I'll find something for you." His breath was warm on the back of her neck.

Talking and smiling and playing her violin that night she felt entirely unlike herself: glamorous, sexy and naked. The dress made her feel naked, and so did the looks from the men present. Chase Campbell was always at her side, ready to fend off any importunate advances.

When he took her home he smiled at her. He was just her height but he made her feel quite overwhelmed by his size when he looked so intently into her eyes. "The dress was a great success. Do you like it?"

"Yes. Please thank your daughter for lending it to me. I'll have it cleaned and give it back to you."

"No, keep it for a while. We've more parties coming up, you'll need a pretty dress. I understand how you women's minds work." His grin was conspiratorial.

"I can't . . . "

"Of course you can. For the orchestra, remember?" His cold lips brushed her cheek.

Shivering, she pulled away. "Good night."

The appearances continued and the money rolled in. The orchestra manager rubbed his hands in glee. Chase Campbell's smile grew broader, and predatory, though his behavior remained avuncular. Images of wolves, fangs bared, drooling, began to haunt Eilidh's dreams.

She longed for someone to talk to but she was too shy to have made friends in the orchestra. The other women regarded her as a threat and competition, for both her beauty and her talent. Ian was studying desperately for exams. And Joe was away in England on another internship, out in the countryside in a primitive cottage without a phone.

When Chase took her home after their last fundraising appearance of the season she was finally able to relax. One more concert and the orchestra would break for the summer and she could go home to Eilean Dubh and her family and Joe. She'd been quite giddy with the thought all evening, had chatted easily with the guests, flirted in a way that was the more seductive for its innocence. She'd even accepted a second glass of champagne, and was slightly woozy from it.

Outside her building she turned to Chase and put her hands in his. "Thank you so much for all you've done this year. The orchestra appreciates your efforts and I am grateful too. It's all your doing. I'd never have had the nerve alone."

"You're welcome. I've enjoyed it." His eyes moved over her speculatively. "I wonder—would you mind if I came up and used your phone? My wife's not been feeling well and I'd like to call her to see if she needs anything from the chemist's." He smiled. "Pills, tissues, you know."

She was too happy to heed the warning bells in her head. The Sight was not strong in her in Edinburgh and she had learned to disregard it. "Aye, come on up."

Inside the flat he looked around. "This is quite cozy." He picked up a paperback book from the table. He smiled at the lurid cover with its half-draped heroine swooning into the arms of a bare-chested, long-haired warrior. "Romance novels. Why do all you women like them?"

Startled at having to defend her taste in reading she said, "It's just a bit of fantasy. And love. The hero always falls in love with the heroine and they live happily ever after. The phone's just there on the table."

"Oh, I don't think I'll need that." He took off his suit coat and draped it casually over a chair. His fingers moved to his tie, loosening it.

"Your wife . . . "

"Is in Glasgow, visiting her mother." He shuddered. "Dreadful woman, her mother. So I'm all alone this weekend, quite the lonely bachelor in my big empty house. Your flat is so much cozier, Eilidh. I think I'll stay here with you."

"But you can't—it wouldn't be right. People would talk."

"They're talking already. Might as well give them something to really talk about." He pulled off the tie and put it carefully on top of the suit jacket.

"What do you mean, they're talking?"

"About you and me. About your pretty new dress and your expensive flat. Wondering how you could afford them on your salary. Coming to the obvious conclusion, when you and I are together so much."

She stammered, "You said the dress was your daughter's."

He looked at her, eyebrows raised. "You actually believed that, didn't you? For your information my daughter is fourteen and I wouldn't permit her to wear a dress like that one if she were your age. Too slutty. But it suits you perfectly." He went back to unbuttoning his shirt. "No, that dress came from a very exclusive shop just off Prince's Street."

He smiled at the memory. Slender, haughty, very young girls had paraded before him in frocks that had caused his groin to tighten as he imagined the delicious bodies beneath them. He'd taken his time in selecting the dress, leering at all the sweet young flesh on display. Madame Elise, the proprietor, had gritted her teeth but without obvious provocation she had no reason to throw him out. Besides, she'd been through this before with him. She wondered who the unlucky recipient of his generosity was this time.

He said softly, "I've been more than patient with you. Now I'm going to have what I want. Take the dress off. The thought of ripping it off you is most appealing but it was too expensive for me to indulge myself that way."

She backed away, bumped into a table and turned her attention from him, involuntarily, when she felt the lamp behind her begin to wobble.

And he was on her. One hand was on her neck, bringing her head close to his, and one hand roamed down the silk dress and seized her bottom. He kissed her hard, his huge tongue battering entrance to her mouth. When she gasped in shock he plunged his tongue between her half-opened lips until she began to choke.

She fought desperately. He grunted with pleasure as her body moved on his. "I love it when you struggle, it just makes me harder. Can you feel me?" He thrust his pelvis against hers.

"Please," she cried. "Don't do this. I thought we were friends."

"Now we're going to be even better friends. I can be very friendly when you're lying naked under me and I'm fucking you. I've waited a long time and it's whetted my appetite. I've had plenty of time to think about what I'm going to do to you."

"I'll scream . . . "

"Oh, you will. From fright and pain and then from pleasure. I'll enjoy hearing you scream. Scream away, no one will hear. The walls are thick in this building; that's one reason why I rented this place for you."

"I pay my own rent!"

"Eilidh, Eilidh, you're such a fool. Quite charming, really, how foolish you are. Did you truly think you could get an apartment like this for the miserable pittance you can afford? I'm paying two-thirds of it. I have an arrangement with the rental agent." He grinned wolfishly. "You're what they call a kept woman."

She froze. She understood now the raised eyebrows, the disbelieving smiles when she'd talked to her orchestra mates about her wonderful apartment. Of course they all knew it was impossible on her salary. They must think I'm a slut, she thought. Tears of humiliation spilled from her eyes.

He licked a tear from her cheek. "Quite delicious, you are. I'm going to have such a good time with you." He hissed into her ear, "You're a virgin, aren't you?"

"Aye."

"I thought so. I haven't had a virgin in a long time, I thought they were extinct. Young girls are such tarts today, aren't they. I think I'll take you hard, the first time, rip away your precious little veil. It'll hurt, you know. But that's part of sex: pain. You'll come to like it, after a while.

"How did you keep your maidenhead, anyway? I thought all you peasant families slept together in one bed to keep warm in the long cold winters. I would have thought your father or that big handsome brother of yours would have had you. Or both of them." He nuzzled her neck. "Ah, well, their loss is my gain."

Horrified and revolted at what he'd said she beat his chest with her fists. "That's wicked! How dare you say such things?" She thought she might be sick down the front of his designer shirt.

"I like it when you fight me." He buried his face in her throat and bit, hard. His hands snaked around behind her and one held the dress while the other pulled the zipper down, almost to her tailbone.

He pulled the straps off her shoulders and the dress slid to her waist. When she tried to cover herself he seized her hands in one of his large ones and pulled them behind her back. "No bra, I thought as much. What a little whore, flaunting your nipples at all the men. You deserve to be punished, to teach you a lesson." His free hand went to his belt, unbuckled it, pulled it out of the loops. "A few stripes on your bottom will teach you modesty."

She went rigid with terror, her mind vacant, frozen.

He stared at her breasts. "You're little. I like a woman with big tits, myself, but yours are pretty even if they are small. They'll be bigger after I've sucked and bitten them; they'll be all swollen and hot in my mouth." He covered one breast with the hand that held the belt and squeezed painfully.

The other hand tightened on one of her arms and twisted it up behind her back. She shrieked. "You should be good to me. I could break your arm, Eilidh. Think of that. A violinist with a broken arm. Or a dislocated shoulder. It might never get entirely well. What would happen to your wonderful career then?"

Cold anger rose in her, warring with the pain and the fear. The champagne mist cleared and her mind was beginning to work. This man was going to hurt her badly, especially if she fought him. But he'd have to kill her; she'd not give willingly what he wanted. What did the woman in the last romance novel she'd read do when she was about to be raped?

She forced herself to soften in his arms, looked at him teasingly from under her lashes, licked her lips seductively. "You don't have to be so rough, you're frightening me."

He looked into the beautiful blue eyes and was mesmerized. Just for a minute he allowed his grip on her arms to loosen. She wrenched them free and brought her leg up, hard, into his groin. Then she stamped down with her heel on his foot.

He gasped for breath, doubling over, fighting the pain. "Little bitch, so you want it rough, do you? You'll be sorry for that."

She pushed him away and he staggered off balance. The dress slithered lower and she grabbed it with both hands, bunching it up as she darted away, struggling furiously to pull the straps back over her shoulders before it tripped her. She reached the other side of the sofa. Rubbing his groin, he advanced on her, a grim smile on his face. Terror filled her again, made her knees weak. Don't give up. Think, she told herself. Look for a weapon, something to hit him with. She'd only get one chance; he was too strong and would easily overpower her.

She gauged the distance to the door and knew she could never make it before he caught up to her.

The phone rang.

She snatched it up and babbled into the receiver, improvising desperately. "Ian, thank God! There's a man in my flat; he's trying to rape me. Can you come at once? Where are you? That close?"

The wrong number at the other end sputtered unhearing apologies and hung up. She cried into the dead receiver, "Break down the door, please, hurry!"

She put the phone down and glared at Campbell. "That was my brother. He's in the pub down the street and he's on his way here. He's six foot six and he'll kill you."

He stared at her. Then he moved casually to the chair and retrieved his jacket, shrugging into it. He tossed the tie around his neck. "Another time, then, Eilidh. And if you want my advice you'll tell your brother you were mistaken about the rape. Tell him you were just trying to scare away an over-eager boy friend."

At the door he turned. "And don't even think of involving the coppers. Who would they believe, you or me? Especially when it turns out I'm paying for your apartment. You'd be seen as a cheap little whore, hungry for all you can get. I'd tell them you were my mistress and you were angry with me. Wanted me to divorce my wife and marry you. Something like that."

He smiled. "Wonderful publicity for the orchestra, don't you think? And a real boost for your career."

He remembered, abruptly, that her six-foot-six brother was on his way and left in a hurry.

She darted to the door and shot the bolt, then leaned against it, trembling. Her eyes roamed around her lovely little flat and she shuddered.

He had forgotten his belt. It lay coiled on the floor like a snake, waiting.

I've got to get out of here, she thought; he'll come back. He'll have a key. He can break through that bolt, she realized, and went cold with terror. She shoved a chair under the doorknob, then a table against the chair.

But he won't come back tonight, he'll think Ian is here. The realization drove her to sudden, furious activity.

She wriggled out of the horrible silk dress, threw it on the floor, wanting to burn it, pour acid on it.

She piled her possessions into her suitcases, packed up everything she owned, her violin, her books, the little statue Jamie had given her for luck, the vase with pebbles from Eilean Dubh. She threw out the food in the refrigerator, filling the rubbish bin. She was never coming back to this place.

She waited out the night, dozing upright on the living room sofa, startling awake at any sound in the building, dropping off again and again into sleep punctuated with terrifying nightmares filled with fear and pain. Early the next morning she called Ian, concocted an excuse for leaving Edinburgh so quickly and made arrangements for him to pick up her things and store them in his flat. She dropped her key in the post for him. She did not dare face him; the hurt and shame were too new and she was afraid she'd blurt out to him what had happened.

And he would go after Chase Campbell and punish him. She couldn't allow that; a run-in with the police of that magnitude over a man of that importance would probably get Ian kicked out of university.

She made one firm decision that morning. She was going to Archie, the orchestra manager, and tell him what had happened. He had a daughter himself, and he was kind, and he would believe her. It was the least she could do for the other girls who were likely to follow in her footsteps as fundraisers.

Archie listened to her quietly. When she was finished he closed his eyes and leaned his elbows on his desk, cradling his head in his hands. He thought of the other young women whom he'd paired with Campbell on the fundraising circuit. There was Sarah, who'd left abruptly in mid-season for a job, less well paid, with an English orchestra. There was Margaret, who'd mailed in her resignation. And there was Tess, who'd simply disappeared. The word was that she'd gone back to her parents in Aberdeen but no one knew why, though there was plenty of speculation.

Rumors had floated around about Campbell and Archie had ignored them. The man was simply too good at raising money and the orchestra needed it badly. Now he had the makings of a sexual harassment suit and a nasty scandal on his hands if Eilidh told anyone about this. Beyond that floated the faces of other young women who'd been victimized, terrorized, raped. He thought of his own daughter and shuddered with guilt and horror.

He said through gritted teeth, "I'll take care of him, Eilidh. He'll not do any more work for us and I'll put out the word—discreetly—in the arts community that he's not to be trusted with young women." He took a deep breath. "If you want to press charges against him, I'll go with you to the police."

She shook her head. "It's his word against mine. I can't prove a thing. Just a few bruises, that's all I have to show." She looked up at him. "I want to go home, Archie, right away. Today. Can you fix it for me so that I can miss the last concert?"

"I'll fix it. Your father's ill, he's in hospital, something like that. Eilidh . . . you'll be welcome back next year. I hope you'll stay with us. Don't let this ruin your career."

She smiled sadly at him. She'd had enough of Edinburgh and her career for the time being. She needed to be back in Eilean Dubh. She took the train to Oban and caught the ferry the next day.

Jamie, on a wakeful prowl through the cottage one evening while Màiri slept soundly, heard the soft sound of sobs from the attic bedroom, Ian's old room, which Eilidh had taken over when she'd come back. He paused at the bottom of the steps, listening intently. He'd known something was wrong when she'd come home early, tight-lipped and exhausted, but he was waiting for her to tell him. He never pried.

Despair, he thought, tasting the air like a bloodhound. And fear, and regret. And a terrible sadness. It made him want to weep with her, for her. He trembled with the need to know what awful thing had happened to his darling Eilidh.

He got his fiddle from its case, stood at the bottom of the steps and began to play the first tune he'd taught her, a traditional Eilean Dubh song. She'd learned it on the little violin that had been Darroch's gift to his honorary niece.

When he finished he heard her violin answering. She played Mozart and he stood, instrument in hand, lost in wonder. His daughter, he thought. So talented, so beautiful, so good-hearted, so gentle. What had happened in Edinburgh?

When she finished he started a lilting reel that the two of them had often played together at *cèilidhean*. He heard her join in and they played together, alternating solos, flashes of brilliance, each teasing the other on to new flights of fancy.

At the tune's end there was silence. Then she came downstairs.

He could see the tears still on her cheeks. "Cup of tea?" he said casually. "We've got some of those chocolate biscuits you like."

At the kitchen table he was finally able to put it into words. "Something wrong, *mo fhlùr*?"

She sighed. She had been crying for Simon, even though he was six months gone, and for the frightening ending of her association with Chase Campbell, though she would not tell her father about that. And for the bitter disillusion that life in Edinburgh had brought her.

"I was in love with a man who turned out to be gay," she said, finally. She could tell him part of the truth, at least.

"Gay?"

"You know. Homosexual."

"Oh. You didn't know? He didn't tell you?"

"No. Not till he was leaving the orchestra. I didn't know he was going to leave, either."

"Oh. That must have been a shock." The bastard, Jamie thought, furious, and covered her hand with his, not knowing what to say.

"Aye. But I'll feel better now that I'm home."

And she did.

Twenty-nine

I shut the door to face the naked truth,
I stood alone—I faced the truth alone,
Stripped bare of self-regard . . .
Christina Rossetti

*E*ilidh finished her story about Chase Campbell.

Joe trembled with anger. He felt a burning desire to go to Edinburgh and shove the villain's teeth down his throat, then cut off his cock and send it after his teeth. Almost afraid to touch her, he took her hand gently.

And suddenly she flung herself into his arms and began to cry. She wept away her fear and disgust and shame. At last she drew her head back from his chest and sniffled. She said, "That's why we have to make love."

"What?"

"I'm afraid. I dream about it. Sometimes he's a wolf and he's going to rip my throat open if I don't let him have me. Sometimes he's on top of me, and I'm naked . . . " She shuddered. "I'm afraid I won't be able to make love and I can't marry you if I can't. If I keep seeing his face and hearing his voice. It wouldn't be fair to you, to have a wife who couldn't enjoy making love."

He understood her intuitively and he knew she meant it. And if he didn't act now he'd never have the courage. *Carpe diem*, he thought. Seize the day. He stood up and held out his hand. "Come on, then. Let's give it a try."

Hand in hand they walked to the bedroom. "I've never done this before. Shall I undress?" she said, her voice quivering.

He had no idea what to do, having never done it before either, but he wasn't going to let her know that. She needed to have confidence in him. "Let me do it." He unbuttoned her blouse with tender hands and slid it off.

He stared at her jeans, wondering what came first: shoes and socks, he supposed. How was he to manage that? "Lie down on the bed," he said.

Obediently she stretched out and looked up at him, eyes frightened but shining with trust. He took off her shoes and her socks, and stared, entranced, at her feet. They seemed yards long and slender, with a preposterously high arch, and her toes were as long and delicate as paintbrushes. He played with her toes and she giggled.

Well, that was a good sign. "Ticklish?"

"Aye."

He moved his hands up her legs until he came to the fly of her jeans. He unbuttoned and unzipped, then pulled the jeans down and off. "Skin the rabbit," he said, and she giggled again.

When he moved to lie down by her she said, "Aren't you going to take off your clothes?"

Damn, he'd forgotten. So much for a sophisticated seduction. He ripped his shirt buttons open, sending one flying, and pulled off shirt and undershirt. He sat down on the bed and took off shoes and socks, then stood up and took off his trousers. He left his shorts on; he didn't have the nerve to take them off yet.

He stretched out beside her and they lay looking into each other's eyes. A thousand things to say came into his mind but his lips refused to cooperate. Finally he managed, "You're beautiful and I love you very much."

Delighted, she whispered, "I love you too, my darling," and moved closer, putting her mouth shyly against his. Within a minute she'd coaxed his mouth open and her sweet little tongue was inside, caressing him until he moaned. That was one thing she knew how to do, Eilidh thought in satisfaction. Simon had taught her how to kiss and now she was pleasing her lover. My lover, she thought and shivered with fright.

Joe felt her trembling and it worried him. He wasn't at all sure he could manage this. "Lie down on your back," he ordered and when she did he lifted himself up on his elbows and leaned over her. Her eyes were wide with terror. Like a little animal, he thought, and his veterinarian's instincts took over.

"You're afraid. If you were a rabbit I'd calm you like this," he whispered and ran his finger up and down her slender nose. She smiled at last and her eyes closed.

He pressed gentle kisses on her face and worked his way over her chin and down her throat. He kissed and petted, murmuring soothingly as he would with a skittish young colt. "Easy there, now, we're going to be just fine," he whispered. His hands slipped under her and found the catch to her bra, opened it awkwardly, and pulled it off.

Like any normal boy he'd seen naked women in the magazines passed around surreptitiously at school but he'd never seen anything as beautiful as her breasts. So dainty, each just the right size to fit in a teacup. "Like two little scoops of ice cream," he said. "With a cherry on top of each." He bent and kissed each nipple, feeling them harden to sharp little points against his lips.

Eilidh gasped, "He said they were too small, he said he'd have to bite them and squeeze them till they were swollen. He said he'd hurt me and I'd like it . . . " The wild look was back in her eyes.

"Shhh. Nothing is going to hurt you. I wouldn't hurt you for the world, Eilidh, I love you so much." He lifted his head from her breasts and put his hand on her flat belly, moving it in circles around her navel, just above her little bikini pants. "Old Dog loves this," he said softly. "He sprawls on his back and his legs spread out and his tongue hangs out of his mouth. And he drools. Are you drooling, darling Eilidh?"

She laughed out loud. "Just about. Do it some more."

He scratched her belly gently, then kissed her navel and continued down her body, down the long slender legs, kissed his way down the long feet to the end of the long toes. "Turn over," he said and when she did he worked his way upwards. She was even beautiful behind her knees, he thought, his mouth savoring the softness of her skin.

"Lie still, relax." Obediently she willed the tension out of her body. He slapped her flanks lightly. "Horses like this, and cows. It's a sign of friendship to them."

He stroked her small bottom, slipping his hand inside the bikini pants. "This is where you pet cats; they love it if they know you well enough to permit it. It reminds them of their mothers cleaning them when they were kittens." He moved up her spine to her shoulder blades.

"I thought you'd have wings here, my darling fairy," he whispered.

"A fairy who falls in love with a mortal loses her wings. They began to shrink when I began to love you."

"How disappointing. I wanted to see them. I thought they'd be fluffy, all trailing feathers."

She giggled. "That's an angel. A fairy's wings are like gossamer . . . like a dragonfly's."

"Iridescent . . . reflecting all the colors of the rainbow?"

"Mostly they were pink."

He took the back of her neck in his mouth, setting his teeth in her carefully. "This is how a stallion holds a mare when he mates with her," he growled.

She wriggled with excitement.

Pansy, the little black cat, jumped lightly up on the end of the bed and settled herself with her paws tucked under her chest. She regarded them benignly out of her enormous violet eyes.

A wave of pure lust enveloped Joe. He'd never felt it so strongly before and it overwhelmed him, frightened him with its intensity. He trembled with need. He sank his teeth in her neck again and she cried out and went limp beneath him, yielding herself completely.

"Turn over," he ordered, and when she did he kissed her shoulder, her throat, then bent to put his mouth on her breast.

A sudden, crippling doubt swept over him and he lifted his head and looked at her. She was so lovely, so gifted. Who was he, to think he could be her lover? To think he could marry her? What would happen to her career, if she married him?

He was just an ordinary man and she was a miracle of beauty and talent. He could never marry her.

He pulled himself up and threw his legs over the edge of the bed. "No, I can't do this, I can't."

"Why not?"

"You should wait for your wedding night, for your husband. For the man you love."

"But you're the man I love. I want to marry you," she said in a small voice.

"It can't be. I'm going to stay here and work with Mr. Cunningham. And your career is in Edinburgh, and Paris, and Vienna, and God knows where else. How could we bear to be separated?"

"But I love you," she insisted stubbornly. "What's happened, Joe, why don't you want me? You were eager enough a few minutes ago."

"Aye." He glanced down at his groin. "Something seems to have dampened my enthusiasm."

He pulled on his jeans, stuffed his feet into his shoes and grabbed a shirt, buttoning it as he stumbled to the door and out of the cottage. He ran down the hill to the ocean.

He stood looking at the waves that rolled and crashed against the rocks. The noise filled him and he wanted to scream his pain to the uncaring sea. A terrible need for quiet overpowered him and the water beckoned. He wanted to walk out into it, let it close over his head, let the cold water bring him silence. Just stand inside the water and fill his head with silence.

But he longed for peace, not death.

He turned away from the water and began to trudge slowly up the hill, past his cottage, with no idea of where he was heading. By the time he neared the top of the hill he could go no further. His stifled sobs were robbing him of breath, crushing his chest. The little garden on his right seemed like a refuge and he opened the gate and staggered in to collapse on the stone bench under the tree.

Thirty

It is the duty of age to counsel youth.
It is the duty of youth to listen.

Eilean Dubh proverb

*J*ean and Darroch had gone to bed early, expecting a wakeful night with Rosie, who, perversely, after sleeping through the night for a month, had gone back to wanting food every four hours. Jean had awoken around eleven, unable to go back to sleep and desperate with a nursing mother's hunger. Unable to banish the thought of a blackberry jam and peanut butter sandwich from her mind, she slipped quietly downstairs.

She fixed her sandwich and was seized by a sudden desire to eat it outside, under the stars. Since she was naked except for her slippers, she pulled on Darroch's long black coat that hung by the back door.

The coat was "bespoke," made to order for him. It came down to Jean's ankles and pooled around her in folds, reminding her how tall and broad-shouldered her darling husband was. She was not small but she could almost wrap it around her twice. She found the belt and fastened it tightly around her waist, enjoying the silky lining against her skin. The coat had the faint odor of peat smoke that she identified with Darroch and it aroused her. Maybe when she came in, she thought, she'd slip into bed and run her hands over her husband's warm body until he stirred and turned drowsily to her.

The only trouble with having a baby was that it limited their opportunities to make love. Thinking of the baby made her breasts tighten to a full heaviness. She hoped she wouldn't leak milk on the coat lining.

Wrapped in the coat she stepped out into the garden. It was not until her eyes had adjusted to the moonlight and the million twinkling stars that she realized she was not alone. Slumped on the bench under the rowan tree was a dark figure. She was frightened, at first, her city reflexes making her think of danger, but Eilean Dubh had no muggers, no rapists, no burglars. It was entirely likely, however, that the figure on the bench was someone who'd had too much to drink down in the village and had chosen their bench for a momentary respite as he staggered home.

The thought made her a little indignant, that someone had intruded into their garden because he could not hold his liquor. On the other hand, he might simply be ill. That was worrying. She decided to talk to him rather than retreating into the cottage. "Hello, there!" she called. "Can I help you?"

Sunk in misery, his chest clenched with sobs, Joe did not hear her soft voice at first. He lifted his head and saw her moving toward him. "Oh, God," he gasped and suddenly realized where he was: he had stumbled into the garden belonging to the Laird and his wife. He forced himself to his feet. "Mrs. Jean, I'm so sorry. I didn't mean to disturb you . . . "

"You didn't disturb me. It's Joe, isn't it. Whatever is wrong?" She peered at him through the darkness.

"Oh, God," he moaned again and sank back down on the bench. "I'll leave. Just give me a moment to sort myself," and he burst into tears again. He lowered his head into his hands in despair. "It's hopeless, I can't stand it. I'm sorry, Mrs. Jean, I'm the biggest prat there is, I just can't help myself."

She sat beside him and put her hand on his back. "Tell me, Joe."

"It's Eilidh."

"Ah." The name explained everything. He was certainly not the first man to be cast into despair, pierced to the heart by the beautiful fairy of Eilean Dubh. "Lovers' quarrel, Joe?"

"We're not lovers. I couldn't do it, I couldn't."

Uh-oh, thought Jean. If it was a physical problem she knew she wasn't qualified to deal with it. "Umm . . . "

"She's a virgin, Mrs. Jean. I couldn't take what she should save for her husband on their wedding night."

Oh, dear, thought Jean. He shouldn't be telling me this and I shouldn't be listening. But she couldn't help it, any more than he could keep himself from talking. "But, Joe, everyone's been saying you're engaged. Isn't it true?"

"No, well, yes. Sort of. She told me she loved me. And I'm desperately in love with her. We talked about marriage. And tonight we started to make love and I realized suddenly that it wouldn't work, we can't get married. How could I ask her to give up her career and live here as a country vet's wife? And how can I take her virginity if we can't get married?" He lowered his head into his hands again, slumped in misery.

Poor lad, so old-fashioned, so sweet, thought Jean, and said, "Come inside, Joe. I'll make you a cup of tea."

"Could I, Mrs. Jean? If I could just talk about it . . . "

How it had happened she didn't know, but she was well and truly into the role of confidant now. "It's Jean, not Mrs. Jean." She shivered as a breeze licked her ankles and stood up decisively. When he did not rise she put her hand on his shoulder. "Come inside. It's too cold to stay out here."

He followed her in and sank down at a chair at the kitchen table. Jean put the kettle on and got out cups. She made tea, brought it to the table and said, "Now, then. When you're ready to talk, I'm ready to listen."

He lifted his head. "I can't marry her. I'm an ordinary guy and I'm going to live an ordinary life as a vet, no glamor, just damned hard work. She's a brilliant musician and she has a wonderful career ahead of her. She belongs in Edinburgh, maybe even London or Paris.

"And she needs someone to look after her. How can I protect her when I'm here on Eilean Dubh? There's no way I'd ask her to give up her music. I know how much it means to her and what she means to music. So here I'll be, stumbling through muddy barnyards in the middle of the night and there she'll be, alone and unprotected at the mercy of God knows whom. She doesn't know how to take care of herself; she's too innocent and trusting."

He hesitated. "There was a man in Edinburgh . . . she trusted him and he tried to rape her. He tricked her into letting him into her flat and it was just God's own luck and her cleverness that she got away from him. He hurt her. He told her he'd break her arm if she fought him. Imagine that, Mrs. Jean. Imagine what that would do to her."

Jean stared at him, appalled, imagining Eilidh's terror. Imagining her own daughter Sally, fighting off a rapist. A wave of anger swept her.

"And she was so afraid, so afraid she'd never be able to stand a man touching her. She said we'd have to make love before she'd marry me, because it wouldn't be fair to saddle me with a wife who couldn't enjoy sex. Tonight we—we worked it through and she wanted me, she wasn't afraid any more. And I just couldn't do it; I realized we can't get married and it's not right to be lovers if you can't marry. It's not the way I was brought up." He lifted his head with dignity and stared off into a corner of the room.

She heard footsteps overhead and Darroch's voice, calling softly from the top of the stairs. "Jean?"

"It's all right, lovie." She stood up and hurried to the spiral staircase.

"Who's that with you?" He came down, tying the belt on his robe. "Joe? What's going on?"

"I found him in our garden," she whispered. "He's dreadfully upset. It's Eilidh."

"Oh." Darroch understood perfectly. He stood staring at his wife.

"You've no clothes on, Jean," he said disapprovingly. "And entertaining a young man in the middle of the night."

She glanced down at herself. "Oh, that's why my ankles were so cold. But I've your coat, lovie. It will always protect me."

"Go up and get dressed, Jean," he said. "I'll keep Joe company while you do."

"Okay," she said and scampered up the stairs.

Darroch walked to the table and looked sternly at Joe. "My wife is nursing our baby. She needs her sleep, Joe. Is this important?"

Joe scrambled to his feet. "Oh, God, I'm sorry. I'll leave . . . "

Darroch put a hand on his shoulder and urged him down. "Have your tea first." He poured himself a cup of tea and stood with it in his hand, leaning against the sink. When Jean reappeared, dressed, he said, "I'll go back to bed, then, shall I, while you have your chat."

"No," said Jean and Joe simultaneously.

Joe said, "No offense, Mrs. Jean, but it might help to have a man's point of view."

To Jean, Darroch was the epitome of common sense and the fount of wisdom. Of course he would find a solution. She summed it up quickly. "Joe and Eilidh are in love, darling, but Joe says he can't marry her."

Darroch looked from one of them to the other and sighed. Trust his tender Jean to get herself involved in a matter of the heart and one that could take hours to unravel. "Why not, Joe?"

"She's brilliant, Laird Mac an Rìgh, she's going to be a brilliant concert violinist. Her life will be in the world." Already thinking like a native-born *Eilean Dubhannach*, he divided the world into two parts: the Island, and outside. He took a deep breath. "I've told Mr. Cunningham that I'll come to work with him on Eilean Dubh. He's offered to make me a partner."

"Is that so?" said Darroch, delighted. "That's *miorbhuileach*. He's been worked into the ground since John Cameron died. He must think highly of you, to make you a partner right away."

Joe shook off the compliment. He said firmly, "It would be unfair to tie

Eilidh to me and ruin her career. She deserves success. And she needs someone who can look after her."

"Does she want to marry you?"

"She says so." He smiled, remembering the moment when she'd said yes. Then tears came to his eyes again and he dropped his head into his hands.

Jean reached out to put a hand on his shoulder but Darroch shook his head. No, he said silently. He said, "You think she needs looking after, Joe?"

"I know she does. She's so gentle, so vulnerable . . . "

Darroch stared at Joe. Then he laughed. Jean looked at him indignantly. He said, "I don't suppose either of you have ever watched Eilidh playing football—that's soccer, Jean. She was the star forward on her side at school, absolutely deadly with her left foot. Ran like a deer, had moves around opposing players so fast she was past them and the ball in the goal before they knew she was coming. And the defenders she couldn't elude she ran into full blast, totally fearless. She had tricks with her elbows and knees that young devil Ian taught her. She terrified defenders."

He chuckled, remembering. "She never got caught. She looks so innocent the referees could never believe she did anything wrong. She was so wicked you didn't know whether to be appalled or to applaud.

"She took her side to two Highland championships, over in Inverness. Her mates called her The Fairy. I think the other teams had different names for her. Like 'that redheaded bitch with elbows like daggers.' And other, more colorful names.

"I've known her since she was born, Joe. She was raised by two strong parents. She has a good head on her shoulders and a firm grasp on reality, for all the novels she reads. She'll make mistakes but she'll learn quickly."

Joe started to protest but Darroch shook his head again. "It's a decent instinct, Joe, to want to protect your womenfolk, and I respect you for it. God knows it's a dominant trait in Eilean Dubh men; we're all obsessed with keeping our families safe. I'm sure my dear, independent, American wife thinks I'm overly protective."

Jean said, "No, I don't." When he looked at her, surprised, she added, "I feel the same way about you and Rosie. It's human nature to want to protect those you love."

Darroch smiled at her and said, "Joe, you don't do a woman any favor when you try to wrap her in cotton wool and protect her from the real world. Sooner or later reality always intrudes. What if you cosset her for years, don't let her grow up and learn how to take care of herself and then you become ill and can't look after her. Life is uncertain, you know. Death and loss are part of it."

He said with conviction, "Eilidh is tough, Joe. Not as tough as old boots, but getting there. She looks like a wisp of thistledown that the first breeze would send flying but her roots are deep and solid."

Joe was silent. He was thinking, suddenly, of how Eilidh's quick thinking had saved her from rape. And hadn't she said she'd kneed her attacker in the groin, and stamped on his foot? And her clever idea when the telephone rang. That wasn't the action of a helpless victim. Perhaps he'd underestimated her.

Darroch said, "Your real problem, if you marry, will be the separation. Eilidh in Edinburgh, you on Eilean Dubh. That will be very, very hard."

Jean said softly, "I can scarcely bear it, love, when you're away."

"Me as well, *m'aingeal*." He took her hand in his and brought it to his lips. "There's no easy answer for that, Joe. Except . . . it's better to have true love part of the time, than not at all."

Joe stared at Darroch. What the Laird had just said echoed in his ears like a thunderclap. Better to have true love part of the time, than not at all. A wild hope began to grow in his breast. "Perhaps I could work something out with Mr. Cunningham. Winter's the quiet time here; perhaps he could manage on his own. I could get a job in an Edinburgh clinic, concentrate on small animal practice. Or take advanced classes at university. Or work in a surgical clinic, become really expert in new surgical practices. We could have some of the winter together, while Eilidh's with the orchestra."

"You'd have to come back in March for lambing season."

"Aye, Mr. Cunningham would need help then. But Eilidh'd be done in May with her music and she could come back home." He frowned. "But what if she's offered a concert tour, or a recording contract . . . or . . . "

"Or what if the sky falls? Or Eilean Dubh drifts away on the ocean?" Darroch grinned at him.

Jean said, "Or a meteorite crashes into the earth?" Or Eilidh gets pregnant, she thought, but wisely did not say it.

A plaintive wail rose above their heads and echoed down the staircase, the sad cry of a baby who knows herself to be abandoned, left starving, wet and lonely. Right on cue, Jean thought, and moved to get up, but Darroch said, "I'll bring her down, *mo chridhe*. Rest yourself a moment longer."

When he had gone upstairs Joe said in awed tones, "He's a very wise man, the Laird. He's made it all clear in my head. There might be a chance for us, Mrs. Jean, if I've got the courage to take it."

"Eilidh needs you, Joe, and you need her. Take the chance. It's the most precious thing in the world, to love and be loved in return."

She got up and went to the leather chair by the fire, unbuttoning her blouse. Rosie would be ravenous and in no mood to wait. Milk sprang to her breasts at the thought.

Darroch brought the baby down and settled her in Jean's arms, and Rosie latched on with enthusiasm. He knelt and got the fire blazing, then drew up a stool and sat at Jean's feet. Totally absorbed in each other and in Rosie, they forgot, momentarily, their young guest and his problems.

Joe stood up uneasily, realizing it was time for him to go. He watched the trio for a few moments, unable to tear his eyes away: the curve of the mother's neck as she bent her head over the baby, the long line of bare skin from throat to breast, ending in the child's small, dark-haired head pressed against her, one tiny hand curled, opening and closing in pleasure as she nursed greedily. Jean stroked the baby's head. Darroch leaned forward, watching them both intently, lovingly. His arm was draped across his wife's thighs, one hand slightly under her skirt.

Joe stared, and wished for his camera.

Even in the shadows he could see the deep purple aura of contentment around them. So much love, he thought, and for a moment he saw Eilidh, holding their baby, and himself in a similar tableau. He trembled with anticipation.

He said, "I'll be going now. Thank you, Mrs. Jean, and Laird Mac an Rìgh."

"Just Jean and Darroch, please, Joe. No titles, just friends."

"Good night, then, Jean. And Darroch. And Rosie." He stumbled to the door and wafted out of it, down the hill, floating on air. Tomorrow, he thought, he'd go to Eilidh and tell her all he'd learned and ask her again to marry him. With courage and conviction, and this time he knew they could make it work.

Inside his cottage he went into the bathroom and splashed some cold water on his face. As he was drying his hands he glanced over his shoulder into the bedroom and caught a splash of red-gold splayed out over the blanket. Astonished, he turned and walked to the bed.

She was curled up half inside the covers and half out. One shoulder was exposed and one long leg. She waited for me, he thought, his heart swelling with happiness. He pulled off his clothes and crawled into the other side of the bed and pulled her to him, nestling his head in her sweet-smelling hair.

Half awake, Eilidh murmured, "You came back."

"Aye, I did." He pulled her closer and draped an arm over her. "I'll not leave you again." They fell asleep together.

Thirty-one

I screamed and—lo!—Infinity
Came down and settled over me . . .
Edna St. Vincent Millay

*W*hen Joe awoke the next morning he was alone in bed. Damn, he thought savagely. It was all a dream. He lay on his back staring at the ceiling, so disappointed that he hadn't the energy to move. Finally he pulled himself together. In the bathroom he brushed his teeth, then took a cold shower.

Walking out of the bathroom damp-skinned, heading for his clothes, he heard the rattle of pots and dishes from the kitchen. He pulled on his jeans and staggered to the kitchen doorway.

He stopped abruptly, staring.

The teakettle was steaming and bacon sizzled in a frying pan. Eilidh, completely naked, but wearing his slippers, was beating eggs in a bowl. As he watched, mouth open in amazement, she put down the bowl just as the kettle started to whistle. She rinsed the waiting teapot, then threw in a practiced number of spoonfuls of tea and filled it with water.

He waited, terrified, for the water in the kettle to splash burning drops on her beautiful bare belly.

She put the kettle on the stove and turning back, caught sight of him. "*Madainn mhath,* darling," she said happily. She skipped across the kitchen and threw her arms around him, turning her face up to his. "Good morning kiss?"

"Eilidh . . . angel . . . " he said helplessly as her soft mouth met his in the most delightful kiss. Her small breasts tickled his naked chest.

"You taste like toothpaste," she said. She whisked her tongue over his lips and then licked her own lips with exaggerated delight. "Yummy." She smiled.

"I have to sit down," he mumbled and moved away from her to collapse in a kitchen chair. Sit down or fall down, he thought; his legs had gone all rubbery.

"Are you all right?" she said anxiously.

"Eilidh, you do realize that you've no clothes on, don't you?"

She looked down at herself. "Of course. At home in my flat I often cook naked. Saves heaps on laundry. I usually wear an apron, though. Do you have one?"

The thought of her front bits covered with an apron and her back bits completely bare was having the most amazing effect on him. He was trembling, sweating and he was hard as a rock and risen as high as a small tree. His jeans were hugging him unbearably.

All that he could think of to say was, "No, I don't have an apron."

"Oh, well, I'll just be careful then." She turned back to the eggs.

Joe staggered to his feet and went into the bedroom. He rummaged in a drawer and pulled out an undershirt. He went back into the kitchen and held it out. "Here, put this on. Instead of an apron."

Too late he realized it was a summer undershirt with straps instead of sleeves. Her beautiful strong violinist's shoulders emerged from the fabric as she pulled the shirt on. It draped around her, clinging to every curve.

It was too short, it barely reached the tops of her thighs and when she lifted her arms to the cupboard to bring down cups and plates . . .

Joe sank down at the table again, put his head in his hands and groaned.

She poured him a cup of tea and brought it and the milk pitcher to the table. "Here you are, my lovie, a nice cuppa. Why, what's the matter, Joe? Do you have a headache?"

He could stand no more. He put his hands on her waist and pulled her down on his lap. He said fiercely, "Do you have any idea of what you've done to me, prancing around naked?"

She wriggled on his lap, feeling his arousal. "I can guess," she giggled. "It's lovely, isn't it." She ran her hands over his bare chest. She wrapped her arms around his neck and kissed him, coaxing his lips apart, murmuring beautiful Gaelic words.

"What are you saying?" he gasped, nearly demented with pleasure.

"I said I can feel how hard you are against my bottom. I said I want to do wonderful things to you with my mouth but I'm not sure what they are because I've never done them before. I want to paint pictures on you with my tongue and play my violin while you bury yourself in me."

"Dear God, where did you learn to talk like that?"

"From romance novels. Do you like it, my darling?"

"It's wicked . . . "

"That's why it's so much fun. Talk to me that way."

He wrapped one large hand around the back of her neck possessively, feeling damp hair ripple over his fingers. She must have showered, too. He thrust his other hand up under the shirt and filled it with her breast. He growled, "I want to devour you. I want to dribble blackberry preserves from your breasts all the way down your body and lick it all off. I want to nibble on your nipples."

"You'll nibble on your breakfast first. I'll fill you up, then you can fill me up."

"Hussy. Aren't you afraid I'll get all fat and logy and sleepy if you make me eat a huge breakfast?"

"Oh, I'm sure I can think of a way of to wake you up." She bounced gently on his lap until he moaned. Then she jumped up. "Got to turn the bacon."

Breakfast was very good. "You're a grand cook, darling Eilidh."

She smiled. "Everyone in our house knows how to cook. My mother's an excellent cook but she is easily distracted. If she gets an idea she'll sit down and start making notes, forgetting what's on the stove. Daddy taught Ian and me—Daddy does it too—to keep an eye on her and stir things if her mind is someplace else. That's how Ian and I learned to cook."

He pushed his empty plate away, thinking how much he enjoyed looking at her. Her wonderful hair was coming loose from the bit of kitchen twine she'd impatiently tied around it while she was cooking. It had nearly destroyed him, watching her lift her arms to tie it, lifting the shirt, drawing it tight against her small perfect breasts. He wanted to loosen her hair completely, spread it around her shoulders and run his fingers through it.

He realized, suddenly, that it was not just to save on laundry that she hadn't put on her clothes. In her artless way she had been trying to seduce him. He grew hot all over, then warm with love.

"Will you marry me, Eilidh?" he said solemnly.

She laughed. "Because I can cook?"

"No. Well, partly. But mostly because I love you. And because I want to make love to you. Now." He stood and walked to her, holding out his hand.

She looked up at him. Then she rose and put her hand in his and he led her into the bedroom.

They stood facing each other by the bed. He reached for the shirt and drew it up over her head. She opened his jeans all the way and pushed them down, her hands warm against his thighs. She cupped him between her hands and he thought he would collapse at her feet in blissful worship.

"You are *miorbhuileach*," she said and he shuddered. She let him go and flung herself down on the bed, hands above her head in utter surrender, just like in one of her romance novels.

He tore off his jeans and threw himself down by her. "You are the most beautiful creature in the world."

She teased, "Pretty as a new-born calf?"

"Even prettier."

His warm brown eyes gleamed and she laughed. She reached out and pulled off his glasses, turned and put them on the bed stand behind her. "You won't need those."

He leaned over her and they kissed for a long time. Her sweet little tongue was avid against his and she wriggled and cooed her delight. "I'll never get tired of kissing you," she said.

He raised himself on one elbow and sent his free hand moving over her body, possessing each small luscious curve while he sucked her tongue deep into his mouth. Honey, he decided. She tasted like honey. He was maddened with desire, shivering and shuddering with it.

God, he had to have her. He wasn't quite sure how to go about it but he was learning fast.

The touch of his hand warmed her all over and she arched herself toward him, purring with happiness. He kissed the long plane of her throat and moved his mouth over her collarbone. "You have wonderful muscles here," he said, "and in your arms."

"Violinist's muscles. It takes a lot of strength to hold a violin and play through a concerto. I lift weights, sometimes, to get stronger."

"My little Amazon." He moved his mouth slowly to one of her breasts and kissed it tenderly.

"I'm sorry my breasts are so small," she whispered. "There's no weights you can lift to make them bigger."

He took her breast in his mouth, shivering with delight when he realized he could take nearly the whole inside and feel her hard little nipple against the roof of his mouth. "They're just right," he said. "They fill my mouth to perfection. Like little apples." His hand moved down and cupped her bottom. "Like apples here too." His hand tightened, squeezed. "I think I'll call you my little apple. How do I say that in the Gaelic?"

It was *miorbhuileach*, the way he made her feel; she could hardly think. "It's *ubhal. M'ubhal*, my apple. *M'ubhal beag*, my little apple."

"You-val." He tested the unfamiliar word, rolling it around. "No, I like apple better. It's got sharp little peaks in it, like your breasts have. My little love apple. No, two little love apples on top and two bigger ones down below. You're a whole orchard. All mine." He nuzzled his face between her breasts and began to work his way south.

He kissed each rib. "You're thin, though. I'll have to fatten you up with my cooking."

She sighed, "You can cook too? What do you cook?" She rolled her eyes in pleasure when his mouth went to her navel.

"Anything that I can make great masses of that last for a week. Spaghetti sauce, stew . . . " He moved his mouth down one wing of her pelvis and licked across her belly to the other one.

"Chili . . . " He parted the curls between her legs and caressed her. "Hot and spicy. And Eilidh for dessert."

He put his mouth on her and growled ferociously like an oversized puppy into the rosy curls.

She screamed something in the Gaelic and her hips arched off the bed. He put his hands under them and brought her hard against his mouth. She stiffened, screamed again and collapsed into his hands.

He lifted his head. "You are incredible," he said. "Nobody ever told me a woman was like that. Why doesn't anyone ever tell you the important things?"

"Well, I know them."

"How?"

"Romance novels. They're like a primer on sex." She laughed giddily when he rose up over her. She put her hands against his shoulders and pushed. "Lie down," she said. "I want to do the same thing to you."

"Eilidh, I don't think . . . " I don't think I can stand it, he wanted to say, but her hands warm on his body and her mouth hot against his nipples robbed him of speech and he collapsed on the bed. "I want to taste you," she whispered and took him in her mouth.

"Oh, God," he cried. "Stop—don't stop—oh, God!" He wrenched himself from her just in time. "I need to come into you now," he growled and she sprawled beneath him, legs parted, the picture of wanton womanhood.

He balanced himself on his elbows over her and thrust carefully.

"Oh, my," she gasped. "I hope there's room. Are you in me all the way yet?"

He had never in his wildest fantasies imagined that a woman would be so tight inside. He tried to go slowly but his control was slipping away and he wanted to bury himself deeper and deeper, lose himself completely and shout his ecstasy to the world.

"Please forgive me if I hurt you," he whispered. "I know it's painful for a woman the first time."

Something was happening inside Eilidh. She felt herself opening and stretching and it was wonderful beyond belief. She cried, "I don't care if it hurts, I want all of you inside me!" She shoved herself against him.

Taken completely by surprise, he answered with an urgent thrust, throwing inhibitions and caution out the window. They both felt it when her virginity was torn away. "Oh, it did hurt," she cried in a pitifully surprised voice and a little sob escaped her.

Joe felt like the worst brute in the world, like the worst kind of criminal. "Darling Eilidh, I'm so sorry. I'll come out of you. Why doesn't anyone teach men how to do this!" he cried in frustration.

Something else was happening to Eilidh. She was beginning to enjoy the feeling of fullness that had been so terrifying a moment ago. "Don't leave me . . . just move a little." She lifted her hips towards him and pulled them away, beginning a rhythm that she'd never encountered in any music she'd ever played. "No, don't leave, come back. Umm . . . deeper now . . . Oh, Joe!" Ecstasy spread through her, beginning between her legs and enveloping her whole body.

Now he felt like a hero, feeling her tightening and rippling against him. "You like it, don't you. Tell me . . . " he whispered in her ear.

"Aye," she said and screamed.

He went over the edge and plunged deep into an abyss of pleasure, shuddering and moaning.

Afterwards they lay quietly together until she said, "I'm glad it was you for my first time."

"And I'm glad it was you, for my first time."

"Really? It was your first time too? Why didn't you tell me?"

He turned his head away from her gaze. "I thought . . . women like an experienced lover. And when I hurt you I thought I was doing something wrong." He shivered. Even now he thought he could have done better, have hurt her less.

But she stretched her arms above her head again and undulated from side to side voluptuously. "Umm . . . I loved the way it hurt. It was like in a lovely romance novel. A bit of pain and then splendor. You were wonderful, darling Joe. I love you so much for saving yourself for me." She enveloped him in her large Skye blue eyes. "Just think of it. The first time for both of us and we came together. Something to tell our children."

"Well, maybe. Our grandchildren, maybe."

He was suddenly afraid he was squashing her. He turned over carefully, keeping himself within her and bringing her to lie on top of him. She sat up gingerly and drew her legs up under her hips.

He was nearly incoherent with pleasure. "Oh, God. How good that feels, my dearest, darling Eilidh. Oh, be careful. Don't take me so deep, you'll hurt yourself."

She leaned backwards, arched her body and put her hands down behind her in the Yoga position called the Camel. She moved and he moved. She writhed and he writhed. He exploded again and she felt something hot scalding up inside her. "Oh!" she cried and climaxed, the sensations this time in an entirely different place.

She threw herself down on top of him and curled up confidingly. In a minute he heard her soft breathing. She had fallen asleep in the sweetest little cat nap imaginable.

He held her close and wept with happiness.

Pansy, the little black cat, jumped gracefully onto the bed and settled herself against Joe's shoulder. Old Dog padded into the bedroom and put his chin on the bed. He would have liked to climb up onto it but his arthritis made it impossible. He circled the bedside rug three times and collapsed onto it with a grunt. They all slept.

Thirty-two

What is the need of Heaven
When earth can be so sweet?
Edna St. Vincent Millay

*W*hen he awoke and found her gone that evening he sprang out of bed and went looking for her, terrified again that it all been a dream.

She was in the kitchen, bent over the small refrigerator, her bare bottom temptingly raised in the air. When she straightened up again her hands were full of food.

"Yum, hummus. I love hummus. Wherever did you find it on the Island?"

"I brought it with me from Edinburgh. There's pita bread on the counter." He couldn't think of food; he was too busy devouring her beautiful body with his eyes.

She spread hummus on the pita bread, murmuring with delight as she crammed it greedily into her mouth. Then she turned back to the refrigerator to rummage through it again. "Grapes . . . apples . . . brilliant! Got any nuts and raisins?"

"In the cupboard. No, the next one."

She gathered the results of her foraging on the counter and surveyed it with delight. "Oh, darling Joe! Are you a vegetarian now?"

"Well, no. I just try not to eat a lot of meat. Are you a vegetarian?"

"Not a very devout one, I love chicken and fish too much." She gobbled more food.

How does she do it, he wondered. She's so slender. He watched, amazed, as her flat little belly began to round gently and expand outward with the quantity of food she was putting into it.

Then she stretched. "I want to brush my teeth. Oh, I don't have a tooth-brush. Yuck, I'll taste nasty when you put your tongue in my mouth."

"I have an extra toothbrush," he said, trembling.

"Goody. Oh, I know what let's do. Let's dance!"

Joe was an excellent waltzer, just as he'd said. He pulled her into his arms and swung her masterfully around the kitchen table, in a loop around the sofa, with a twirl in the space between the two rooms. Round and round they went, both hearing music in their heads. They didn't hear the same tune, but it didn't matter.

Pansy was curled up on the wide window seat sound asleep, paws tucked tidily under her chin and her tail wrapped around her nose. But Old Dog lifted his head and watched, and thumped his tail in rhythm.

At last Joe spun her into the bedroom. They fell into bed together and the rhythm continued and intensified. Just before he climaxed Joe heard a different tune, an old Gaelic song he'd never heard before but somehow knew. Where can that be coming from, he thought, perplexed. Cemetery Hill is at least three miles away; I could never hear them from here.

Then the beautiful girl in his arms arched her back, pressed herself up against him, crying his name. He still heard the music, but no longer cared where it came from. It was enough that it was there.

On the morning of the next day both were completely exhausted from their innocent, greedy passion. Joe lay in bed looking at his flaccid cock. It was too exhausted to rise. Eilidh complained that her sex was sore and he found something in his veterinary kit and rubbed it carefully into her while she purred with pleasure. "My nipples are sore, too," she teased and he rubbed the balm into them.

"What is that stuff?" she asked.

"Udder balm," he said.

"Udder bliss," she sighed.

Joe smiled. Then he laughed and laughed while she watched him, delighted at her joke.

He bent over to taste her mouth. "I suppose your lips are sore as well. Would you like some balm rubbed there?"

"No," she said and looped her arms around his neck. "Kiss them and make them better." Then she got up and fixed a huge breakfast of scrambled eggs, bacon (forgetting that she was sort of a vegetarian), toast and a pot of tea.

"What day is it?" he mumbled as he ate.

"Tuesday, I think."

"After breakfast we'll go and see your parents." She looked puzzled. "I want to ask your father—and your mother, too—for your hand in marriage."

She was so pleased by that idea that she jumped up, ran around the table and sat on his lap. "Darling, you're so sweet and old-fashioned. Daddy will love it." They kissed, the flavors of egg, toast and each other mingling in their mouths. He squeezed her breast possessively. Mine, he thought. She's mine. Finally he said, "Get dressed, my angel, and we'll walk up to your house."

"If I can still walk," she giggled.

He wondered uneasily what her parents would say about the two days she'd spent with him. But then, they'd not come after her and she'd assured him she'd told them where she was going to be.

When they walked into *Taigh Rois* they found not only Jamie and Màiri, but Darroch as well.

"If we're interrupting . . . ," began Joe.

Màiri leaped to her feet. "Eilidh, where have you been?" she demanded.

Eilidh looked defiant. "I've been with Joe."

"For two days and two nights?" said Màiri in astonishment.

"Aye."

Joe braced himself for recriminations, denunciations, a furious father, a weeping mother. But Jamie and Màiri just looked at each other, then back at Eilidh.

"So that's how it is," said Jamie. He had suspected as much, and had tried to reassure his wife. "That's all right, then."

Màiri nodded. "I'd not have worried, Joe, if I'd known she was with you."

Joe looked sternly at his *inamorata*. "You said you told them where you were."

"I left a message saying I was with a friend," she muttered. "I don't have to say which friend."

"Oh, Eilidh," mourned Joe. This was the last thing he wanted, to get off on the wrong foot with his future in-laws. "You shouldn't have done that. It's not right to worry your parents."

All four of them looked at him and he blushed. "Well, it isn't. If one of my sisters had done that to my mother I would have told her off good."

He'd felt an enormous responsibility for his young siblings. It was Joe who'd instilled in the two girls an awareness of treating their hard-worked mother with respect and consideration.

Eilidh said, "Aye, my darling. I'm sorry, Mummy. I'm sorry, Daddy."

Joe smiled at her, then said awkwardly, "If you're busy, Mr. and Mrs. MacDonald, and Darroch, we can come back later."

The three exchanged glances. Jamie said, "No, go ahead. What is it?" He had a strong feeling he was going to like their news.

"I can leave if it's something personal," began Darroch.

Eilidh said, "No, stay. I want everyone to know. I love Joe and he loves me and we're going to be married!"

"Oh, Eilidh," said Joe mournfully. "I had my speech all prepared. Would you please let me talk?"

"I'm sorry, darling," she whispered. "You go right ahead. Everybody forget what I've already said."

The older three looked at each other. Jamie grinned. "She always did blurt out whatever was on her mind. She takes after you in that, *m'eudail*," he said, looking at Màiri. "All right, young Joe. Go on with what you were saying."

Determined to get it out properly, Joe began, "Sir, and Mrs. MacDonald, ma'am, I have the honor to ask for your daughter's hand in marriage."

"I see," said Jamie, keeping as straight a face as he could, under the circumstances, and trying to look surprised. "And do you love my daughter? And does she love you?"

Eilidh, bubbling, opened her mouth to blurt out something else but Joe stilled her with a look.

Hmm, thought Darroch, he does that just like Jamie does to Màiri. This has the makings of a promising relationship.

"Aye, sir. We love each other. And I can assure you that I'll look after her. I have a good profession and I can take care of my wife."

"I suppose you'll want to live in Edinburgh," said Màiri sadly.

"Mummy, I already live in Edinburgh."

"But not all the time. You still come home to us every summer, after the orchestra season is over."

"Ma'am," said Joe, asserting himself again, "I have been offered, and accepted, a position as junior partner to Mr. Cunningham, the vet here on Eilean Dubh. I intend to make the Island my home."

"*Miorbhuileach!*" exclaimed Jamie.

"So you'll be living here?" said Màiri hopefully.

Eilidh and Joe looked at each other, suddenly serious. "Part of the time. She'll be in Edinburgh for the winter, for the orchestra. We've accepted that we'll have to live apart, part of the year."

"How awful . . . "

"How will you manage?"

"Well," said Joe. He gave Darroch a private look. "Someone once told me that it's better to have part of what you love than none of it. And we think that's true. We're going to do the best we can."

"Very wise," murmured Darroch.

"When do you want to get married?" asked Màiri.

"Right away. Next week," bubbled Eilidh.

Màiri looked slyly at Jamie. "Takes after you in that, she does."

"People have been whispering that you two were engaged, and we've wondered why you haven't told us." The foreboding that had been in Jamie's mind for weeks suddenly came to fruition and sent a chill through him. He took his daughter's hand and stared into her eyes. "Something is wrong, Eilidh, something happened. What was it?"

Eilidh could hide the truth no longer; she'd never been able to keep a secret from her father when he looked at her that way. "I've wanted to marry Joe for ages but I was frightened . . . about making love." She hesitated, looked at Joe, and then stammered, "I left the orchestra early because there was a man who tried to rape me."

Jamie said blankly, "What?" Even with the Sight, he had not expected this.

The words spilled out. "He's an important fundraiser and the orchestra asked me to make appearances with him at cocktail parties and places where people with money get together. I'd play a couple of tunes, smile at people and he'd hit them up for money." She swallowed hard. "He was always really nice to me, he's twice my age and he's married. I thought he was safe. Then after our last fundraiser, he asked if I would let him come in to use the phone. He said he had to call his sick wife."

Reliving it, she was cold with terror. She groped blindly with her hand and Joe took it in one of his, then wrapped his other arm around her. She said, "When he came in he said he wasn't going home. That I must know what he wanted, that he'd given me enough signs and that he was tired of waiting.

"I told him I was a virgin and begged him to leave me alone but he said it had been a long time since he'd had a virgin and that he was quite looking forward to it. He said it would hurt, but that pain was part of sex and the more it hurt the more I'd like it."

Jamie was trembling with fury and Màiri, white with shock, was weeping.

Darroch was as angry as Jamie; he was gritting his teeth so hard that they felt as though they'd snap off. This was what Joe had told Jean, he realized suddenly. No wonder she'd been upset.

"I said I'd scream and he told me to go ahead, the walls were so thick no one would hear me." She hung her head in shame. "I asked how he knew and he said he'd been paying most of my rent for months. He called me a fool for thinking I could get an apartment like mine for what I was paying. All of a sudden I realized that everyone must know, that's why they'd looked at me so oddly when I talked about how lucky I was to have such a nice place and so cheap. They all probably thought I was sleeping with him. That I was a slut, out to get what I could from a rich married man."

She shuddered and Joe pulled her closer. "Then he leaped on me. He said he wanted to tear my clothes off but the dress was too expensive. He twisted my arm behind my back. He said he'd break it and asked me what would happen to my music then. Nobody'd want a violinist with a broken arm, he said."

She turned to Joe and buried her head against his chest and wept.

"Oh, *mo nighean*," said Màiri helplessly. She walked over and put her arms around both of them and the three cried together.

Jamie and Darroch looked at each other, speechless with rage and outrage.

At last Jamie said quietly, "How did you get away from him, darling Eilidh?"

Joe said, "The phone rang and she snatched it up. It was a wrong number but she pretended it was her brother and that he was just five minutes away. She said he should break the door down, that someone was trying to rape her."

"You are clever, *m'eudail*," said Jamie in admiration.

Darroch said, "Did he hurt your arm?"

"It was sore for a few days and I was terrified he'd wrenched something. But it's all right now."

Jamie rose like a python uncoiling. "He's a dead man," he said pleasantly, rubbing one fisted hand into the palm of the other.

Darroch nodded. "I'll come with you. Can't let you have all the fun."

"Glad to have your company. I hate to travel alone."

Joe looked at the women, expecting them to remonstrate against this bloodthirstiness. But Màiri was nodding her head in grim agreement and Eilidh was running across the room to throw her arms around her father's neck. "Thank you, Daddy," she whispered. "I've been so afraid that he'll hurt another woman."

He whispered something back, looking at her intently.

Eilidh said, "No, I'm all right. Joe made me all right, with his wonderful loving."

Jamie said, "Thank you, young man. Eilidh, you should have come to me with this."

She hung her head. "I was ashamed, at first. I thought I'd done something wrong, that I'd led him on. That it was my fault. I couldn't tell any of you. Except finally Joe."

Darroch stood up. "If we're all settled, I'll nip on home and tell Jean I'm off to Edinburgh tomorrow." Near the door he paused and turned back. "I shouldn't think we'd have to kill the bastard, Jamie."

"No?" Jamie raised his eyebrows.

"No. I've no fancy to see the inside of an Edinburgh jail."

Jamie said in astonishment, "They'd put us in jail? For killing the man who tried to rape my daughter?" Darroch nodded solemnly and Jamie said, "Of all the damn fool Lowlander ideas. How the devil do they protect their womenfolk?"

Darroch shrugged his shoulders. "I've no idea. We'll talk on the chopper, think of something interesting to do to him." He grinned wickedly.

Joe stared from one man to the other. Surely they had been joking; they'd not really entertained thoughts of murder. But they seemed perfectly serious and he had the Lowland Scot's inborn wariness of what mad things wild Highlanders might do.

He blurted, "I'm going with you."

"Of course," Jamie said; he'd taken it for granted.

Joe said awkwardly, "I'd best be going home, then, and get ready."

"Chopper leaves at eleven. I'll call Murdoch and have him save three seats. Meet us here at nine for breakfast."

"Right. Well, goodbye, everyone." His eyes were on Eilidh.

"I'll walk you to the gate," she said demurely.

At the gate they kissed and clung to each other. Eilidh whispered in his ear, "When you come back, darling, we'll spend another two days making love. Maybe three."

Feeling very responsible, he said, "I'd better get some condoms in Edinburgh."

"Ugh, nasty plastic. I'll have Mummy take me to the doctor and he can give me those pills. After all, we're going to be married next week."

He shook his head. "I'll have to have time to tell my mother and sisters so they can all come. I can't be married without my family here."

"Of course, darling Joe. I'll put Mummy to work on that too, she loves to organize things."

Thirty-three

Now's the day and now's the hour;
See the front o' battle lower . . .
Robert Burns

The secretary heard the fierce wave of whispers that swept through the department well before she heard the beautiful deep voice. "Good morning," the voice said.

She looked up. Twenty-five feet and seven hundred pounds of Scottish manhood stood before her desk. One was the handsomest man she'd ever seen, one was the angriest, one looked like an oversize Greek god and one was uncannily familiar. Four pair of eyes, three blue and one brown, stared down at her.

She gulped. "Umm . . . may I help you?"

"We're here to see Mr. Chase Campbell," said Darroch pleasantly.

"Do you have an appointment?" she babbled.

"No." Darroch smiled.

"Well, he's a very busy man. I don't think he can see you without an appointment. I'll take in your names, though, and your business."

"You may tell him it's a young lady's fiancé, father, brother and honorary uncle," said Darroch, raising his voice deliberately. "And our business is private." The beautiful voice rumbled with menace and carried to the farthest desk in the department.

Three pretty, very young women smiled grimly. So the bastard was finally going to get what was coming to him, they all thought. All three hoped it would be violent. And loud, so that they could hear all of it.

Joe, growing impatient, jerked his head towards the nearest closed door. "Is that his office?"

"Yes," the secretary stammered and jumped to her feet as the four turned toward the door in one fluid motion. "Let me tell him you're here."

She rushed to put herself in front of the door and found herself taken by the shoulders and gently set aside by the Greek god. He smiled at her and she trembled with pleasure. "Dinna fash yersel', lassie," Ian said in the old way. "We'll announce ourselves."

The man behind the desk looked up and his jaw dropped. "Who the hell are you?" he demanded. His eyes flicked over the four nervously.

Darroch said, "Good morning, Mr. Campbell. This is Mr. Joseph Munro, Eilidh MacDonald's fiancé. Mr. James MacDonald, her father. Mr. Ian MacDonald, her brother. And my name is Darroch Mac an Rìgh. I'm a sort of honorary uncle."

Chase Campbell went deathly pale but he managed to say, "Ah. Eilidh's family. And how is the dear child? I heard she'd gone back to her Island. Is she ill?"

"Sick of you," snarled Jamie.

Darroch shook his head reprovingly at Jamie. "So you know about our Island. I wonder perhaps if you know what the penalty there is for rape?"

Chase Campbell turned even whiter. "Why would I?"

"It's death. Traditionally meted out by the victim's family. Now in your case . . . " Darroch considered him carefully. "It's attempted rape. The penalty for that—in the old days, of course, we're much more civilized now—was only castration. The would-be rapist's balls are squeezed in a very large pair of pinchers until they ruptured." He smiled. "There's a set of the pinchers in our Museum. Nasty looking equipment. Must have been extremely painful. It did cross my mind to bring them with me."

Campbell was shaking but he was determined to brazen it out. "I don't know what you're talking about but I'd advise you to get out of my office before I call the police. If you're accusing me of rape . . . "

"Attempted rape," Darroch corrected. "The young lady was clever enough to convert a simple wrong number into a phone call from her brother."

"A wrong number. The cunning little bitch," Campbell snarled, forgetting himself.

A rumble of anger arose from three throats and three men took a step forward. Darroch raised his hand for restraint. "I should be very careful how you refer to Miss MacDonald," he advised. "Eilean Dubh men are particular about how our women are addressed."

Campbell snapped, "Why don't you go to the police if you think you have a complaint against me. Otherwise get the hell out."

"I'm well aware the police require proof. Fortunately, all we require is Eilidh's word. And we have it on her authority that you attempted to take advantage, in the most evil way, of her innocence." He shook his head. "To threaten to break her arm . . . And you call yourself a music lover."

He smiled at Joe. "Thanks to her fiancé she seems to have suffered no lasting harm. We intend to see that remains the case. If we hear of any attempt to sabotage her career—and believe me, we'll hear—we will not be lenient the next time.

"And another thing: Eilidh's told the orchestra's manager exactly what happened. He's very sensitive to sexual harassment issues, as everyone should be these days, and he will ensure that other arts organizations know about your unfortunate tendencies. He will see that your career of victimizing young women is over. Finished. You may, of course, continue to raise funds for these groups. In fact, I encourage you to do so. We're all supporters of funding for the arts.

"I believe our business with you is concluded. We'll say good morning." The glares and clenched fists of the other three told him they were far from finished with Campbell but Darroch shook his head at them. "Come along, mo chàiradean," he said firmly and moved toward the door. Reluctantly they turned to follow.

Campbell walked from behind the safety of his desk. As Darroch had anticipated, he had to have the last word. He mumbled defiantly, "Little teasing slut, I know she wanted it."

All four turned back but Jamie's reaction was the swiftest. His punch started from his toes and carried him across the room to plant his fist in Campbell's belly. He crumpled to the ground at Jamie's feet, gasping for breath, tears rolling down his face.

Jamie looked down at him with scorn. "Your gut's soft, man. You need to get more exercise."

Joe was beside him suddenly. "Get up," he snarled. "It's my turn."

Obligingly Darroch reached down and hauled up the other man, whimpering with terror, by the scruff of his neck.

They faced each other. Joe said, "You damned bastard." He raised his

fist and aimed it at Campbell's face. For a long moment, they stood sus-
pended in time. Joe looked into the other man's eyes and read anger, pain
and something else . . . It was frustrated lust. He had really wanted Eilidh,
Joe realized. He knew what his punishment would be.

He gripped Campbell tightly by the throat and leaned forward to
whisper in his ear so only the two of them could hear. "She's beautiful
naked, with her hair rippling down over her breasts. She screams with
pleasure when I make love to her. And she's as sweet as honey between her
legs and you'll never have a taste of her." Campbell shuddered with desire.

Joe said, releasing him suddenly so that he fell back against the desk, "I
wouldn't dirty my hands with you."

Darroch hated violence. He nodded his approval at Joe and put a hand
on his shoulder. "Well done, lad," he murmured.

Ian stepped forward. "Fortunately, I'm not so fastidious." He slapped
Campbell with his enormous open hand. The other man's head jerked sideways with the blow and he collapsed at their feet again.

Darroch sighed. "Everyone's had a piece of you except me. What'll it be,
I wonder?" He looked around thoughtfully, then took a piece of paper from
the desk and with his long slender fingers folded it into an admiral's hat. He
set it carefully on Campbell's head.

The other three burst into laughter.

"Suits you, it does," said Ian.

"Come along, lads," said Darroch, shepherding them out. He opened
the door wide so that the entire office, watching avidly, could see their tyrant
boss collapsed on the floor wearing a silly paper hat.

Darroch paused at the door. "So long, sailor," he said, whipping off a
mock salute. The laughter of the four rang through the office and was
echoed by the other employees. A great gale of laughter rose up through the
ranks and followed them as they stalked out.

Out in the sunlight, the four smiled at each other. "How about a pint,
lads?" said Darroch.

"Aye," said Jamie. "Intimidation is thirsty work."

"There's a grand little pub near here, just off Prince's Street," said Ian,
who knew almost every pub in Edinburgh. "Best pickled onions in the city."

Ensconced in the pub with plates of bread and cheese in front of them,
they waited for their beers. Ian passed around the bowl of pungent pickled
onions. Darroch shook his head and Jamie shuddered but Ian popped two in
his mouth. He offered the bowl to Joe. "Eat up," he said. "They're delicious."

Joe took one and valiantly put it in his mouth. A lightning bolt of pickle, garlic and onion seared the delicate membranes and brought tears to his eyes. "Wonderful," he mumbled through the pain.

When the pints arrived, Darroch lifted his in the air. "To the four muske-teers," he said. "*Slàinte mhath.*"

Joe looked at the other three. He'd lost his father when he was very young. At university he'd so immersed himself in his studies that he'd not had time for close male friendships. Now the unfamiliar pleasure of mascu-line bonding swept over him. He was part of a family now, he realized. He had a father, a brother and an honorary uncle.

Tears welled up again, from emotion this time, and spilled down his cheeks. He put down his pint and pulled out his handkerchief and dabbed at his eyes, unashamed.

Ian said kindly, "Those pickled onions are fierce, aren't they. Have another?"

Joe shook his head. He raised his glass. "The four musketeers. Slan-jah vah!"

After a while Jamie was well into his third pint with no discernible change in voice or behavior. Darroch nursed his second. Their conversation had slipped into the Gaelic and they sat, a Hebridean island, in an Edinburgh pub.

Joe sipped cautiously at his first pint; he wasn't much of a drinker. Ian drained his third. He had demolished a huge plate of steak pie, bridies, chips and beans and now looked at the world and his future brother-in-law with cheerful enthusiasm.

Buoyed by his acceptance Joe ventured to ask the question that had nagged at the back of his mind. "Ian, I wonder if you might know . . . where I could buy . . . uh . . . condoms."

Ian said absently, "Chemists. Have to ask for them, they keep them under the counter. Damned Puritans." Then his eyes narrowed. "Why?"

"In case the Island doctor won't give Eilidh the Pill until we're married. It would be wrong of me to get her pregnant, so soon."

Ian said dangerously, "You've been sleeping with my sister."

Joe lifted his head. "Aye, I have that honor. We're lovers. If you have a problem with that I'll be happy to discuss it with you outside." They glared at each other.

As an actor Darroch was always sensitive to the change in people's voices. He glanced their way and said to Jamie, "The puppies are snarling at each other."

Jamie said lazily, "Aye. You're closest. Just give that young whelp of mine a knock on the top of his head to settle him down."

"I will not. He might take exception, and he's twice as big as me."

"He's twice as big as everybody," Jamie muttered. "I wish to God I knew where he gets it."

Darroch considered. "Màiri's grandfather on her mother's side. Biggest man the Island ever saw, a veritable giant."

"I'm glad he comes by it honestly. I was thinking a cloud of radiation had maybe drifted over from Dounreay."

The young men's voices had lowered alarmingly and Jamie raised his. "Here, you lot," he snapped and growled a command in the Gaelic.

Ian's head jerked around to his father. "Aye, sir. I'm sorry, sir." He turned to Joe. "Sorry. No business of mine. No offense." He held out his hand to Joe who shook it gravely.

"None taken," he replied.

The waitress had been hovering around their table all evening, to the dismay of her other customers who'd been clearing their throats, glaring and finally waving their arms in a desperate attempt to gain her attention.

She ignored them. She was sure she'd seen the dark-haired man on television and she had a hopeful feeling that the biggest one was the man who'd starred in that movie about Rob Roy. He was much handsomer, and much younger, in person. The one with glasses was probably a film executive, she thought hopefully.

She didn't care who the fourth man was. She was just enjoying looking at him.

The five women at the table next to them had given up all attempts to carry on a conversation and were watching and listening avidly, wondering why they could not understand what the two older men were saying. "French," whispered one. "No, I think it's Czech, or Russian," said another. All five wondered why they'd not been able to gain even a flicker of attention from the men, despite sideways glances with fluttering eyelashes and skirts discreetly hiked just above the knees.

"Maybe they're gay," hissed the third.

"No, they can't be. They're too big."

"What's that got to do with it?" asked the fourth.

The waitress hovered. "Can I get anything else for you?" she said hopefully to Ian.

He held up his glass to ask for another round but Jamie said firmly, "Coffee, love. For all of us."

Wounded, Ian looked at his father. Jamie snapped in the Gaelic, "You've had enough, you great pillock. Do you think we want to drag you home through the streets of Edinburgh in a shocking state of drunkenness? In front of all these Lowlanders?"

"Aye, sir," said Ian meekly and turned limpid blue eyes on the waitress. "Coffee, *m'aingeal*, and have you anything sweet in the kitchen, besides yourself?"

She fluttered. "There's apple bramble tart, sir."

Ian stared at her mouth and drawled tenderly, "A piece of the tart, then." His eyes flickered up and down her in appreciation. "A big one. And cream." He grinned at her and she staggered away, nearly running down several customers.

Oh, he's good, thought Darroch, remembering his own days as a charmer.

In the end it was only Jamie's furious glare that kept Ian from bursting into triumphant song as they wended their way back to his flat for the night.

Thirty-four

*T*he four musketeers returned to Eilean Dubh, to find wedding arrangements in full cry. Joe consulted his mother and sisters and a date was set. Màiri booked the Rose for the reception and she, Sheilah and Eilidh began planning the food.

The only piece of the puzzle remaining was where they were to be married, and by whom, since none of the three MacDonalds belonged to a kirk. "Registry office for the wedding, I suppose," said Màiri.

Joe shook his head. "Minister Donald will marry us at the kirk."

Jamie said, "But we're not members. He probably won't . . . "

Joe said, "I'm a member of his kirk," and they all stared at him in disbelief. "And I've already asked him, and he's said yes."

Joe was a committed Presbyterian and a regular churchgoer and on his arrival on Eilean Dubh he had checked out both Minister Donald and Minister Tòrmod's kirks. He was at a disadvantage, since both services were in the Gaelic. But there was something about Minister Donald's kirk and the Minister himself that he liked.

He made an appointment to see Minister Donald and expressed his desire to join his kirk. "I must tell you frankly, Minister, that I am not a Free Presbyterian, and there are some aspects of your beliefs with which I am not in agreement. Perhaps I might come see you occasionally and we could talk."

Talk? About theology? The Minister was astonished. He rarely met anyone with an interest in religion beyond their weekly attendance at kirk.

Even Darroch, with whom he used to have stimulating arguments, had his mind full of other matters, now that he had a wife and baby.

"There is one other thing," said Joe. "Since I do not have the Gaelic I cannot understand your sermons. Would it be possible for me to get an English translation from you each week?"

The Minister smiled, delighted. "Of course."

Joe began a regular pattern of visits at the Manse. On one of them, in answer to a question from Minister Donald, he confessed that he had seriously considered becoming a minister himself, at one time.

"Why did you change your mind?" Donald asked.

Joe smiled gently. "I had no problem with writing sermons or conducting services. It was the giving of advice. I never felt that I was wise enough myself to tell others how to live their lives. So I decided my ministry should be with the animals. They never ask for advice. Remember, Minister, what Job says:

But ask now the beasts, and they shall teach thee;
And the fowls of the air, and they shall teach thee;
And the fishes of the sea shall declare unto thee.
Who knoweth not in all these that the hand of the Lord
has wrought this?
In whose hand is the soul of every living thing,
and the breath of all mankind.

"I prefer to be the one who is taught, not the teacher." Joe smiled again.

The Minister looked at his young friend with admiration. A loss to the clergy, he thought. Humility of the soul was a rare and touching attribute.

The wedding took place within a month and the reception was followed by a rousing cèilidh at the Citizens' Hall. There was fiddling and singing and dancing, and plenty of food and whisky. It went on to the wee hours of the morning.

Joe and Eilidh slipped away in the middle of the party and went home to their little cottage and their animals. Pansy and the birds were soundly asleep but Old Dog pulled himself painfully to his feet to come to the door and greet them, as was his right and his duty.

The newlyweds let him out and waited until he was ready to come in. They put out fresh food and water for the animals, then went to bed, made glorious, passionate love and fell asleep nestled together spoon-fashion.

The peace of Eilean Dubh fell over the cottage and all was silent, within and without.

PART III

Ian and Sally

Thirty-five

It gets to be kind of lonely
But at the same time off-putting,
Counterproductive, as you realize once again
That the longest way is the most efficient way,
The one that looped among islands . . .

John Ashbery

Ian MacDonald's life so far had been shaped by three factors: he was Màiri and Jamie's son, he was Eilidh's twin, and he was—and had been since the age of six—the tallest boy and man on the Island.

His remarkable height was accompanied by a muscular build. He had never been thin or reedy, never been less than strong. Being tall and strong meant never being intimidated by a bully, never having to fear the challenge of another boy. And it meant he developed a remarkable sense of self and self-confidence from a very young age. He was also stubbornly hard-headed.

Fortunately he had also learned calmness and self-control from Jamie and kindness and compassion from Màiri. She ingrained in him as well her deep love of her Island and her sense of responsibility for its well being. Between them, they created a man who was both strong and gentle.

He learned music, every Eilean Dubh child's birthright, from both parents. Jamie started the twins on miniature fiddles when they were five years old. Ian, asserting himself, refused to try, so Màiri put him on the piano even though his legs barely reached the pedals. He didn't like that either, so they contented themselves by teaching him to sing. Then at the age of seven he demanded to learn to play the drums.

Jamie said to him, "Whomever will we get to teach you?"

Ian said, "I'll teach myself."

Jamie said, "Wherever will we get a set of drums?"

Ian said, "I'll make one for myself." And he did. Old Angus Mac-a-Phi helped him.

He fell in love with Sheilah Morrison of the Rose Hotel when he was nine years old, and figured out that getting her husband Gordon to teach him how to play the button-box accordion was a way to be around her. Within three months he'd fallen in love with the accordion as well. Then he decided he did like music after all and Màiri had him playing piano by the end of the year.

And then he discovered the bagpipes. That was his chosen instrument from then on and he was very, very good.

Besides music, he loved sports and his studies. As he grew older, science classes captured his imagination. His attic bedroom became both workshop and laboratory and a constant source of worry to his parents, who feared he'd either set the cottage on fire or blow it up. Fortunately they did not know about his collection of live insects and small rodents. He cleaned his own room just to keep his mother out of it, figuring that the less she knew about its contents the happier she would be.

He loved chemistry and thought he'd be a chemist when he grew up, then a biochemist, then a medical researcher. Then it dawned on him: to pursue any of these careers he would have to leave his Island. He was too much his mother's child to entertain that as a possibility. He worried and thought for weeks, and then he woke up one morning with his mind made up.

He would be a doctor, and he would live and work on Eilean Dubh. It was as simple as that.

Having made his decision he caught the post bus up to Airgead one day and installed himself in Ros MacPherson's waiting room. "He's all booked today, Ian," said the worried receptionist, noting the determined look on the boy's face. "He really can't see you, unless it's an emergency."

Ian waved his hand in dismissal. "It is all right, I will wait. I will wait until his appointments are completed, all afternoon if necessary. I wish to speak to him about becoming a doctor."

She relayed this conversation to Ros MacPherson. Intrigued, he instructed her to send Ian in at his tea break. Despite his heavy workload, he always paused briefly for a cup of tea in the afternoon. Otherwise he found he got so overwhelmed that he was in danger of mixing up gall bladders with pregnancies.

Ian wasted no time. "I am going to become a doctor, Mr. MacPherson, and if you permit, I would like to work with you here on the Island after I qualify. Can you tell me how to go about it?"

Flabbergasted, Ros took a deep breath. These were words he'd been waiting all his working life to hear. He'd never had an assistant for any long period of time. He'd made do with students from Edinburgh and the occasional newly-graduated physician who swiftly determined that country life as personified by a tiny Gaelic-speaking Island was not at all what was wanted. He'd even made the mistake, once, of hiring a retired doctor from Glasgow who turned out to be an alcoholic of the most appallingly sodden kind, who'd thought that he could practice both his profession of doctor and his avocation of drunk in an undemanding rural setting. He was swiftly sent packing.

Ros had finally given up on doctors and concentrated on getting Eilean Dubh girls off to nursing school on the mainland, since girls were easier to lure back home, bound as they were by family ties. He'd developed quite a good corps of nurses and a nurse midwife, and they'd trained aides to help out.

It worked and the Island's medical needs were met, but Ros still felt as though he were on a moving sidewalk that would throw him off if he didn't keep marching briskly forward. He needed help and he wanted a colleague, someone with whom to discuss cases and exchange advice. It was lonely, being Eilean Dubh's only doctor, and he craved companionship.

And here sat Ian MacDonald, the brightest young man in the High School, and he wanted to become a doctor. Ros sent up a prayer of thanks to the One Who Listens, and leaned forward towards the new recruit. They spent so much time together that day that Ros' appointment schedule was set back severely, but at the end of the interview Ian had the information he needed to chart both his education and his future career. And he had a job: he would help out at the Clinic after school.

He completed High School with a stunning array of A-levels and went off to Edinburgh to university and to medical school. He never looked back.

Thirty-six

How often does a man need to see a woman?
Once!
Once is enough, but a second time will confirm if it be she,
She who will be a fountain of everlasting mystery . . .
Walter James Turner

*J*ean's daughter from her first marriage, Sally Abbott, came to Eilean Dubh when baby Rosie was about a month old. She had finished spring semester at the University of Wisconsin and hopped on a plane, eager to see her new sister and to help her mother with the baby. She'd gotten a job with Sheilah at the Rose Hotel, to further her experience in culinary matters, and moved into Jean's little thatched cottage, at the head of the lane.

She was at *Taigh Rois* one day, sitting on the sofa with the baby. Rosie was half asleep, lying flat on Sally's lap, looking up at her with a baby's drowsy expression guaranteed to win the hardest hearts. Sally's heart was particularly soft. She was talking to the baby in the absurd doting way loving adults talk to babies.

Rosie burped. A dribble of milk ran out of her mouth and she choked. Sally swept the baby up onto her shoulder, patting her back vigorously. Rosie coughed and sputtered and burped again, loudly. A hiccup of milk transferred itself to Sally's shoulder. She sighed and looked around for help.

The door had been left open for the breezes and for Mairi's cat to wander in and out. The shadow that darkened the doorway was enormous. Sally stared.

"*Feasgar math*," a deep voice said. Sally found herself staring at the largest man she had ever seen. He ducked his head to pass through the threshold and stopped there.

He looks just like Jamie, Sally thought, bemused, devastatingly handsome, with thick blond hair and a sturdy muscular frame, but he was about six inches taller and broader in proportion. He was taller even than Darroch Mac an Rìgh.

He, for his part, saw a slender, beautiful girl with a cloud of red-brown hair, holding a baby.

He did not have the gift of the Sight, like his father and his sister, but something about this woman's appearance burned itself into his mind. Destiny, sitting on the couch with a baby in her arms. Bells clanged.

He advanced into the room. Sally clung to the baby. They stared at each other.

Sally whispered, "Hi. Would you mind getting me a fresh diaper—I mean, nappy. They're on the kitchen table."

He brought one to her. While she wiped her shoulder and positioned the clean part of the diaper under the baby's head he said, "That's Rosie. You must be her sister from America."

"Yes. My name is Sally."

Sal-lee. The unfamiliar name reverberated in his mind. He bent his great length over her and touched the baby lightly, murmuring in the Gaelic.

"Who are you?" Sally said.

"I'm Ian MacDonald. Màiri and Jamie's son."

"Oh, sure. I should have figured that out. You look just like your father. But you're so much bigger," she blurted.

He grinned. "They say I take after my grandfather, my mother's father. He was the biggest man on the Island in his day."

Sally smiled at him and his heart contracted with pleasure. She said, "I'm glad to meet you." Testing her knowledge of the unfamiliar Gaelic, she ventured, "I suppose they call you Ian . . . more. Is that right?"

"Yes. Ian *Mór*, big Ian. And they call you *breagha*. Beautiful."

Sally blushed and ducked her head. This was too much for her. With all her flirtatious expertise with men she could think of nothing to say. She was usually glib when she met a new man but something about this one hobbled her tongue.

He said abruptly, "Are you married?"

"No."

"Engaged?"

"No." Sally relaxed. She was on familiar ground now. Next he would ask her for a date.

But he didn't. "May I hold the baby?" he asked. When she nodded he sat down beside her and scooped Rosie up off her lap. His large hands brushed the tops of her thighs and the contact sent small electric shocks through her.

He swung the baby up to his shoulder and murmured in her ear. Sally felt a twinge of envy, imagining his hands on her shoulders, his breath against her skin. She blushed again.

The elder MacDonalds and Mac an Rìghs came into the cottage. He rose gracefully for such a large man, handed the baby to Sally and went forward to put his arms around his mother. Màiri disappeared into his embrace, almost smothered by his hug. Then he embraced his father and they spoke in the Gaelic.

He nodded respectfully to Jean, then extended his hand to Darroch, who said, "*Fàilte*, Ian. Jean, you remember Ian, don't you?" Ian's appearances on the Island had been few, the last two years, because of his deep involvement with medical school. And he'd missed Darroch's and Jean's wedding because he'd had a rare opportunity to help out in a clinic in Africa.

Jean said, "Of course. Have you and Sally introduced yourselves?"

He turned to grin at Sally and said, "I have been making the acquaintance of both your beautiful daughters." His tone was possessive and Jean stared in surprise. Jamie raised his eyebrows.

Darroch said, "Aye, they are, aren't they." His tone too was possessive. He moved into the room and sat down by Sally and told her, "Ian is home from medical school in Edinburgh. Back for his summer holidays."

"How's school going, Ian?" asked Jean.

"Very well, Mrs. Jean." He sank into a chair. "We are now at a most interesting part in the curriculum. " And he began to describe his current courses in physiology and anatomy, cheerfully assuming all his listeners would find them as fascinating as he did. When he reached the part about dissections, everyone stirred uneasily.

Darroch, noting the expression on Jean's face, stood up. He knew she was still subject to occasional twinges of nausea, left over from her pregnancy. "Time for us to go, *mo chridhe*. Baby needs her feed and a nap." And I need Jean in bed with me, he thought happily. After the long abstinence of late pregnancy and post-delivery healing, he and Jean had only just begun to make love again, and sex was all he thought of lately. And sleep. Sex and sleep and not necessarily in that order.

He gathered Rosie from Ian's arms and turned to Jean, eyebrows raised.

"Coming, lovie," she murmured, gathering up baby gear. "See you later, folks."

"I should go, too," said Sally.

"Are you staying in Darroch's mother's cottage? I will walk you there," Ian announced, unfolding himself up from the chair.

Pleased, Sally gave him her patented smile that had never yet failed to fascinate a man and headed for the door, Ian close behind her. Bemused by the smile, he almost forgot to duck his head at the lintel and narrowly escaped a hard bump on his forehead.

Sally had recovered her self-possession, now that the smile had worked, and she chatted gaily all the way to her cottage. Ian said little. He was absorbing her presence at his side even as he listened to her sweet voice. At the cottage, he turned to her, noting her height with pleasure. And she had beautiful long flowing hair that was the color of an Islay whisky, sparkling green eyes and her body had all the right curves and indentations.

Ian liked long hair. He adored lovely eyes. And he was crazy about a full bosom and well-rounded hips. He could hardly believe his luck, to find such a woman, unattached and here on Eilean Dubh, and obviously intrigued by him.

He fancied he knew something about Americans, having made friends at his university with a student from Texas. They like the direct approach. "You are lovely," he announced.

Sally stopped in mid-spate, then smiled uneasily. "You don't waste any time."

"No. Will you go to the pictures in Airgead with me tonight?"

"Umm . . . okay." She'd already seen that particular film twice, once in Milwaukee and once last week with Eilidh and Joe, but she didn't care about that.

"Good. I will pick you up at seven." He turned and marched off down the hill.

Sally scampered inside to the kitchen window and watched him all the way back to *Taigh Rois*. Now that, she thought, is one delicious hunk of man.

After the movie, sitting together in the Airgead fish-and-chips shop, she found out that he was brainy as well as beautiful. He was able to talk intelligently on any subject she introduced, and though he was opinionated, he was willing to listen to her arguments and be swayed. It was quite the most challenging and interesting evening she'd ever spent with a man.

Increasingly in the days following Ian was to be found wherever Sally was. They took long hikes together. They visited Eilidh and Joe and both sets of parents. They took Rosie for walks down to the seashore at the end of the lane so that Jean and Darroch could have a bit of peace and quiet.

They talked and argued and told each other jokes; both of them loved to tell jokes and each had a large repertoire. Soon they'd learned each other's jokes and it needed only the punch line spoken to crack them both up into intimate, delighted laughter.

They gathered with their elders at *Taigh Rois* and made music. Because he was not allowed to play his bagpipes in the house (to keep the roof in place, Jamie said), Ian got out his button-box accordion and played that. Sally was coaxed into singing American folk songs in duet with her mother.

Ian appeared at Sally's cottage one morning with brushes and buckets. "Your cottage needs a fresh coat of lime wash," he announced, and proceeded to swab it down. Sally kept him supplied with cups of tea and glasses of soft drinks while he worked. She lingered, wide-eyed, to watch his graceful, powerful movements and the way his clothes, wet with sweat, outlined his superb muscles. He was so gorgeous that her body tingled.

She admired the sparkling white cottage when he was finished. "How about some supper?" she asked. While he was working she'd slipped down to Murray the Meat in Ros Mór, flying along on her bicycle, and bought a big piece of steak. She thought a man deserved meat after such hard work.

"*Miorbhuileach!* I am starved," he announced. "I have brought a change of clothes," he said, fishing in his backpack. "May I use your shower?"

"Umm . . . sure." The thought of Ian, naked and wet and just a few feet away, sent shivers through her. You need to get a grip, girl, she told herself.

But she almost lost her grip when he came out of the bathroom in fresh clothes that clung damply to him, his blond hair gleaming with drops of water, smelling faintly of lemons. "I used your shampoo. I hope you don't mind," he said.

He lowered himself into a kitchen chair, which immediately assumed the appearance of a child's toy beneath him, and stared appreciatively at the plate of grilled steak and creamy mashed potatoes that she set before him. "There is nothing more *miorbhuileach*," he said solemnly, "than a beautiful woman who can cook."

Sally blushed.

And a woman who blushes is quite captivating, Ian thought.

After dinner they moved to the sofa which Ian angled so that they could watch the television. There was an important Scottish Cup football match on, between Inverness Caledonian Thistle and Heart of Midlothian. Inverness were Ian's favorite team, since they were Highland, and one of their younger players was from Eilean Dubh.

Ian adored football. He marveled that Sally knew so much about the game, even though in her American way she persisted in calling it soccer. She was as vehemently partisan as he was for his team and she was adept at dissecting plays and strategy. When he commented on that she said, "Oh, yes. I played soccer in high school and at the University. I love the game."

"Perhaps you would care to come with me tomorrow morning to the High School. Some of us are getting together to play a friendly with the lads from Airgead." He held his breath. Many women would not care for such an outing, sitting outside on hard benches in cool breezes that mussed their hairdos.

But Sally said enthusiastically, "Sure, I'd like that."

The next morning she found herself sitting on the High School football pitch's wooden benches, along with Màiri, Jean and Rosie, Eilidh and Ian's Catrìona and several other women.

All the men from their lane were involved. Darroch was the captain and a stalwart in midfield, where he directed play. Jamie and Joe, rugged and tough, were defenders. Ian, with his great height and long arms, was in goal. Several men from Ros Mór filled in at other positions.

Ian the Post was the sole forward. Diffident and shy in real life, on the football pitch he was cunning, swift and elusive, darting around the other side's defenders as though they were wearing clay boots. He scored two goals before the game was fifteen minutes old and the Airgead side were looking hard-pressed.

Minister Tormod from Airgead was the referee. When the two sides played in Airgead, Minister Donald refereed to keep things fair. Now Donald paced up and down the sidelines, shoulders hunched, shouting advice and commands at his team.

The ladies watched intently, cheering and groaning as appropriate. Sally whispered something to Catrìona and she nodded in agreement. When the two teams took a break, Sally ran around behind the goal on the pretext of bringing Ian water. She said to him, "I've been keeping an eye on their right fullback. I think they'd like to pass the ball to him and let him try a shot."

He looked at her sharply, then nodded. When, several minutes later, the right fullback came out of nowhere with a hard shot, Ian was there, stopping it with a stunning dive to the left goal post.

He turned and gave Sally the thumbs-up sign as she cheered wildly.

"Nobody gets anything past Ian," said Màiri smugly and Sally grinned.

At the end of the match Ros Mór were up three-nil, Darroch having put the last goal past the dispirited Airgead side. Talking, laughing, shaking hands with their opposite numbers, the players came off the pitch and headed for the High School's showers. Afterwards everyone went to the little pub on the square for a pint and nosh.

Sitting at the table, Sally realized she was having the time of her life. Here she was with her darling mother, the world's sweetest baby and the nicest women she'd ever met. Across the table from her, talking football and laughing with the lads from Airgead, sat the five sexiest men on the Island, all of them except for Ian in happy, deeply committed relationships.

There was Darroch, not conventionally handsome, but Sally'd been in love with those glorious blue eyes and that long elegant nose ever since she'd been nine years old and had watched him on television in *The Magician*. It was more than obvious that her mother adored him and he adored her, and they both worshipped Rosie.

There was Bonnie Prince Jamie, just as crazy about his wife as he'd been when they'd gotten married over twenty years ago. Sally had watched Jamie find Màiri at *cèilidhean* and slip away home with her, his intentions perfectly clear from the way he wrapped his arm around her waist and steered her to the door.

There was Joe, sweet, gentle and shy. Eilidh had shared with her the story of how Joe had loved away her fears after her experience with the almost-rapist. Sally thought she'd never heard anything so romantic.

There was Ian the Post, with his open honest face and his loving looks at his Catrìona, which were returned in full measure.

And then there was Ian *Mór* MacDonald, six foot six of muscle and dynamite, the only unattached man in the bunch. He was sitting next to her, his long legs almost touching hers, his arm draped across the back of her chair in a proprietary manner.

I wonder what he would be like as a lover, she thought, then blushed, because she was not used to thinking about men that way. She had an old-fashioned attitude towards sex before marriage: she disapproved. She'd made that perfectly clear to the men she'd dated, and if it lost her a boyfriend, she didn't care. Men were like streetcars; there'd be another one along any minute.

But there was something about Ian that made her think about scenes in romance novels. Hot kisses, removal of certain bits of clothing, intimate touches. Her lips quirked up at the corners at the thought.

As if he'd read her mind, he bent and said softly in her ear, "And what are you thinking about that brings that smile to your lips?" She turned red. Ian grinned. "Must be good, whatever it is. I hope I'm in it."

"Wouldn't you like to know?" said Sally, too rattled to think of anything clever, falling back on the trite.

"If you'd like to tell me I'd love to listen," Ian whispered, his breath tickling her neck and ruffling her hair. "Will you tell me, Sally?"

"Maybe." She gave him an intimate little smile. Although he often caught her off guard, she was enough of a flirt herself to recover quickly. That was what made her association with Ian so stimulating.

Jamie observed this exchange and murmured in the Gaelic to Darroch. They looked at the couple, then at each other, then smiled. Now there's a good match, thought Jamie, and glancing at Darroch, knew he agreed.

Had he known what they were thinking, Ian would have agreed as well. Sally had occupied the prominent place in his thoughts ever since he'd met her and he'd come swiftly to the conclusion that she was the one with whom he wanted to spend his life. They understood each other intuitively. Sally was as smart as he was, she had a sharp sense of humor, and she had a serious side to her nature that cared deeply about social causes. She would fit in perfectly with his plans to serve his Island as its doctor. She would make him the ideal wife.

And, as a bonus, she was beautiful and sexy, and her sweet mouth and curvaceous body promised a world of pleasure.

Their association had always been that of man and woman, never guy and gal pal, buddies or mates. Each was intensely aware of the other's sensual attractions. But it made Sally uneasy that Ian had never tried anything with her. Every man she'd dated had tried to make their relationship physical within the first few dates. She wondered if she was losing her touch.

True, Ian had lately begun to salute her, on both meeting and parting, with a kiss on each cheek, a gesture employed by the Island's alpha males, her stepfather Darroch and Jamie MacDonald, with women whom they admired and respected. All the women so saluted knew that it was a tribute to their stature on Eilean Dubh, and that it meant only friendship.

Ian MacDonald, an alpha male-in-training, carefully watched his elders and imitated them when he dared. So far Sally was the only recipient of his greeting kisses. He was working his way up to Jean, Sheilah, and beautiful Ian's Catrìona.

What this relationship meant and where it was going, Sally didn't know. Ian had a healthy interest in her body; she'd caught him looking at her longingly any number of times, almost licking his lips in appreciation. Sooner or later, she figured, he would make his move.

She didn't know what she'd do then. But she was damn sure she was going to hold on to her virginity. She was keeping full custody of her body, and hoping to hang on to her emotions as well.

Thirty-seven

He's a bonnie laddie, a fine bonnie laddie,
Such a bonnie laddie!
How can I tell him nay?
Lady Grizel Mac an Rìgh

*W*hen Ian turned up at her cottage one Wednesday night after dinner Sally was a little miffed, because he hadn't been around since Sunday.

"Hello, stranger," she said coolly.

He noted the coolness with amusement. He truly had been very busy, helping his father, but it was good to know she'd noticed his absence. It had been hard to stay away from her but he calculated that it would fan the fire a little, assuming there was a fire. It had certainly fanned it in him. His dreams lately would have made an experienced roué blush.

"It seems like eons since I've seen you, Sally," he said tenderly.

She tossed her head. "Does it?"

"I've wanted to come over but my father has been keeping my nose to the grindstone." He sighed. "He's got some maggot in his head about his damned Jacob's sheep. I've been knee-deep in fleece and dung for three days, holding each sheep while he examines them. I swear he's counting their teeth."

Sally laughed, absurdly happy to know he did have a valid excuse for ignoring her. "Has he found anything wrong with them?"

"Damned if I know. He got Joe up to the flock yesterday and the two of them spent the morning mumbling and poking while I struggled to hold on to each animal they poked. Jacob's sheep don't like being poked, you know. I thought that huge old ram was going to take out my balls with his horns. He's twice as big as I am and meaner than a Tory politician."

"I imagine Joe was a real help."

"Aye, it's grand to have a tame vet in the family. My father's fair chuffed about Joe and Joe thinks Dad's the greatest man in the world, and besides he adores Jacob's sheep, God knows why. Quite the mutual admiration society, Dad and Joe and those sheep."

He stretched. "I'm all over aches and pains. I suppose you wouldn't want to put me in a hot bath, then massage my back and legs, would you?" He looked at her teasingly.

At last, and moving right along and not wasting any time, thought Sally, and met his advance with a feint of her own, a counter-attack through his stomach. "No massage, but I've got a chocolate torte I just baked, a new recipe. Would a piece of that help?"

"May I have it on your sofa, with a cup of tea?"

"Coming right up."

After he'd eaten his cake he said hopefully, "Would you let a poor tired shepherd stretch out on your sofa and put his head in your lap? Just for comfort, mind you."

She considered the request. "I might, as long as it's just for comfort."

They arranged themselves on the sofa and Ian relaxed into her lap with a contented sigh. His long legs dangled over the sofa arm.

Sally could not help stroking the thick blond hair, brushing it back off his face. He was undeniably gorgeous with those clear blue eyes looking up at her, a promising sexy glint in their depths. "So that's where you've been the last few days."

He said, self-assurance in every syllable, "Did you miss me?"

"Yes." Then, before he could get too conceited about that she added, "I baked cookies yesterday and thought I'd have to eat them all myself, instead of counting on you to demolish a dozen or so."

He smiled, enjoying the skirmishing. "Aye. I have a rare appetite for your cooking." He said softly, "I have other appetites too."

Thrust and counter thrust. Sally trembled, well aware what the next move would be, and not sure how long her defenses would hold. "I don't know if I could do anything about those."

"Would you be willing to try?"

"I might." To hell with resistance, she thought, she was going to meet the invader on his own ground. She'd kissed guys and always kept her head.

"God, that mouth of yours has been driving me crazy for days," he growled and sat up suddenly. Her last coherent thought was "Uh-oh," just before he swept her into his arms and his lips descended on hers.

His was a generous mouth, in proportion to his size, and it covered hers completely, hard and passionate and gentle all at the same time. He finished the kiss by sucking her lower lip inside his and biting it. Then he kissed the corners of her eyes and the tip of her nose.

The electricity between them was so strong that Sally felt her hair standing on end. "You're quite a kisser," she gasped.

"You inspire me." His tongue flicked over her lips, coaxing her mouth open and she froze, remembering how she'd hated it when a guy did that, thrusting his tongue inside until she thought she'd choke. But Ian was using only the tip, like a paintbrush, caressing the inside of her lips and her teeth. She let her tongue touch his and he took it between his lips and sucked it tenderly. She sighed, on the brink of yielding more.

His arms tightened around her like steel bands and she quivered with alarm and pushed him back, her hands on his chest. Too fast, he thought, but it was getting harder and harder to contain his passion. He'd felt the electricity too and it wasn't his hair that was standing on end.

But she was trembling.

"What's wrong, Sally?"

"You're scaring me a little. You're so big and so strong. I feel like you could just swallow me up."

He rocked her and crooned, "Wae's me, yer unco' thrawn. Hush yer blether an' dinna skirl, ma sonsie wee quean. Ian Mór winna scaith ye. We maun gae gey thick thegither."

"What?" He had distracted her from her apprehension, just as he had intended. She looked at him quizzically. "What language is that?"

"Scots. Perhaps you prefer the Gaelic." He began to talk to her in that language and this time he was really enjoying himself, since she had no idea of what he was saying. He could praise the sweetness of her mouth, the fullness of her breasts and the roundness of her bottom without worrying about being slapped. You've got the tastiest hips, he told her, one hand straying down to caress her there. The kind of hips that make a man think about being inside you, the kind of hips that would welcome a man's loving invasion.

"What on earth are you talking about?" she asked, shivering from the heat of his breath in her ear.

"Nothing on earth. Heaven. Paradise." He toyed with the idea of translating what he'd said, but good sense prevailed. For a first effort it was going pretty well but he'd better not push his luck. He let his arms slacken around her and noticed with interest that she wasn't pulling away from him. Always leave a woman wanting more, he thought. "I'd best go home, Sally," he said. "Thank you for the cake. And the kisses."

"You're welcome." She gave him her little teasing grin. "I'm glad you enjoyed both."

The grin nearly pushed him over the edge. He wondered if she knew how potent it was, how it made him want to pick her up in his arms and carry her off to bed and kiss the smirk off her face, turn it into a look of astonishment just before she screamed with pleasure.

They shook hands solemnly at the door, Ian foregoing the cheek kisses in order to keep his passion in check. On the way home he opened his coat and let the cold breeze blow around him to cool him down. Instead of going into *Taigh Rois* he kept walking, down to the seashore, his mind processing what he'd learned about Sally so far.

He was almost sure she was in love with him and damned sure he was in love with her. Tonight's encounter had confirmed what he'd known from the first time he'd seen her, holding Rosie in her arms. This was his woman, everything he wanted.

Jamie had told him about sex, the first time he'd asked. Told him simply and calmly, using all the right terms for male and female parts of the anatomy, explaining it all. He finished by saying, "That's how babies are made. When you're older I'll tell you about the rest of it. It's called making love."

"How much older do I have to be?"

Jamie considered him carefully. "In your case, fifteen." His own sexual initiation had come at the age of sixteen but kids today were precocious.

The day after his fifteenth birthday Ian managed to catch his father alone in their cottage. "It's time for you to tell me the rest of it, Dad." He'd been dying of curiosity for months.

"And what would that be?"

Ian said impatiently, "You know. What you said you'd tell me when I was fifteen."

"Ah." Jamie made a pot of tea while Ian waited, squirming with impatience. He poured them each a cup, then sat down. "That would be about men and women."

"About making love, aye, please, Dad."

"Aye. Well, it's the greatest pleasure a man and woman can feel with each other and it should be reserved for someone you truly love." It was like Jamie, not to mention marriage.

"The first thing you have to learn is that the woman must always be willing and you must always be gentle. A loving, willing woman is the greatest gift God ever gave a man, and you must be worthy of her. You must know how to please her. Your own pleasure should be secondary, for it's easy for a man. A woman needs more." He went on to explain, in tender detail, what a woman needed and how to satisfy her natural hunger.

Ian listened in awe to his father's soft voice. So beautiful, he thought. He could not yet imagine himself doing all the things with a woman that Jamie spoke of.

Reading his mind, Jamie said, "You're too young for all of this. Making love is for adults, not children. No experimentation, mind. Promise me that." Jamie had learned the hard way, was ashamed of his own youthful Jack-the-lad reputation and intended that his son should grow up to be a man of principles and high morals.

"Aye, sir. I promise."

"Making love is sacred. It's a solemn covenant between a man and a woman. There's nothing wrong with a few kisses, if the girl fancies it. But save the rest for the one you truly love. Be sure about it."

Jamie's counsel stayed with Ian throughout his teenage years and he stood by his promise to his father. Kissing was as far as he went with any of the girls he dated. It made him wildly popular. Eilean Dubh girls learned quickly that they'd never have to fight off Ian *Mór*; virtue was safe with him. And he was lots of fun to be with and a wizard at kissing.

It wasn't until he went off to university in Edinburgh and let himself be seduced by the wife of one of his professors that he lost his virginity. He'd thought he was truly in love with her, and the humiliating end of that affair, with the knowledge that she'd just wanted the attention and the body of a handsome young man, made him realize that his father had been right about being sure. He'd let lust and vanity rule him and lead him into committing adultery. He was deeply ashamed and terribly confused after it ended. How were you supposed to know if it was real? How did you keep your body from betraying you?

This was definitely a relationship, no doubt about that, and Sally knew it. She could feel the air of approval emanating from her mother, her stepfather, and Ian's parents.

They were considered a couple. Ianandsally, all run together in one word. "Call Ianandsally and see if they want to go to the pictures with us," their friends would say. "Are Ianandsally coming up for supper tonight?" Jean would ask Darroch.

It flattered her ego that she'd caught the most eligible man on the Island but now that she'd caught him she wasn't sure what to do with him. And she wasn't sure he'd stay caught. Maybe he'd wiggle off the hook, with his trademark grin and it would be another one of his jokes. "Ha, fooled you, Sally," he might say.

She was in love with him, as she'd never been before. How could she not be in love with a huge gorgeous guy with a dynamite sense of humor, a brilliant brain, a kind and gentle heart, who kissed like a movie star?

But what possible future could they have together?

Thirty-eight

He has ta'en my heart away,
In his arms he bids me stay,
Stay and love him for alway,
How shall I tell him nay?

Lady Grizel Mac an Rìgh

Ian wasn't in the least confused about Sally. He loved her and he wanted her. He understood now what his father had meant about the sacredness of making love. But how was he going to get Sally to understand that they were meant to be together?

He would have to seduce her, Ian thought. Eilidh had never been able to keep secrets from her twin when it involved the family, and she had shared with him Màiri's confidences regarding her first sexual experience with Jamie.

Their mother and Darroch had been in love, the twins knew, and they would have married, if he hadn't wanted to leave the Island for an acting career, and if Màiri hadn't been so determined to devote her life to Eilean Dubh.

She'd been lost and miserable when she parted from Darroch until two years later, when she'd met Jamie MacDonald at Sabhal Mór Ostaig, the Gaelic college on the Isle of Skye. Jamie, with his gift of the Sight, had recognized her right away as his lifelong mate, and had wooed her intensely for a week until she succumbed, on the hill at Tarskavaig above the college. He had known instinctively that she would be his forever once she let him make love to her; she would not give her body away without committing her heart and mind.

Ian, not sure of his next step in the wooing of Sally, decided he would do just as his father had done: make love to his woman. Then she would be his without question. It had worked for Jamie and it should work for him. And if Jamie had done it, it had to be the right thing to do.

Aye, sex was the answer. His parents, rather to his surprise, had a full and active sexual relationship, despite their advanced age. He remembered another conversation with Eilidh, when he'd said jokingly, "I think I put a crimp in my father's love life whenever I come home from Edinburgh. He can't tell me to go off and play with my friends when he wants to be alone with Mother."

Eilidh had said, "Aye, they still like to make love, don't they. It's sweet."

Ian had grinned. "Dad gets a certain look in his eye. Remember when I first understood it? I'd say, 'We'd really enjoy going to the pictures, Dad, but we haven't got any money.' And he would dig in his pocket and pull out a few pound notes. Then I would say, 'Could I use the car? It's so far to walk, we'd never make the start of the film.' And Dad would pull out his car keys and toss them to me. And he never even growled at me if we stopped in at the chippie and came home late."

Eilidh giggled. "We were wee devils. I don't know how they put up with the two of us."

Now that Ian had the answer to his Sally dilemma, he planned his campaign as carefully as any general. It involved flowers and a bottle of wine, and a meal he would prepare for her in her cottage. He made a very good risotto; an Italian student at his university had taught him how.

Sally hadn't had risotto since she'd left Madison and her mouth watered at the thought. She was entranced, watching him cook, his big hands capably slicing and stirring. She thought it was sexy if a man could cook.

Afterwards they sat in front of the fire with their coffee. Drowsy and contented, she let her head drift to his shoulder.

Aha, he thought, and wrapped his arms around her. What else would she like, he thought. Sweet words in her ear, in the mysterious Gaelic, of course, and tender kisses. He cooed and murmured. He put his hand under her chin and turned her face up to his and kissed her. When she responded he swept his arms under her and lifted her as though she was weightless onto his lap.

It turned Sally on. She was not a small woman, at nearly six feet tall, and though slender she had a well-developed figure. Ian with his great size and his strong arms made her feel fragile and dainty. She hadn't felt dainty since she'd been twelve years old.

She let him tilt her back in his arms and kiss her passionately, enjoying every minute, feeling herself become warm and yielding.

Time to make his move, Ian thought. He murmured in her ear, "I want you, Sally. Come to bed with me, let me make love to you."

Sally was brought abruptly back to reality. Damn, it was decision time and it had come so swiftly she was unprepared. Why couldn't he have worked a little slower? She hadn't expected him to rush the final fence. But she managed to draw herself up straight, no easy feat since she was on his lap and surrounded by his arms. "No. I'm saving myself for the man I will marry."

He drew back and looked at her. "You are a virgin?" At her nod his face broke into a glowing smile. "But that is *miorbhuileach!* You've saved yourself for me. I am the man you're going to marry."

Furious, she wriggled off his lap, long legs and skirt flying, and went to stand by the fire, her back to him, her shoulders rigid. "Really, Ian," she said disdainfully, "I didn't think you'd try that old line. Not with me, anyway."

He protested, "It is not a line. Look at me, Sally." He crooned her name, drew it out slowly: Sal-leee.

That deep purring note in his voice usually got him the attention he wanted, from Sally, anyway. She turned.

"Come sit beside me," he coaxed. He patted the sofa by his side.

Her feet moved her to the sofa and she sat down on the far end, as far away as she could get.

He reached for her hand and she gave it reluctantly. "I want to marry you, Sally. You are meant for me. I've known it from the first moment I saw you." When she looked away, chin high, he added, "I would get down on my knees and propose to you, *m'aingeal*, but it would not be dignified. It would be like a bear kneeling in front of a fairy. You would laugh."

Her lips twitched. I probably would, she thought. Every neuron in her body screamed to her to say yes to both requests. She had a sudden vision of herself in bed with him, his mouth and hands working magic on her body. She turned scarlet. Her hand tingled and she snatched it from his grasp.

"I don't know. It's too soon . . . Oh, I'm so confused." She knew she was babbling and it infuriated her.

"Aye, I seem to have that effect on you." He smiled smugly.

Annoyed, Sally snapped, "You do not."

His smile grew. Sally wanted to slap him. None of the other men who'd been after her had affected her the way he did and she hated losing control of a situation.

"Sally, come closer to me," he coaxed. "Meet me half way."

He smiled and she melted. Then he reached for her and pulled her into his arms, against his broad chest and into his lap again. He seemed to feel that was where she belonged. "Marry me, Sally," he crooned. "I love you so much."

"You're going too fast." He kissed her again and her mouth opened to him and her arms went around his neck. "Oh, Ian, I do love you."

"*Miorbhuileach*. Say you'll marry me and let's go to bed to celebrate."

Indignant, she pushed him away. "No, no and no. What part of no don't you understand?"

He looked at her blankly. "What?"

"No, I am not going to bed with you. You make it seem so simple and it's not at all simple, this marriage thing. What are we going to do if we get married?"

"Make love all the time. Imagine it, Sally. In our own bed, loving each other."

She could imagine it all too clearly. "There's a lot more to being married than making love."

"Oh, aye. There will be talking and laughing and music. And making babies. I want a big family. Four or maybe five babies and us here on the Island in our own little love nest. Happily ever after."

"Ian, you don't understand. Suppose I don't want to live on the Island with you and five babies."

He considered. "I would settle for four. Maybe even three. We'll start with three and see how it goes. Perhaps twins for the first batch."

Sally shuddered, remembering Màiri's stories about the horrors of raising twins. "Oh, Ian." She sighed, wondering how to make him understand. "I love you, and I like the Island very much, but I want more out of life than being a wife and mother. I haven't seen anything of the world. I want to travel. I want a career. I want to make something of my life. And I'm American and maybe I don't want to live in the Scottish boondocks."

Puzzled, he said, "What is a boondock?"

"The back of the beyond. I'm a city girl."

"But your mother was a city girl and she loves it here."

She snapped, "I am not my mother."

"Of course you aren't. You are my own sweet, beautiful Sally. Such a delicious body, and lips swollen from kisses, like little plums."

Somehow he had gotten her blouse unbuttoned and his hand was caressing her breast through the thin fabric of her bra. "Breasts like melons," he whispered. Then, when she looked at him indignantly, he amended, "Little melons. Perfectly round and ripe. Do you know how I like to eat melons?'

He found the front catch on her bra and opened it one-handed. "First I remove the rind." He pulled the bra open. Sally looked down and saw his large hand cradling her breast. She felt herself being tilted back in his arms again. He whispered, "Then I dive right in and gobble them up."

When his mouth surrounded her nipple she thought she would go straight up in the air like a skyrocket. "Please," she whispered and had no idea whether she was asking him to stop or continue what he was doing. Because what he was doing felt marvelous.

He moved his mouth over that breast in widening circles, burrowing his face in the valley between, then moving to the other one. "Oh, Ian," she gasped and filled her hands with blond hair. The harder he suckled the harder she pulled, unconsciously, until he lifted his head and said, "Ow. You're hurting me, sweet Sally."

She let his hair go. "I'm sorry. I just got carried away. I've never felt anything like that before."

"Has no one ever kissed your breasts before, *m'aingeal*?"

She went all hot, remembering. "Just once." She'd been in high school, he'd been a wild, undisciplined, exciting boy she was crazy about and they'd been necking on her parents' sofa. She could have made love with him, probably would have, if she hadn't heard the car pulling into the driveway. She'd pulled away and jumped up, hastily buttoning her blouse. She'd just gotten the lights and television on before her parents walked into the house.

She was red with embarrassment, remembering Jean coming into the living room, her quick look from her blushing daughter to the defiantly guilty boy. Luckily her father had gone right upstairs.

She'd never gotten that carried away again, the memory of her mother's apprehensive face in her mind. But Jean's face wasn't visible now to protect her from indiscretion and Ian was turning her on like a thousand-watt bulb. He was so big and solid and hard with muscle, especially the part she could feel beneath her.

They could make love right there on the sofa, Ian thought, but it was old and the springs sagged. "Come to bed with me, Sally, let me have you," he crooned into her ear. He kissed her again and his big hand moved down her body, pulling her skirt up, easing her panties down to her ankles. Then he slipped his fingers between her legs.

Shocked, she yelped, twisted away violently and fell off the couch, her bottom and elbow landing hard on the floor.

Ian yelped. Sally's knee had hit him in a spot that was vulnerable, especially right now. Cautiously he assessed the damage, and decided he was more surprised than hurt. He looked down at her, and was shocked to see the tears running down her cheeks. "*M'aingeal*, are you all right?"

The funny bone in her elbow was throbbing, her bottom hurt, and she was overwhelmed with embarrassment and humiliation. She struggled awkwardly to her feet. When Ian reached out to help her she pulled away and stumbled, tripped by the panties. Angrily she kicked them off, sending them flying. She lost her balance and landed hard on the sofa on her aching bottom.

Ian did the unforgivable: he laughed. It was a nervous laugh, fueled by the expression on Sally's face and her uncontrolled movements, but it was a laugh nevertheless.

It made Sally furious. "So you think it's funny, do you?" she snarled, rubbing her elbow.

He realized his mistake at once. "No, of course not. Come here, *m'aingeal*." He wrapped his arms around her, intending to be comforting, but her body in his arms turned him on again. He groaned with lust and tried to recapture lost ground. "Please, Sally, come to bed with me. I'll make you feel better."

"You're not going to make me feel anything." She put her hands against his chest and shoved. "Get away. You're squashing me and I can't think when you're so close."

"What do you have to think about? You want me and I want you, and we're going to be married." He stared at her stubbornly.

"You're so damn sure of yourself. Haven't you listened to anything I've said?"

How was a man supposed to think when his woman's blouse and bra were half off and her breasts in full view? "Cover yourself, then, if you want me to be rational," he snapped.

She looked down at herself, blushed and fastened up her clothes, her fingers shaking. Ian sighed as the beautiful sight disappeared from view. This was not going at all as he had expected.

"Give me back my underpants," she demanded.

He looked at the sofa, then down to the floor. He took the tiny bikini bottom between two fingers of each hand and stared at it. "Is this what you wear all the time?"

She snatched at the pants but he eluded her. "No, those are just plain cotton for everyday. I have little lacy ones for best."

"Smaller than these? *A Dhia*, it's hardly decent." He was very, very hard, just thinking about it.

"Well, no one's supposed to see them. Give them back."

"No, I don't think I will. I'll just keep them. Maybe sleep with them under my pillow." He tucked them inside the waistband of his jeans, pushing them all the way inside. "Come and get your knickers if you want them," he invited.

Sally sputtered with indignation and reached for him, her fingers slipping inside his waistband before she realized what she was doing. She turned redder and tried to snatch her fingers away but he captured them and held them where they were. "Feel what you're doing to me," he said softly and moved her hand down his jeans. *"Tha thu 'gam chur às mo chiall."* You're driving me daft.

"Oh, my goodness. You're so big."

"Aye. Well, I'm a big man and it's all in proportion."

"How could we ever . . ."

He crooned, "Don't be afraid, *m'aingeal*. I'll take you slowly, take as long as you need for you to get used to me. I've never hurt a woman yet."

She yanked her hand free and eyed him suspiciously. "Just how many women have you had?"

He decided to be perfectly honest. "Three. The first was the wife of one of my professors."

Her eyes widened. "But that's adultery."

It was his turn to go red in the face. "Aye, and I'm not proud of it. She told me her husband was impotent but she couldn't divorce him because she felt sorry for him. She offered herself and I wasn't strong enough to say no. I found out later that she picked out a fresh student every year to try it on with. I was humiliated. I broke it off with her."

"What about the other two?"

"The second was Elizabeth. She was a first year medical student, like me. It wasn't sex at first; we just decided to live together to save on expenses and help each other with our studies. One thing led to another and after a week we moved into the same bedroom. We were together about a year; then she decided to be a microbiologist instead of a doctor. She went to England to go to school there.

"The third was a woman I've gone out with three times. She wanted to do it on the second date. She's one of those women curious about a big man, wanted to know if I was big all over. On the third date we went to her flat and spent the whole evening fucking." He said bitterly, "I wouldn't dignify it by calling it making love. She had no particular feeling for me except lust and that's what I gave her in return. What she wanted. And just that once.

"I'd about given up on women until you came along. I knew right away about you, Sally."

"Knew what?"

"I knew that I was going to fall in love with you, that I would love you forever, and that I was going to try my damnedest to get you to marry me." What the hell, he might as well confess. "I figured if I could get you into bed you'd marry me. I didn't know that you are a virgin but I knew damn well you wouldn't give yourself to a man if you didn't love him, if you wouldn't commit to him."

"That's blackmail. I won't give myself to you even though I do love you. I believe in waiting till I'm married."

"So do I, but we're going to get married, so why wait?"

"You're so sure of yourself. Listen to me, Ian: I won't marry you unless I'm sure we want the same things. And that means living here and being the doctor's wife, because that's what you want."

"If we love each other that's all that matters."

"It isn't." She took his face in her hands and stared into his eyes. "I'm a person too. It wouldn't be doing either of us any favors if we don't look sensibly at the future and make sure we're right for each other. I want my marriage to be forever."

"I don't understand any of this. You love me, but you won't marry me. You want me, but you won't go to bed with me." He shook his head in despair. "Women," he said.

Sally stood up. "I think you'd better go home, Ian. We don't have anything else to say to each other."

Ian stood up. "I think you're right. Good night, Sally."

"Good night, Ian. Thank you for the wonderful dinner."

He stared at her until she trembled. "Thank you, Sally. For the kisses. For the taste of your breasts. And for saying that you loved me, even though it doesn't matter worth a damn." He stalked to the door.

"Goodbye, Sally." He strode through it dramatically.

Torn between laughter and tears, Sally thought, wow, what a performance. Maybe he should be an actor instead of a doctor. Then she went into the bedroom, threw herself on her bed and sobbed for an hour.

Thirty-nine

Mother knows best.
Universal proverb

Sally couldn't help it, she had to talk to someone, and the obvious person was her mother. She went down to Jean and Darroch's cottage the next day, helped start a load of wash, and tidied the kitchen while her mother nursed Rosie.

Finally Rosie was down for her nap and she had her mother's undivided attention. She moved restlessly around the room. Finally she looked at Jean and blurted, "Mom, I don't know what to do about Ian."

Surprised, Jean said, "What do you want to do?"

"I don't know that either." She flung herself into a chair and stared at her mother. "Look, I'm sorry, but I really need to talk to someone and I don't have any girl friends my own age here except Eilidh and I can't talk to her about her brother. Besides, she's so crazy about Joe that her advice wouldn't be rational."

"I'll be glad to listen, dear," said Jean, feeling motherly.

"He wants to make love to me."

Jean swallowed hard and lowered the teacup from her lips very slowly. It rattled on the saucer when she put it down.

"And he's very sexy and when he puts his arms around me he just sweeps me away. I don't know what to do."

Jean cleared her throat and said, "Um . . . Sal, I don't know if I'm the right person to advise you about this."

"Well, who else can I turn to? I'm so confused."

Jean got a grip on herself. "Sally, what do you want to do?"

"Well, what did you want to do at my age? In fact, what did you do at my age?"

Jean turned scarlet and looked at the floor. "Well, I certainly wouldn't advise you to get pregnant at nineteen like I did."

Sally looked at her. "That's another thing. He wants babies."

Jean said, "Does marriage figure into any of this?"

"Oh, yes, he wants us to get married. And he wants a lot of babies; we haven't agreed on how many," she said darkly. "He wants me to stay here on the Island and be the doctor's wife. And he wants to make love to me now and he wants me to come and live with him in Edinburgh until he finishes medical school."

"That's a lot of 'Ian wants,'" said Jean.

"Well, he's so forceful, Mom. And he's so possessive."

"I think that's a characteristic of Eilean Dubh men. Darroch is like that, too."

"How does that make you feel?"

"I rather like it, especially after your father's attitude toward marriage. It's not owning, it's belonging. We belong to each other."

"Hmmm. That's nice, the way you put it." She was thoughtful for a moment, then said, "I never have, you know. Made love, I mean. I'm a virgin."

"That's good, dear."

"He's not, he's had three affairs. What's it like, making love? I don't have anyone else to ask. I'm sorry if it embarrasses you but I have to know. I'm sort of afraid. He's so big. I've touched him through his clothes, when we were, you know, fooling around. Will he hurt me?" She was wringing her hands in agitation.

Jean was trying very hard not to be freaked. This discussion had happened so suddenly that she was unprepared. It was not the calm, rational talk they'd had about sex all those years ago, when she'd answered—thought she'd answered—all of Sally's questions. "Well, I wouldn't worry about that. You . . . stretch, you know. And I'm sure he'd be gentle; he's that sort of man."

"Tell me what it's like, Mom."

Jean decided to be perfectly frank. "Well, I've only had two lovers. With your father it was very nice but he tended to be rather . . . quick. With Darroch it's slow and sweet. He takes his time; he makes sure I'm enjoying it.

And he talks to me; he whispers in my ear in the Gaelic. It was a real incentive for me to learn the language, to understand what he was saying when he was making love to me."

She chuckled. "In fact, I remember the first time I actually figured out something he had said . . . " She stopped abruptly, remembering just what he had said. She was pretty sure her face was red. "He's very passionate and he is there with me, if you know what I mean. It's me he's making love to, not just a woman. It's quite lovely, really."

"Umm." Sally was wide-eyed. "That sounds nice. When Ian kisses me and touches me I feel wonderful and really turned on. He talks to me too; it's so sexy. I have a hard time keeping myself together around him. And I keep wondering if I should go ahead with him, someone I really like and trust, or save myself—God, that sounds dumb but it's how I feel—for my husband."

"But I thought he wants to marry you."

"Yes, Mom, but do I want to marry him?" she cried. "Do I want to stay here on this Island and be the doctor's wife? I'm only twenty-one; I haven't done anything with my life. How do I know I want to stay on Eilean Dubh? It was all right for you when you came here. You'd already experienced life; you were old."

"I beg your pardon," Jean said indignantly. "I was forty and that is not old. And I'm forty-two now and that's not old either."

"Oh, Mom, you know what I mean. You'd done things, you'd gone to college, you'd seen the world . . . "

Jean had always regretted that she had married so young and it was disconcerting to hear herself described as a woman of experience. "I understand. It would be quite drastic for you to decide to spend your life here."

Sally shuddered. "I'm afraid of being trapped. Suppose I wake up ten years and several children later and decide this isn't what I want at all?"

"Sal, I can't answer that. Only you can decide. How do you feel about him?"

Sally clasped her hands together, a rapt expression on her face. "I adore him. He is the most wonderful man I've ever met, the sweetest, the smartest. You wouldn't believe how smart he is. He just blows me away when he talks.

"But how do I know it's really love? He's so intense, so dominating. Sometimes I have to pick a fight with him just to assert my personality so he doesn't swallow me up. We fight a lot."

Alarmed, Jean said, "What do you fight about?"

"Everything. It's as natural to us as breathing. Well, it's not really fighting, it's arguing. We argue about politics and religion and everything. And he loves to argue and he changes sides constantly. One week he'll be arguing from a radical point of view and the next week he'll be conservative. He does it to keep his mind limber, he says. He's in the debate society at his university. I get the impression he's their star."

"Yes, " said Jean. "A combination of Mairi's fire and Jamie's cool logic, both of them as smart as whips. He is formidable."

Sally sighed. "I don't know how much longer I can resist him, Mom. What shall I do? The idea of making love with him is so tempting . . . "

Jean said slowly, "I think you should go back to Milwaukee."

Sally stared at her. "Why?"

"Go back to school. Finish your degree. Enjoy being with your father, being in America. See how you feel about leaving and coming to live in Scotland. But finish your education, this phase anyway. And experience being away from Ian. If you really love him I think that will tell you what you need to know."

"Maybe you're right, Mom. He'll be in Edinburgh in medical school, anyway. If I can't stand to be away from him I'll come back. And it will give us both time to think things through. But how can I bear to leave him? And you? And Rosie?"

"It has to be done, and you'll find the strength to do it."

I sure hope so, thought Sally dubiously.

Forty

*It is easier to change the flow of the tide
than to change a stubborn woman's mind.*
Eilean Dubh proverb

*N*ow all she had to do was tell Ian her decision. But they'd been avoiding each other since the ill-fated dinner party. Ian was as hard-headed as she was. Finally she overcame her pride and made the first move: she called *Taigh Rois*. When Jamie answered she asked him to tell Ian that she'd like to see him.

Now what, thought Jamie. Those two had looked to be settled but Ian'd been going around with a face like doom for the last three days and there'd been no sightings of Sally near their cottage. A gloomy Ian would eventually mean the bagpipes, his usual way of expressing his emotion, and it would not be stirring marches this time; it would be slow airs and laments. Jamie and Màiri expected it daily, and dreaded it with both their souls. There was nothing more depressing than an unhappy piper.

When he gave Ian the message he was touched to see his son's face light up with joy. "She wants to see me, Dad? Did she say where or when?"

Poor devil, thought Jamie. "Ian, if I can help in any way . . . "

"Thanks, Dad, but if she wants to see me it must mean she's changed her mind." He grinned broadly. "Women, you know," he said from his lofty heights of expertise. "They do change their minds, especially when they're wrong."

Jamie shook his head and resolved to see if the chemist up in Airgead stocked earplugs. He didn't often experience the Sight when it involved his own family, but he had a strong presentiment that bagpipe laments would follow soon.

Ian tracked Sally down to the Rose Hotel, where she was working the lunch time shift for Sheilah, who was giving her cooking lessons in exchange for her help. When Sally went into the dining room to check for new arrivals she saw him sitting at a table. She trembled in anticipation and forced herself to be cool and to bring him a menu as if he were any old customer.

"Hullo," he said, looking up at her.

"Hi." She thrust the menu at him. "We've some good things today. I hope you're hungry."

He stared at her, not touching the menu. "You know I am," he said softly.

She threw the menu down on the table and fled into the kitchen.

"New customer?" said Sheilah, who was stirring a chocolate custard on the stove.

"Just Ian *Mór* MacDonald," she muttered.

"Oh. What does he want to eat?"

"I don't know. Why don't you go ask him? He'll have had time to look at the menu by now."

"The custard . . . " Sheilah began but Sally took the spoon out of her hand. "I'll do it."

Sheilah gave her a puzzled look but went into the dining room. "Hi, Ian. What will you have for lunch?"

The menu lay untouched. "Anything," he muttered. "Cook's choice. Have Sally choose for me; she knows what I like." And what I want, he thought.

Sheilah reported the conversation, back in the kitchen. Sally glowered, then said something under her breath. Sheilah had no idea what was going on but she was finding it fascinating.

Still mumbling, Sally took a warmed plate and scooped potatoes onto it, arranging them artistically. She lifted several veal collops from the baking pan and added them, dribbling a little gravy on the potatoes. Then she took a generous serving of asparagus tips and fanned them out on the other side of the plate. As a finishing touch she placed one of her lemon roses on the veal. She showed it to Sheilah for approval.

"Wonderful," said Sheilah, glancing at the plate, then up at Sally who was pink from the heat of the kitchen and something else.

Sally stalked into the dining room and thrust the plate under Ian's nose. He looked at it admiringly, then up at Sally with his heart in his eyes.

"Eat every last bit," she ordered and walked away.

When she returned ten minutes later the plate was clean. Ian looked at her longingly. "Delicious," he said and Sally turned even pinker. When she took the plate he said, "Could I have some coffee, please?" As she moved away he said, "And will you have a cup with me? Please?"

In the kitchen Sally said, "Do you mind if I sit with Ian for a few minutes?"

"No, of course not. Just take these custards out for table six when you go." Sally loaded the custards onto the tray with their coffees.

She seated herself by Ian and looked at him grimly.

"Was the veal yours?" When she nodded he said humbly, "You are a fantastic cook, Sally."

"Thank you." She sipped her coffee.

"May I walk you home?"

"I'm not going home. I have to help with the cleanup and then I have to do my marketing."

"I will come with you and carry your basket," he said, in a tone that did not allow for argument.

When they had finished their coffees he stood up, swept the cups into his hand and headed for the kitchen with Sally scampering behind him. There he picked up a dishtowel. "I will dry," he announced.

"No, no, the dishes dry in the dishwasher. Health regulations," said Sheilah, alarmed, and plucked the towel from his hand. She looked from Ian to Sally and back again. "I can finish, Sal, if you want to go."

"It is my job," began Sally and Ian interrupted. "Quite right. I will wait for you." He sat down in a chair, dwarfing it, and folded his arms. He watched them as they worked.

The silence was getting on Sheilah's nerves so she discussed with Sally the menus for the next day's meals. She was relieved when the cleanup was over and these two worrisome young people could be sent on their way.

When they left the kitchen Ian took Sally's arm. She shook him off. He looked at her with his scolded-puppy-dog expression. "Are you angry with me, Sally?"

She was ashamed of her behavior. "No." He smiled and took her arm again. She sighed. He was not going to make this any easier for her. "Let's go some place where we can talk," she said.

"Your cottage?"

"No." She needed somewhere neutral, where she would not be tempted to dissolve into his arms. "Let's go into the public bar. It's closed now but I have the key." She led the way down the hall.

A prickle of unease filled Ian. The public bar did not seem the proper romantic spot for Sally to confess that she could not live without him and would marry him as soon as he wanted.

"Have a whisky," said Sally, in a tone that brooked no dissent. She poured a good measure for him, writing the amount and brand down on a piece of paper and sticking it on a spindle by the cash register.

She brought it to the table where he sat.

"I'm leaving," she said. There was no reason to sugar-coat it.

"Leaving?"

"I'm going back to Milwaukee to finish my college degree. I figure if I take an extra-heavy course load I can graduate next July."

"Sally . . . "

"It will give us time to think about our commitment to each other."

He snarled, "That's ridiculous. My commitment to you is unshakable: I want to make love to you, marry you, have babies with you, live with you the rest of my life. I don't need to think about it. It's not going to change."

"Oh, Ian." Tears spilled from her eyes. She'd been a fool to think that she could get through this without hysteria. "I do love you so much. You're so uncomplicated."

"Is that an insult?"

"No, of course not." She took his hands in hers. He pulled them away, picked up the whisky and downed it in a single swallow. Sighing, she got up and brought the bottle of Bruichladdich over to the table, with a glass for herself.

Sally said, "Please try to understand, Ian. I have to finish school. I have to have my degree. Then I can go to graduate school or get a job."

He said stubbornly, "You don't need a job. I can look after you and our family. I won't make a fortune being a doctor here but it's secure; we'll never have to worry. We can live in your cottage until we have children and need a bigger place."

"Suppose I want a career?"

"You'll have a career. My wife, and mother to my children."

She poured herself a large whisky and took a healthy swallow. "Why do I feel like I'm living in a Dickens novel? Ian, I have to be somebody other than your wife and your children's mother."

"Our children's mother, Sally. Two boys and two girls." He said wistfully, "Growing up here on Eilean Dubh, with my family and yours. All of us together. And you and me in bed each night."

God, she was tempted. Rosie was so sweet that she could just see herself with a baby like that, or two, and Ian adoring her and cuddling her tenderly every night. Being good friends and neighbors with her mother and Darroch, and Ian's parents. Working with Sheilah at the hotel and becoming the very best cook she could possibly be.

"I love you, Sally. I worship you. I'll devote my life to making you happy. Why isn't that enough?"

"I don't know. Maybe it will be. Just give me space to find out."

He said urgently, "Promise me you'll come back, when you've finished your schooling. Promise me you'll give me a chance."

"Oh, Ian." She dissolved in tears, wept helplessly until he got up from his chair and came to kneel by her. He stretched his arms up to her and she collapsed into them. "I'm going to miss you so much."

Ian thought, how can I live without knowing that you'll be mine one day? He held her and petted her and comforted her, feeling his heart breaking.

It finally dawned on him. He had to let her go if there was ever to be a chance that he'd get her back one day. It's called growing up, he realized. Knowing that you can't always get what you want.

Forty-one

The dawning of morn, the day-light's sinking,
The night's long hours still find me thinking
Of thee, thee, only thee.

Thomas Moore

*G*ood-byes at the helicopter pad were somber. Sally embraced Darroch, then, weeping, her mother and Rosie. Then she turned to Ian who stood rigid and gloomy.

He held out his hand. "Goodbye, Sally," he said, his tone formal.

"Oh, Ian." She flung her arms around his neck and kissed him. "I'll write, darling. Please write back."

His resistance crumbled and his arms wrapped around her, crushing her to him, his mouth on hers tender and hard at the same time. "Don't forget me."

She laughed through her tears. "How could anyone ever forget you, Ian *Mór*?"

Màiri and Jamie were awakened next morning with the sound of the pipes being played very close to them, in their front garden in fact. The tune was "The Flowers of the Forest", a funeral tune and the saddest one in a piper's repertoire. Màiri groaned, "I knew it," and buried her head under her pillow.

Jamie growled, "That great pillock. What does he think he's doing at this hour of the morning?" He squinted at the clock. It was not as early as he'd thought but he was still being cheated of an hour of sleep. "I'll sort him." He swung his feet out of bed and sat up.

Màiri said, "*Mo gràdh*, don't be too hard on him. He's very unhappy."

"So will I be, if he keeps this up. And he'll wake the whole lane. What will the neighbors say?"

"Darroch and Jean will understand and so will Eilidh and Joe. And the ocean will drown him out so the Andersons won't hear. I'll talk to him later. Come and lie back down. Since we'll not get any more sleep this morning we may as well make good use of the time."

Diverted, he looked down at her. "What did you have in mind?"

She smiled and opened her arms. It was an offer he couldn't refuse.

Ian agreed that it was, perhaps, unfair to everyone for him to play the pipes so close to the house at such an early hour. "I'll go across the road into the pasture," he announced.

"What about my sheep?" said Jamie, alarmed.

"You've always said they like it when you play to them."

"The fiddle's civilized. It's not a bloody great instrument of war," Jamie muttered.

What Jamie's prized Jacob's sheep thought of the piping was obvious from the first few notes. The alpha ram gave the universal sheep alarm signal, a sort of snort-sneeze, and they stampeded to the far end of the pasture and arranged themselves in a defensive circle, ewes and lambs in the center, rams around the edge, facing out. They watched Ian carefully.

He paced up and down. A good piper could never play properly standing still. Mournful notes flowed over the pasture and the sheep shivered with apprehension. But in *Taigh Rois*, Jamie and Màiri slept happily undisturbed.

Eilidh woke early one morning and her sharp ears picked up the distant sound of the pipes. She crept out of bed and dressed and walked up the hill to the pasture. Arms resting on the stone wall, she stood and listened. At the far end of the pasture sheep's heads turned around to watch her suspiciously, but they did not break formation.

When he stopped she climbed over the wall and went to him. "What was that tune? I don't know it."

"It's a *piobaireachd* I'm composing."

"Hmm. Parts of it sound more like a *pioghaid*"—a magpie—"or a *piorradh*"—a squall.

Ian said, unoffended, "Well, I'm just making it up as I go along, I haven't got it right yet." He lifted his head and stared dramatically towards the ocean. "I'm going to call it "*Cumha dha* Sally.""

Lament for Sally, Eilidh thought and her heart went out to him. Poor baby, she thought. But sympathy was not what he needed, he felt sorry for himself enough already. She said matter-of-factly, "I liked the *urlar*"—the ground—and she hummed it. "But not the variation that goes . . . " She hummed again.

Ian winced. "You're right, that's terrible." He picked up the pipes and stared at them thoughtfully. "Maybe if I tried . . . " He hummed a new variation.

"Aye, that would work better. Tell you what, why don't I bring some staff paper tomorrow and note it down for you? It'd be easier to see what works."

"Would you, darling Eilidh? That would be *miorbhuileach*, if you'd do that for me." He smiled at her gratefully and she realized it was the first real smile she'd seen from him since Sally had left.

She brought her staff paper the next morning and she and Ian worked on his lament diligently. Intrigued, the next day she brought her violin and began improvising with him. They played and she scribbled and they played some more.

In a few days enough music was on paper that they could play it in Joe's and Eilidh's kitchen on her violin and the bagpipe chanter, just the way they'd played music together as youngsters under their parents' tutelage.

Joe listened in awe. "That's wonderful. It's so sad, but there's that lovely happy bit too. And it's different. It's unusual, fiddle and bagpipe together."

"Aye," said Eilidh thoughtfully, an idea growing in her head. Several days later she coaxed Joe into coming with her with his tape recorder for their morning *seisean*. He taped their playing, one of Ian's drones capped off so the pipes didn't drown out the violin. Back in the kitchen, they listened to it. Then they took the tape up to *Taigh Rois* to play for the elder MacDonalds and the Mac an Rìghs.

Jamie said slowly, "I've never heard anything like that. Where did you get that piece of music?"

"It's Ian's *piobaireachd*. He wrote it for Sally."

Four heads swiveled around to look at Ian, who blushed.

Darroch said, "It's quite *miorbhuileach*. Play it tomorrow night at the *cèilidh*."

The reaction at the *cèilidh* was one of total, astonished silence. Joe taped this performance, along with the excited murmur that came next and rose to shouts of approval. Eilidh mailed the tape off to the conductor of her orchestra, who she knew was looking for different, exciting new pieces of music for the next season.

He liked it. In fact, he loved it, got the music from Eilidh and gave it to the orchestra's arranger to score parts for supporting instruments. Woodwinds, said Eilidh, and a piano. He would premiere it at a matinee concert that fall and recommended to Eilidh and Ian that they consider entering it into that year's contest for new music from young Scottish composers.

Ian was lifted momentarily out of his gloominess. He sent off a copy of the tape to Sally, with the implied message, see how you're making me suffer. But she'd written back enthusiastically, delighted at the music, flattered by the title and thrilled that he had found a new interest to keep him occupied while she was gone. She was deep into creativity, having discovered in herself a new talent for writing.

Music distracted him, working with Ros MacPherson in the Island clinic distracted him, but nothing kept the deep loneliness from closing in at the end of the day. He lay awake for hours at night, thinking about Sally, wondering if she would ever come back to him.

Forty-two

But, bid the strain be wild and deep,
Nor let thy notes of joy be first!
I tell thee, minstrel, I must weep,
Or else this heavy heart will burst . . .

Lord Byron

*M*isery needed company.

To Jamie's delight, Joe Munro was both enthusiastic and experienced when it came to the inner workings of automobiles. Out of economic necessity he'd kept his mother's ancient Austin running long after it should have shuddered to a well-deserved death.

The men were gathering at *Taigh Rois* Saturday afternoon. Jamie had invited Joe up for what promised to be a long delightful afternoon under the bonnet of Jamie's old truck, which was making an interesting series of new noises. Darroch was coming, too. He didn't know the first thing about motors but he could be trusted to keep a conversation going and the teapot filled while the other two poked and prodded in the truck's innards.

Màiri, Eilidh and Jean were off to Airgead for several hours of mysterious female errands, culminating in tea at a pleasant little café renowned for its pastries.

Darroch had been entrusted with the care of Rosie. It was his first solo outing and he was nervous. Jean had expressed a bottle of breast milk for Rosie's afternoon feed and a spare in case she was really hungry, had packed plenty of fresh baby shirts and nappies, and for extra insurance Darroch had brought along a cassette of Jean singing the baby's favorite lullabies. That never failed to soothe the savage Rosie.

He felt confident, elated and apprehensive. Rosie's moods were unpredictable. When she was happy she was all delightful sunshine but when something displeased her she could produce ear-splitting thunder and lightning. And it was not always possible to predict what would displease her.

So Darroch was happy to be at *Taigh Rois*, in the company of Jamie, an experienced father. He rather hoped that Ian, almost a doctor, would be around too, for extra insurance, even though it came accompanied by gloom. He glanced at Rosie, snoozing peacefully near the fireplace in her Moses basket, which had been a gift, unsurprisingly, from the Minister, with appropriate Biblical quotations. Baby had been asleep since he had walked up with Jean half an hour ago. So far, so good, he thought.

The three were starting out their afternoon with a plate of Jean's chocolate chip cookies, warm from that morning's baking, and tea, poured by Jamie into the sturdy mugs he always favored when Màiri wasn't around to insist on teacups.

They were chatting happily when Ian came down the stairs from his bedroom, drawn by the hope of sympathetic male company. All three sighed when they saw his expression.

He sat down at the table, dwarfing the chair, and said nothing. Jamie poured him a mug of tea.

Conversation came to a halt as they watched him apprehensively. Clearly, he had much on his mind.

Finally he blurted, "Women!" and the other three jumped.

"Women," he growled again. "What do they want?"

Recovering first, Darroch said, "They want what men want."

Ian said, "Not so. Men are simple. Men want a hot meal and a hot body in bed. That's all men want."

"Not so," said Darroch indignantly. "I certainly want more than that. I want love. And laughter."

"Music," said Jamie. "Sex and music."

"Companionship," murmured Joe, thinking of long walks, holding Eilidh's hand. Stopping to look at wildflowers and to exchange kisses.

"Intellectual stimulation. Arguments," said Darroch.

"Making up after arguments," said Jamie, with a secret smile.

"Books," said Joe. "Reading a fine book while Eilidh plays her violin." Thinking of his darling Eilidh, Joe sighed deeply and happily, then blushed when the other three looked at him and grinned.

"Newlyweds," said Jamie affectionately.

"We're right back where we started," said Ian, forgetting his woes momentarily in the pleasure of getting a good argument going. "Sex. That's what matters to men. Look at him," he said, gesturing at his scarlet-faced brother-in-law. That's what he's thinking about right now."

Jamie said, "No one's denying that sex is important to men, Ian, least of all the three of us. We're just saying that it's important to women too."

"Ha," said Ian triumphantly. "Then why wouldn't she let me make love to her?"

Darroch said, astounded, "Are you referring to my stepdaughter?"

Not heeding the warning, Ian said, "Aye, of course. Who else has been making me miserable these last three months?"

"Just what did you try on with her?" Darroch growled, his protective instincts toward his womenfolk rising.

"I didn't try anything on. I asked her to go to bed with me." Then, realizing he was in dangerous waters, he added hastily, "So she would marry me."

"What?"

Ian explained patiently, "I knew she'd marry me if she gave herself to me. She's that kind of girl. She'd only give her body to the man she meant to marry. So it seemed that making love to her was the best way to get her to commit herself to me." As the three stared at him in disbelief, he added, "You know, Dad. Like you did with Mother. You made love to her six days after you met her so that she'd agree to marry you."

Jamie choked on a mouthful of tea.

Darroch was furious. Màiri's quick capitulation to Jamie was a sore spot with him, probably always would be even though he was happily married now, and he certainly didn't like hearing it discussed in public.

Joe was shocked, fascinated and embarrassed. He didn't know where to direct his eyes.

Jamie coughed and sputtered and Ian slapped him on the back. "All right now, Pop?"

Jamie snarled, "How the hell did you know that? And don't call me Pop."

"Sorry, Dad. Mother told Eilidh and Eilidh told me. She thought it was sweet. It is, sort of."

"Women," said Jamie bitterly. "No concept of a secret, no idea of privacy when they get together to wag their tongues. Is there nothing they won't tell each other?"

"I think it's sweet, too," said Joe shyly, braving Jamie's and Darroch's glares.

"It's private, you great young prats. Not to be talked about." Jamie said a few other well-chosen words in the Gaelic that left Ian squirming.

"I'm sorry, sir. I didn't think . . . ," said Ian guiltily.

"Do you ever?" Jamie said.

Hoping to defuse the situation Darroch said, "Well, it's all water under the bridge now. All right, Jamie? Ian?"

Joe said hesitantly, "I think women need to be wooed . . . "

"You're the one to talk, aren't you?" said Ian. "You hopped into bed with my sister damned fast."

It was Joe's turn to glare. "There was a reason for that. Besides, she asked me. She was afraid . . . "

"And you took advantage of that." Ian smiled triumphantly.

Joe rose, his fists clenched. "Damn you, Ian, you know what the situation was with that bastard in Edinburgh. And it's none of your damn business anyway. Step outside and I'll show you just how little of your damn business it is."

Rosie stirred and mewled loudly in her sleep.

Alarmed, the four looked in the direction of the Moses basket and lowered their voices guiltily. "She's not waking up yet, is she?" said Jamie in terror. He'd heard Rosie in full cry.

"I hope not." Darroch tiptoed to the basket and bent over his daughter. He fussed with her blankets, then came back to the table and sank down into his chair. "She's all right."

"Thank God." Jamie sighed, relieved.

Darroch said, "Let's try to remember it's our wives and daughters we're talking about . . . "

"And my sister," muttered Ian.

Joe, who had sat down, scowled at him.

Darroch continued patiently, "And show some respect. We all know what it's like to want a woman and not be able to have her . . . "

Ian said, "Except Joe, who got what he wanted right away."

Joe rose again, his face contorted with rage. "Outside, Ian. Unless you want your mother's rug covered with blood."

"Shut up, you lot!" snapped Jamie. "Darroch's right. The next one that says anything disrespectful about our women is going face first out that door."

"Sorry," Ian said.

Joe muttered something under his breath.

Darroch began again, "A woman needs time to think about it and a man has to be patient . . . "

The devil had hold of Ian's tongue and he could not stop himself from saying, "What the hell do you know about it? Jean fell into your arms like a ripe plum."

Darroch stood up and shouted, "She was married when we met and I waited months to have her. And it took months after that to get her to marry me! *A Dhia,* Ian, I'll flatten you myself, six foot six be damned!"

"I'll help you," snarled Joe.

Jamie blinked, marveling as always at his son's ability to stir up trouble. Darroch, known for his calm, self-contained-to-the-point-of-stuffiness demeanor, and Joe, quiet and shy, were both on their feet, fists clenched, glaring at Ian.

"It's my fault," Jamie mourned. "I should have beaten the smart mouth out of him when he was a teenager." He had never laid a hand in anger on either child, would never have even thought of it. He growled, "Listen, you. If you don't want to sleep on the beach tonight and eat seaweed for supper you'll apologize and keep a civil tongue in your head from now on."

Ian looked around at the other three. He had not intended to get himself in so deep and he certainly had not intended to alienate the men he was relying on for comfort and advice. He dropped his head into his large hands and mumbled something.

"What did he say?" asked Joe.

"He says he's sorry," said Jamie. He spoke briskly and firmly to his son in the Gaelic.

Ian lifted his head. "Aye, sir. I'm sorry, I don't know what got into me. I couldn't stop myself. I'm miserable, if you must know."

Darroch dropped back into his chair and Joe followed his example. "Well, I think we've already figured that out."

"If any of you can tell me what to do . . . I'm at my wit's end. I dream about her, I think about her constantly, I'm knotted up inside wanting her." Ian said despairingly.

Darroch said, "When I was desperate for Jean I used to walk down to the sea in the middle of the night without a coat, let the wind and the sea spray get me thoroughly chilled. I'd get so cold my balls would crawl up inside me for comfort. Then I'd run up the hill, tear my clothes off and throw myself in bed. It was the only way I could get to sleep, sometimes."

"What ever happened to cold showers?" said Jamie, amused in spite of himself.

Darroch grinned. "Those quit working when I started imagining Jean in the shower with me and thinking of ways to warm her up."

Joe said, "There's nothing more wonderful, is there. Having your own woman to love." He brushed brown hair out of his eyes and adjusted his glasses. "I never dreamed anyone like Eilidh would ever belong to me. She's—well, I don't have the words." His face glowed with love.

Darroch and Jamie looked at him, then at each other, thinking of their own hard-won happiness with their beloved wives. All three smiled.

Ian said, through gritted teeth, "This is not helping me, watching the three of you grinning, lusting for your women."

Darroch said gently, "There is no help for you, lad. Only hope. Did she give you hope?"

"I think so. She said she loves me, she still says it in her letters. She says she adores me, in fact. She just can't commit herself to life here on the Island."

"Compromise," said Joe. "Eilidh and I have had to work it out one step at a time. Darroch said . . . " He glanced shyly at the older man. "It's better to have part of what you love, than nothing at all. You've got to find a way to be together that suits you both."

"Damned if I can figure out what it's going to be. I've given my word to Ros MacPherson to make my future as a doctor on Eilean Dubh. I could get on with a practice in Edinburgh or even down in England, but it's not right for me. I have a commitment to Eilean Dubh."

"Just like his mother," said Jamie proudly.

"And if Sally doesn't want to live here with me . . . " He sighed.

The other three sighed in sympathy.

Rosie stirred and uttered her trademark banshee wail. The men nearly fell off their chairs in shock and Darroch sprang to his feet. "Warm her bottle, for God's sake, Jamie. It's in your fridge." He scurried to the Moses basket and lifted Rosie out. "There, there, *m'aingeal, mo fhlùr*," he crooned. "Hush, baby, Daddy's here." He patted her back and she burrowed her head into his sweater, rooting. "Aye, love, I know you're starving. Uncle Jamie's getting your bottle; it'll be all right soon. Daddy's just going to change your nappy and you'll be warm and dry."

Joe and Ian watched, bemused. "That'll be us someday, Ian," said Joe.

"God willing," Ian mumbled. He had wanted four children. Right now he would settle for the promise of just one.

But he felt better after he'd shared his misery with the other men. If they'd had the same experience perhaps his situation would end happily too. If it didn't—he tried not to think about that. If he didn't win Sally he'd never be happy again and he couldn't bear to think about losing her.

He went back to school in Edinburgh and buried himself in his studies. When she was ready they'd talk about it again.

She had promised him that and he clung to hope.

PART IV

Ruth and Russ

Forty-three

I will find out where she has gone,
And kiss her lips and take her hands;
And walk among long dappled grass,
And pluck till time and times are done
The silver apples of the moon,
The golden apples of the sun.

W. B. Yeats

No one really knew whose idea it had been, but Jean thought that it had started with the article Sally had written for the travel magazine.

Shortly after her arrival in Milwaukee Sally began to have dreams of Eilean Dubh. They were not just about Ian, and her mother and Darroch, and Rosie. They were dreams that drifted and swept over the mountains of the Island, down to the sea and back again to the cozy rank of lime-washed cottages that lined the coast at Ros Mór. In the dreams she could smell peat smoke and wildflowers. And they always ended in her own cottage, by her fireplace, under her thatched roof. They were dreams that brought her a deep contentment while she slept and a deep sense of loss when she woke up.

She had expected to miss Ian dreadfully, and did, but now she realized that she also missed Eilean Dubh. It was disturbing, to feel such attachment to a place where she'd only spent a few months.

Desperate to exorcise the Island, she took her Creative Writing professor's advice and began to use what she was experiencing in what she was writing. The professor read one of her pieces, an exercise in description in which she'd written about the view from Cemetery Hill, and was impressed enough to suggest that she expand it and submit it to a travel magazine that liked to run picturesque essays.

She wrote Joe for pictures he had taken of the Island, and submitted them along with her manuscript. It was accepted.

Now she sat staring at the cover of the magazine, seeing Joe's picture of the sea at the end of their lane. And her article inside, and her byline, and more of Joe's pictures.

The magazine editor wrote her that the article had produced an enthusiastic response from readers and expressed an interest in more material about Eilean Dubh. Little cozy islands always went over big with travel fans.

"I've been thinking, Mom," she began in her weekly phone call with Jean on the Island. "Why couldn't we put together a book about Eilean Dubh? We could use your fairy tales and Joe's pictures."

Jean said enthusiastically, "And music. Maybe a folk tune or two. Or something new from Jamie."

"And a recipe from Sheilah."

"And folk remedies. Everyone's interested in them."

"And maybe include a CD by *Tradisean*."

Darroch liked the idea, too, and ran it by Liz, his agent. She thought that interest in Eilean Dubh, spurred by their recording's success and fueled by *Tradisean's* sudden disappearance, was still high. She talked to a publisher. He liked the idea well enough to come up to the Island for a chat, and at the end of his stay offered a book contract.

Amazed and appalled by what she'd gotten herself into, Jean phoned the good news to Sally.

Sally went immediately to her computer and began to sketch out an outline for the book. She and Jean e-mailed ideas back and forth.

Enthusiasm ran high. Joe carried his camera everywhere, taking pictures like a crazed Margaret Bourke-White, and studied the pictures he already had. Sheilah searched through her recipes, wondering which ones to share. Jamie polished tunes he had written and Eilidh noted them down for him. Jean polished her fairy tales and collected folk remedies. Anna Wallace wrote a piece about Island wildflowers to go with Joe's photos.

Sally worked on the narrative that would tie it all together. *Eilean Dubh: Celebration of a Small Island* became her working title.

Sally had kept her nose to the grindstone. She had never worked so hard and accomplished so much. Though it wasn't easy juggling the book and her class work as well as coping with her yearning for Ian, she completed all her courses and was ready to graduate at the end of summer session. After graduation she would go to Eilean Dubh and finish the book. And sort out her love life.

Ian called Jean and asked humbly, "May I go with you to Sally's graduation?" In the past he would simply have announced that he was coming, but the time without Sally had taught him patience and humility.

"Yes, of course, Ian. I'm sure she'll be glad to see you."

Ian thought glumly that he hoped so.

He slumped in his seat all the way on the long flight to Milwaukee, worrying about his reception. He had asked Jean to keep his arrival secret. He wanted to see what Sally's face would show him when they met again.

She was waiting at the gate for them when they got off the plane. She wrapped her arms around her mother, kissed Rosie, embraced Darroch, and suddenly noticed who was looming behind him.

"Hello, Sally," said Ian.

Sally turned white, then red, and longed to throw herself into his arms. But she was determined to play it cool. "Hi, Ian," she said, trembling. She'd never realized how expressive his eyes were, and the message they were sending was heavy with meaning. Decision time, Sally, she thought, and stretched up to give him a tender kiss on the cheek.

Ian shivered when her lips touched him.

Well, that's a good sign, she thought, and her heart went all soppy.

The man standing beside her cleared his throat, reminding Sally to introduce him. "This is my friend Charlie. Daddy had an unexpected crisis at work and he couldn't come to meet you so Charlie filled in for me. He borrowed his mother's minivan so there'd be room for everyone." She smiled at him and he blushed.

When it came Ian's turn to shake hands he gripped Charlie's firmly and stared into his eyes. Who are you, he said with his gaze. What do you mean to my Sally?

Charlie quailed at the stare, but returned a firm handshake. He was crazy about Sally but was aware he did not have her full attention. And now, standing before him, was the reason why: six foot six, uncompromisingly Scottish and grimly determined.

Charlie glanced at Sally, caught her expression and knew his suit was doomed.

The Abbott house, Jean's home for the twenty years she was married to Russ, was spacious, with high ceilings, but Darroch and Ian *Mór* cut it down to size. Sally led her mother's party to their room, then turned to Ian, following behind.

"I wasn't expecting you," she said. "I don't have a room prepared."

"I can sleep on the sofa," he began but Sally said, "Nonsense. This house has five bedrooms. Come on, we'll find one for you."

They went down the hall into the room opposite Sally's. "The room's clean but the bed needs sheets." She got linens and they made the bed together. Then they stood looking at each other across it.

For once in his life Ian was at a loss for words.

So was Sally, and being in a bedroom with him wasn't helping. Finally she blurted, "Aren't you going to kiss me hello?"

He moved around the bed and took her in his arms. They kissed passionately. The bed beside them loomed large in both their minds.

If we could just lie together, Ian thought desperately, I could tell her everything that's in my head, everything I've thought about during this wretched time apart.

But the bedroom door was open. Sally pulled away from him, knees trembling, lips tingling.

"Do you still love me?" he demanded. He knew it was the most important question he'd ever asked anyone.

"Yes, of course. More than ever." She flung her arms around his neck and whispered in his ear, "Do you still love me?"

Words failed him, in English anyway. He poured out his heart to her in the Gaelic, knowing that he was babbling, and not caring.

Sally looked at him, chuckling. "I take it that's yes."

Overwhelmed with love and passion, he picked her up in his arms and sat down on the bed with her in his lap, kissing and cuddling her. In another moment he would have her down on the bed, making frantic love to her.

Conscious of the open door, Sally tore her mouth from his and said, "Later, sweet thing. Right now I have to go down and help Ruth with dinner."

"Who's Ruth?"

"The lady next door. She's Daddy's special friend. She and her daughters are going to eat with us tonight." She wriggled off his lap and onto her feet and in a moment was out the door, leaving Ian sitting on the bed.

He heard Jean and Darroch leaving their bedroom, where they'd tucked Rosie up for a nap. Darroch, glancing through the bedroom door, spotted Ian.

"Go ahead, *mo chridhe*, I'll be down in a minute," he said to Jean, and knocked on the open door. "All right, Ian?" he said.

Ian lifted his head. "Aye. At least I think so." He could still feel Sally's warmth in his arms and he was still desperately aroused.

Darroch walked in and sat down in a chair by the bed. "How did it go?"

"*Miorbhuileach*. She says she loves me."

Darroch smiled sympathetically. "Hellish, isn't it," he said. When Ian did not reply, he said, "Take your time, get yourself sorted. Then come downstairs for a drink. You look like you could use one." He got up and left, shaking his head, wondering if his stepdaughter was in the same state as Ian. Probably worse, he thought.

Forty-four

*The time will come
When, with elation,
You will greet yourself arriving
At your own door, in your own mirror
And each will smile at the other's welcome.*

Derek Walcott

*J*ean walked into the kitchen and was startled to find Ruth from next door, an apron around her waist, busily chopping cabbage for cole slaw. They hadn't seen each other for two years and Jean remembered, resentfully, that Russ had slept with this woman after Jean had fled to Scotland, while they were still married. "Hi," she said.

Ruth turned from the chopping board, wiped her hands on a paper towel, and said, "Hello. Welcome back." She extended a hand. "Nice to see you again."

Jean shook her hand. "It's fun to be back." They looked at each other for a long awkward moment. Then Jean said, "Can I help with anything?"

"Well, you could slice bread and put it on a plate. The rest is done."

Jean looked admiringly at the plump loaf of bread. "Did you make this?"

"Yes. It's not as good as what you make. I've just started baking bread because Russ likes it. He missed yours." She blushed, suddenly realizing what she had revealed.

Aha, thought Jean, and picked up the cue. "You and Russ . . . you're an item, then?" What a stupid thing to say, she thought; you sound like a silly gossip columnist.

"We're very fond of each other." Ruth said anxiously, "I hope you don't mind."

Astonished at the comment, Jean realized that she did not mind. If Russ had found another woman it would relieve her last little niggling guilt about leaving him. "No, that's great. He's been lonely, I'm afraid."

"So was I. For years, after Walter died." Ruth smiled. The smile made her quite pretty. She was small, verging on plump, with dark brown hair and eyes, not in the least glamorous, not the type Jean had imagined Russ would want, now that he was free to roam the world of unattached women. "My girls like him a lot."

"How are your daughters?" said Jean, relieved to be able to steer the conversation into neutral territory. And Ruth began to talk proudly of the oldest daughter in nursing school, the second at university, the third in high school, the fourth an eighth-grader.

"Three of them will be joining us tonight. Carol's got hospital duty so she can't be here but the others will come. Eating up everything in sight and talking their heads off. Russ says it's like being inside a beehive when they all get going. I hope your husband doesn't mind."

"When has a man ever minded pretty young girls?" Jean was remembering, now, that all of Ruth's daughters were attractive and smart and very, very talkative. Bemused, she imagined Russ in the middle of five women. Like a sheikh, she thought: he's probably the center of attention and loves it.

Sally came in from setting the table in the dining room and saw with relief that her mother and Ruth seemed to be getting along fine. She'd blurted out to Jean, months ago, her experience in coming home unexpectedly from school one morning and finding her father and Ruth in their bathrobes, drinking coffee. It had been obvious that they'd spent the night together.

She'd been afraid that Jean would be angry with Ruth, or standoffish. But they were chatting like the old friends and neighbors they were, having lived side by side for fourteen years.

Then Darroch came into the kitchen and was introduced to Ruth. Two of Ruth's daughters bounced in, talking furiously, and the eighth-grader followed them, wailing, "Where's Russ? My computer's eaten my English paper! I need Russ to find it! I couldn't possibly do it all over again."

"Not home yet, darling. Relax. Russ will fix it." Ruth smiled reassuringly.

Voices rose, talking, laughing. Bedlam, thought Jean, imagining Russ in the center of such commotion. Suddenly she could not wait to see him again.

The kitchen door swung open again and Ian came in. He stopped abruptly at the sight of so many pretty girls.

Ruth and her daughters stared in awed admiration. Ian always evoked that kind of reaction from women, Sally thought, and introduced him. "This is my friend Ian," she said. "This is Ruth from next door and these are her daughters: Liz, Annie, and Jennie."

Ian smiled disarmingly. If there was one thing he knew how to do it was to enchant women. There was a low "wicked!" from one of the girls and a giggle from another. They shook hands shyly.

"Would anyone like a drink?" asked Sally.

"Aye, please," said Ian. "A large whisky."

Darroch said, "I'll have the same, please, Sally."

Sally took drink orders and went to the liquor cabinet in the dining room. She'd bought a bottle of Glenfiddich, knowing what the Scots would like. As she was pouring Russ came in. "Hi, Daddy. Everyone's here. They're in the kitchen."

Russ sighed happily. "What a racket. I can tell the girls have arrived." He went into the kitchen. Jean noted with interest that his gaze lingered tenderly on Ruth, before he kissed Jean and shook hands with the men.

At dinner the din increased as the girls all talked at once and the adults put in a word whenever they could. By the end of the meal, when they took their coffee in and sat in front of the fireplace, everyone was well acquainted.

Just like being back on Eilean Dubh, Jean thought, remembering get-togethers in Jamie and Màiri's kitchen. Only noisier.

Forty-five

My true love hath my heart and I have his,
By just exchange one for another given;
I hold his dear, and mine he cannot miss,
There never was a better bargain driven.
My true love hath my heart and I have his.

Sir Philip Sidney

*C*onscious of Ian's longing looks, Sally made an excuse to be alone with him after dinner. "Let's take a walk around the block, Ian," she said. "You can get a look at a typical American neighborhood."

They walked hand-in-hand, saying little. Now that they were together again they were a little unsure of what to say to each other, how to re-establish their relationship. Ian, used to blurting out whatever was on his mind, found himself unexpectedly tongue-tied. When Sally suggested they go around the house and sit on the swing on the side porch he accepted eagerly.

They sat, carefully not looking at each other. Then Sally said, "I've really missed you, sweet thing."

"Oh, Sally," he said. He pulled her into his arms and kissed her fiercely.

When she came up for air she said, "Have you missed me?"

"Don't tease me, Sally. You know I have." He stared at her. "And you know what I've come here . . . to hear."

"Yes."

"I'll ask you again, and this time for the last time. Will you marry me?"

"Yes."

The answer was given so quietly and with such conviction that he was stunned. "You will?"

"Yep. I've figured it all out . . . " He grabbed her again and it was several minutes later before she could add, "Don't you want to know what I've planned?"

"All that I care about is that you're going to be mine."

She grinned. "So if I say that I want you to stay in America and be a doctor here that's all right?"

Ian grimaced. It would be like cutting out his heart to have to leave Eilean Dubh but he'd learned in their months apart that Sally was absolutely necessary for his happiness. If she wanted him to stay in the States he was resolved to agree and to endure it, at least until he could talk her into going back to the Island. "Aye," he said firmly. "I will have to qualify over here, of course. Is that what you want?"

"No, of course not. I want to live with you on Eilean Dubh. The doctor's wife. And mother to all those children you want to have." She gazed at him demurely. "We'll still have to negotiate the number of children, though."

Overwhelmed, he reached for her but she drew back. "You haven't heard all of it. I'm going to be a writer. I'm going to do travel writing. I've sold a magazine editor on the idea of a series of pieces about Britain. They're always popular in travel magazines.

"I'm going to take trips all around Britain and find unusual places to write about, quirky things like weird monuments and ghosts and little festivals and . . . "

She said a great deal more but Ian had stopped listening to all the details she was pouring out so eagerly. It was all going to come true, all the dreams and plans he'd made for the two of them. He'd have his Sally and his Island and his career as a doctor. He was the happiest and the luckiest man in the world.

"Of course after I have a baby, I'll need to stick closer to home and then I'll start writing fiction. Maybe love stories; I'll try them out on Eilidh. I like writing fiction; I have a short story out now to a little literary magazine." She sighed happily. "That's the great thing about writing. You can do it anywhere, even on a funny little Scottish island."

Her voice hummed in his ears like the song of a thousand birds singing in harmony. He pulled her onto his lap, covered her face with kisses and petted every inch of her he could reach, until she stopped talking, breathless, and kissed him back.

"Come to bed with me, Sally. I can't wait any longer."

"What, right now?"

"Tonight, after everyone's gone to sleep."

But she was feeling shy. "Let's get acquainted again. Then we'll see."

It was his turn to sigh.

Forty-six

You will love again the stranger who was your self.

Derek Walcott

Jean, Darroch and Ian were beginning to feel at home in Milwaukee. There was plenty of time for little chats between various members of the party.

Ian confided to Darroch that Sally had said yes to marriage.

Sally told Jean what she had told Ian and Jean was quite breathless at the idea that her darling daughter would be coming to live on the Island. She considered Ian as a future son-in-law and decided that he would do very nicely.

Russ told Jean that he was thinking of asking Ruth to marry him. "I don't want to spend the rest of my life alone."

Jean shook her head. "Not a good reason, Russ. Do you love her?"

He didn't answer.

It was all very gratifying to Jean, so many loose ends being wrapped up so tidily. Sally's graduation the previous week had been an occasion of great pride for her parents, but for Jean it was not an ending to the parenting phase of her life, as she had sadly anticipated years ago when Sally had started college.

Instead, she was starting all over with a new baby and a wonderful new man to raise her child with her. She had a grandchild, to carry on the Greer and Abbott family lines. And Sally was going to marry Ian, a fine choice for a husband, and they would be living right up the lane in the thatched cottage that had brought Jean so much happiness. One day, soon if Ian had his way, there would be children from that marriage, and they'd be right next door for her to pet and love.

Eilean Dubh, thought Jean. Her life had been changed, all thanks to her MacChriathar ancestor Ùisdean's sad parting from his lover Mòrag Mac an Rìgh, and his forced emigration to America two centuries ago. Now she'd brought her family back to the Island where it would flourish again. A circle closed. That, surely, was worth a prayer of thanks to the One Who Listens, Jean knew.

It was time for her to make her final farewells to her home in Milwaukee. She went out for lunch with a group of her girlfriends, leaving Darroch in charge of Rosie, and they spent a wonderful two hours talking and laughing.

She was dropped off in front of the house and remembered that she had no key. She walked around to the side, hoping that the door would be unlocked, and was astonished to see Darroch stretched out on the chaise longue in the garden.

He was wearing one of Russ' old bathing suits. Russ never threw out any of his clothes and he had a collection of swimsuits in various sizes, purchased as his body had changed and matured. This one, Jean estimated, was about ten years old, and fitted Darroch perfectly, wrapping itself around his slim hips.

She had never seen him dressed like that. It was too chilly on Eilean Dubh to lie around in a swimsuit, even in summer, and men there never even took off their shirts when working outside.

She stared in admiration. What a man, she thought, and he's all mine. And then with a start of alarm she remembered the baby. "Where's Rosie?" she demanded.

Darroch opened his eyes drowsily and focused them on his wife. "*Feasgar math, mo chridhe.* Did you have a good time with your friends?"

"Yes, lovely. Where's Rosie?"

"She's in the kitchen. Ruth's quite fallen in love with her; she asked if she could feed her lunch." He smiled. "She adores children, you can see it in her. I wonder if Russ knows. We might not be the only forty-year-olds in the family with a new baby when they get married. That is, if Russ ever gets around to proposing to her."

Jean was silent, thinking over what he had said. Not the part about the baby, although that was enough to bemuse her, thinking of Russ starting all over again with middle-of-the-night feedings and dirty diapers.

It was the fact that her husband had mentioned, so casually, about them all being part of one family. And it was true, they were all related in a way:

Jean, Darroch, Rosie, Russ, Ruth and her girls; Rod and Lucy and grandson Andrew Russell, Sally and Ian. And Jamie and Màiri, as much as Jamie might dislike the idea of being in the same family with Russ. They were all related, and she was the center of it. They were all related because of her. Ten degrees of Jean, she thought, and the idea made her a little dizzy.

She shook it off and said, "Where did you get the suit?"

"It's Russ's. Ruth found it; she said he wouldn't mind if I borrowed it. Why don't you go change into a swimsuit, Jean, and take in some sun?"

"Okay." She went into the house and peeped into the kitchen. Ruth was sitting facing her and the baby was in a high chair, her back to Jean. Ruth was talking to her lovingly and feeding her spoonfuls of something from a little baby food jar.

Jean put her fingers to her lips and smiled at Ruth to continue. She closed the kitchen door quietly and went upstairs.

She'd left her swimsuits at the house, not expecting to need them on Eilean Dubh, and they were packed in a box at the back of the closet in the bedroom she'd once shared with Russ. She found it and pulled out a one-piece and a modest bikini that she'd bought for a trip to the Caribbean they'd planned years ago. It had been cancelled when Russ had had an emergency with the business.

After some hesitation she put on the bikini. The top was a little skimpy because of the expansion of her breasts from nursing but she decided she looked all right. And it was only for their back yard. She didn't think she'd wear it out in public, though.

Back outside she was pleased to see Darroch's eyes widen at the sight of her in the bikini. "Very nice," he said. "Are you sure no one can see us back here?"

She stretched out on the second chaise. "Yes. Why?'

"I'm not used to having so much of my wife exposed to public view."

"Oh, it'll be handy for nursing," she said, and right on cue Ruth appeared with the baby who chortled happily and held out her arms at the sight of her mother. Rosie latched on to Jean's breast, more for comfort than food, since she was full of baby sweet potatoes.

"She's such a darling, Jean," said Ruth wistfully. "She's been good as gold."

Jean and Darroch exchanged glances, each thinking of Rosie's unpredictable moods. "Yes, she's a little love, aren't you, my sweetie," she said. "Most of the time, anyway. Hope she'll be as good for me the rest of the day. Otherwise I might have to call on you for reinforcements, Ruth."

Ruth said eagerly, "I'd love it; call anytime. What's it like, having a new baby?"

"At my age, you mean. Well, it's interesting," Jean began.

Darroch interrupted. "Quite wonderful," he said firmly. "Exciting, and maddening, but always *miorbhuileach*. I have never had any experience with babies before. I am quite enjoying it."

"Darroch's a great help with her," said Jean. "I wouldn't want to do it with a man who doesn't help out." A word of caution was in order, she thought, remembering what Darroch had said. Russ had not been the most eager helper in the world with Rod and Sally when they were tiny.

"Yes, I suppose so," said Ruth but her expression was still wistful.

Forty-seven

. . . down by the brimming river
I heard a lover sing
Under an arch of the railway:
"Love has no ending . . . "

W. H. Auden

Sitting in the sun porch with Russ one evening Darroch picked up a large coffee table book of Frank Lloyd Wright's work and leafed through it with growing interest. What amazing ideas the man had had, he thought; what wonderful houses he'd built.

Russ was a Wright enthusiast and noted Darroch's involvement in the book with approval. "Like that, do you?" he said.

"Aye. I've always admired him."

"Ever seen a Wright house in person?"

"No," said Darroch with regret. "There aren't any in Britain."

"Oak Park, Illinois," said Russ. "Suburb of Chicago. Fantastic collection of Wright houses all in one neighborhood. Like to drive down and see them?"

"Very much," said Darroch.

"I try to get down there at least once a year. I park the car and walk around enjoying them. None are open to the public; they're private residences. But it's fun to see the outsides." He sighed. "I thought once I'd like to become an architect, but I had to take over my Dad's business."

He hesitated, then said, "We could do that tomorrow if you like. It's a couple hours drive to Chicago. Traffic's terrible so we'd need to get an early start."

Darroch agreed with alacrity and within an hour the party was organized. Ruth wanted to go, too, and Jean and Rosie of course. And Ruth's youngest daughter Jennie, who thought she'd take photos and notes and write a paper on Frank Lloyd Wright for a class at school. They'd take Ruth's van since Russ's sports car would only hold two.

That left Sally and Ian. Dubious, they looked at each other across the dining room table. Ian, with his height, was never comfortable in a car for long periods of time, unless he was its only occupant and could push the seat back to its full extension. Long-legged Sally had the same problem. Neither looked forward to a three-hour car ride to Chicago.

Ian had as much interest in Frank Lloyd Wright as the average medical student, which was to say none. He announced, "I will stay home. That will make more room for all of you."

Sally glanced around the table. "I'll stay home, too. It wouldn't be right to leave our guest here all alone."

Ian brightened.

Russ looked at Ian suspiciously. He had not bargained on leaving his only daughter alone in the house all day with this Scottish sex fiend, who he knew damn well was interested in more than Sally's mind. "Uhhh . . . ," he began, trying to think of an excuse to abort the excursion.

Sally, quicker-witted than her father, said, "Ian and I will fix dinner and have it all ready when you get home. What would you like, Daddy? How about pork chops? Or a lovely roast chicken, with my orange dressing? And cornbread? And I'll make something special for dessert. Maybe a pie."

Russ felt his mouth begin to water. Sally was a superb cook and a special meal from her was not to be turned down lightly. His resolve to keep the two young people apart weakened. With all that cooking they'd not have time to get into trouble.

Sally clinched the deal by saying, "And in the morning Ian and I will go swimming. Or play tennis."

Great, thought Russ; they'll get too tired to do anything but cook.

The party set off the next morning, the van packed with people, baby supplies, and lunch. Sally and Ian waved good-bye.

Then he turned to her eagerly. "What shall we do now, Sally?" he said, hoping against hope she was going to drag him up to her bedroom. A whole day of privacy, he thought eagerly, a whole day alone with his darling girl.

She studied him, then announced, "Tennis. I'll get the rackets. You can use Daddy's. The court's just a half mile away, up the hill."

She gave him such a good game that after a while he forgot she was a woman and threw himself hard into it, managing at last to squeak out a win.

Then they went into the ice cream shop across the street and Sally introduced Ian to sundaes.

Back home, Sally marched into the kitchen and began dinner preparations. She'd decided on the roast chicken, and she put Ian to work chopping oranges and grating bread crumbs while she sauteed herbs to season the dressing.

Then he set the table while she made iced tea and an apple pie. At last everything was ready and she slid the chicken into the oven.

Then she turned to Ian. Her eyes were wide, her palms were sweaty and she was sure her knees would knock together if she tried to walk. But she gathered her courage and said, "Let's go upstairs to bed."

Ian stared, wondering if he'd heard her or if his thoughts had suddenly acquired a voice. He'd hoped, of course, but had almost given up on a delightful afternoon of lovemaking. She'd kept them both so busy.

Sally said, "Of course, if you'd rather not . . . "

Ian blinked and came back to life. "Of course I would." He took a decisive step towards her and she stepped back, then nimbly cut past him, headed for the staircase. She thought if she didn't get upstairs immediately she'd lose her nerve. Ian followed, breathless at the turn events had taken.

Outside her bedroom she paused, her hand on the doorknob. "I'm going to take a shower. I'm all sweaty from playing tennis and cooking."

"*Ceart math*," said Ian, reverting to the Gaelic in his agitation. "I'll shower, too."

"Meet you in my room in a few minutes, then." She fled.

Ian leaned against her door, willing his knees to quit shaking and carry him across the hall to his room. When at last he was able to move he did so slowly, feeling each joint creak like an old man's.

After he'd dried off, he went across the hall to Sally's room. He knocked, then opened the door and went in. She was still in the shower; he could hear splashing and singing. He listened for a few moments, pleased that she sounded so cheerful. He felt more than a little apprehensive, and eager about what was to come.

He stepped further into the room and looked around, eager to learn all that her room could tell him about her.

The bedroom had pale, sunshine-yellow walls, lace curtains and three small oriental rugs, glowing like jewels on the polished wood floor. It was not a frilly little-girl room but it was definitely feminine. He bent to look at the contents of a large maple bookcase, wondering what she liked to read.

There were well-worn copies of *Little Women* and *Anne of Green Gables. The Jungle Book* and *Good Night, Moon,* both very old. *Bridget Jones' Diary,* next to Maeve Binchy, Rosamunde Pilcher and Nick Hornby. A dictionary and French textbooks. Books on Scottish history and wildlife, all purchased after her mother had gotten involved with Eilean Dubh. Two books about sex and marriage. He pulled one of those out and glanced through it, chuckling. So his virgin darling knew the basics. He looked forward to expanding her knowledge.

He wandered around the room, looking at another shelf with a collection of glass animals, all well dusted, and on the shelves below Beanie Babies and a group of teddy bears. The bear that was tattered and missing an eye held pride of place in the center.

There was a small collection of sports trophies, two for swimming and one for tennis that made him remember her smashing backhand with its wicked topspin that he'd met this morning. And a trophy that commemorated her high school's soccer team's first place finish in the state tournament for girls.

He stood in the center of the room and gazed around, and at last let his eyes rest on her bed. The sheets had been drawn down invitingly and the lemon-yellow quilt was neatly folded across the bottom of the bed.

He went to it, picked up a pillow and held it to his nose, and breathed in the cool fresh scent of lavender. His body tingled to his toes.

The bathroom door opened and Sally stepped out, wrapped in a beautiful mid-thigh length yellow robe, semi-opaque, and very sexy. Her whisky-colored hair flowed over her shoulders and her eyes were bright with apprehension, and something else.

He stared, dazzled. It was as though a ray of sunshine had entered the room.

She took one look at him and began to giggle. "Where did you find that?" She recognized the robe he was wearing as one of Rod's old ones. It was ancient, faded terrycloth and miles too small for Ian. The sleeves reached just below his elbows and the robe itself came only midway down his thighs. A great deal of Ian, long muscular arms and legs, stuck out and the robe barely met around his chest and belly.

He looked down at himself. "I found it hanging on the back of the closet door. I didn't want to walk around your father's house naked. It didn't seem right."

She drew a deep breath. "Well, you're in my room now. Take it off."

He gave her a long look, pulled off the robe and let it drop to the floor.

Sally stared, wide-eyed. "I've never seen a naked man before, a real one, I mean. Not a painting or a statue." Both her father and her brother had been very modest around her, keeping themselves carefully covered, even on camping trips.

She drifted closer, her eyes running over him with a touch of uneasiness. Naked, he seemed even larger than he did in clothes. How were they going to do this without him squashing her? Her eyes went lower and she shook her head dubiously. "I just don't see how you're going to fit inside me."

Ian sighed. Why did she always have to analyze everything? The other three women he'd made love with had been all too eager to get him into bed. Even Elizabeth, the medical student with whom he'd lived, who'd wriggled furiously and complained bitterly about his size, had quickly melted under his onslaught and wrapped her legs around him to pull him deeper.

"We'll take it slowly, and I'll stop if you don't like it." Up to a point he could stop, he thought. He hoped she'd make her mind up before he reached that point. He put his hands on her hips and drew her closer.

The yellow robe, softly patterned with large pale flowers, was deliciously soft under his hands. She'd bought it at the mall last weekend for just this very occasion.

He said, "You look like that pastry we had after dinner last night."

"Lemon meringue pie? I look like a lemon meringue pie?"

"Entirely edible." He bent down to nibble the side of her neck and she shivered.

She was pliant under his hands and he could tell she was willing but he had to give her one last chance to say no. 'If you don't want to . . . if you want to wait till we're married, that's all right, Sally," he said valiantly.

"It's okay. I'm just a little nervous."

"It's only me, *m'aingeal*. You've no reason to worry about me."

"I know. It's just that . . . I've never done this before."

"I won't hurt you. I promised Dad I'd not do anything to hurt or frighten you."

"Wait a minute. You talked to Jamie about—umm—well, this?"

"Well, I could hardly talk to your father."

"Why did you have to talk to anybody?"

"It's a man's thing. I'm not surprised if you don't understand." Then, as she opened her mouth on an indignant reply he seized the opportunity and kissed her. She was rigid but began to soften as his lips explored hers tenderly.

Seizing his opportunity to retaliate he murmured in her ear, "You talked to your mother, didn't you?"

"That's different," she said indignantly.

"How is it different?"

"Well . . . " She had all sorts of reasons but forgot them as he moved his mouth to her throat.

"Do you want to try it?" he whispered.

"Okay. What do we do next?"

"This." He put his arms on her shoulders and turned her around so that her back was to him. He reached around her waist and untied her belt. When it fell loose he eased the robe off her shoulders, folded it carefully and draped it across a chair.

She was standing in profile to him, her hands clasped at her waist, valiantly resisting her impulse to cover herself with them. Her back was a long elegant curve, ending in the softly rounded bottom.

Ian stared and felt love and lust and tenderness all at the same time.

Suddenly she turned, took two steps forward and flung herself into his arms. Ian gasped with delighted shock. *A Dhia beannaich mi*, he thought. It was really going to happen, what he'd fantasized about for so long. He hoped his heart could take it.

Sally realized slowly that she was enjoying the close contact very much. Ian was satisfying large and strong and very masculine, as evidenced by the hard object pressing against her belly. She remembered how her girlfriends had drooled over him. This might be fun, she thought; I might even like it. "Come on," she said. "Let's do this thing."

She detached herself from him, turned to the bed and crawled in. He stretched out by her and they gazed into each other's eyes.

"You are so beautiful," he said. She had an athlete's body, with wide shoulders, flat belly and long strong legs, all tempered and honed by sports.

"I bet you say that to all the girls," she teased.

"I do not," he said with dignity. "Because no one is as beautiful as you, no one even comes close." Then, to tease her in return, he said, "I especially admire your hips. So wide and your pelvis so deep."

Sally did not consider a remark about wide hips a compliment, and as she sputtered indignantly, Ian went on, "The pelvic bone is my favorite in the body."

He sat up. He put his hands on her belly while he crooned in an uncanny combination of lover and medical school professor, "The pelvis cradles and protects many vital organs: bladder, liver, kidneys and in the female, the uterus and the ovaries. It is a classic example of the wonderful architecture of the human body." He looked down at her dreamily, then began to caress the area he was talking about.

Sally was enjoying the caresses more than the rambling discourse, although she had to admit that it was interesting. Talking during sex was apparently an Eilean Dubh custom; she remembered her mother saying that Darroch talked while he made love to her. Somehow she doubted that Darroch would have given a lecture on anatomy, though.

She was brought out of her musings by the sudden realization that Ian's hands had moved downward.

"Here is the ultimate mystery of the female," he murmured. "Within is the small hidden channel that can open to take a man's penis, that can open even wider to let the head of a baby through." He raised his head from his contemplation and smiled dreamily into her eyes. "You are a wonder, Sally, a masterpiece of engineering."

"You make me sound like the Eiffel Towel," Sally complained. "Whatever happened to all that stuff guys are supposed to say?"

He raised his eyebrows at her. "Such as?"

"Well, you know. How beautiful my hair is. Or my eyes."

He changed instantly from the professor to the cool seducer, and said in his sultriest, sexiest voice, "Your breasts are exquisitely tempting." He bent and put his mouth on one and his hand on the other.

Sally heard herself begin to moan. Her hands clutched the bedsheets convulsively. "Oh, wow. Oh . . . "

He suckled harder and felt her writhe with pleasure. All right, he thought in satisfaction. The rest should be easy. Oh, my Sally, he thought, this is going to be *miorbhuileach*.

But he was keeping a tight rein on his growing lust. He was determined this would be an experience she'd always remember with love and pleasure. This was the beginning of their real relationship, he thought, and he had to do it the right way.

He kissed and caressed her till he felt her body become softly inviting, felt her arch up to him, heard her crying out his name. Then he moved on top of her and positioned himself at her entrance.

He looked down at her, searching for any sign of alarm or fright. But her eyes were closed and her expression was dreamy. Suddenly she opened her eyes and looked up. She reached for him and drew him down to her.

He needed no further invitation. He entered her slowly and felt her open to him. Encouraged, he slipped deeper.

Sally said, "Ummm . . . " in surprise, then in satisfaction.

He pushed again. She was very tight but so far he had encountered no barrier. He pushed deeper, slowly, and deeper, hearing her soft murmurs of pleasure, then realized he had almost all of his length inside her. He stopped, puzzled. He knew she was a virgin, but where was the barrier he'd worried so much about?

Then his medical training gave him the answer: she was an athlete, had played tennis, soccer, biked, probably had ridden horses. Her hymen, stretched by vigorous activity, had parted and shrunk away gradually and naturally. He felt an enormous surge of relief. He wasn't going to hurt her after all.

Liberated, he pushed in the final distance and lay quite still above her, luxuriating in the tight heat surrounding his cock, realizing that she had taken all of him inside her. "All right, Sally?" he crooned.

"Oh, yes, this is really nice." Her voice became a breathless whisper. "There sure is a lot of you."

"Perhaps I should come out . . . " He withdrew almost all the way, just to tease her. She said in alarm, "No, don't do that, come back."

"Oh, I will." He plunged back in again, then withdrew, then began the age-old pattern of movement that all lovers know.

Sally shuddered and began to move with him.

He was fast approaching his own climax but was determined to take her with him. He slipped his hand between her legs to pet her and heard her piercing orgasmic cry just as he found his own release.

They lay quietly together in post-climax languor. Then Sally sighed, "Now I know why people enjoy making love so much." She added, puzzled, "Why didn't it hurt? All the books say it will."

"Don't believe everything you read," said Ian and in a surge of triumphant happiness he rolled over, taking her with him, ending up with her on top of him.

Sally gasped with surprise and wriggled to adjust herself to this new position. He was still inside her, though somewhat diminished, and it felt wonderful. She said, "If I'd known it would be this much fun, I would have started sooner."

He looked up at her. "It wouldn't have been fun for you, Sally," he said solemnly. "For you it would only be fun with someone you love. And that's me. I'm the first man you've ever loved, aren't I."

She bent to kiss him. "Yes, you are."

"And you're on top now. You're in charge. You can do whatever you want with me." He grinned.

He was teasing again. She knew how to deal with that. She raised herself up on her elbows and gave him a calculating look. "Whatever I want. Hmm. What do I want? Maybe a little of this?" She lifted and lowered her hips, then rotated them over his body until he moaned. "Or this." She put her lips against his and when he moaned again she tickled his lips with her tongue.

Driven to the limits of his endurance Ian rolled her over again. They had reached the other side of the bed and were lying crosswise, her head precariously balanced on the edge and her hair trailing over it.

"Feeling playful, are we?" said Ian. He bent and nipped her earlobe.

She giggled. "It's the most extraordinary feeling, having you inside me. I feel like a toaster with half a loaf of French bread stuck inside."

Ian picked up on the game. "I'm like one of those sausages you eat over here. A hot dog, that's it, inside a bread roll, warm from the grill."

Sally said in her sexiest voice, "Like a burrito wrapped around hot chili peppers. The really hot ones. Jalapeño."

He leaned down to purr in her ear, "A stick of peppermint rock candy, in a warm wet mouth that sucks it slowly and lovingly." He lifted his head and gave her a knowing grin.

"Oh, I love it when you talk like that." She wiggled invitingly. "Come on, let's do it again."

"Steady on, Sally. I'm not a machine, I need time to recover."

She narrowed her eyes and stared at him appraisingly. "How much time?"

He assessed the state of his body. "About fifteen seconds," he said and grinned.

She began to count. "One, two, three . . . "

"Fifteen," said Ian, and plunged deep. Sally gasped with shock, then screamed.

Afterward they cuddled in each other's arms until Sally turned her head and caught sight of the clock. "Oh, damn. Look at the time. Let me up, I've got dinner to finish." She wriggled furiously.

"Let's call your father on his mobile phone. Tell him something, anything. Tell him you've burned the dinner and they should all go out to a restaurant." He didn't want to move, he wanted to lie there forever with her lovely body trapped under his.

"Burned the dinner? Me?" she said indignantly. "I don't burn dinners. Why should I tell him that?"

"We'd have another hour or two to make love."

"We can't do that. They'd all know. Let me up, let me up."

Sighing, he rolled off her. It had been worth a try, he thought.

As she scampered towards the bathroom to dress she called over her shoulder, "Make the bed for me, please, sweet Ian. I've got tons to do downstairs."

"Sally . . . may I come to you tonight?" he said coaxingly.

She grinned. "You bet."

He lay there for a few minutes, thinking of all the lovely things that he would do with her tonight to continue her education in lovemaking. Then he sprang up and made the bed, and hustled downstairs to peel potatoes.

When the others returned, Darroch made a point of being first inside the house, wanting to make sure the lovers were in order before Sally's father saw them. He was quite sure that Ian would take advantage of the opportunity of an afternoon together. He walked into the kitchen and saw Sally at the stove, stirring something in a large pot. The smell of baking cornbread wafted to his nostrils.

"Hullo. Have a nice afternoon?" he said and then thought, fool. How tactless can you be?

But Sally smiled serenely. "Hi. Yes, it's been very pleasant."

Ian, sitting at the table with a bowl of potatoes on his lap, looked at Darroch, smiled and nodded his head slightly to signify, man to man, that all had gone well. Then he blushed a bright scorching red, an errant schoolboy's blush.

Uh-oh, thought Darroch. One look at Ian's face and Russ would know right away what they'd been up to and all hell would break loose.

But one of Ruth's daughters bounced in next, then Ruth and Jean, inquiring about dinner and what they could do to help. By the time Russ had fixed drinks and brought them into the kitchen everything was under control.

That night Ian slipped across the hall and carefully opened Sally's door. She was waiting for him with open arms.

Forty-eight

We know what is coming, that we are moving
Dangerously and gracefully
Toward the resolution of time . . .

John Ashbery

Seven A.M. was Rosie's favorite time of day. She awoke at seven like an erupting volcano, with a howl that rivaled a volunteer fire department's siren. After being awakened twice by that banshee wail Jean and Darroch had trained themselves to wake up a few minutes before seven so that Jean could be ready to thrust a nipple into the hungry mouth as it opened to scream for nourishment, love and a clean diaper.

It was ten minutes to seven when Jean woke. She looked at her husband, still deeply asleep. They had made love three times last night, with cat naps in between each *seisean,* stimulated by the freedom of someone else's house, the king-size American bed and the sound sleep of their offspring. Must be a full moon, thought Jean. They had not bothered with foreplay the last time. He had whispered her name and she had opened her arms and pulled him to her.

Thinking to let Darroch have a nice lie-in, she slipped out of bed and into her robe, an eye on the clock, and scooped up a drowsy Rosie and the diaper bag to take downstairs. She tiptoed to the door, opened it with exaggerated care and slipped through.

As she closed the door behind her she saw Russ, his shoulders taut with what she recognized from twenty years of experience as rising fury, and heard him snarl, "What the hell are you doing in my daughter's bedroom?"

She saw Ian just outside Sally's door, dressed in a ridiculous terry robe that left most of his long arms and legs exposed. She saw him brace himself against Sally's door as though expecting gale winds. Guilt was all over his face. Jean was fascinated to see there was no trace of shame. Shock, defiance, but not shame.

She felt the baby stir in her arms. "Ian, go to your room," she said crisply. "Russ, come downstairs."

Both men stared at her. Neither moved.

Exasperated, Jean repeated, "Ian, go to your room at once. Russ . . . "

The baby gave a warning hiccup. Raised voices were not what she expected at this time of day. She drew breath for her first piercing cry. Ian glanced at the baby in alarm and moved quickly to his door and inside it.

"Hurry up, Russ. I can't hold her back very long and she'll wake the house. Probably the people in the next block as well," she added ominously.

Russ had heard Rosie's morning cry only once and it had been quickly stifled. He remembered, shuddered and moved with alacrity to the stairs.

Jean felt in the pockets of her robe for a pacifier and popped it into Rosie's mouth. The baby blinked in surprise but accepted it. She rolled her eyes up at her mother in warning that this paltry substitute would not satisfy her for long.

Jean scampered down the stairs. "Kitchen," she called over her shoulder to Russ.

In the kitchen Jean handed Rosie to Russ. "I'll make coffee," she said.

Russ looked down at Rosie in his arms. "Uhhh . . . hi, peanut." She gave him a calculating stare and stopped sucking the pacifier. It wobbled in her mouth. He said hastily, "You take her, Jean. I'll make the coffee."

She had forgotten that Russ had learned to cook after she had left him. She took the baby and swiftly changed her diaper.

Rosie let the pacifier drop. Relieved of that nasty wet rag between her legs and that nasty rubber thing in her mouth, warm and dry again, Rosie unbent enough to give her mother her most charming baby smile. Delighted, Jean cooed and cuddled.

Rosie remembered abruptly that she was starving and it was minutes, possibly hours past her breakfast time. She opened her mouth and uttered a plaintive, despairing wail that was even worse than her fire engine siren.

Jean scuttled into a chair, opened her robe and offered Rosie her breast. The baby clamped down like an alligator. Jean gasped. Rosie began to suckle vigorously, milk began to flow and mother and child relaxed into their favorite shared occupation.

Russ, turning to look, was struck by a flood of memory: Jean and Sally, twenty years ago. A wave of emotion swept over him and tears came suddenly to his eyes. He brushed them away and moved to Jean's side. Resting one hand on her shoulder, he bent to look at the baby and saw the sweet curve of Jean's breast and the pink edge of the nipple held firmly in Rosie's jaws.

The feeling that engulfed him was sexual only in the most primitive way. He wanted to kneel by Jean, rest his head on her thigh and stare at the miracle of mother and baby.

Instead, he forced himself to turn away and pour Jean's coffee, adding milk and a dab of sugar, just the way she liked it.

She sipped and smiled at him gratefully. "How good a cup of coffee tastes. We drink mostly tea, gobs of it, on Eilean Dubh."

Eilean Dubh. Russ snapped abruptly back into reality. Jean was not his, Rosie was not his and they belonged in an entirely different life.

Sally was his, though, and some explanations were due. "What was that damned young rascal doing in our daughter's bedroom?" he demanded.

Jean sighed. Why the hell hadn't Ian been more careful? Still, there was no point in trying to hide the truth from Russ. The kitten was out of the strudel and the knöpchen were in the fat. "I would imagine that he was making love to her," she said calmly.

Russ stared. "Don't you care, Jean? Your only—I mean—our only daughter is being debauched in your own house and you aren't concerned?"

She had never realized it before but Russ had a flare for the melodramatic that rivaled Ian's. For a moment she was tempted by the thought of letting the two of them have it out. But that would not be fair to the other inhabitants of the house, and would embarrass Sally to tears and fury.

She began, "It's not like that at all. Ian and Sally have been in love for months. They've been talking about getting married. But she wouldn't make love with him until she was sure. She told me she was saving herself for the man she was going to marry. If they're lovers now it's because she's decided she'll have him for a husband."

"What? She can't do that, she's too young."

"She's older than I was when I married you."

Russ harrumphed and tried a new angle. "They shouldn't be sleeping together until they're married," he said in self-righteous indignation.

Jean looked at him. "Like you and me?"

"Jean, it's not the same thing."

I've had this conversation before, she thought uneasily. "How is it different?"

"Well . . . " The silence stretched out as he tried to think of something else to say. "She's my daughter."

Jean sighed. "I suppose that's how my father felt."

Russ smiled unexpectedly. "I guess. Poor old Dad Greer. He was furious with me, remember? I wonder if he's looking down at me now and laughing."

"Probably." She grinned.

Russ took a large swallow of his coffee and forced himself to accept the inevitable. "Well, tell me about this guy."

Jean said, "He's Sally's age, he's a medical student in Edinburgh, and he's Jamie's and Màiri's son."

Russ grimaced. "Jamie, huh. We don't think much of each other, you know. At least I know he doesn't like me."

"That's all water under the dam, or whatever," Jean said firmly. "Jamie and Màiri are fine people and they love Sally. She's like another daughter to them. And Ian is a wonderful young man: he's smart, he's talented, he's absolutely devoted to Sally. He will treat her like a queen, like Jamie does Màiri. Eilean Dubh men are very loyal and loving. We couldn't ask for a better son-in-law."

"Yeah, okay. Guess I've got to go with your judgment. He'll have to come and talk to me, though," Russ said firmly.

"Ian's very traditional. I'm sure he's already planning to do that. If you haven't frightened him out of his wits, that is."

"What? All I did was ask him what he was doing in Sally's bedroom. Any father would have done that."

"Yes, I suppose so. Try to treat him gently, Russ. He's not used to American fathers."

"I'm sure not used to a big blond lump of a Scotsman, either, especially one who's fooling around with my daughter. Have a little sympathy for me, Jean."

Jean smiled at him. "Oh, I do, Russ, I do." Rosie dropped from the nipple, satiated. Jean covered herself and put baby to her shoulder for burping.

"I suppose they'll all be stirring around wanting breakfast pretty soon," said Russ. "I'll get some pancakes started."

After a breakfast that was tense for all participants Russ stood up and glared at Ian. "I'll see you in my study," he said ominously, and stalked out of the dining room.

"Uh . . . where is his study?" asked Ian uneasily.

Sally said, "I'll show you, sweetie pie. Do you want me to come in with you and talk to him?"

"Certainly not," Ian said with dignity. "This is between me and your father."

Russ, seated behind his desk, was an imposing figure and the look he turned on Ian was enough to frighten the bravest suitor. "Sit down and quit looming over me. Out with it now. What's going on between you and my daughter?"

"Mr. Abbott, sir, I want to ask you for your daughter's hand in marriage." Ian stammered.

"I should think so. Sneaking into her bedroom at all hours of the night. What's wrong with you boys today? Ever heard of waiting till marriage?"

"I'm sorry, sir. We've just—we didn't—we never have, before yesterday." Ian straightened his back and sat up. "Yesterday was the first time. She wanted to wait until she was sure about marrying me, and now she's sure. I've waited months, sir; she's been driving me mad, but I didn't rush her. She's—she was—innocent. I wouldn't take advantage of her. It was her decision and I respected that."

"So it's Sally's fault, is it? She seduced you?"

"No! I didn't mean that. And there was no seduction involved. We are both adults, sir; we are old enough to decide for ourselves," Ian said bravely, meeting Russ's glare. "We made a mutual decision to become lovers."

"Using condoms, are you?" Russ snapped.

"Uh—well, we will, from now on. Yesterday was not entirely planned."

"See that you do. I don't want you getting her pregnant right away, especially before the wedding."

"No, sir. You are absolutely right, sir." Ian tried without success to conceal the tremor in his voice. He was glad that he and Sally would be living three thousand miles away from her terrifying father.

"Take care of her, can you? Got a job?" Even though he remembered what Jean had told him, he was enjoying making this cocky young devil squirm.

Relieved to be back on solid ground Ian stammered eagerly, "Oh, aye. I'm a medical student; I'm first in my class. I have employment waiting for me when I graduate. I will join the practice of our doctor on Eilean Dubh."

That damned Island again. "So you're going to take my only daughter away from me, halfway around the world?" Russ growled.

Ian drew himself up and said firmly, "Aye. I'm sorry about that, sir. I have made a commitment to work on Eilean Dubh, where I am needed. And

Sally is happy with that; I would not do it otherwise." He took a deep breath and made the ultimate sacrifice. "You would always be most welcome to visit us. Sally will miss you very much."

They stared at each other. Then Russ stood up. Ian jumped to his feet. "All right. You have my permission. I'll expect you to look after her." He thrust out his hand.

Ian extended his hand, wiping the nervous sweat off on his trousers first, and they shook hands. "Aye, I will. Thank you, sir."

"Now run along. I have work to do." Russ sat down and started shuffling papers on his desk.

Ian walked out of the room with as much dignity as he could muster. Then he staggered down the hall and collapsed against the kitchen door. Sally, who'd been waiting anxiously, jumped up in alarm.

"What happened? Is everything okay?" she cried.

Ian pulled himself together and managed to smile, though the corners of his mouth quivered. "Everything is fine. Your father has given me permission to marry you."

"Permission? Well, of all the medieval ideas."

"This is the way men do these things, Sally," said Ian grandly. "We have talked, man to man."

"For heaven's sake." She smiled. "Put you through the wringer, did he. Good old Daddy. Well, kiss me, you big lummox. I guess I'm yours."

After dinner that night, with Darroch, Jean, Russ and Ruth seated around the fireplace, Ian stood up and went to stand by the mantel. "Come here, Sally." When she joined him, he put his arm around her shoulders and said to the group, "We have an announcement to make. Sally has agreed to be my wife. And Mr. Abbott has given his consent."

"Well done, lad," said Darroch.

Jean smiled. "For what it's worth, you have my . . . umm . . . permission as well." She got up and hugged them both. "Welcome to the family, Ian."

His nose a little out of joint, Russ got up. "Well, I've got an announcement to make, too. Ruth and I are going to get married." He smiled in triumph, having recaptured center stage.

Everyone exclaimed and looked at Russ, except for Jean, who looked at Ruth, at her expression of amazement that swiftly turned into anger.

Ruth said coolly, "I can't imagine where you got that idea, Russ." She stood up. "I'm going home. Goodnight, everyone."

No one spoke until they heard the front door close firmly behind her. Then Jean said, "You just assumed. You haven't asked her yet, have you, Russ."

"Ummm . . . no."

Sally said, "Oh, Daddy. How could you?"

"Uh-oh," said Darroch.

Ian said, "Oh, Mr. Abbott, that is a big mistake. Women like to be asked, you know. Sometimes you have to ask them over and over," he said, looking at Sally. "They take a while to make up their minds; you know how women are. They say yes in the end, of course, but they must be asked first." He was quite prepared to expound on the subject until he saw the expression of total fury on his future father-in-law's face. "Umm—that is—uh, that's what I think. Uh, sir."

Russ turned to Jean. "Go and talk to her, Jean. Make her see reason."

Jean stared at him, aghast.

Darroch said firmly, "She will not. This is between you and Ruth."

Jean sent him a glance of thanks and said, "That's right, Russ. You have to work it out with her yourself."

"That's right, Daddy," echoed Sally and when she heard Ian clear his throat, ready to add his bit to the conversation, she glared at him until he closed his mouth and looked away. "It's nobody's business but yours and Ruth's."

"Go to her, man. Talk to her," urged Darroch. "Right now, before this gets any worse."

Russ looked at the faces all staring at him and said crossly, "Yeah, all right." He turned and left the room.

Darroch said, curious, "Has no one ever told him no before?"

Jean said, "I don't think so. I never did, anyway. It wouldn't have done any good. He always does just what he wants to do."

Sally said, "Daddy always gets his own way. Except when you left him, Mom, and right now."

Ian said, "Well, I think . . . "

"Shut up, Ian," said Darroch and Sally simultaneously.

Forty-nine

Gather ye rosebuds while ye may;
Old time is still a-flying . . .
Robert Herrick

Jamming his hands in his pockets, hunching his shoulders, Russ stalked down the front sidewalk and up the walk to Ruth's house, determined to pound on the door until she came out. But she was sitting in the swing on the porch. "Hi," he said uneasily.

"Hello."

"Okay if I sit down?" At her nod he flung himself down on the end of the swing. "Guess I was out of order, huh? Should have asked you first."

"Yes."

"Okay, then, let's make it official. Will you marry me, Ruth?"

"No."

"What? Why not?" he said indignantly.

"There's a lot of reasons."

"Like what?"

"To begin with, you haven't said you love me."

"Would I ask you to marry me if I didn't?"

"I don't know," she said unhappily. "You're lonely, you want someone to run your house, you want someone for sex and I'm convenient."

"You love me, don't you?"

"Yes."

"Well, then." He moved to take her in his arms but she pulled back.

"I need to be more to you than a convenience."

"Damn it, Ruth . . . "

"I would prefer it if you didn't swear at me," she said.

"What the hell do you want from me? You're driving me crazy."

"I'm sorry," she said, although she really wasn't. They were at an important point in their relationship and he needed to understand that, if she could make him understand. "Marriage is a real commitment. I have to be sure we're on the same wave length."

When he stared at her, uncomprehending, she added, "For one thing, there's the question of being faithful. I know you were unfaithful to Jean and I won't put up with that, any more than she did."

"Told you, did she," he said bitterly.

"No, she didn't have to. I figured it out for myself, why she left you. I'm not going to expose myself and my daughters to that kind of heartache."

Russ said, "You don't have to worry. I wouldn't wreck another marriage just to play around. I learned my lesson."

"But if you still want other women it might be too much for you, after the charm of marriage wears off."

"It won't happen." He turned away and stared out into the empty street in front of the house. "I mean it. I've done a lot of thinking about what went wrong between Jean and me and I take full responsibility for it. I used to lie awake nights, thinking about what I did to her and how I ruined our marriage. I wouldn't take that kind of chance again." He smiled wryly. "I guess maybe I've grown up."

He turned and looked her straight in the eye. "One woman's enough for me, Ruth, as long as it's you."

A shudder of relief went through her. She believed him. "That's a start, anyway."

"What else do you want?" he said, baffled.

What did she want? She loved Russ deeply, she wanted to marry him, but on her terms. Otherwise he'd dominate her the rest of her life and she'd been alone and independent too long to allow that. And he was the kind of man to value more something that he'd had to work to get. "Let's take it a day at a time and talk about things, until we're sure."

"I'm sure now," he mumbled.

She smiled suddenly and his heart leaped with pleasure. Maybe he was getting through to her after all. "Come here," he said, and opened his arms.

She moved closer and let herself melt into him, giving him back kiss for kiss until he groaned with lust. "Let's go to bed," he whispered.

"We can't. The girls are still up."

"Come over to my house, then."

"With all those people? They'll know."

"Who cares?"

"I do," she said with dignity.

Russ sighed. "Have it your way, then. Maybe tomorrow afternoon, when the girls are off to school. I'll come home early from work."

"You're incorrigible, Russ."

"No, just horny." He pulled her closer and whispered in her ear, "It's so good with you, baby. I love making love with you, you're so sweet and hot."

Ruth sighed. "Go home, Russ. It's getting late and I have to get Jen off to school at seven tomorrow."

"Okay, babe. Tomorrow afternoon, don't forget." She could hear him whistling tunelessly as he swung jauntily down the sidewalk.

She stared after him and sighed again. Oh, we've got a long, long way to go, she thought.

Fifty

*It was desire, not affection, which bound you to me,
the flame of lust rather than love.*

Heloise to Abelard

Russ felt, uneasily, that his life was changing beyond his ability to control it. He was going to lose his daughter; she was going off to Scotland. And his comfortable relationship with Ruth was undergoing a metamorphosis.

He had had it in mind for several months that he might marry her. He was fond of her, he was comfortable with her and he enjoyed her daughters. And he liked the idea of a ready-made family to replace the one he would lose when Sally followed her mother to Scotland. His big house was lonely, and would be even lonelier, without Sally.

But it was hard to give up the freedom he'd acquired, unwillingly, when Jean had left. Did he really want to commit himself again to one woman? He'd be faithful to her, he knew that, and that meant giving up all kinds of possibilities that might come along.

While Ruth was making up her mind, he would take the time to make up his, to be sure of what he wanted. It wouldn't be fair to marry Ruth if he still had an eye for other women.

Alice, the woman who presented herself in his office the next morning for a job interview, staggered him and shook his resolve to marry. She was petite, blonde and dressed in a suit so smart he thought she'd stepped out of one of those women's fashion magazines. It had an upper-executive air to it, and so did she and the resume she presented.

"This is pretty impressive," he said to her, tapping the portfolio on the desk in front of him. "Why do you want to come to work for me? With credentials like these I'm sure one of those large software firms would snap you up. I'm small potatoes compared to them. And I can't offer you the kind of salary they can."

"I want a challenge and that's what your firm specializes in. I don't want ordinary jobs that anyone fresh out of college could handle. I've done my share of those. I want to work where I have to use my brain, not just rattle off stuff in my sleep."

"The tough ones are what I get so I know what you mean. I like them too." He smiled back at her, ratcheting the charm up a notch. He thought he could really enjoy having a woman like this around the office. "If that's what you want, the job's yours." He wrote the proposed salary down on a piece of paper and pushed it over to her.

Alice looked at it and said ruefully, "It's a good thing I'm not in it for the money."

"Yeah, well, that's just for starters. After we get used to each other I'll see what I can do. The benefits are excellent, though, and I can offer you more vacation than you'd get someplace else. I'm easy-going about time off. If you're available when I really need you, I won't care when you get here in the morning or about long lunch hours."

"I'm always early to work and I don't take long lunch hours. I eat at my desk."

"So do I, when I have time to fix lunch to bring. Tell you what, we can eat together. We can order pizza in for lunch or get deli takeout." Her smile became a little more distant at the intimacy of the suggestion that they'd share lunch. Russ added hastily, not wanting to rush his fences, "Sometimes the staff and I do that."

"Of course." She stood up. "If we're agreed, I'll be on my way. I'm sure you're busy; I won't take up any more of your time. When would you like me to start?"

"You'll want to give notice where you're working now."

"I've already done that. I left them a month ago."

Pretty sure she'd get a new job easily, he thought, and she was right. Any company would snap her up. He was just lucky she'd chosen him. She was a real find, and gorgeous and sexy, too. "You can start as soon as you like."

"Fine. I'll come in tomorrow and get my desk organized so I'll be ready to begin on projects on Wednesday. There is just one thing, though: I'll need two weeks off three months from now, and I'm afraid that's non-negotiable. I'll give you the dates and plan my work so that I'm all caught up before I take the time."

She was cool, asking for vacation before she'd even started. "Something special happening?"

"Very special. I'm getting married." Her smile lit up her face and made her look very young.

She was only a little older than Sally, Russ realized suddenly. What was he doing, lusting after a girl like that? He felt like a silly old fool, or worse, a dirty old man. "Oh. Uhh, that's great. No problem with the time. I suppose you have a lot to do."

"That's why I left my job a month ago, so I could arrange the details. We're having the works: formal dress, St. John's Cathedral, Paris honeymoon. The orange blossom special. It's all organized," she said efficiently. "If anything comes up, my wedding planner and I can work it out over the phone. Now I can sit back and enjoy it."

"Great." They shook hands and she left. Russ sank back down into his chair. There'd be no sophisticated seduction there, he thought. Alice, the smartest, most beautiful young woman he'd met in years, and she was already spoken for. He had his standards; married women were off limits to him. And he realized, uneasily, that this young woman had shown no interest in him whatsoever, except as an employer.

Suddenly he felt very old, and alone. He reached for the phone and dialed Ruth's number. "Hi, baby," he said into the answering machine. "I'll see you around three. And I'll be waiting for your answer to that important question."

He knew, suddenly, that he was ready to settle down.

Later that afternoon, lying in Ruth's arms in the soft afterglow of love-making, he nuzzled his face against her hair and whispered, "You're wonderful, baby," and meant it. There was something about her that conjured up memories of Jean. Both women were warm, loving and passionate. And grown-up.

And Ruth was a friend, just as Jean had been his friend. You were a fool once and ruined it, he thought. Are you going to be a fool again? "Marry me, Ruth," he crooned.

She looked at him and then over his head to the clock on the bedside table. "Oh, dear, look at the time! Jen will be home any minute!" She sprang out of bed.

Lying alone he listened to the sound of her footsteps running down the stairs. Damn, he thought savagely. Then he got up, dressed and went downstairs to pour himself a large whisky.

Fifty-one

God knows I never sought anything in you except yourself;
I wanted simply you, nothing of yours.

Heloise to Abelard

Ruth knew that what she was waiting for was for Russ to say he loved her. She wasn't going to tell him what she wanted; he had to figure it out for himself. She despaired that he ever would.

She and Jean had fallen into the comfortable habit of coffee together mid-mornings while Darroch took Rosie for long walks in a stroller that Ruth had borrowed from a friend. He had an endless curiosity about America and Americans and he loved walking the neighborhood, looking at the big old houses. It was all so different from Eilean Dubh. Actor-like, he soaked it all up and stored it in his memory.

Jean was concerned about Russ and Ruth's relationship, which had seemed so perfect and now had stalled in its tracks. She hadn't liked to ask but this morning her curiosity got the better of her. "Umm . . . how are things going between you and Russ?"

Ruth said, "Your guess is as good as mine."

Jean said, "Oh." Then, after a pause, which Ruth wasn't filling, she said, "What seems to be the trouble?"

"Oh, you know. Men. The usual."

"Yes." Jean looked at the woman whom she now regarded as a friend. "Well, no. What's wrong, Ruth?"

"I don't know if he loves me."

Astonished, Jean said, "He wants to marry you."

"Why does he want to marry me?"

"Because he loves you."

"Does he? Why hasn't he said so?"

"He hasn't said so?"

"No." Ruth dropped her head.

Russ, you fool, thought Jean.

Ruth blurted it all out, almost too fast for Jean to follow. "If he loves me why doesn't he tell me? What does he want? Maybe he's just worrying about being alone after Sally leaves. Maybe it's because you and Darroch and Sally and Ian are so happy. Maybe he's just jealous, just wants to feel included. Everyone's getting married; why shouldn't he?"

Jean could not think of anything to say.

"If he loves me he should have told me before he asked me to marry him. Maybe he's regretting that he asked me, maybe he got carried away, maybe it was just a spur of the moment impulse." Ruth said bitterly, "I sleep with him, I'm his hostess, his partner, his confidant. I already give him everything he wants. Why would he commit himself? I'm not young or glamorous. He could find someone else any time."

She lifted her head and looked Jean straight in the eye. "If I marry him without him loving me what's to keep him from chasing other women?"

Jean said, "He wasn't much for telling me that he loved me. It's not his way."

"I don't care. I need that from him; I need to know. I'm not just the woman next door who stepped into his ex-wife's shoes when he wanted someone." She said, "He's not the first man I've had a relationship with since Walter died. There was someone about five years ago. I was in love with him and I thought he loved me. I thought we were going to get married.

"Then he told me he'd decided it was all too much for him, marrying a woman with four children. It was too complicated, too much responsibility. He broke my heart, he really did. And the girls liked him, too. Imagine what it was like, trying to explain why Bill didn't come around any more."

Ruth bowed her head. "I can't go through that again."

Jean said, appalled, "No, of course not. How dreadful."

"I have plenty of money, you know, I don't need a man to support me. Walter left me independent; it was almost as though he knew he was going to die young. He had a huge life insurance policy and he'd already set up trusts for the girls when each one was born to pay for their education. I took the money from the insurance and with the help of his broker and his tax adviser and a lot of books I taught myself about investing. I enjoy it and I'm a good investor, smart, conservative. Mostly blue chips although I had a little flyer with the high-tech stuff and got out of that in time with a profit. I've got security.

"That's why I've never had to have an outside job; I've been able to stay home with the girls. I don't need a man to look after me. I want an equal partner, a man who loves me. And who respects me enough to say so."

Jean shook her head, overwhelmed. "I don't know what to say, Ruth."

"Don't say anything to Russ. He doesn't know all this and it doesn't matter. The only thing that matters is whether or not he loves me. As I love him. And I don't want anyone coaching him about what to say. Promise." She glared fiercely at Jean.

"Oh, no, I wouldn't dream of it," said Jean, although she had been thinking about doing precisely that. "You're right. He has to work it out in his own head."

"Yes," Ruth said. Then she smiled, the mask of control firmly back in place. "Would you like another cup of coffee? Try these cookies, I just made them this morning." She sighed. "They're Russ' favorite."

Jean thought about it all day. She wanted to talk to Darroch and see what he thought but she couldn't betray Ruth's confidences. It was between the two of them. And she realized that Ruth was right: Russ had to work it out for himself.

Fifty-two

*R*uss came home the next night tired out, wanting a few minutes to himself before he dealt with the members of what had become a large and noisy household. He went into the dining room and poured himself a whisky, then opened the humidor next to it and took out one of his cherished stash of very expensive cigars. Cigars were one of his little indulgences after Jean left. Smoking them around her would have brought endless worried lectures, in her most earnest voice, that would have made him feel guilty and quite destroyed the pleasure of the smoke.

He clipped the cigar, then took it, a lighter, an ashtray and the whisky into the sun porch. It was nearly dark and he thought he was alone until he heard a voice.

"Good evening, sir." Ian was sitting in a corner of the porch.

"What are you doing here?" growled Russ.

Ian sat up straight and said nervously, "I'm sorry, sir. I'll leave if you'd prefer to be alone."

"It's all right. Stay put." Might as well get to know the kid, Russ thought. "Want a cigar?" He waved the one in his hand.

Ian shuddered. "No, thank you, sir. I have watched the dissection of a number of smokers' lungs. You would not know that they belonged to human beings." He warmed to his subject. "There is considerable destruction of the air sac walls in the pulmonary tissue, and a large amount of black carbon deposits derived from tar. There may be free blood in the bronchial lumen and . . . "

Russ felt a wave of nausea and hastily laid the cigar down. "Yeah, all right, that's enough about that." He changed the subject quickly. "Why are you in here by yourself?"

Ian settled back in his chair. "I was just sitting here thinking."

"What about?"

"Sally, of course."

Russ could hear the smile in the young man's voice. "Where is she?"

"She is out shopping with her girlfriends." Telling them about me, Ian thought happily. He knew that she was breaking the news of her engagement. She planned to take him to a party that Saturday, to show him off, she said.

"So what were you thinking about Sally?" said Russ suddenly.

Ian jumped. He had been reliving the experience of a few days ago when he and Sally had first made love but of course he couldn't tell her father that. He improvised quickly, "I was thinking about the first time I kissed her." Well, that was partly true.

"Hummph," said Russ.

"And thinking how much I love her and how happy I am that she's going to marry me. And how hard it was waiting for her decision." Ian sighed deeply.

That was something Russ could relate to: waiting for a woman to make up her mind. He said gruffly, "Yeah, women. What made her finally decide to marry you?"

Ian said slowly, "I think it was because she sorted in her mind what she wanted to do with her life. She is a fine and independent spirit, Mr. Abbott. She did not want to become just an appendage to me, just the doctor's wife. She has to be her own person. And I respected that, even though it tore me apart, the waiting. All I could do was hope that it would all work out as I wished."

"Yeah." Russ sighed. "It's hard to know what's going on in women's heads." He took a deep breath. "Take Ruth, for example."

"She is still deciding, is that it, sir?" said Ian delicately.

Russ burst out, "What the hell do women want?"

Ian said, remembering a conversation he'd had on Eilean Dubh, "They want what men want." Jamie, Darroch and Joe would have been proud of him.

Russ ranted on, unheeding. "She says she loves me. We're great in bed. And her girls and I get along fine. Why won't she marry me?"

"Perhaps she too is afraid of losing her independence."

"Hell, I'm not going to chain her to a wall! And I'm certainly not dragging her off to some God-forsaken island like you are with Sally."

Ian swallowed the insult to his beloved Eilean Dubh and said, "Aye. Mrs. Ruth has established her own personality. She knows who she is." He said sympathetically, "It is hard for men these days, isn't it. We are always told that what women want is to get married, but it isn't true. It wasn't true for Sally or Jean and it's not true for Mrs. Ruth."

Russ said, "What's that about Jean? She didn't want to marry Darroch? I thought she was crazy about him."

"Oh, aye, she loves him very much. It was that marriage had failed her once and she didn't believe that having a union sanctioned by church and state meant anything any more. She wanted them to be lovers." Ian had quite forgotten that the man next to him was the cause of the failure of Jean's marriage.

Russ squirmed with guilt and took a deep gulp of his whisky.

"Of course such a relationship is not acceptable on Eilean Dubh. It would have been scandalous, not at all appropriate for the Laird and his lady. So they handfasted themselves to each other. It was not until she got pregnant that she agreed to marry him. This is what Sally has said to me."

Ian peered sympathetically through the dusk at the other man. "I do not know what to suggest, sir. Except to be patient and wait, and keep telling her you love her."

"Think that'll help, do you?"

Ian smiled. "Well, it certainly won't hurt, will it, sir."

The front door opened and closed and Sally's voice caroled, "Ian!"

Ian jumped up. "Excuse me, Mr. Abbott."

Left alone in the dark Russ sat thinking deeply. Just tell her you love her, he thought. Do I love her? How do I know? He thought about that for a while.

He tried imagining life without Ruth. If they couldn't work out the marriage thing they'd have to end their relationship; they couldn't go back to being just friends. He'd be alone for a while but the world was full of women. Could he replace her? He thought about Alice, the beautiful young girl he'd just hired. What would it be like to start an affair with a woman like that?

It would be exciting. It would be challenging. It would also be, he realized, very tiring.

Being with Ruth was comfortable. Making love with Ruth was wonderful. Talking with Ruth was both relaxing and stimulating.

Was that love or friendship?

Did it matter?

Fifty-three

You alone have the power to make me sad,
to bring me happiness or comfort.

Heloise to Abelard

At dinner that night Russ watched the couples at his table. Jean and Darroch, Ian and Sally. What did they have between them?

The younger couple was playful with each other. Sally smacked Ian's hand with her fork when he tried to steal the last spear of asparagus from her plate. Ian teased Sally about a mishap she'd had with a soufflé on Eilean Dubh months ago. Once in a while their eyes would meet and they would exchange a secret smile.

Hmm, thought Russ, that's just sex. And kid stuff. Silly kid stuff.

Jean and Darroch were taking turns feeding Rosie who sat between them in her high chair, whacking her spoon rhythmically on the tray and opening her mouth like a bird in the nest. Once Jean looked away, distracted by something Russ had said, and the spoonful of baby carrots ended up on Rosie's cheek instead of in her mouth.

The baby opened her mouth for a wail of protest and Darroch made a face at her, wiggling his eyebrows, wrinkling his long elegant nose. Rosie, taken by surprise, chuckled instead.

Jean moved in with a napkin and wiped baby's face, cooing sympathetically. Rosie, mollified, opened her mouth for another spoonful. Jean and Darroch grinned at each other over her head.

Teamwork, thought Russ. That's part of it too.

There was an intimacy between each couple that he envied. He felt left out, and longed for Ruth. If she was there they too could grin at each other like a couple of silly kids. He missed her. Why the hell wasn't she here with him?

Damn it, she should be here. She was supposed to be at his side, she was his friend, his lover. His woman. Thinking about her absence he got quite angry and scowled furiously.

Jean caught his expression and grew anxious. She looked at Darroch and raised her eyebrows. He shook his head.

"Stop it," said Russ in frustration, scarcely realizing he'd spoken aloud.

Ian and Sally had been playing footsie under the table and both jumped, wondering how Russ had known and why he cared. "Sorry, Daddy," said Sally. "Sorry, sir," said Ian, turning a slow, deep red.

"What?" said Russ, baffled.

The members of the dinner party looked at each other uneasily and then down at their plates. Everyone was silent.

Rosie banged her spoon on her tray and shouted, "Mumph!"

That meant more food. Jean pulled herself together, scooped up a spoonful and thrust it in the baby's mouth. Everyone but Russ relaxed.

After dinner Sally and Ian volunteered to do the dishes. Russ thought, from the giggles that accompanied the offer, that it was more so they could be alone than from a genuine desire to be helpful.

Darroch said, "Time for your bath, *mo fhlùr*," and swung baby up out of her high chair. "All that lovely American hot water to play in. You'll get quite spoiled."

When Jean turned to accompany him Russ said, "Jean, could I talk to you a minute?"

Jean thought, oh, dear. Russ was clearly undergoing some sort of mental or spiritual crisis and she was the one he'd elected to deal with it, just like in the old days. She sighed, "Yes, of course," and followed him to the sun porch. He took her hand and drew her down to the sofa beside him. Then he seemed at a loss about what to say.

Thinking of Rosie splashing merrily in her bath, Jean said, trying not to show her impatience to join her husband and baby, "What did you want to talk about?"

"Ruth."

"Oh, dear," said Jean aloud, remembering her promise. "What about Ruth?"

"I don't know," said Russ unhappily. "I'm up against a brick wall. I don't know what to think any more, or what to do."

He leaned forward suddenly and stared at her. "Jean, did you ever love me? Really love me?"

Astonished, she said, "Yes, very much. Starting when we were in high school and continuing for twenty years of marriage."

"Why did you stop loving me?"

"I think I grew up."

Russ said angrily, "What the hell does that mean?"

She said, "I realized I was responsible for my own happiness. When you betrayed me, when I couldn't depend on you, I had to depend on myself. I had to make a new life for myself, away from my family and my home. And I did it. Along the way I realized that if I couldn't trust you, I couldn't stay married to you and that's when I decided on the divorce."

"He talked you into it, didn't he," said Russ accusingly.

"If you mean Darroch, no, he had nothing to do with it. We didn't realize that we were falling in love until after I made my decision about you." She said suddenly, "Did you ever really love me, Russ?"

"Sure I did. Remember the good times we used to have? Talking till all hours, making love the rest of the night. Laughing, playing with the kids, camping trips, stuff like that. Where did it all go, Jean? Why did it disappear? What happens to love?"

"I don't know what went wrong, Russ. I used to lie awake at night after I'd left you, wondering about that." She was silent, remembering those anguished nights. "Perhaps we didn't talk enough. Darroch and I talk to each other all the time. Maybe you should talk more with Ruth. And listen to her."

He shook his head impatiently. "Talk, chatter, blah-blah-blah. What has that got to do with anything?"

"Women like to talk; it's important to us. One of the nicest things about Darroch is that he talks to me, even when we're making love."

"Okay, so if I babble my head off she'll realize she loves me? That I'm a really sensitive guy and she can't wait to marry me? Come on, Jean, get real. There's got to be more to it than that. The trouble is that I don't understand what love is. You told me once that you really love Darroch. What does that mean?"

She was on surer ground now; she could talk easily about her love for Darroch. "We're best friends. When we're apart I miss him desperately because I want to be with him all the time. We help each other. We take care of each other. We laugh and sing and cook together. I have more fun with him than I've ever had with another person."

Oh, God, thought Russ in despair, I'm hooked. That's how I feel about Ruth. "Jean, what am I going to do?" The wall of ice that he'd constructed around his heart dissolved abruptly and to Jean's complete astonishment he burst into tears, bending over and hiding his face, his shoulders shaking with sobs.

She moved closer and put her arms around him. "What's wrong, Russ?"

"Damn it, I love her," he mumbled. "I never wanted to love anyone again. I wanted to be free, to be able to walk away first so nobody could walk away from me. It's like diving into a bottomless pool, like being lost in an endless forest." Words tumbled out of him. "I just wanted to be friends. We could get married because we're friends; I don't have to be in love with her. I'm frightened, Jean. " He talked on and on while Jean, baffled, tried to sort what he was saying into some comprehensible order.

Darroch had tired of waiting for Jean and he'd come in search of her. Baby was done with her bath and she was lying in her crib, talking to her fingers. This ideal state of affairs would not last long. Any minute she would decide she was ready to nurse and would scream for her mother. He heard Jean's voice in the porch and went to the door.

Darroch's jaw dropped when he saw his wife holding her ex-husband in her arms, rubbing his back tenderly, his face nestled between her breasts. A wave of jealousy swept over him. He frowned. "Jean, what's going on?"

Jean looked up and mouthed something at him.

"What?"

Get Ruth, she mouthed frantically.

Understanding at last, he went to the living room phone and called next door. "Carol, is your mother available? Can you send her right over?"

"Sure. She's on her way."

Darroch went to the door and waited until Ruth came hurrying up the front walk. "What's wrong? Is it Russ? Has something happened to him?" Her voice, normally so strong, trembled with anxiety.

He led the way without words to the sun porch. Jean and Ruth stared at each other. Then Jean detached herself from Russ, got up and Ruth slipped into her place. She pulled Russ into her arms and crooned to him.

Jean whispered to Darroch, "Go upstairs. I'll be along in a minute."

A glance over her shoulder told her that Russ was alternating fierce kisses with words babbled between the kisses. She went to the kitchen and pushed the door open to discover Ian and Sally locked in a passionate embrace. Sally's left leg was wrapped around Ian's right one and his hand was on her bottom, pressing her against him.

A dish towel lay forgotten on the floor.

Oops, thought Jean. "Excuse me."

Ian and Sally leaped apart. Ian turned brick red. Sally clutched at her unbuttoned blouse and pulled it together over her breasts. "Hi, Mom," she gasped. "We didn't hear you come in."

Obviously, thought Jean, but said only, "I came to tell you not to go into the dining room. Your father and Ruth are having a private—uh—conversation in the porch."

"Really?" said Sally, her eyes wide, stretching the word out into multiple syllables. "What's happening, Mom?"

"I don't know, but let's hope for the best." She smiled, left the kitchen and went to the staircase. On the way she paused and cocked an ear towards the sun porch. There were unmistakable sounds of incoherent babbling coming from it. She grinned and headed up the stairs. Finally got it, did you, Russ, she thought.

In the porch Russ was now focusing on one thought. He slipped to his knees in front of Ruth and seized her hands. "I love you."

"Oh, Russ . . . "

"We're friends, you know that; we have been for a long time. But we're more than friends now. I love you. I want us to be together for the rest of our lives."

He drew a deep breath and the old, cold, self-assured Russ vanished and the nice guy that had been lurking inside him, squelched for years, reappeared. "I love you and I need you, Ruth. I promise I'll look after you and the girls, and I want you to look after me, always. Please marry me."

Ruth looked down at him. What on earth had brought about this transformation? It was real; there was no mistaking the honest emotion in his face and the sincerity in his voice. The opinionated arrogance was gone. She believed every word he'd uttered. "I love you, Russ. Yes, I'll marry you."

"Oh, baby!" he cried. He threw himself back up onto the sofa and scooped her into his arms. A few happy minutes later he lifted his head and said, "Come on. We're going to bed so I can make love to you properly. And you're staying the night with me. So we can talk and make wedding plans." He'd waited long enough, he thought. Like the good businessman that he was, he was going to clinch the deal right now.

"I can't! The girls . . . "

"Carol's there. She knows where you've gone, right? She'll look after the kids and she'll know what to tell them. This is our time." He got up and held out his hand. "I want to make love to my beautiful fiancée." Fiancée, he thought happily, all confusion and indecision gone. The word had a great ring to it; it meant Ruth as his at last. He'd won his woman. He felt as triumphant as if he'd climbed a mountain or run a race, and almost as breathless. It was like being seventeen again.

He put his arms around her and kissed her tenderly. "Shall we go to bed, my Ruth?"

For the second time that night, Ruth said, "Yes, Russ."

That night three couples consummated their love. The passion inside raised the temperature outside the house several degrees.

Early the next morning Ruth tiptoed out of the bedroom, shoes in hand, and crept down the stairs. She was halfway out the door when she realized she'd not brought her keys with her in her haste last night. Her house would be locked. There was no way she could sneak back inside it and pretend that she'd been there all night.

She stood for a moment, considering. Then she shrugged her shoulders, picked up the morning paper and went into the kitchen to put the coffee on.

When the rest of the household assembled a short time later in the dining room they discovered that the table was set and delicious odors were wafting out of the kitchen.

Ruth appeared, coffeepot in hand. "Sit down, everyone. Breakfast is ready."

"Can I help?" asked Jean.

Ruth shook her head. "Nope. This is my show."

"What a wonderful woman," said Russ. He looked around the table. "Everyone have a good night?" He grinned broadly. "We sure did," he said.

His eyes met Ruth's and they exchanged smiles. Rosy-faced, she disappeared into the kitchen.

Sally looked at Ian and blushed, thinking of their night together.

Darroch gave Rosie a spoon to bang on the tray and smiled to himself, remembering how he'd held Jean naked in his arms while she nursed the baby and he'd kissed and played with the breast that Rosie had already emptied.

Russ leaned over to Jean and said, *sotto voce,* "I babbled like a brook, Gina."

She smiled, delighted. "I'm glad, Russ."

He said, grinning, "That was good advice. You ought to write one of those columns. You know, Mother Jean's advice to the lovelorn."

Jean looked at him in surprise. He was teasing her. The old Russ was back, the Russ who had gradually disappeared years ago, the man who could tease and laugh and have fun. Wonders never ceased.

Ruth came back into the dining room, bearing a baking pan. She'd found Sally's box of cornmeal and had made cornbread, Russ' favorite. She put it on the table with a flourish and turned to go back into the kitchen.

Russ rose and caught her around the waist before she could leave. "We've got an announcement to make," he said. "A real one, this time. Tell them, baby."

Ruth said shyly, "We're going to get married."

"You heard it from her," Russ said. "So it's legit. You can't go back on it, babe. I've got witnesses." He threw his arms around her and kissed her with a resounding smack.

Ruth giggled unexpectedly, then murmured, "I'll get the eggs."

"Let me," said Sally, jumping up. "You sit down, Ruth. You cooked it. I'll serve."

"This is a special occasion," announced Russ. "Sal, bring that bottle of champagne that's in the back of the fridge, the one I always keep for emergencies."

Jean got glasses from the sideboard and Russ popped open the champagne. He poured for everyone and announced, "A toast. To Ruth, my wife-to-be. Soon, I hope."

Darroch put his finger in his glass and wet Rosie's lips with a drop of the champagne. He raised his glass with the others and said, "*Slàinte mhath*, Ruth. And Russ too. You're a lucky man."

"Yep," chortled Russ. "Lucky and happy."

After breakfast, while they were clearing the table, Jean said, "All right, Ruth?"

Ruth sighed. "Yes, I'm fine. I feel a little like I've been run over by a truck, though."

Jean grinned. "Get used to it. That's how Russ operates."

Fifty-four

The only sanity is a cup of tea.
Gwendolyn Brooks

*N*ow that both romances had come to completion, all the women involved realized that it was past time to make wedding plans. Ian was due back at medical school in seven weeks; Jean and Darroch were due in California in ten days because he was going to make a television commercial for the American Dairy Association, just as he had in Britain for the Milk Marketing Board. If everyone was to attend, two weddings had to be arranged without further delay.

Ruth and Russ's was the easiest. Neither wanted a big fussy event. Ruth wanted a small service in her church with a few friends, and a reception at her house. She sent out invitations, ordered flowers, and bought a rose silk suit with a matching hat and veil.

Sally and Ian's wedding was more complicated, and made even more so by their differing expectations. Sally wanted to invite all of her considerable circle of friends, enjoy showers and pre-nuptial parties, and have a lovely white dress and a long lacy veil. One of her friends told her that wedding dresses had to be ordered and took months to receive, and she panicked until Jean came up with the idea of having her own dressmaker produce the perfect dress. So they selected a pattern and fabric, and hurried to the dress-maker, who promised the dress within four weeks.

Sally consulted her minister and they selected a date, and booked the church social hall for the reception. She hired a caterer that another friend recommended, selected a menu, created wedding invitations on her computer and had them printed at the local copy shop.

Five days after she'd started her whirlwind of planning, she triumphantly announced after dinner that evening that all the decisions had been made, and they would be married in five weeks in her church.

"Umm," said Ian nervously. "I thought . . . I hoped . . . "

Everyone looked at him quizzically except Rosie, who was on Darroch's lap, playing with his shirt buttons and sending delightful baby smiles up at him.

"I expected . . . "

"Spit it out, sweetie," demanded Sally. "What's on your tiny Scottish mind?"

He glanced at her, offended, stuck his nose in the air with dignity and announced, "I had thought that we would be married on Eilean Dubh."

"Oh, no," said Ruth. "A bride always gets married in her own home." Then she glanced around nervously and added, "Sorry. I didn't mean to interfere."

"Absolutely right, baby," proclaimed Russ. "With her father by her side to give her away." Remembering how he felt about giving his daughter to this interloper, he glared at Ian.

Sally said, "My friends are here in Milwaukee and I want them all to come to my wedding." She'd felt a warm glow of satisfaction every time her girlfriends had eyed Ian admiringly, and looked forward to parading him in his wedding finery—his kilt, of course—for her whole world to see.

"My friends are on Eilean Dubh," announced Ian firmly, "and my sister and her husband." Then, looking around challengingly, he added, "And my parents."

Uh-oh, thought Jean, and exchanged a nervous glance with Darroch.

"Well, they can all come, can't they? I mean, I did plan to invite your family," Sally said with a twinge of sarcasm.

Ian voiced the thought that had been lurking in Jean's mind. "My mother will not leave Eilean Dubh."

"Afraid to fly, is she?" asked Russ. "I don't like it either, but for such an important event she has to get over it." Satisfied that he'd solved the problem, he looked around at the others. "She just has to get on the damn plane and do it."

"You do not understand," said Ian unhappily.

Darroch understood, and so did Jean. They were both remembering how Màiri had balked at the idea of going to London, and both were well aware of how stubborn she could be. Get her to fly to America? They might as well try to persuade the sun not to set at night.

"I don't get it. Both your folks like me, don't they? I mean, they wouldn't object to our getting married, would they?" said Sally in an uncertain voice.

"Of course not," said Ian. "They both have been hoping that you would say aye."

"Well, what is it, then?" demanded Sally.

Like her, both Russ and Ruth looked puzzled.

Ian heaved a great sigh, and said, "My mother does not leave Eilean Dubh. It is an article of faith with her, that she has nothing to do with the outside world. I am not even sure that she believes that America really exists outside of television programs."

"That's nuts," snorted Russ. "I remember your mom. She's that red-headed firebrand, right? She didn't seem to me to be a shrinking violet."

"It is not that she is frightened," said Ian, and stopped. He understood in his heart his mother's feelings, but had no idea how to explain them to those who didn't know and love her.

Darroch tried. "Màiri is a special case. She thinks she will be . . . corrupted by the outside world . . . " He stopped, too. There was simply no way to put it into words.

Jean said, "Maybe you could have one ceremony here, and another on the Island."

"I don't think my wedding dress could travel to Scotland in a suitcase without being ruined. I'd look awful." Bride-nervous to begin with, Sally saw her dream of wowing the world in her wedding finery dissolve into a crumpled heap of satin and tulle. Her eyes filled with tears.

"You could wear something else," began Ian. "You could get a dress that would pack without wrinkles." Noticing the stricken expression on Sally's face, he shut up.

"Well," said Ruth, in a soothing voice. "What a dilemma." She looked around at the others, hoping someone would come up with an acceptable solution.

"No, it isn't," said Russ crossly. "Sally will get married here, and anyone who doesn't care enough to come can just stay on their damned little Island and pout."

Ian snarled, "My mother does not pout. It is a matter of principle with her, not leaving Eilean Dubh."

Russ snorted. Ian glared, for the first time ready to take on his maddening father-in-law-to-be, in defense of his beloved mother. Sally sniffled and dabbed at her eyes. Ruth twisted her hands nervously, suddenly aware she was in the middle of some very uncomfortable family dynamics.

Jean glanced at Darroch for help, realizing that the situation was escalating. He shrugged his shoulders helplessly.

Rosie said, "Da-duh." Everyone looked at her in shock.

Jean cried, "Oh, lovie, her first word, and it's Daddy!"

His ears turning pink with pleasure, Darroch grinned a proud father's grin. "So it is." He lifted the baby and nuzzled her tenderly in her belly.

Rosie gurgled and her arms and legs waved wildly. "Da-duh! Ah da-duh!" she babbled over and over. Then she spotted Jean. "Ma-muh!" she shouted.

"Oh, boy," said Jean helplessly. "Two for the price of one." She went to sit by Darroch and the two of them cooed and giggled, and Rosie cooed back.

Relieved at the fortuitous interruption, Ruth stood up. "Time for me to say good night," she announced, and noting that Russ looked ready to take up the cudgels again and that Ian looked more than willing to oblige him, added, "Walk me home, Russ, dear."

The party broke up. Jean and Darroch took their miraculous offspring upstairs for her bath, and Sally and Ian were left sitting at the dining room table, staring at each other uneasily. "What are we going to do?" he asked in despair.

"I don't know, sweet thing. Maybe we should call off the wedding and just agree to live together. Get handfasted, maybe, like Mom and Darroch."

Ian shuddered. "And just how do you propose we explain that to your father?"

"Oh, boy," said Sally, just like her mother before her.

In the clear light of morning the situation still seemed unresolvable. Ian admitted to himself that Sally was quite within her rights to insist upon being married in Milwaukee, and he was equally sure that his mother would consider it within her rights not to leave Eilean Dubh. It made him a little cross, to think of his mother immuring herself like a nun on her Island, oblivious to her only son's wedding plans.

It was not until mid-afternoon that it dawned on him what to do.

His father would intervene. Jamie, in the majesty of his role as head of the family, would simply tell Màiri that she was going to America, and that would be that. Jamie had been known to put his foot down before—not often, but when it was truly necessary, as in the case of *Tradisean's* recording in London and their tour of Britain—and surely he could prevail on this occasion.

His mother was strong-willed, independent and stubborn, but she retained in her heart and mind enough of the old Island tradition that a man was ruler of the household and that his decisions should be obeyed, to make her bow to Jamie's will.

Sure he'd found the solution, Ian fretted until five o'clock, when he knew that the six-hour time difference between Eilean Dubh and Milwaukee meant that it was eleven at night on the Island, and that his mother, an early riser, would have gone to bed. Ian knew his father often stayed up later to read. He would broach the subject of wedding attendance to him in a private call, and let him deal with Màiri.

Jamie was predictably delighted when he heard that Sally had consented to marry Ian and spent the first few minutes of the phone call expressing himself volubly in the Gaelic, congratulating his son on his good fortune and outlining his thoughts on marriage.

When Jamie paused for a moment, Ian explained his problem. "Sally wants to be married in Milwaukee and we want you and Mother to come to the wedding." Then, into the stunned silence, he added, "And Eilidh and Joe, too."

"I am sure that they would be delighted to come, and me as well. I have often longed to visit *Ameireaga*. But your mother . . . that is an entirely different situation. It took months for her to forgive me for making her tour with *Tradisean*, even though I am convinced she enjoyed it. Part of it, anyway." He hesitated. "Could we not just leave her home, and take lots of pictures to show her when we get back?"

"No!" Ian shouted, like a little boy. "I want my mother at my wedding!"

Jamie sighed. "*Ceart math*. I will try," he said, although he was beginning to think he was getting too old to find the energy to make Màiri do something she did not want to do. He had a sudden, horrendous vision of himself pushing his wife by the shoulders onto an airplane while she braced herself, dug in her heels like a stubborn donkey, and shouted abuse at him. Why didn't I marry a biddable woman? he thought to himself, and then realized that no matter how much of a termagant she could be, he would always love Màiri with all his heart and soul. But sometimes she was easier to love than others, and this was not going to be one of those times.

Ian, Sally, Jean and Darroch waited anxiously for Jamie's call the next afternoon. When it came, Ian could tell the answer by the defeated sound of his father's voice.

"She has said no, that under no circumstances will she come to *Ameireaga*."

Ian relayed the dread news to the other three, and faces fell. Then he said, "Wait a minute, Dad has another idea." He listened, nodded, then said, "Dad says that Darroch should talk to her."

Darroch had half expected as much. He sighed deeply, cast a despairing glance at Jean, walked to Ian and took the phone. In resigned tones, he greeted his redheaded nemesis.

He talked to her in the Gaelic for ten minutes. The others could hear her shouting on the other end of the phone. Darroch's beautiful actor's voice reasoned, cajoled, challenged, and finally changed to a deep, coaxing purr that raised the hackles of jealousy on the back of Jean's neck. She told herself sensibly that there was no reason to be jealous, that Darroch and Màiri would always have a special bond of communication between them, because of their past relationship as lovers. Hell, she thought, Russ and I will always have a special bond, like it or not. Twenty years of marriage had done that.

Finally they saw a small smile of triumph curl around Darroch's mouth as his voice sank to a soft loving whisper, and the shouting on the other end ceased.

Darroch pulled out his handkerchief and wiped his brow, then handed the phone to Ian. "It is all right, she will come. Tell your father the details."

Sally flung herself into Darroch's arms. "Thank you, thank you, thank you! You are wonderful, my darling stepdaddy!"

Jean came forward to embrace her husband. "Lovie, what on earth did you say to her that changed her mind?"

Darroch shook his head. "I don't know exactly." He grinned. "But it might have been the part about how the Americans—especially Russ— would think that she was too frightened to visit a big city. She could not endure being thought a coward."

He smiled gently at Ian. "Or it may have been that she really wants to come to her son's wedding, and just wanted to shout a while before she would let herself be talked into it."

"Good Lord," said Jean, after they'd all had a reviving dram of Russ's whisky. "Where are we going to put all these people? There'll be . . . " She counted on her fingers. "Fourteen of us. I think."

"My family can stay in a hotel," said Ian. "My mother hates hotels," he added dubiously.

"Certainly not," said Jean. "We've got five bedrooms in this house; we'll all fit in here somehow."

Sally said, "Ruth's got five bedrooms, too. Maybe I could move next door, bunk in with one of her daughters."

Consulted when she arrived a few minutes later, Ruth agreed whole-heartedly. "The girls can double up. And Russ and I will be married by then, so he'll share with me. That leaves two rooms at my house."

"And two at our house," Jean added.

Ian said enthusiastically, "I can move in with Sally if that would help," and he received a quelling look from all the adults present.

In the end it was agreed that Jamie and Màiri could go into Russ's room, Eilidh and Joe would take the unused bedroom at the Abbott house, and everyone else would stay where they were.

Jean said, "That'll work . . . Oh, no! We forgot Rod and Lucy and little Andrew. They'll already be here for Russ and Ruth's wedding! Let's start all over again. If Ruth's girls double up, Eilidh and Joe can stay at Ruth's and that leaves one extra room here for Rod's family. That puts both babies in the same house. Keeps all the racket under one roof. And I can play with my new grandson, and Rosie will meet her nephew."

Jean and Ruth smiled at each other, well pleased. "This will be fun," said Ruth. "I love being part of a large family. We'll all get to know each other."

"Just so Adrienne and the Prince don't show up," Darroch whispered to Jean.

"How are we all going to get around?" asked Sally. "There's Dad's sports car, and my little Miata, and Ruth's minivan. Oh, Carol has a car too . . . "

And the counting began all over again.

Fifty-five

This poem
Could go on a long time,
But you've already understood it;
You got the point some time ago,
And you'll get it again.

Mark Halliday

Russ and Ruth's wedding was sweet and quiet. Both glowed with happiness and everyone present could see their love for each other. All their children, Ruth's girls and Sally and Ian, Rod and Lucy with baby Andrew, made a smiling semi-circle around them as they said their vows. Everyone applauded when the ceremony was over and Ruth and Russ were pronounced "husband and wife."

Jean felt a particular sense of satisfaction: Russ was now somebody else's responsibility, and she no longer had to feel guilty about having dumped him.

The newlyweds went to Chicago for a weekend, then returned, postponing a proper honeymoon until Sally and Ian's wedding was over.

Jean and Darroch went to the airport to meet the Eilean Dubh party on their arrival. Eilidh and Joe came up the jetway first, then Jamie, carrying his precious fiddle case, and carriers holding his and Ian's kilts. There was no sign of Màiri.

"Oh, no," cried Jean. "She didn't change her mind, did she?"

Before Jamie could reply, two more people appeared: an immensely tall man in a cowboy hat and a fringed leather jacket, and on his arm, Màiri. "Here we are, little lady," said the tall man expansively. He swept off his hat and swung it in a wide arc. "Welcome to America, ma'am. Fal-chur, you'd say, I reckon."

She looked around appraisingly, nodded her head in a queenly manner, then turned to her escort. "I am pleased to be here," she said grandly. "I have enjoyed talking to you on the plane, Rex."

"It's been my pleasure. Meer-vo-luch, as you'd say in the Gaer-lick. I surely do hate to say goodbye; that was the most interestin' plane ride I've ever had. Now don't forget, if ya'll ever get down to San Antonio, I want ya'll to come stay on the ranch with me for a good long visit." He made her a little bow. "Feas-gur mah, Miz Màiri."

"We'll look forward to seeing you on Eilean Dubh next year," said Màiri. "You all take care, now, honey."

As the Texan walked away, replacing his hat and turning once to wave, Darroch hissed in Jamie's ear, "Who is that woman and what have you done with Màiri?"

"I don't know," said Jamie helplessly. "Something happened at thirty-three thousand feet—maybe the cabin pressure changed—and she turned into the queen vamp of the Middle Hebrides. You should have seen her effect on the male flight attendants. They were so busy chatting her up I couldn't get a drink out of any of them." He paused thoughtfully. "Except for Betsy, the little blonde. She was most attentive. And Jane, the brunette. Lovely girls."

"I'll bet," said Jean, gazing at Bonnie Prince Jamie and imagining his effect on women confined with him in a small space for ten hours. "I wonder what the other two hundred passengers did for booze and peanuts."

Jamie said morosely, "Her behavior was certainly peculiar. It's enough to make a man get religion, trying to figure out a woman. Maybe I'll have a little chat with Minister Donald when I get back."

Màiri looked from one of them to the other, and demanded, "Well? Are we going to stand here forever?"

Jamie and Màiri's meeting with Russ was guardedly pleasant. Safe on his own ground, Russ was relaxed and gracious and plied his guests with the fine assortment of single malt whiskies Ian had helped him select. Ruth and Sally had prepared a traditional American dinner of fried chicken, mashed potatoes, corn on the cob, and chocolate cake. By the end of the meal, cordial relations between MacDonalds and Abbots had been established, and Mac an Rìghs sighed in relief.

The week preceding the wedding was filled with feasting, merriment and family togetherness. The babies, Rosie and Andrew, received so much loving attention that they were in a fair way towards being spoiled, and took the combined efforts of both sets of parents to get them settled down at bedtime.

Later each evening the Abbott living room rang with music. Ruth revealed a hitherto unknown talent at the piano, and she and Màiri took turns at the

Abbott baby grand, Màiri nodding her approval of the other woman's playing. Jamie provided his usual dazzling fiddle solos. Jean and Darroch sang, and got Sally to join in. Ian mourned that he'd left his bagpipes at home, and contented himself with keeping time on the coffee table with a wooden spoon from the kitchen.

Even Russ, not much of a music lover, was lured into the gaiety and on the fourth night was coaxed into singing a solo rendition of "My Darling Clementine," which made Jean, Sally and Rod wistfully tearful, remembering camping trips from years ago.

Russ, rebuffed politely by the four Scots when he offered to take them golfing (only Joe had ever played), settled for hiring a boat to take his guests on a fishing trip on Lake Michigan. Each man caught his limit, and they all returned sunburned, happy and at peace with each other.

Even Jamie seemed reconciled to the idea of being related to Russ. "The man's a grand fisherman," he confided to Darroch. "And he was modest enough about that beauty he reeled in. Didn't gush at all."

The wedding was a splendid affair, the presence of the kilted Scots causing a fair amount of fluttering amongst the lady guests, and raised eyebrows from the men. "Why would a guy want to wear a skirt?" they muttered to each other.

Flutters and mutters changed to whispers of admiration when Sally floated down the aisle on the arm of her handsome, doting father, and wafted up the steps to stand by her handsome, awe-stricken bridegroom. She was resplendent in a snugly-fitting gown of white silk with a demi-train, and a full lace veil over her blushing face.

Everyone agreed that she had never looked more beautiful.

Jean had splurged on a green silk mother-of-the-bride suit, with a blouse that opened down the front in case Rosie needed a snack during the wedding. The baby wore a pink dress trimmed with strawberry appliqués, and a matching bonnet. Her dislike of anything perched on her black curls was well known to her mother, and Rosie's expression and roaming fingers indicated that the bonnet would not remain in place for very long.

Darroch had brought his kilt along for his television commercial appearances, and was his usual debonair, distinguished self in black jacket and shirt with lace frills. A number of the guests thought they recognized him, and the public television fans knew why. "He's an actor. He was in *Wuthering Heights* on *Classic Theatre* last year," hissed one of them, and others wondered if it would be appropriate to ask for an autograph.

The other *Eilean Dubhannaich* excited their share of awed whispers from the American guests. They're so exotic, so different, thought the watchers.

Màiri had managed, to everyone's surprise, to include in her suitcase an elaborately trimmed antique blouse and her sash and full-length kilted skirt in her MacDonald tartan, and with her red-gold hair streaming down her back she looked like a princess from some ancient fairy tale.

Eilidh, her hair like a flickering flame, was a lovely bridesmaid in a simple long blue dress, and the devotion on the face of her husband Joe, Ian's best man, brought sighs of envy from the watchers.

Bonnie Prince Jamie was himself: stunningly handsome. The ladies moaned with admiration, and thought about how they could contrive a few minutes to talk with . . . and look at him.

Rod entered the church proudly with his wife on one arm and his son tucked into the other. Lucy, like her mother-in-law, was wearing a blouse that opened easily. Luckily, for Andrew decided that he was hungry halfway through the service, and his whimpers were stilled as soon as he was put to his mother's breast.

The reception concluded with the band playing gentle waltzes, having exhausted themselves earlier by playing newly-learned versions of "Scotland the Brave," and "Flower of Scotland," guided and led by Jamie's fiddle. The *Eilean Dubhannaich* couples grinned at each other as they waltzed sedately, all envisioning the joyous *cèilidh* with Scottish country dancing and wild music that would celebrate Sally and Ian's wedding when they got home.

Sally and Ian went up to the Abbott family cabin on the Door Peninsula for a five-day honeymoon, and Rod and his family departed for California. The remaining couples were left to entertain each other.

Màiri shocked everyone by announcing what a grand time she'd had in *Ameireaga*. "It is a fine country," she said graciously. "Perhaps we will return some day. I should like to see the Grand Canyon and the Statue of Liberty. I hear that they are quite *miorbhuileach.*"

Jamie, stunned, threw an overwhelmed look at Darroch.

"You have been a fine host, Russ," Màiri added. "And Ruth has made us very welcome. We have enjoyed our visit."

Darroch and Jean could only wish that Ian had been there to hear his mother's remarks.

Russ, coming uneasily to a relationship of mutual respect with Darroch and Jamie, now that they were related not only through Jean but also through Sally, invited them to tour his software company's offices. He was justifiably proud of what he had achieved in his years in business and was anxious to show off his achievements to the other two alpha males in the family.

The offices, housed in a converted warehouse, were attractively decorated in soothing shades of pale green, cerulean blue, and warm gray, and colorful paintings hung on the walls. Each employee's desk featured family pictures and favorite memorabilia, and potted plants flourished in front of the two large window walls.

When Darroch commented on how pleasant the offices were, Russ said proudly, "Yep. The only thing we don't have is a great view." He was standing by the windows, which overlooked a shabby section of Milwaukee's warehouse district. "Sure would be nice to look out on Lake Michigan, or even the Milwaukee River," he said, "but there's no affordable space available."

It was then that Darroch got his great idea, conceived by the reference to the water views. "You are so successful, Russ," he said. "Have you not thought of expanding the business?"

"Yes, I'd like to," admitted Russ, a classic American entrepreneur. "But I can't do it alone. I'd need Rod's help, and so far he's not interested in joining the firm. Kid's too darned independent to work with his old man. Besides, I've pretty well cornered the market in my field; there's no place else to go."

Except abroad, thought canny Darroch. Late that evening he used the bedroom extension phone and his credit card to phone Eilean Dubh. He reached Barabal Mac-a-Phi, the current chair of Eilean Dubh's governing council. "*A Bharabal*, you ken Russ Abbott, who was at Jean's and my wedding last year?"

"Hmmm . . . " Barabal said. "Would he be the arrogant, high-nosed Yank who used to be married to your Jean, and thought himself so much above us humble Scots?"

"The very one. His and Jean's daughter Sally, my stepdaughter, has married the MacDonalds' Ian."

"Never!" said Barabal. "Jamie couldn't stand the sight of the man. There's fireworks to come there."

"Aye, it's happened, but no fireworks, for we're all staying at Russ's house: Jamie, Màiri, Jean and myself, and Ian and Sally. We're as close as clams, the lot of us."

"Wonders never cease," said Barabal.

"Aye, Russ has got himself a fine new wife, who has mellowed him considerably, and a handsome grandson. He's also got a successful business that's set me thinking. He fixes computer software."

"I didn't know computer software got broken," said Barabal.

"It does, and I'm thinking if it gets broken in the States, it must get broken in Scotland as well. So why shouldn't yon Russ expand his business into our country?"

"Meaning what?" said Barabal.

"Why should he not establish a wee branch of his firm on Eilean Dubh?"

"A wee branch?"

"If he did it would provide employment for those young computer whizzes the High School turns out with no place to go for work but off the Island."

"Hmmm." Barabal thought it over, and said, "They could go to university for training, and a good job would lure them back home."

"My notion exactly."

"A grand idea, if a bit daft. How do you reckon on accomplishing this miracle?"

"You ken the fine building the woolen mill used to occupy, with its retail space for sweaters and all and the café, that's about two miles from Airgead?"

"Aye."

"Could you go and have a wee keek at it, and let me know the state it's in, and what it would take to put it into the shape that would make it attractive to a great American businessman?"

"Refurbished with the help of the Trust . . . "

"Aye, and with Trust scholarships to send our young folk off to the mainland for schooling in the repairing of software."

"A bonnie idea. I'll just be going down there the day."

The next day Darroch phoned Barabal for her report.

"The building is a wee bit musty, given it's not been used since that mainland businessman gave up on the sweater business, our Island not attracting the number of tourists he'd hoped for. But it's sound, good roof, no leaks."

"And does it have, as I remember, a view of the ocean?"

"A fine one, from the big front windows."

Darroch sighed in pleasure. The next day he said to Russ, dropping the idea casually into a conversation he'd initiated about business, "Have you never thought of expanding overseas?"

"Hmmm?"

Darroch was not a golfer, but like all *Eilean Dubhannaich* he had a lot of experience in fishing. He cast out his lure. "A fine branch office in Scotland, providing a real service to British businessmen, repairing their broken software."

Russ was interested, as Darroch had hoped.

"As I understand it, your company can perform its services anywhere."

"Well, yes, but I'd need a headquarters . . . "

"A modern building, with a reasonable rent and low taxes, financial help to fix it up, and the potential for purchasing the property outright. A pool of young talent, smart and motivated, for employees."

Intrigued, Russ said, "And where might I find such a paradise?"

"We're looking for new businesses to establish themselves on Eilean Dubh, and we could make you a very attractive proposition, should you care to give us a try."

The fish eyed the hook cautiously. "I'd need a good person to run it, someone sharp and dependable, since I've no intention of moving to Scotland."

Sensing a nibble, Darroch twitched the lure. "Aye, right enough. Some fine young lad or lassie, someone you could rely on entirely. Someone like your Rod, perhaps."

Russ was struck by the idea. His hope had long been to lure his independent-minded son into joining the family business, and here was a way to do it: give the boy complete responsibility for a new venture, away from his father's overwhelming presence. He bit, but with reservations. "Why would I want my grandson so far away from me, over in Europe?"

"He's in California now. Is that any closer?"

"Now that you mention it, I don't think it is. And I'd have plenty of excuses to run over and visit the Scottish branch of the firm. Tax-deductible trips, in fact."

The fish was well and truly hooked. Darroch was immensely pleased with himself. Not only was he on the verge of securing new jobs for Eilean Dubh, he might also have arranged for Jean's grandchild to be on the Island with her. She'd been tearful at the thought of having to leave young Andrew so many miles away. This would score him big points with his loving wife.

Russ reminded him that Jean would have to approve, too, as she was co-owner of the business. Darroch said, his actor's training allowing him to remain straight-faced while he grinned inside, "Aye, of course. You'll have to talk to her. But you're good at persuading women."

Russ preened.

Rod would have to be convinced of the benefits of the move, of course, but he'd like the idea of running his own part of the company. Lucy would help convince him, too; she'd been starry-eyed over the Island when she'd visited it at the wedding, and sighed sadly when they'd had to leave. The gentle, relaxed way of life in Eilean Dubh would suit her down to the ground.

There was a fighting chance, Darroch thought, that the thing might work. And if it did . . . he'd have his Jean and she'd have her son and daughter and grandchildren nearby. And baby Rosie and baby Andrew could grow up together. One grand family, all of them on Eilean Dubh. He'd be a real Magician if he could pull that off, and Jean would adore him forever, even more than she already did.

The three senior couples sat around the Abbott dining room table after dinner a few days later, reminiscing about the exciting events of the last several weeks. That caused Russ to remember an important omission.

"Baby!" he exclaimed suddenly to Ruth. "We haven't had a proper honeymoon!"

"We had the weekend in Chicago."

"That was just a warm-up," Russ said dismissively. "We owe ourselves a real getaway." Then, when Ruth opened her mouth to protest, he said, "No arguments, baby. Carol can look after the younger girls, and your sister can check in on them. Alice is really sharp; she can run the business for a couple of weeks. Let's take some time off. Where would you like to go for your honeymoon?"

As she hesitated, he said, "Just name the place. Anywhere you like."

Ruth said, "Anywhere?"

"Yep," Russ said, expecting her to choose Paris, or San Francisco, or even Tokyo.

"Well then . . . " Ruth looked around at her fellow diners, and smiled shyly. "In that case, I'd like to go to Eilean Dubh."

Darroch regretted ever afterwards that he had not had a camera to capture the expression on Russ's face. He looked from Ruth to Jean to Darroch, with a detour to Jamie and Màiri, and back to Ruth again. "What is this, a conspiracy?" he demanded, to Ruth's bewilderment.

"Why, no," she said. "It's just that I've heard everyone talk about it so much, and I'm the only one who's never been there."

Still suspicious, Russ said, "Yeah, that's right." He brightened, thinking that this would be an opportunity to check out Darroch's business proposal. A certified workaholic, he always liked to combine business with pleasure.

He cheered up even more when he remembered that it would also mean that he could enjoy the comforts of the Rose Hotel, and Sheilah Morrison's gourmet cooking.

Maybe it wasn't such a bad idea, after all. Russ said grandly, "If that's what you want, baby, you've got it. Your wish is my command."

Return to the Dark Island

A lift to the heart, a light in the eye,
A lilt to the step at the miles gliding by.
Soon Beinn Mhic-an-Rìgh looms into view,
And I behold Eilean Dubh.

Beanntan MhicChriathar rise high to the west.
Rudha na h Airgid beckons me to my rest.
There is the sight I've been longing for
As I sail into port at Ros Mór.

I've been to places, both great and small
The isle of my heart is the prize of them all.
Home is the traveler, joyous the view
As I behold once again Eilean Dubh.

Return to Eilean Dubh

Jig

Snow on the Mountain

Scottish country dance, Jig for 3 couples in a longwise set

Devised by Lara Friedman-Shedlov in Autumn 2003
for *The White Rose of Scotland*

Tune: "Return to Eilean Dubh" by Sherry Wohlers Ladig

1-4   1st couple cross giving right hand and cast to 2nd place.

5-8   1st couple dance half a figure of eight, 1st woman up around 2nd woman, 1st man down around 3rd man, finishing by dancing into the middle of the set and pulling right shoulders back to end back-to-back.

9-16 Petronella-double triangles: 1st couple dance bars 9-14 as for regular double triangles. On bars 15-16 they rotate a quarter of the way around to finish back-to-back, 1st woman facing up and 1st man facing down. Meanwhile, 2nd and 3rd couples set as for regular double triangles on bars 9-10, petronella one place anti-clockwise around the set on bars 11-12, set as for regular double triangles on bars 13-14, and petronella one place anti-clockwise around the set on bars 15-16.

17-20 1st woman with 3rd couple (who are in 1st place), 1st man with 2nd couple (who are in 3rd place), dance right hands across.

21-24 3rd man, followed by 3rd woman and 1st woman; and at the same time 2nd woman, followed by 2nd man and 1st man, chase clockwise halfway around the set, finishing in the order 2nd couple, 1st couple, 3rd couple, all on own sides and flow into:

25-32 Circle six hands round and back.

Fifty-six

And I walked, I walked through the light air;
I moved with the morning.
Theodore Roethke

The flight from Milwaukee to Glasgow, packed though the plane was with *Eilean Dubhannaich* and their constituency, was uneventful. The flight attendants were too busy to flirt with Màiri and Jamie, and there was no Texan on board for Màiri to enchant.

No one recognized Darroch as a television star, and he and Russ were able to spend plenty of time with their heads together, talking business. Jean was considerably bemused by this, since Darroch had not shared his grand scheme with her, keeping it as a surprise, and she'd not thought of him and Russ as bosom buddies. She couldn't imagine what they'd found to talk about.

Jean got Rosie to nurse as the plane was taking off, so baby did not scream at the sudden change in cabin pressure. Màiri and Ruth sat with Jean in a middle row of seats and all three took turns cuddling Rosie to keep her happy. Jean was even able to slip away for a bit and sit with Sally, Eilidh and Joe, and discuss their book, *Eilean Dubh: Celebration of a Small Island*. There was editing and organizing yet to do, but they felt confident that their manuscript would be ready by the publisher's deadline.

Ian was the only one unhappy during the flight, because there was not enough leg room to accommodate him in his seat. He finally pulled one of his medical textbooks from his carry-on and stood in the back of the plane, leaning on the bulkhead, reading.

At Glasgow the travelers caught a train to Oban, and stayed the night there. The next day everyone boarded the Caledonian-MacBrayne ferry. Two islands later, they were at Eilean Dubh.

Ruth's eyes went wide as the boat neared the Island. "Oh, my," she said. "It looks so mysterious, rising up out of the water that way. It's like it's floating."

"There's always a wee bit of fog around Eilean Dubh," said Darroch. "That's what gives it that effect."

Jean put her fingers to her lips. "Don't destroy the illusion with facts," she whispered in his ear, and he grinned. "*Ceart math*," he said. "The Brigadoon bit."

"Everyone's entitled to some fantasy in their lives," she replied. "And where better to find it than on a tiny Scottish island?"

Ruth, still entranced by the view, cried, "Look at that big mountain in the west! Is that snow, that white stuff around the peak?"

"Aye, there's snow on it year around. That's *Beinn Mhic-an-Rìgh*," said Jean. "Mac an Rìgh's mountain, in English."

"Hmmph," said Russ. "I suppose it's named after you-know-who."

"His great-greats," Jean answered.

Ruth sighed. "It's like the books I've read and the movies I've seen about Scotland." She took a deep breath. "The air smells like pines and sea and . . . "

"Wildflowers," said Jean. "The Island is full of wildflowers."

"Oh, I love wildflowers!"

Eilidh, coming up behind them, said, "Joe and I can show them to you, if you like. We know where all the special places are."

Sally was right behind her, hand-in-hand with Ian. "We'll organize a picnic and go flower hunting."

"I would love that," said Ruth, her eyes shining.

"Why is it," said Russ, "that whenever I get near this Island with any of my family I hear this giant sucking sound?"

"I don't know what you mean," said Darroch innocently.

Russ gave him a suspicious glance. "Oh, I think you do."

The ferry docked, and the travelers scampered off, the *Eilean Dubhannaich* giving a collective sigh of pleasure at being home again. "I feel as though I should kneel and kiss the ground," said Jean.

"Don't do that," said Darroch in alarm. "Everyone will think you're a gusher."

Barabal Mac-a-Phi, Darroch's co-conspirator, was waiting on the dock. She ran an eye over the arriving passengers and quickly picked out the stranger in their midst. She stepped forward. "*Fàilte gu Eilean Dubh,*" she said, and presented Ruth with a bouquet of heather.

"How lovely," breathed Ruth.

"Aye," said Barabal. "That's heather, picked just this morning. The sprig in the middle is white heather. Very rare, and it's special good luck."

"Thank you," said Ruth.

"*Tapadh leat.* That's the Gaelic for thank you. You'll want to learn a wee bit of the Gaelic while you're visiting Eilean Dubh," said Barabal.

"Will I?" said Ruth innocently, and repeated the phrase. "Tapp-uh lot. Is that right?"

"That's grand," said Barabal. "You've a real ear for the language."

Russ raised his eyebrows and looked at Darroch. "I know when I'm beaten. I suppose you've got a pen and a contract in your back pocket, ready for signing."

Darroch grinned. "Barabal has it. But let's not talk about business yet. Let's just enjoy being home on the Island."

To his surprise Russ grinned back. "Okay. I have to admit it, I don't mind being here. Take me to the Rose, give me one of Sheilah's special meals, and a few—drams, is it?—of whisky, and I might be—just might be—putty in your hands."

Darroch gave him a friendly slap on the back. "You're a fine fellow, Russ. We'll make an *Eilean Dubhannach* out of you yet."

Russ rolled his eyes. "Maybe, but don't think you're going to get me to learn that weird language."

The travelers were grouped in a circle on the dock. Jamie said, "Isn't it *miorbhuileach* to be home. I feel as though we should all be singing 'The Emigrant's Lament' to welcome us back."

"That's so sad," said Jean. "What we need is a happy tune, a returning-to-Eilean-Dubh happy sort of tune. Why don't you compose one, Jamie?"

Jamie considered. "Aye, I might just do that. Will you write words for it, *a Shìne, mo luaidh?*"

She said, "Aye, I just might do that, *a Sheumais,* my main man."

Jean looked at the friends and loved ones surrounding her, then at the bustling dock, the town beyond so full of life, and the dark mysterious mountains in the west. She felt Darroch's arm go around her shoulder, and she looked up into his amazing blue eyes, full of sweetness and love. Rosie, in Darroch's arms, wiggled around to face her mother, and gave her a charming baby smile.

Jean took Darroch's hand in hers and said, "I've got a lot to write about. And a lot to be thankful for, here on Eilean Dubh. Now, and forever."

An Deireadh

Read another Scottish Island story,
Magic Carpet Ride,
a tale of Cape Breton and Minneapolis.
Check the web site, www.scottishislandnovels.com,
for publication date.

Acknowledgements

*M*òran taing to . . .

As always, my family, Mike, Michael, Anita and Aaran, and John and Carla, for their help, encouragement, good advice and laughter (mostly at my expense).

Carla McClellan, for another beautiful book cover, and John McClellan, for technical support to both Carla and me. He's also a great book salesperson!

The St. Andrews Society of Minnesota, for awarding me the Andrew Simon Fraser scholarship for my first book, *Westering Home*.

Cindy Rogers, my editor. Right on target, once again.

Sherry Wohlers Ladig, Becka Schafer and Don Ladig, who are the musical group, Dunquin. Five of Sherry's wonderful "chunes" grace *The White Rose of Scotland*. She's almost written enough for a Dunquin Eilean Dubh CD! Sherry is an awe-inspiring musician and composer, and a dear and helpful friend, who always gets to read my manuscripts first and whose advice is always sound.

Lara Friedman-Shedlov, a most accomplished dance deviser. Thanks for another delightful creation!

Bob Lies, past Pipe Major of the Minnesota Pipes and Drums, for his enlightening advice and fascinating conversation about bagpipes, the *urlar* and the *piobaireachd*, and his loan of MacNeill and Richardson's useful book.

Reverend Alex J. MacDonald of the Free Church of Scotland, minister of Buccleuch and Greyfriars Free Church in Edinburgh, for his helpful information on Presbyterian practices. Any misinterpretations of the Church's practices and teachings are entirely my own, and I apologize for any errors.

Donnie MacDonald, from the Isle of Lewis, Scotland, a noted folksinger and member of *Men of Worth*, for his help with the Gaelic. Again, any errors are mine, and my apologies.

The Hat Ladies: Judith, Sherry, Màiri and Deb. Great tea-drinkers, conversationalists, and sources of inspiration and wise counsel.

Milt Adams for creating Beaver's Pond Press, and Judith Palmateer, for all her hard work and encouragement.

Teresa Jensen, because I forgot to thank her for the golf quotes in *Westering Home*!

Twm Siôn, the world's best kitty.

Literary Notes and Other Miscellany

Jacob's sheep: Jamie's favorite breed. They are small, multi-horned, black or lilac in color with white spots, and their meat, fleece, pelts and horns are highly marketable. The name is Biblical in origin, relating to the patriarch Jacob, who requested from his father-in-law all the spotted sheep in his flock, in lieu of wages. Jacob gave his favorite son Joseph a coat of many colors. Was it spun from the wool of a Jacob's sheep?

Lady Grizel Mac an Rìgh (176?–1826) was the only daughter of the Mac an Rìgh chief, and received a most unusual and superb education from the Jacobite refugee Douglas MacShennach, who was the chief's scribe/secretary, and fluent in both Gaelic and English. Lady Grizel learned English from him, and it was he who discovered her extraordinary gift for poetry and encouraged her writing.

Sailors returning from mainland Scotland brought back books as gifts for Lady Grizel, including Robert Burns' first book of poetry, *Poems, Chiefly in the Scottish Dialect*. Both Lady Grizel and Douglas were immediately entranced, and the next voyage over to the mainland carried a selection of her poems and a letter to Burns.

He replied at once and thus began a correspondence between the two poets. After the fashion of the time, each assumed a *nom-de-lettre*. Burns became Hercules, and he christened Lady Grizel the Goddess Thistleonia. Only two letters survive, those of Hercules to Thistleonia, and they are preserved in the Island library at Airgead.

Burns' early death, a murder by medical decree, was a terrible shock to both Lady Grizel and MacShennach, and their shared grief may have turned friendship into something deeper, as her work thereafter was mainly love poems. The chief permitted his daughter to wed her Douglas, and their children were the beginnings of the MacShennach clan on Eilean Dubh.

Hugh MacDiarmid (1892-1978) is the pseudonym of Christopher Murray Grieve, one of Scotland's greatest poets. Many of his works are written in Scots. His poem "The Little White Rose" has inspired the adoption of the white rose as the emblem of the Scottish Nationalist Party.

"She Walks in Beauty" is a poem by Lord Byron.

Robertson's Relics and Anomalies of Scotland, 1923: Eilean Dubh occupies the longest chapter in Sir Iain Robertson's weighty tome. The arduous five-hour voyage he undertook to get there, in a fisherman's boat through choppy seas, did not seem to have dampened his enthusiasm, for he speaks repeatedly of how enchanting the Island is.

Other reference books consulted include:

Douglas, Ronald MacDonald. *The Scots Book of Lore and Folklore,* W. and R. Chambers, 1953.

Keay, John, and Keay, Julia. *The Collins Encyclopedia of Scotland,* Harper Collins, 1994.

MacNeill, Morag. *Everyday Gaelic,* Gairm, 1986. I have discovered that this helpful book is for sale in the gift shop at the Gaelic College of Arts and Crafts, St. Ann's, Nova Scotia. I highly recommend it to Gaelic learners. The college's web site is: www.gaeliccollege.edu

MacNeill, Seumas, and Richardson, Frank. *Piobaireachd and its Interpretation,* John Donald, 1987.

Munro, Michael. *The Patter: a Guide to Current Glasgow Usage,* Glasgow District Libraries, 1985.

Notes on Piping

When Jamie refers to the bagpipes as a "bloody great instrument of war," he is speaking the literal truth. Scottish bagpipers led their clans into battle, and an ancient form of the bagpipe was popular with the Romans. It was "the instrument of war of the Roman infantry," according to the Byzantine historian Procopius.

Ian is composing for Sally a *piobaireachd,* an art form which Seumas MacNeill calls "the classical music of the Highland bagpipe. It consists of a ground or *urlar* (which is itself a variation on a basic theme) followed by a number of other variations on this theme. The ground is played slowly and is usually the most interesting and satisfying part of the whole composition."

The combination of bagpipes and fiddle, and the scoring of the piece for piano and woodwinds, is my own invention, and has caused some raised eyebrows among my musician friends. But this is fiction, after all.

Gaelic–English Glossary

Terms and Phrases

Fàilte gu Eilean Dubh: Welcome to Eilean Dubh.

Fàilte gu mo thaigh: Welcome to my house.

A Dhia! Oh, God! *A Dhia beannaich mi!* Goodness gracious me!

A bheil Gàidhlig agad? You have the Gaelic?

breagha: beautiful.

Cal-Mac ferry: Caledonian MacBrayne Hebridean & Clyde have provided ferry services to twenty-two islands and four peninsulas in the west of Scotland since 1878, giving rise to the saying, "The earth is the Lord's and all it contains, except the Western Isles and they are MacBrayne's."

Cumha dha Sally: lament for Sally.

ceart math: okay.

cèilidh: a social evening of music, dance and storytelling.
Plural: *cèilidhean.*

chan'eil Beurla agam: I don't speak English.

a charaid, mo charaid: oh friend, my friend. Also, to a woman: *mo bana-charaid.*
Plural: *mo chàiradean.*

chat up: flirt with, try to pick up (British slang).

ciamar a tha sibh an diugh: how are you all today?

cock-up: to make a complete mess of something (British slang).

craic: talk, chat.

cù aosda: old dog.

an deireadh: the end.

diabhol: devil. *bana-dhiabhol:* female devil.

eileanach: islanders.

fair chuffed: very pleased, happy (British slang).

feasgar math: good evening. *oidhche mhath:* good night.

gabh mo leisguil: excuse me.

Gaelic mince: Gaelic chatter, nonsense.

glé mhath: very good.

gormless: clueless (British slang).

Jack-the-lad: brash young man out for a good time; a ladies' man; a rake (British slang).

madainn mhath: good morning.

mar sin leat: bye for now.

misneachd: courage.

miorbhuileach: marvelous.

mòran taing: many thanks.

pioghaid: a magpie.

piorradh: a squall.

piobaireachd: anglicized to pibroch. See the Notes on Piping.

Radio One: "BBC Lite."

Scottish country dancing: traditional social dancing of Scotland, done with a partner, usually in a longways set of four couples. An ancestor of American square dancing.

seiseanan: music jam sessions.

s' math sinn: great, terrific, smashing.

slàinte mhath: good health (traditional Gaelic toast).

smoor the fire: cover it over at night with peats to keep the fire till morning. The procedure is accompanied by a prayer that originally asked the protection of the goddess Brighid, because the household fire is sacred to her. Now more commonly addressed to St. Bridget or Mary, or, on Eilean Dubh, to the One Who Listens.

take the mickey: to tease, mock, make fun of (British slang).

tapadh leat, tapadh leibh: thank you. Second phrase is plural, formal or respectful.

tapadh leat gu dearbh: thanks very much.

thà gu dearbh: yes indeed.

tha mi gu math: I'm fine.

tha mi duilich: I am sorry.

tha mi toilichte a bhith an seo: I am happy to be here.

tha thu 'gam chur às mo chiall: you're driving me daft.

Tony Benn-ish: Anthony Wedgewood-Benn is a British politician who renounced his title when he inherited in order to keep his seat in the House of Commons. (A peer would have to move into the House of Lords.)

tradisean: tradition.

tri-coig-tri-coig: three-four-three-four (telephone number).

try to pull my wife: make a pass at, try to seduce (British slang).

urlar: term for the ground, or theme, in a pibroch. See the Notes on Piping.

People

ban-Uibhisteach: a woman from Uist.

Eilean Dubhannach: a native of Eilean Dubh. Plural: *Eilean Dubhannaich.*

mo leadaidh: my lady.

Sasannachan: English people.

Sìne: Jean. Pronounced "sheenuh." When aspirated (an h is added after the s) it becomes *Shìne*; pronounced "heenuh."

Somhairle Mac-a-Phi *as sine:* the elder Somhairle.

Somhairle Mac-a-Phi *as òige:* the younger Somhairle.

an Tighearna Dearg: the Red (Socialist) Laird.

A Mhic an Righ: formal way of addressing the Laird.

Terms of endearment

m'aingeal: my angel.

mo chridhe: my heart.

m'eudail: my darling.

mo fhlùr: my flower.

mo ghràdh: my love.

mo ros beag: my little rose.

mo nighean: my daughter.

m'ubhal beag: my little apple.

Places

a' chreag: a cliff.

àite laighe: helicopter pad (literally, a resting place).

Ameireaga: America.

Beanntan MhicChriathar: the MacChriathar hills.

Beinn Mhic-an-Righ: MacRigh's mountain.

Cladh a' Chnuic: Cemetery Hill.

an Eaglais Easbuigeach: the Episcopal Church.

an Eaglais Chaitliceach: the Catholic Church.

an Eaglais Shaor: the Free Kirk.

Rudha na h Airgid: Airgead Point.

Sabhal Mór Ostaig: the Gaelic college on the Isle of Skye.

Taigh a Mhorair: the Laird's house.

Taigh Rois: the Rosses' house.

A note on the Gaelic: in certain circumstances some initial conso-
nants aspirate, that is, are followed by an 'h'. One instance is after
the word *a,* the usual form of address which precedes names and
titles, and means 'oh'. For example: *A Dharroch* – oh, Darroch.

Scots expressions

Scots is the third language of Scotland, used most notably by the poets Robert Burns and Hugh MacDiarmid. Its roots stretch back to the twelfth century. It grew out of the Scandinavianized Northern English spoken by emigrants from England to southern Scotland. It has been heavily influenced by Gaelic and French.

dinna fash yersel': don't trouble yourself.

hush yer whist, wummin: hold your tongue, woman.

keek: look.

peely-wally: pale, ill-looking.

stramash: a confused tussle.

What Glaswegian Jimmy Buchan says to Jean and Darroch regarding obtaining the certificate she needs to marry in Scotland:

> "Gie's a coupla weeks. Tha high heid yins in Edinbro 'll hafta hae a nebby. Ah'll put the wind up, rummle 'em a bit, and we'll get ye fixed aout the week or twa. Gaun on w' yer plannin'; it'll aw cum right."

In English, roughly:

> "Give me a couple of weeks. The big shots in Edinburgh will have to have a look at it. I'll stress how important it is and get them right on it, so we'll have approval in a week or two. Keep on planning; it'll be okay."

What Ian Mór says to Sally:

> "Wae's me, yer unco' thrawn. Hush yer blether an' dinna skirl, ma sonsie wee quean. Ian Mór winna scaith ye. We maun gae gey thick thegither."

In English, roughly:

> "Woe is me, you're dreadfully stubborn. Hush your idle talk and don't fuss, my toothsome little lass. Big Ian won't hurt you. We must be very friendly with each other."

Ian fancies himself a bit of a linguist, and likes to use Scots phrases now and then.

Soccer (football) talk

boots: shoes worn for playing soccer.

match: game.

nil: zero.

pitch: the playing field.

play a friendly: an informal match.

side: a team.

Partick Thistle, Heart of Midlothian, and Inverness Caledonian Thistle are all Scottish soccer sides. Plural verbs are always used with the name of a team, as in, "The Airgead side were looking hard-pressed."